1 9 8 7

THE GRAYWOLF

SHORT FICTION SERIES

Family

STORIES FROM THE INTERIOR

Edited by

GERI GIEBEL CHAVIS, Ph.D.

Graywolf Press : *Saint Paul*

Publication of this anthology is made possible in part by a grant
from the Bigelow Foundation. Graywolf Press receives generous
donations from governmental and private sources. Graywolf is
a member agency of United Arts, Saint Paul.

Library of Congress Catalog Card Number 87-80014
ISBN 0-915308-93-2

This is a work of fiction. All characters and incidents in this work
are fictional, and any resemblance to any person, living or dead,
is coincidental.

Published by GRAYWOLF PRESS, 2402 University Avenue
Suite 203, Saint Paul, MN 55114. All rights reserved.

Fourth Printing

ACKNOWLEDGMENTS

SHERWOOD ANDERSON. "Unlighted Lamps." Copyright © 1921 by B. W. Huebsch, Inc. Copyright renewed 1948 by Eleanor Copenhaver Anderson. This story appears in *The Triumph of the Egg*. Reprinted by permission of Harold Ober Associates Incorporated.

TONI CADE BAMBARA. "Raymond's Run." Copyright © 1970 by Toni Cade Bambara. Reprinted from *Gorilla, My Love* by Toni Cade Bambara, by permission of Random House, Inc.

PHYLLIS BENTLEY. "Mother and Daughter." Copyright © 1960 by Phyllis Bentley. This story appears in *Kith and Kin: Nine Tales of Family Life* (Victor Gollancz Ltd., 1960). Reprinted by permission of A. D. Peters & Co., Ltd.

GINA BERRIAULT. "The Houses of the City." Copyright © 1982 by Gina Berriault. This story appears in *The Infinite Passion of Expectation* (North Point Press, 1982). Reprinted by permission.

ELIZABETH BOWEN. "Coming Home." Copyright © 1950 by Elizabeth Bowen. Reprinted from *The Collected Stories of Elizabeth Bowen*, by permission of Alfred Knopf, Inc.

GWENDOLYN BROOKS. "The Young Couple at Home." Copyright © 1971 by Gwendolyn Brooks. This story appears in *The World of Gwendolyn Brooks* (Harper & Row, 1971). Reprinted by permission.

HORTENSE CALISHER. "A Christmas Carillon." Reprinted from *The Collected Stories of Hortense Calisher*, copyright © 1975 by Hortense Calisher. Reprinted by permission of Arbor House Publishing Company.

WILLA CATHER. "The Sentimentality of William Tavener." Copyright © 1965, 1970 by University of Nebraska Press. This story appears in *Willa Cather's Collected Short Fiction, 1892-1912* (Rev. Ed.), with introduction by Mildred R. Bennett, edited by Virginia Faulkner (University of Nebraska Press, 1970). Reprinted by permission.

JOHN CHEEVER. "The National Pastime." Copyright © 1953, 1981 by John Cheever. Originally published in *The New Yorker*. Reprinted by permission of International Creative Management.

COLETTE. "The Sempstress." *From My Mother's House and Sido* by Colette. Copyright © 1953 by Farrar, Straus and Giroux, Inc. Reprinted by permission of Farrar, Straus and Giroux, Inc.

DALE EUNSON. "The Hero's Son." Copyright © 1973 by Dale Eunson. This story appears in *Parent and Child in Fiction* (Brooks/Cole, 1977). Reprinted by permission.

ERNEST J. GAINES. "The Sky Is Gray." Copyright © 1963 by Ernest J. Gaines. From *Bloodline*. Reprinted by permission of Doubleday & Company, Inc.

ANGELICA GIBBS. "Father Was a Wit." Every effort has been made to locate the author of this story which appeared in *Story Magazine* (Vol. X, No. 54, January 1937). If the author reads this, please contact Graywolf Press.

LIBBI MIRIAM. "Maiden Names." Copyright © 1987 by Libbi Miriam. Reprinted by permission of the author.

IRENA NARELL. "Papa's Tea." Copyright © 1969 by Irena Narell. This story appears in *The Woman Who Lost Her Names*, edited by Julia Wolf Mazow (Harper & Row, 1980). Reprinted by permission.

FLANNERY O'CONNOR. "Everything that Rises Must Converge" from *The Complete Stories by Flannery O'Connor*. Copyright © 1961 by the Estate of Mary Flannery O'Connor. Reprinted by permission of Farrar, Straus and Giroux, Inc.

HELEN HARRIS PERLMAN. "Twelfth Summer." Copyright © 1951, 1978 by *The New Yorker Magazine, Inc.* Reprinted by permission.

MARSHA PORTNOY. "Loving Strangers." Copyright © 1983 by Marsha Portnoy. This story appears in *McCall's* (January 1983). Reprinted by permission.

JAMES PURDY. "Encore." Copyright © 1957, 1961 by James Purdy. This story appears in *Children Is All* (New Directions, 1961). Reprinted by permission.

CYNTHIA MARSHALL RICH. "My Sister's Marriage." Copyright © 1955 by Street & Smith Publications, Inc. This story first appeared in *Mademoiselle*. Reprinted by permission.

JANET BEELER SHAW. "In High Country" and "The Trail to the Ledge." Copyright © 1985 by Janet Beeler Shaw. These stories appear in *Some of the Things I Did Not Do* (University of Illinois Press, 1985). Reprinted by permission.

ELAINE MARCUS STARKMAN. "Anniversary." Copyright © 1980 by Elaine Marcus Starkman. This story appears in *The Woman Who Lost Her Names*, edited by Julia Wolf Mazow (Harper & Row, 1980). Reprinted by permission.

WALLACE STEGNER. "The Blue-Winged Teal." Copyright © 1950 by Wallace Stegner. Copyright renewed © 1978 by Wallace Stegner. Reprinted by permission of Brandt & Brandt Literary Agents, Inc.

JOHN UPDIKE. "Man and Daughter in the Cold." Copyright © 1968 by John Updike. Reprinted from *Museums and Women and Other Stories* by John Updike, by permission of Alfred A. Knopf, Inc.

CONTENTS

Introduction / xiii

Husbands and Wives

Mothers and Daughters

Fathers and Daughters

Fathers and Sons

Mothers and Sons

Siblings

Family

STORIES FROM THE INTERIOR

INTRODUCTION

THERE ARE FEW SUBJECTS of greater interest than the family. Everywhere we turn, social commentators and mass media writers are exploring the impact of the family system on our lives and speculating on the future of marriage and the family as institutions in our society. As individuals, we are all deeply colored by the families we have emerged from and the new ones we create as adults.

Vivid literary works focusing on family relationships can indeed be an invaluable resource for us as we seek to learn more about the ways families function. Sigmund Freud and Abraham Maslow, along with many others, acknowledged the power of literature to expand our understanding of psychological realities. In her book *Family Insights through the Short Story*, Rose Sommerville, social science educator, underscores the value of literature, pointing out that family life educators "could hardly find a more appropriate resource than that of imaginative literature."

Family: Stories from the Interior gathers together works of short fiction that are moving, well-written, and alive with people whose emotions, thoughts, and behavior are not unlike our own. Each story takes us on a journey inward to the heart and marrow of family life, shining the spotlight on the various relationships within families: those between husbands and wives, mothers and daughters, fathers and daughters, fathers and sons, mothers and sons, and siblings. Since it is the very nature of the modern short story to present characters upon the brink of change, to capture moments of crisis and revelation in the lives of individuals, this anthology of twenty-five stories is filled with the drama of family living.

This collection is designed primarily for those who enjoy reading short fiction and who want to learn more about what makes families tick. It is for men and women who wish to explore their personal feelings and expectations in relation to family members and to identify the themes that persist in their own particular families. But this is also an anthology for educators and their students. It is an ideal text for thematically organized literature courses on the college and advanced high school levels and for courses in psychology, family therapy, family life education, and women's studies. Moreover, this collection is an excellent resource for mental health professionals who work with families and family-related problems and who wish to share therapeutic reading materials with their clients.

While richly diverse, the experiences of the family members populating the pages of this book highlight two basic themes: ambivalence and the ebb and flow of merging and separateness that characterize family relationships.

In defining the "family connection" in *Psychoanalysis and Fantasies of the Unconscious*, D. H. Lawrence writes:

> The connection is as direct and as subtle as between the Marconi stations, two great wireless stations, all adjusted to the same, or very much the same, vibration. All the time they quiver with the interchange, there is one long endless flow of vitalistic communication between members of one family, a long, strange rapport, a sort of life-unison....But all the time there is the jolt, the rupture of individualism, the individual asserting himself beyond all ties or claims.

As Lawrence's words imply, we depend on family members to meet our needs for belonging and security, but we fight these very same individuals when our wishes for independence are frustrated. Daily, we enact the archetypal drama of escaping from and returning to the people who influence strongly who we are and how we behave.

While reading this anthology, we will meet children idealizing

and demythologizing their parents and will observe parents holding on to and letting go of offspring heading down the path to
maturity. We will watch spouses circling in a not always graceful
dance of pursuit and distancing, and will experience the feelings of
siblings caught between defending blood ties and carrying the
banners of their uniqueness. While the stories gathered here are
not intended to reflect the full range of family types to be found in
today's society, there is, within each section, variety in the stories'
narrators, the characters' life stages, and the composition of the
particular families. Readers will also find here works reflecting
both the negative and positive dimensions of family life. Taken
together, these stories weave an intricate family tapestry in which
the colors of joy and sorrow and the threads of conflict and reconciliation are tightly interwoven.   G.C.

Husbands

&

Wives

INTRODUCTION

Focusing on the married couple, this opening section includes works that together provide a balance between the husband's and wife's perspective on the marriage relationship. As a group, these stories capture what renowned sociologist Jessie Barnard has noted, namely that "there are actually two marriages in every marital union — his and hers — which do not always coincide." In relating to one another, a husband and wife have expectations and reactions that are often not directly communicated but certainly affect their daily interactions.

Spouses' attitudes and behavior toward one another reflect not only their temperamental differences and diverse past experiences but also the numerous myths of marriage that permeate our society. One of the most fundamental myths is the belief that marriage is supposed to make couples totally happy and secure, that the exchange of marriage vows ensures the end of loneliness and the satisfaction of nearly all one's emotional, social, and physical needs. The fairy tale ending, "And they lived happily ever after," is deeply ingrained in the psyche of even the most sensible couples embarking on their wedding journeys. Another widespread notion is the idea that the individuality of two spouses ought to take a back seat to the couple's merged identity. Marriage has been ideal-an experience of togetherness in which two people feed on the perpetual manna of romantic ecstasy, sharing everything — from everyday events and goals to all their earthly possessions. Related to these common notions are the beliefs that love automatically solves all problems, married couples instinctively know how to meet one another's needs, and disagreement between spouses is a destructive element to be avoided.

Inevitably, all of these idealized notions carry with them the seeds of disillusionment, a disillusionment that may account for the equally prevalent cynical myth that getting married is the surest way to destroy the romance in a relationship. According to the perpetuators of this stereotype, marriage breeds boredom and imprisons the couple, particularly the husband whose wings of carefree bachelorhood are clipped at the moment he is foolish enough to utter the words "I do."

This blend of diametrically opposed views on marriage in our society is mirrored by the ambivalence couples experience as they struggle to keep their marriages viable and oscillate between feelings of love and resentment, satisfaction and despair.

The "complete togetherness" notion is a particularly powerful and disturbing one affecting couples' interactions, since spouses are individuals needing to exercise some degree of autonomy. Every man and woman in an intimate relationship must grapple with the challenge of discovering the particular blend of connectedness and independent action that is both comfortable for each personally and acceptable to the other. When couples relate, there is typically a rhythm of intimacy and distancing, with spouses finding ways to approach one another and the means to gain breathing space.

In this section, we see how five different couples discover or have already established ways of connecting and separating. We meet young couples such as those in Shaw's "The Trail to the Ledge" and Brooks's "Young Couple at Home," who are defining their relationship to one another and working out rules for living together. In Starkman's "Anniversary," Calisher's "A Christmas Carillon," and Cather's "The Sentimentality of William Tavener," we encounter older couples more set in their ways, yet evolving new patterns in responses to mid-life circumstances. We watch as all these couples face the predictable and react to surprises.

The couples we meet in the five stories are partners who are temperamentally very different and whose differences help create balance, stir up conflict, and foster growth. As readers, we have the opportunity to perceive how these various couples avoid and confront one another and communicate, both verbally and nonverbally, their desires, resentment, caring, and loneliness.

The opening story, "The Trail to the Ledge," highlights the inner struggles of an introverted young husband whose need for privacy clashes with the expectations of his demonstrative wife. Less serious in tone than Shaw's story, "The Young Couple at Home" provides us with a wife's inner responses to her husband's intrusiveness. Brooks' story reveals the unspoken disappointment and quiet resignation of a young wife whose husband's tastes and habits differ sharply from her own.

Shifting back to the husband's views in "A Christmas Carillon," we follow the thoughts of a man embarking on a psychological trip home to wife, children, and the family hearth after a six months' legal separation. Calisher's story captures vividly a husband's turmoil when his need for freedom clashes with his yearning for connectedness.

Like the husband in Calisher's story, the wife in "Anniversary" craves the freedom to realize her personal potential and vacillates between escape fantasies and a renewed commitment to her fifteen-year-old marriage. Experiencing a wide range of emotions as she reviews past events, the heroine in Starkman's story moves toward present discoveries in relation to her self and her spouse.

Discovery also characterizes the wife's experience with her husband in "The Sentimentality of William Tavener." Here, we see how a middle-aged couple, grown accustomed to a lack of intimacy, are drawn together in an unexpected new way. Along with "A Christmas Carillon," this story shows us how children can affect a marital relationship. Cather's story, however, also provides a good example of how coalitions or alignments involving spouses and children persist, yet can change, in the dynamic process of family living.   G.C.

Janet Beeler Shaw

THE TRAIL TO THE LEDGE

G AIL WASN'T in their cabin at Camp Berry, but she'd left him a note taped to the fridge: "Took the jeep to get some groceries. Back soon. Your wife, Gail." They'd been married for six weeks and Gail got a kick out of calling herself "your wife." Jim pulled the note from the fridge and laid it on the drainboard by the little sink as he opened himself a can of Coke. Her big scrawled letters took over the whole piece of torn notebook paper. In the narrow space below her name she'd made large X marks for kisses. Like a little kid, Jim thought. But Gail was twenty. He held the chilled Coke can against his forehead a moment and then settled down at the pine table, glad to be alone.

He was the tennis coach this summer and was with the kids from eight-thirty in the morning until dinnertime. Gail was usually waiting for him when he got back to their cabin in the counselors' section. She was teaching drama and dance and wanted to talk about her day and hear all about his. They'd taken the jobs at the camp so they could share their experiences, she reminded him. She'd found the job openings in the Sunday *Times* and applied right away — two sheets of notebook paper in her big scrawl. Within a week they'd received a phone call. Their background was excellent and the director liked the idea of a married couple. It would add stability to the camp situation for the younger campers.

Jim opened the latest copy of *Sports Illustrated* and took a gulp of his Coke. There was a good article on Jimmy Connors. Studying Connors's follow-through on his serve, Jim thought he could tell that it was probably his second serve; he could see Connors was trying to control the ball with spin. He turned his wrist like Connors's to confirm his guess and heard the jeep pull up by the cabin porch. Gail beeped the horn twice and he went to the window. She'd tied her hair back with an orange scarf and was wearing her green croupier's eyeshade for sunglasses. She'd left her really wild stuff packed away so they could fit into the camp atmosphere better, but she was wearing one of her tie-dyed tee shirts without a bra. He could see her dark nipples through the lavender cotton. He'd told her several times that he didn't think it was a good idea with so many young boys around.

"Want help with the groceries?" he called.

"Nope. I can manage, honey." She swung out of the jeep and grabbed a bag in each arm. Her hiking boots were loud on the bare floor of the cabin porch. He held the screen door open for her and she made kissing noises at him as she passed. "Little hick grocery," she said. "No fresh stuff at all." She dropped the bags on the narrow shelf by the sink and flung herself down in the canvas chair by the door, pulling the scarf from her hair and shaking her head so that her thick, dark hair fell free around her face. She reached for his Coke and took a long drink.

"I'm not especially hungry anyway," he offered. After he'd finished coaching he'd gone over and swum in the large pool. It had felt good to him to count the laps of his freestyle, to feel the water cold on his sunburned arms, his legs and back getting tired. For a while he'd forgotten he was working at the camp and he was lost in the body memory of working for his Senior Lifeguard exam when he was sixteen. The other swimmers had offered him some cookies one of the mothers had sent — swimmers were always sugar hungry. He'd felt pleasantly guilty eating the heavy cookies, licking icing from his fingers, knowing he wouldn't be hungry for supper.

She bent to unlace her hiking boots. "How was your day, Jimmy?"

"Good. A good day."

"I think we're settling into the routine," she said. "My little princesses have gotten used to working their tails off."

"You had a good day?" he asked politely, watching her finish his Coke.

"We did some truly creative stuff in the drama group. I had them act out life situations. One gutsy girl, the blonde I told you about, took the part of an alcoholic. Wow, was she *in* it. Really transformed herself. I was so proud!" She settled back, stretched, and tipped her chin up to laugh with pleasure in the memory of her student. For a moment he saw her as he liked her best — clothed in the sheen of her own animal energy. He admired her because she liked herself so well. He'd thought of himself as second-rate most of his life. It made him feel free and good to be with her when she was enjoying her own enthusiasm. He wanted to be like that.

Stripping off her knee socks she wiggled her toes, rubbed her big, powerful dancer's feet, all muscle. "Tell me about your day." It wasn't a question.

"No superstars," he said promptly. "Three, maybe four, really strong guys. One good girl. Hits them deep and hard." He couldn't think of anything creative that they'd done. Just the usual routines. He'd always pushed himself to do a disciplined drill, his own kind of compulsive drive. He'd had to depend on routine and unfailing discipline because he had no natural brilliance. He guessed he coached the same way. Still, that kind of discipline steadied the really good players and the mediocre kids got better through the drills. There wasn't too much to talk about there.

She watched him expectantly. After a while she said, "Maybe you'd like to invite your kids to have hot dogs with us here some night. I was thinking of having some of my drama kids here. We could play theater games and interact with each other. Know each other better. What do you think?"

He shook his head, no. He didn't want to get to know the kids better. He spent all day with them, that was enough. What would they say to each other? He was an adult to them, not a buddy. He'd hated the phony friendship of one of his coaches and admired another who stood back from him, who stayed in the role. "I guess I really don't want that," he added, trying for candor because he knew she liked that.

"I hear you," she said at once. "You value your privacy. I admire that, Jimmy."

"I want to keep my distance," he said.

"Right, honey. But you understand that I want to get closer to my students. We're different that way." She leaned toward him, her face flushed with intensity. She got excited when they talked about "real" things, as she called them — their differences, their feelings, who they were. "I love you for your sense of your own privacy," she added. "You're a complicated, simple guy."

She had called him a "complicated, simple guy" the first time she'd pulled his face to her breasts. He guessed she was right — he didn't understand his complications very well, but he liked simple things. He liked making love and really good steaks. He liked his records. He loved tennis. And he liked silence. He'd begun to realize that he'd spent most of his life in silence. He liked it that way. "I guess I'm tired right now," he said.

She stood and stretched. "I'm going to take a quick shower before I fix supper. Would you get me one of the secret beers?" She leaned to pat his thigh as he reached into the back of the fridge. "Jimmy, you've got the most gorgeous legs in the world. My tall, blond, silent man! I married you for your legs." She took her beer and padded toward the bathroom, unzipping her cut-offs as she walked.

They'd gotten married because she thought she was pregnant. She was taking the pill, but she thought somehow she'd slipped. By the time she'd confirmed that this wasn't so, they'd planned a simple wedding and told their parents. She had wanted his baby, she said. He liked that idea. He liked to hear her say, "Baby. Your baby, Jimmy." When she knew she wasn't pregnant after all, she said, "It felt right. Let's go ahead." He was doubtful, but she was so full of purpose. She loved him for his aloneness, she said. "I need someone cool," she said. "And you need someone warm." His friends in the fraternity told him he was a lucky guy. They said she was something special. He thought they sensed she was somehow better than he deserved.

The thing that worried him the most now that they were married were the nights. Of course they'd made love a lot before — in his car, on her dorm bed, on blankets in the woods — but they'd never slept together all night. Sleeping with Gail was a different thing, and it frightened him. She was neither tall nor heavy, but her weight tipped him toward the center of the bed. She seemed enormous and dark. Even asleep he was aware of her hips and breasts, of her feet tangling with his. Sometimes she woke in the middle of the night and wanted to talk. He wanted her to be quiet and cool, then. He wanted to sleep. Sometimes when he felt especially anxious and couldn't escape her breath or the pressure of her legs, he took the quilt and lay spread-eagled on the floor by the bed. He told her that it was too hot to sleep and the breeze moved on the floor. She'd reach down and rumple his hair, but in a few minutes she would fall asleep and he could move away from her hand. Somehow he hadn't counted on her being with him all night. Nothing had prepared him for the weight of a woman against his sleep.

And she slept naked. Her skin gave off a scent of her musk perfume and of her sweat. He could feel her body heat even if she was several inches away. He'd always slept in his briefs and a tee shirt. He asked her if she didn't want to let him buy her a nightie. But she said no. She'd always slept naked. Once, on their honeymoon, she'd asked him to sleep naked with her. He'd waked in terror. For a moment he had been unable to tell where his body ended and hers began. He felt he'd lost his outline, that he had blurred, melted into her. He'd gotten up at once and put on his underwear. But he felt her heat even through the cotton, and if she moved to his pillow her loose hair stuck to his throat and his shoulders. He didn't know what he was going to do about the nights if he didn't learn to sleep with her.

Gail liked to read in the quiet time after the all-camp activities around the campfire in the early evening. He'd gotten in the habit of going down to the tennis courts and hitting balls against the backboard, enjoying the feel of a light sweat coming up again and the breeze chilly on the back of his neck. He thought the exercise might help him sleep. When he'd return to their cabin it would be almost ten-thirty, and he'd take a quick, cool shower and embrace Gail while he was still wet. She said once that she liked that. She also said they must be careful not to get into a rut with sex. "I like counting on it," he said. It was good to have a pattern to his days.

Tonight she blew him a kiss as he started down toward the tennis courts. She was reading a paperback novel, absently lifting and smoothing the hair at her nape. He stopped in the doorway and looked back at her stretched out in the canvas chair, her amber legs propped up on the railing. He'd managed to eat the eggs she'd fixed — enough anyway. "You're a good girl," he said abruptly, surprising himself.

She smiled. "I love you to pieces and you know it."

He took a side trail down to the tennis courts in the valley below the cabins, checking in his shorts pocket to make sure he had the key to the court lights. He swung at the pine shadows with his racket. He should build up his wrists more, he thought. He'd have more control if his wrists were stronger. There was no chance of his being a pro — it looked like he'd end up in his dad's insurance business. But he'd like to play well. It was important to do something really well.

The court was like a rectangle of dark, unreflecting water. When he turned on the lights the pine trees lit up with an almost artificial green. There was only the sound of the whippoorwills and the steady thud of his tennis balls. No one had ever seemed to notice that he was on the courts at night. The young girls in the cabins on the hill above the courts laughed and teased each other until lights out — thirteen-year-olds — he knew he didn't bother them.

But once on the courts he was bored. Two weeks into the ten-week session and already he was bored. He was hitting strongly enough, but it was an effort for him to try to control the ball. Maybe he was just too tired. He would try to get a nap before supper; maybe that would help him stay in shape. When he lobbed the ball over the backboard and into the woods he decided to quit. He hadn't even broken a sweat yet, but it wasn't worth it. He switched off the court lights and stood still in the darkness, letting his eyes get used to the night. It felt good to be alone. He didn't want to go back to their cabin yet. In the soft silence he could hear the girls laughing in the cabins above the tennis courts.

Without really deciding, he started up the trail that led to the ledge by the cabins. It was farther back by that trail, but he hadn't been gone very long. He realized that he was walking very quietly. When he saw the cabin lights flickering in the pines above him, he made himself breathe more quietly. He remembered the delicious freedom of running through the summer nights as a boy, rhododendrons slapping his arms, the backyards dark and deserted, bright figures glancing out of lighted windows, unable to see him.

The trail led above the counselors' cabin for that section — Eagles Roost. Then there were four cabins for the girls. The highest one was just below the rocky outcropping on which the trail ran. The trail here was in total darkness, but he made out the marker just off the trail — Cabin Four.

There was the flash of colored towels hanging inside the long screened windows of the cabin below the trail. He heard the soft sounds of the girls laughing. He crouched down on the path, the scent of hot pine needles rising in the breeze. The canvas drop cloths that were the sides of the cabin had been rolled up to the top, and he could see the four girls sitting cross-legged on their cots. They wore panties and tee shirts and were eating potato chips. One of the girls seemed to be reading a letter aloud. When her voice paused, the laughter of the other girls rose through the yellow mosquito lights like moths, fluttery and without menace. He glanced back down the trail — no one coming. But to make sure that he wasn't discovered, he crawled off the trail behind a boulder and lay on his belly on the ledge of rock above the cabin and opposite the screened sides. He was about ten feet from the cabin, but in dark shadow of the ledge.

He only watched them for a few minutes. Not much happened, but he hadn't expected anything. He felt a diffused excitement — he was doing something he shouldn't be doing. The feeling of danger made his senses alert and sharp. He thought he could smell the Noxzema one of the girls rubbed into her arms. He heard electricity crackle when the girl with long blonde hair leaned forward and whipped her brush through her hair.

At ten-fifteen the cabin lights blinked — the signal that there was one minute before lights out. The red-haired girl put away her letter, and without speaking, the four girls turned away from each other to pull off their shirts and panties and pull on their pajamas. He caught his breath when he realized that they chose to withhold themselves from each other's sight, each girl alone on her own bed, quickly stripping and changing, her back to the others. The red-haired girl was facing him, her face childish and solemn. He saw that her nipples were flat and pale and that she had a pale, pinky down between her legs. Her shoulders and hips looked like a boy's. Then the lights went out and he heard them calling goodnight to each other in the dark.

He climbed back to the path carefully, moving as stealthily as he was able. His heart was pounding and his face was hot. He had a tightness in his chest that felt like joy. He thought of the girls' innocent restraint. Boys that age grabbed at each other's balls and slapped each other with towels. He hadn't liked that. He didn't want to be pushed around that way. These girls didn't touch each other at all. Each one seemed singular, surrounded by a haze of light. He wondered briefly if Gail would understand his feeling for them. Then he decided that he would say nothing. There was nothing really wrong about what he'd done. But the vision was something that belonged to him alone.

He felt as full of energy and as loose-limbed as if he'd been running. When he came onto their porch he took Gail around from behind and laid his cheek against the top of her head. "Are you going to take a shower?" she asked, looking back and up at him.

"I guess I won't, tonight," he said, and she stood up at once and hugged him. "Oh, wow," she said.

After they made love and she'd fallen asleep, he untangled himself from her warm arms and laid the quilt on the floor. He lay on his back, arms behind his head, and thought about the girls in Cabin Four. He thought about the bones in their shoulders and how their skin shone under the yellow bulb. After all, they were very young and quick and shy.

In the days that followed he developed a regular routine on which he could depend. He and Gail would have their early supper, and if she came back tired or was late, he cooked so that they wouldn't linger over it too long. He learned to make good hamburgers and hot dogs with cheese. "I can't decide which I like best," she said, "looking after you or your looking after me." He made sure to help her clean up the pans so that they wouldn't be late for the campfire activities.

Some nights the girls and boys from her drama group gave skits; some nights there was square dancing. He was intensely aware of the girls from Cabin Four, but he was careful not to look directly at them. They were always together – sometimes they even walked four abreast, arms around each others' waists. When they sat on a log near the fire he could glimpse their narrow knees glowing in the firelight. Two of the girls were blondes, one with braids and the smaller one with loose hair that she wore back in a band. The tallest girl had short, dark hair and dark down on her arms and legs. The red-haired girl, heavier than the others, seemed to be the leader. He didn't want to know their names.

After campfire he and Gail would share a beer and talk. He told her everything he could think of that he'd done that day. He surprised himself with the amount of detail he could remember. "I love the way you're sharing yourself with me," she told him, leaning toward him, her chin on her fists. Then he'd listen to her talk. He kept his eyes on hers and was careful to follow what she said in case she asked him how he felt about anything she'd been doing. He wanted to be good to her. She was a good person. By nine-thirty he was frantic to get away.

He'd take his racket and tennis balls and the key for the lights and start down toward the courts. His mouth was always dry when he stood on the dark courts and heard the laughter and sounds of music from the cabins on the hill above, but he made himself hit for a while. He timed himself: fifteen minutes at least. Never less. It was part of his discipline. And it enhanced his anticipation. He imagined the girls settling down, brushing each others' hair as they liked to do. If he reached the cabin by ten o'clock, he could watch them for fifteen minutes before lights out. He was never late.

Lying belly down against the warm stone ledge, he discovered that they had a very simple routine. Sometimes they tried on makeup, helping each other with glosses that made their lips look large and shiny. Sometimes they trimmed each others' hair. There was usually a letter to read aloud or one to be written, and they helped each other think of witty things to say about camp food. The small blonde often did backbends on her bed, looking straight at him through the screen, upside down and unaware. Mostly they sat on their beds and talked. And each night when they undressed, he held his breath as they turned from each other, stripped off the triangles of panties and their printed tee shirts. Each one was serious and composed, utterly alone in the simple task. They seemed to him in those moments to be shining, quivering like flames.

When the lights went out he crept back to the path. Usually his hands had stopped trembling by the time he reached their cabin. But sometimes he had to run for a while before he went back — he was too short of breath to explain in any other way.

He slept less well all the time. Even lying on the quilt on the floor, often he couldn't fall asleep until he heard the earliest birds begin to sing. He knew that if he was discovered looking in on the girls, there would be a terrible scandal. But he also knew how harmless he was to them — all he wanted was the vision of their cool purity. Who would believe that? And he knew he was betraying Gail in some way that he couldn't quite understand. Lying awake, he either planned his next visit to his ledge by the cabin, or rehearsed the disaster that would fall upon him if he were discovered. The need to see the girls and the need not to be found out seemed to be two equal weights nailed in his chest.

Once, in the middle of the night, Gail reached down for him and he caught her hand before she touched his face. "You're still awake?" she whispered.

"Yes."

"Want to talk, Jimmy? Bad dream?"

"No. My stomach's upset."

"Camp's over next week," she murmured. "I guess we're both ready for a change."

He lay listening to his heart speeding up in his chest, a dull sound that drowned out the early birdsongs. He'd tried not to be aware that time was passing. His routine had seemed beyond time, somehow. But camp would be over next week — he had to face that. He knew the pressure of his guilt would be over, then. But he would lose the girls. He didn't want to be back at college in married housing with only the memory of the warm stone ledge and the sweet, uncomplicated scenes inside the girls' cabin. The memory wouldn't be enough. What would he do then? The thought made him feel helpless. Before he could manage to fall asleep he decided that since it was the last week it would be all right to go to the cabin a little earlier, to give himself more time with his girls.

The next evening Gail was designing a stage set in her notebook and he could slip away earlier than usual. He didn't bother to go to the courts at all, but took the path directly to the cabin by the trail along the top of the ridge. It was a still night and the air smelled of hay and pine, reminding him of a time when he'd been a boy – not innocent exactly, but free both of such need and such duplicity.

Even before he had reached his place on the ledge by the cabin, he realized something was different. Someone was crying. He moved into his position and discovered that it was the red-haired girl who was sobbing, her face in her hands. The taller blonde girl was sitting on the cot beside her, her thin arm around the red-haired girl's solid shoulders. The small blonde sat on her own cot, her chin on her knees, rocking back and forth. The dark-haired girl lay on her belly, sniffing. Had they been fighting? He'd never heard them raise their voices to each other.

Listening intently, he began to decode the bits of conversation. The girl's dog had been run over; her mother had written to tell her so she could be prepared when she came home and found the dog gone. The tall blonde ran her hand up and down the crying girl's back. Perhaps that was how her own mother comforted her when she cried. The crying girl bent double and would not be comforted.

He had never wanted to touch the girls before. He wanted them to stay remote and lovely. But now he felt a powerful urge to enter the cabin and take the crying girl in his embrace. He wanted to run his hands down her freckled arms, rest her head against his chest. He understood that he loved them all in some way he hadn't known. He didn't want any harm to come to them. He felt remote but powerful. If he went inside to her now, he would know how to comfort the crying girl. After all these nights of watching, he *knew* her. She was more than the pure and wavering spirit he had seen at first. She was an unhappy girl. His throat was tight and he knew he must go back to his own cabin in case he moaned out loud. He wanted to think about this new feeling.

When he turned and started to crawl back up to the trail he realized that there was someone standing by the boulder looking down at him, a shadow form. In the moment before she spoke he saw that it was Gail.

"I chased you. You forgot the key for the lights," she whispered, and then she began to cry.

She ran down the trail back to their cabin. He ran after her, afraid that he would catch her after all. After the first wave of guilt that made him catch his breath, he had felt a burst of gratitude toward her — if she'd found him out at least no one else would catch him now. And then he felt a flood of anger — after all, what had he done wrong? It was her fault, somehow — she shouldn't have followed him!

When he reached their cabin she was hunched down in the canvas chair, crying hysterically. He'd never seen her cry before and the violence of her sobs frightened him. He sat down across the table from her and said her name but she wouldn't look at him. Her face was red and blotched and he saw that her eyes would be swollen. She had snot on her upper lip and she didn't try to wipe her face. He got her some tissues but she wouldn't take them from him. Then he got a washcloth dampened with warm water and she took that, burying her face in it. His hands shook worse than hers did. He said her name again, but she kept her face in the warm washcloth.

"Is that part of your bag?" she asked through the washcloth. "Little girls?" She started sobbing again but he was afraid to reach for her. Her whole body shook and her eyes looked at him wildly over the blue cloth. "You'll get in trouble, you know that?"

When she was quieter he tried, "I don't know what it is, but it's over. It's all over."

She shook her head, staring at him. "I don't know what it is, either, but it's not over. Not until you tell me. Not until we work it through."

"I can't talk about it," he said.

"But I want to *understand*." She wiped her throat with the washcloth and flung her hair back over her shoulders.

He rested his forehead on his fists. The pine table smelled of bacon grease. He closed his eyes, feeling the constriction in his throat. "It's nothing. I just watch them for a few minutes. That's all."

"Every night?" she asked.

Before he realized that she couldn't have known that, he said, "Yes. Every night."

"Oh, God!" She started to sob again. "You've got to tell me! What's going on?"

"Nothing's going on." He didn't want to look at her anymore, her face red and her mouth slack from crying.

"Maybe it's nothing you understand," she gasped, "but something is going on." Her silver earrings swung crazily, reflecting the overhead light. "What hurts me the most is that you have this secret," she said softly, as if to herself. "It's not the little girls. It's the *secret*. Do you see that?"

He shook his head. Nothing he could tell her would be enough. She reached for his hand and he suddenly found himself furious with her. She'd followed him, after all! Spied on him! Now she wanted to turn his vision inside out, make it something that it wasn't at all, possess that as well. He jerked his hand away from her. "What about my privacy!" he hissed. "You said you loved my sense of privacy!"

She jumped up, her hip hitting the table. "I didn't mean from *me*! That wasn't the agreement!"

"Your agreement. Yours!"

She ran into the bedroom. He heard her opening drawers and in a little while she came out with her satchel. She had washed her face and tied back her hair. She looked exhausted but she'd put on eyeliner. "I'm going to stay in town tonight. I've got to think things through. I just can't get hold of this."

He realized that he was relieved. He wanted her to leave. He was very, very tired, and maybe he could sleep if he was alone in the bed.

"But we've got to talk about this in the morning, Jimmy. We've got to understand. It'll finish us if we don't." She turned, started out the screen door, a moth darting around her head.

He moved after her, thinking he would tell her that he'd try to make her understand. But he found to his horror that he had picked up an empty Coke can and was hurling it at her back. She ducked behind the screen door and began running toward the jeep. The can hit the screen and bounced back by his feet, leaving a trail of sticky water. "Bitch!" he cried at her as she started the jeep. "Leave me alone, bitch!" He didn't want her to come back later and catch him crying.

Gwendolyn Brooks

THE YOUNG COUPLE AT HOME

PAUL HAD SLEPT through most of the musicale. Three quarters of the time his head had been a heavy knot on her shoulder. At each of her attempts to remove it, he had waked up so suddenly, and had given her a look of such childlike fierceness, that she could only smile.

Now on the streetcar, however — the car was in the garage — he was not sleepy, and he kept "amusing" Maud Martha with little "tricks," such as cocking his head archly and winking at her, or digging her slyly in the ribs, or lifting her hand to his lips, and blowing on it softly, or poking a finger under her chin and raising it awkwardly, or feeling her muscle, then putting her hand on his muscle, so that she could tell the difference. Such as that. "Clowning," he called it. And because he felt that he was making her happy, she tried not to see the uncareful stares and smirks of the other passengers — uncareful and insultingly consolatory. He sat playfully upon part of her thigh. He gently kicked her toe.

Once home, he went immediately to the bathroom. He did not try to mask his need, he was obvious and direct about it.

"He could make," she thought, "a comment or two on what went on at the musicale. Or some little joke. It isn't that I'm unreasonable or stupid. But everything can be done with a little grace. I'm sure of it."

When he came back, he yawned, stretched, smeared his lips up and down her neck, assured her of his devotion, and sat down on the bed to take off his shoes. She picked up *Of Human Bondage*, and sat at the other end of the bed.

"Snuggle up," he invited.

"I thought I'd read a while."

"I guess I'll read a while, too," he decided, when his shoes were off and had been kicked into the kitchen. She got up, went to the shoes, put them in the closet. He grinned at her merrily. She was conscious of the grin, but refused to look at him. She went back to her book. He settled down to his. His was a paperback copy of *Sex in the Married Life*.

There he sat, slouched down, terribly absorbed, happy in his sock feet, curling his toes inside the socks.

"I want you to read this book," he said, " – but at the right times: one chapter each night before retiring." He reached over, pinched her on the buttock.

She stood again. "Shall I make some cocoa?" she asked pleasantly. "And toast some sandwiches?"

"Say, I'd like that," he said, glancing up briefly.

She toasted rye strips spread with pimento cheese and grated onion. She made cocoa.

They ate, drank, and read together. She read *Of Human Bondage*. He read *Sex in the Married Life*. They were silent.

Five minutes passed. She looked at him. He was asleep. His head had fallen back, his mouth was open – it was a good thing there were no flies – his ankles were crossed. And the feet! – pointing confidently out (no one would harm them). *Sex in the Married Life* was about to slip to the floor. She did not stretch out a hand to save it.

Once she had taken him to a library. While occupied with the card cases she had glanced up, had observed that he, too, was busy among the cards. "Do you want a book?" "No-o. I'm just curious about something. I wondered if there could be a man in the world named Bastard. Sure enough, there is."

Paul's book fell, making a little clatter. But he did not wake up, and she did not get up.

Hortense Calisher

A CHRISTMAS CARILLON

ABOUT FOUR WEEKS before Christmas, Grorley, in combined shame and panic, began to angle for an invitation to somewhere, anywhere, for Christmas Day. By this time, after six months of living alone in the little Waverly Place flat to which he had gone as soon as he and his wife had decided to separate, he had become all too well reacquainted with his own peculiar mechanism in regard to solitude. It was a mechanism that had its roots in the jumbled lack of privacy of an adolescence spent in the dark, four-room apartment to which his parents had removed themselves and three children after his father's bankruptcy in '29. Prior to that, Grorley's childhood had been what was now commonly referred to as Edwardian — in a house where servants and food smells kept their distance until needed, and there were no neurotic social concerns about the abundance of either — a house where there was always plush under the buttocks, a multiplicity of tureens and napery at table, lace on the pillow, and above all that general expectancy of creature comfort and spiritual order which novelists now relegated to the days before 1914.

That it had lasted considerably later, Grorley knew, since this had been the year of his own birth, but although he had been fifteen when they had moved, it was the substantial years before that had faded to fantasy. Even now, when he read or said the word "reality," his mind reverted to Sunday middays in the apartment house living room, where the smudgy daylight was always diluted by lamps, the cheaply stippled walls menaced the oversized furniture, and he, his father and brother and sister, each a claustrophobe island of irritation, were a constant menace to one another. Only his mother, struggling alone in the kitchen with the conventions of roast chicken and gravy, had perhaps achieved something of the solitude they all had craved. To Grorley even now, the smell of roasting fowl was the smell of a special kind of Sunday death.

Only once before now had he lived alone, and then too it had been in the Village, not far from where he presently was. After his graduation from City College he had worked a year, to save up for a master's in journalism, and then, salving his conscience with the thought that he had at least paid board at home for that period, he had left his family forever. The following year, dividing his time between small-time newspaper job and classes, living in his $27 per month place off Morton Street, he had savored all the wonders of the single doorkey opening on the quiet room, of the mulled book and the purring clock, of the smug decision not to answer the phone or to let even the most delightful invader in. Now that he looked back on it, of course, he recalled that the room had rung pretty steadily with the voices of many such who had been admitted, but half the pleasure had been because it had been at his own behest. That had been a happy time, when he had been a gourmet of loneliness, prowling bachelor-style on the edge of society, dipping inward when he chose. Of all the habitations he had had since, that had been the one whose conformations he remembered best, down to the last, worn dimple of brick. When he had house-hunted, last June, he had returned instinctively to the neighborhood of that time. Only a practicality born of superstition had kept him from hunting up the very street, the very house.

HE HAD HAD over two years of that earlier freedom, although the last third of it had been rather obscured by his courtship of Eunice. Among the girl students of the Village there had been quite a few who, although they dressed like ballerinas and prattled of art like painters' mistresses, drew both their incomes and their morality from good, solid middle-class families back home. Eunice had been the prettiest and most sought-after of these, and part of her attraction for some, and certainly for Grorley, had been that she seemed to be, quite honestly, one of those rare girls who were not particularly eager to marry and settle down. Grorley had been so entranced at finding like feelings in a girl – and in such a beautiful one – that he had quite forgotten that in coaxing her out of her "freedom" he was persuading himself out of his own.

He hadn't realized this with any force until the children came, two within the first four years of the marriage. Before that, in the first fusion of love, it had seemed to Grorley that two could indeed live more delightfully alone than one, and added to this had been that wonderful release from jealousy which requited love brings – half the great comfort of the loved one's presence being that, *ipso facto*, she is with no one else. During this period of happy, though enlarged privacy, Grorley confided to Eunice some, though not all, of his feelings about family life and solitude. He was, he told her, the kind of person who needed to be alone a great deal – although this of course excepted her. But they must never spend their Sundays and holidays frowsting in the house like the rest of the world, sitting there stuffed and droning, with murder in their hearts. They must always have plans laid well in advance, plans which would keep the two of them emotionally limber, so to speak, and *en plein air*. Since these plans were always pleasant – tickets to the Philharmonic, with after-theater suppers, hikes along the Palisades, fishing expeditions to little-known ponds back of the Westchester parkways, whose intricacies Grorley, out of a history of Sunday afternoons, knew as well as certain guides knew Boca Raton – Eunice was quite willing to accede. In time she grew very tactful, almost smug, over Grorley's little idiosyncrasy, and he sometimes heard her on the phone, fending people off. "Not Sunday. Gordon and I have a thing about holidays, you know." By this time, too, they had both decided that, although Grorley would keep his now very respectable desk job at the paper, his real destiny was to "write"; and to Eunice, who respected "imagination" as only the unimaginative can, Grorley's foible was the very proper defect of a noble intelligence.

But with the coming of the children, it was brought home to Grorley that he was face to face with one of those major rearrangements of existence for which mere tact would not suffice. Eunice, during her first pregnancy, was as natural and unassuming about it as a man could wish; she went on their Sunday sorties to the very last, and maintained their gallant privacy right up to the door of the delivery room. But the child of so natural a mother was bound to be natural too. It contracted odd fevers whenever it wished and frequently on Sundays, became passionately endeared to their most expensive sitter or would have none at all, and in general permeated their lives as only the most powerfully frail of responsibilities can. And when the second one arrived, it did so, it seemed to Grorley, only to egg the other one on.

There came a morning, the Christmas morning of the fourth year, when Grorley, sitting in the odor of baked meat, first admitted that his hydra-headed privacy was no longer a privacy at all. He had created, he saw, his own monster; sex and the devil had had their sport with him, and he was, in a sense that no mere woman would understand, all too heavily "in the family way." Looking at Eunice, still neat, still very pretty, but with her lovely mouth pursed with maternity, her gaze sharp enough for *Kinder* and *Küche*, but abstract apparently for him, he saw that she had gone over to the enemy and was no longer his. Eunice had become "the family" too.

It WAS as a direct consequence of this that Grorley wrote the book which was his making. Right after that fatal morning, he had engaged a room in a cheap downtown hotel (he and Eunice were living out in Astoria at the time), with the intention, as he explained to Eunice, of writing there after he left the paper, and coming home weekends. He had also warned her that, because of the abrasive effects of family life, it would probably be quite some time before "the springs of reverie" — a phrase he had lifted from Ellen Glasgow — would start churning. His real intention was, of course, to prowl, and for some weeks thereafter he joined the company of those men who could be found, night after night, in places where they could enjoy the freedom of not having gone home where they belonged.

To his surprise, he found, all too quickly, that though his intentions were of the worst, he had somehow lost the moral force to pursue them. He had never been much for continuous strong drink, and that crude *savoir-faire* which was needed for the preliminaries to lechery seemed to have grown creaky with the years. He took to spending odd hours in the newspaper morgue, correlating, in a half-hearted way, certain current affairs that interested him. After some months, he suddenly realized that he had enough material for a book. It found a publisher almost immediately. Since he was much more a child of his period than he knew, he had hit upon exactly that note between disaffection and hope which met response in the breasts of those who regarded themselves as permanent political independents. His book was an instant success with those who thought of themselves as thinking for themselves (if they had only had time for it). Quick to capitalize upon this, Grorley's paper gave him a biweekly column, and he developed a considerable talent for telling men of good will, over Wednesday breakfast, the very thing they had been saying to one another at Tuesday night dinner.

Grorley spent the war years doing this, always careful to keep his column, like his readers, one step behind events. With certain minor changes, he kept, too, that scheme of life which had started him writing, changing only, with affluence, to a more comfortable hotel. In time also, that *savoir-faire* whose loss he had mourned returned to him, and his success at his profession erased any guilts he might otherwise have had — a wider experience, he told himself, being not only necessary to a man of his trade, but almost unavoidable in the practice of it. He often congratulated himself at having achieved, in a country which had almost completely domesticated the male, the perfect pattern for a man of temperament, and at times he became almost insufferable to some of his married men friends, when he dilated on the contrast between his "continental" way of life and their own. For by then, Grorley had reversed himself — it was his weekends and holidays that were now spent cozily *en famille*. It was pleasant, coming back to the house in Tarrytown, coming back from the crusades to find Eunice and the whole household decked out, literally and psychologically, for his return. One grew sentimentally fond of children whom one saw only under such conditions — Grorley's Saturdays were now spent, as he himself boasted, "on all fours," in the rejuvenating air of the skating rinks, the museums, the woods, and the zoos. Sundays and holidays he and Eunice often entertained their relatives, and if, as the turkey browned, he had a momentary twinge of his old *mal de famille*, he had but to remember that his hat was, after all, only hung in the hall.

IT WAS ONLY some years after the war that Eunice began to give trouble. Before that, their double ménage had not been particularly unusual — almost all the households of couples their age had been upset in one way or another, and theirs had been more stable than many. During the war years Eunice had had plenty of company for her midweek evenings; all over America women had been managing bravely behind the scenes. But now that families had long since paired off again, Eunice showed a disquieting tendency to want to be out in front.

"No, you'll have to come home for good," she said to Grorley, at the end of their now frequent battles. "I'm tired of being a short-order wife."

"The trouble with you," said Grorley, "is that you've never adjusted to postwar conditions."

"That was your nineteen-forty-six column," said Eunice. "If you must quote yourself, pick one a little more up-to-date." Removing a jewel-encrusted slipper-toe from the fender, she made a feverish circle of the room, the velvet panniers of her housegown swinging dramatically behind her. She was one of those women who used their charge accounts for retaliation. With each crisis in their deteriorating relationship, Grorley noted gloomily, Eunice's wardrobe had improved.

"Now that the children are getting on," he said, "you ought to have another interest. A hobby."

Eunice made a hissing sound. "Nineteen-forty-seven!" she said.

In the weeks after, she made her position clear. Men, she told him, might have provided the interest he suggested, but when a woman had made a vocation of one, it wasn't easy to start making a hobby of several. It was hardly much use swishing out in clouds of Tabu at seven, if one had to be back to feel Georgie's forehead at eleven. Besides, at their age, the only odd men out were likely to be hypochondriacs, or bachelors still dreaming of mother, or very odd men indeed.

"All the others," she said nastily, "are already on somebody else's hearth rug. Or out making the round with you." Worst of all, she seemed to have lost her former reverence for Grorley's work. If he'd been a novelist or a poet, she said (she even made use of the sticky word "creative"), there'd have been more excuse for his need to go off into the silence. As it was, she saw no reason for his having to be so broody over analyzing the day's proceedings at the U.N. If he wanted an office, that should take care of things very adequately. But if he did not wish to live *with* her, then he could not go on *living* with her. "Mentally," she said, "you're still in the Village. Maybe you better go back there."

Things were at this pass when Grorley's paper sent him to London, on an assignment that kept him there for several months. He was put up for membership in one or two exclusively masculine clubs, and in their leonine atmosphere his outraged vanity — ("creative" indeed!) — swelled anew. Finally, regrettably near the end of his stay, he met up with a redheaded young woman named Vida, who worked for a junior magazine by day, wrote poetry by night, and had once been in America for three weeks. She and Grorley held hands over the mutual hazards of the "creative" life, and on her lips the word was like a caress. For a woman, too, she was remarkably perceptive about the possessiveness of other women. "Yes, quite," she said. "Yes, quite."

When she and Grorley made their final adieu in her Chelsea flat, she held him, for just a minute, at arm's length. "I shall be thinking of you over there, in one of those ghastly, what do you call them, *living rooms*, of yours. Everybody matted together, and the floor all over children — like beetles. Poor dear. I should think those living rooms must be the curse of the American family. Poor, poor dear."

On his return home in June, Grorley and Eunice agreed on a six-month trial separation prior to a divorce. Eunice showed a rather unfeeling calm in the lawyer's office, immediately afterward popped the children in camp, and went off to the Gaspé with friends. Grorley took a sublet on the apartment in Waverly Place. It was furnished in a monastic modern admirably suited to the novel he intended to write, that he had promised Vida to write.

HE HAD ALWAYS liked summers in town, when the real *aficionados* of the city took over, and now this summer seemed to him intoxicating, flowing with the peppery currents of his youth. In the daytime his freedom slouched unshaven; in the evenings the streets echoed and banged with life, and the moon made a hot harlequinade of every alley. He revisited the San Remo, Julius's, Chumley's, Jack Delaney's, and all the little Italian bars with backyard restaurants, his full heart and wallet carrying him quickly into the camaraderie of each. Occasionally he invited home some of the remarkables he met on his rounds — a young Italian bookie, a huge St. Bernard of a woman who drove a taxi and had once lived on a barge on the East River, an attenuated young couple from Chapel Hill, who were honeymooning at the New School. Now and then a few of his men friends from uptown joined him in a night out. A few of these, in turn, invited him home for the weekend, but although he kept sensibly silent on the subject of their fraternal jaunts, he detected some animus in the hospitality of their wives.

By October, Grorley was having a certain difficulty with his weekends. His list of bids to the country was momentarily exhausted, and his own ideas had begun to flag. The children, home from camp, had aged suddenly into the gang phase; they tore out to movies and jamborees of their own, were weanable from these only by what Grorley could scrape up in the way of rodeos and football games, and assumed, once the afternoon treat was over, a faraway look of sufferance. Once or twice, when he took them home, he caught himself hoping that Eunice would ask him in for a drink, a chat that might conceivably lead to dinner, but she was always out, and Mrs. Lederer, the housekeeper, always pulled the children in as if they were packages whose delivery had been delayed, gave him a nasty nod, and shut the door.

For a few weekends he held himself to his desk, trying to work up a sense of dedication over the novel, but there was no doubt that it was going badly. Its best juice had been unwisely expended in long, analytic letters to Vida, and now, in her airmail replies, which bounced steadily and enthusiastically over the Atlantic, it began to seem more her novel than his. The Sunday before Thanksgiving, he made himself embark on a ski-train to Pittsfield, working up a comforting sense of urgency over the early rising and the impedimenta to be checked. The crowd on the train was divided between a band of Swiss and German perfectionists who had no conversation, and a horde of young couples, rolling on the slopes like puppies, who had too much. Between them, Grorley's privacy was respected to the point of insult. When he returned that night, he tossed his gear into a corner, where it wilted damply on his landlord's blond rug, made himself a hot toddy — with a spasm of self-pity over his ability to do for himself — and sat down to face his fright. For years, his regular intervals at home had been like the chewed coffee bean that renewed the wine-taster's palate. He had lost the background from which to rebel.

Thanksgiving day was the worst. The day dawned oyster-pale and stayed that way. Grorley slept as late as he could, then went out for a walk. The streets were slack, without the twitch of crowds, and the houses had a tight look of inner concentration. He turned toward the streets which held only shops, and walked up-town as far as Rockefeller Center. The rink was open, with its usual cast of characters — ricocheting children, a satiny, professional twirler from the Ice Show, and several solemn old men who skated upright in some Euclidian absorption of their own. Except for a few couples strolling along in the twin featurelessness of love, the crowd around the rink was type-cast too. Here, it told itself, it participated in life, here in this flying spectacle of flag and stone it could not possibly be alone. With set, shy smiles, it glanced sideways at its neighbors, rounded its shoulders to the wind, turned up its collar, and leaned closer to the musical bonfire of the square. Grorley straightened up, turned on his heel, smoothed down his collar, and walked rapidly toward Sixth Avenue. He filled himself full of ham and eggs in one of the quick-order places that had no season, taxied home, downed a drink, swallowed two Seconal tablets, and went to bed.

The next morning, seated at his desk, he took a relieved look at the street. People were hard at their normal grind again; for a while the vacuum was past. But Christmas was not going to catch him alone. He picked up the phone. At the end of the day he was quite heartened. Although he had not yet turned up an invitation for Christmas Day, he had netted himself a cocktail party (which might easily go on to dinner) for two days before, a bid to an egg-nog party on New Year's Day, and one weekend toward the middle of December. A lot of people did things impromptu. A phone call now and then would fix him up somehow.

But by Christmas week he was haggard. He had visualized himself as bidden to share, in a pleasantly avuncular capacity, some close friend's family gathering; he had seen himself as indolently and safely centered, but not anchored, in the bright poinsettia of their day. Apparently their vision of him was cast in a harsher mold; they returned his innuendoes with little more than a pointed sympathy. Only two propositions had turned up, one from a group of men, alone like himself for one reason or another, who were forming a party at an inn in the Poconos, and one from a waif-like spinster – "Last Christmas was my last one with dear Mother" – who offered to cook dinner for him in her apartment. Shuddering, he turned down both of these. The last thing he wanted to do on that day was to ally himself with *waifs* of any description; on that day he very definitely wanted to be safely inside some cozy family cocoon, looking out at *them*.

FINALLY, THE DAY before Christmas, he thought of the Meechers. Ted was that blue-ribbon bore, the successful account-executive who believed his own slogans, and his wife, a former social worker, matched him in her own field. Out of Ted's sense of what was due his position in the agency and Sybil's sense of duty to the world, they had created a model home in Chappaqua, equipped with four children, two Bedlingtons, a games room, and a part-time pony. Despite this, they were often hard up for company, since most people could seldom be compelled twice to their table, where a guest was the focus of a constant stream of self-congratulation from either end. Moreover, Ted had wormed his way into more than one stag party at Grorley's, and could hardly refuse a touch. And their Christmas, whatever its other drawbacks, would be a four-color job, on the best stock.

But Ted's voice, plum-smooth when he took the phone from his secretary, turned reedy and doubtful when he heard Grorley's inquiry. "Uh-oh! 'Fraid that puts me on the spot, fella. Yeah. Kind of got it in the neck from Sybil, last time I came home from your place. Yeah. Had a real old-fashioned hassle. Guess I better not risk reminding her just yet. But, say! How about coming up here right now, for the office party?"

Grorley declined, and hung up. Off-campus boy this time of

year, that's what I am, he thought. He looked at his mantelpiece crowded with its reminders — greetings from Grace and Bill, Jane and Tom, Peg and Jack, Etcetera and Mrs. Etcetera. On top of the pile was another airmail from Vida, received that morning, picture enclosed. Sans the red in the hair, without the thrush tones of the assenting voice, she looked a little long in the teeth. Her hands and feet, he remembered, were always cold. Somehow or other, looking at the picture, he didn't think that central heating would improve them. "The living room is the curse," she'd said. That's it, he thought; that's it. And this, Vida, is the season of the living room.

He looked down into the street. The Village was all right for the summer, he thought. But now the periphery of the season had changed. In summer, the year spins on a youth-charged axis, and a man's muscles have a spurious oil. But this is the end toward which it spins. Only three hundred days to Christmas. Only a month — a week. And then, every year, the damned day itself, catching him with its holly claws, sounding its platitudes like carillons.

Down at the corner, carols bugled steamily from a mission soup-kitchen. There's no escape from it, he thought. Turn on the radio, and its alleluia licks you with tremolo tongue. In every store window flameth housegown, nuzzleth slipper. In all the streets the heavenly shops proclaim. The season has shifted inward, Grorley, and you're on the outside, looking in.

He moved toward the phone, grabbed it, and dialed the number before he remembered that you had to dial the code for Tarrytown. He replaced the receiver. Whatever he had to say, and he wasn't quite sure what, or how, it wasn't for the ears of the kids or the Lederer woman. He jammed on his hat. Better get there first, get inside the door.

GOING UP to Grand Central in the cab, he pressed his face against the glass. Everything had been taken care of weeks ago — the kids had been sent their two-wheelers, and he had mailed Eunice an extra-large check — one he hadn't sent through the lawyer. But at five o'clock, Fifth Avenue still shone like an enormous blue sugar-plum revolving in a tutti-frutti rain of light. Here was the season in all its questionable glory — the hallmarked joy of giving, the good will *diamanté*. But in the cosmetic air, people raised tinted faces, walked with levitated step.

In the train, he avoided the smoker, and chose an uncrowded car up front. At his station, he waited until all the gleaming car muzzles pointed at the train had picked up their loads and gone, then walked through the main street which led to his part of town. All was lit up here too, with a more intimate, household shine. He passed the pink damp of a butcher's, the bright fuzz of Woolworth's. "Sold out!" said a woman, emerging. " 's try the A&P." He walked on, invisible, his face pressed to the shop window of the world.

At Schlumbohn's Credit Jewelry Corner he paused, feeling for the wallet filled with cash yesterday for the still not impossible yes over the phone. This was the sort of store that he and Eunice, people like them, never thought of entering. It sold watches pinned to cards, zircons, musical powder-boxes, bracelets clasped with fat ten-carat hearts, Rajah pearl necklaces and Truelove blue-white diamonds. Something for Everybody, it said. He opened the door.

Inside, a magnetic salesgirl nipped him toward her like a pin. He had barely stuttered his wants before he acquired an Add-a-Pearl necklace for Sally, two Genuine Pinseal handbags for his mother-in-law and Mrs. Lederer, and a Stag-horn knife with three blades, a nailfile, and a corkscrew, for young George. He had left Eunice until last, but with each purchase, a shabby, telephoning day had dropped from him. Dizzy with participation, he surveyed the mottoed store.

"Something...something for the wife," he said.

"Our lovely Lifetime Watch, perhaps? Or Something in Silver, for the House?" The clerk tapped her teeth, gauging him.

He leaned closer, understanding suddenly why housewives, encysted in lonely houses, burbled confidences to the grocer, made an audience of the milkman. "We've had a — Little Tiff."

"Aw-w," said the clerk, adjusting her face. "Now...let me see...." She kindled suddenly, raised a sibylline finger, beckoned him farther down the counter, and drew out a tray of gold charms. Rummaging among them with a long, opalescent nail, she passed over minute cocktail shakers, bird cages, tennis rackets, a tiny scroll bearing the words, "If you can see this, you're too darn close," and seized a trinket she held up for view. A large gold shamrock, hung on a chain by a swivel through its middle, it bore the letter I. on its upper leaf, on its nether one the letter U. She reversed it. L.O.V.E. was engraved across the diameter of the other side. The clerk spun it with her accomplished nail. "See?" she said. "Spin it! Spin it and it says I. L.O.V.E. U!"

"Hmmm…" said Grorley, clearing his throat. "Well…guess you can't fob some women off with just a diamond bracelet." She tittered dutifully. But, as she handed it to him with his other packages, and closed the glass door behind him, he saw her shrug something, laughing, to another clerk. She had seen that he was not Schlumbohn's usual, after all.

As he walked up his own street he felt that he was after all hardly anybody's usual, tonight. It was a pretty street, of no particular architectural striving. Not a competitive street, except sometimes in summer, on the subject of gardens. And, of course, now. In every house the tree was up and lit, in the window nearest the passerby. Here was his own, with the same blue lights that had lasted, with some tinkering on his part, year after year. Eunice must have had a man in to fix them.

He stopped on the path. A man in. She was pretty, scorned, and – he had cavalierly assumed – miserable. He had taken for granted that his family, in his absence, would have remained reasonably static. They always had. He'd been thinking of himself. Silently, he peeled off another layer of self-knowledge. He still was.

He walked up the steps wondering what kind of man might rise to be introduced, perhaps from his own armchair. One of her faded, footballish resurrections from Ohio State U., perhaps: Gordon, this is Jim Jerk, from home. Or would she hand it to him at once? Would it be: *Dear*, this is Gordon.

The door was unlocked. He closed it softly behind him, and stood listening. This was the unmistakable quiet of an empty house – as if the secret respiration of all objects in it had just stopped at his entrance. The only light downstairs was the glowing tree. He went up the stairs.

IN THE BEDROOM, the curtains were drawn, the night light on. The bed was piled with an abandoned muddle of silver wrappings, tissue paper, ribbons. He dropped the presents on the bed, tossed his hat after them, let his coat slip down on the familiar chair, and parted the curtains. It had a good view of the river, his house. He stood there, savoring it.

He was still there when a car door slammed and the family came up the path. The Christmas Eve pantomime, of course, held every year at the village hall. Georgie had on one of those white burnooses they always draped the boys in, and Sally, in long dress and coned hat, seemed to be a medieval lady. He saw that this year she had the waist for it. Eunice and Mrs. Lederer walked behind them. He tapped on the glass.

They raised their faces in tableau. The children waved, catcalled, and disappeared through the downstairs door. Mrs. Lederer followed them. Below, Eunice stared upward, in the shine from the tree-window. Behind him, he heard that sound made only by children — the noise of bodies falling up a staircase. As they swarmed in on him, she disappeared.

"You shoulda been to the hall," said Georgie, seizing him. "Christmas at King Arthur's court. I was a knight."

"Was it corny!" said Sally, from a distance. She caught sight of herself in a pier glass. "I was Guinevere."

"Had to do some last-minute shopping," said Grorley.

"I saw my bike!" said Georgie. "It's in the cellar."

"Oh...Georgie!" said Sally.

"Well, I couldn't help seeing it."

"Over there are some Christmas Eve presents," said Grorley.

"Open now?" they said. He nodded. They fell upon them.

"Gee," said Georgie, looking down at the knife. "Is that neat!" From his tone it was clear that he, at least, was Schlumbohn's usual.

"Oh, Dad!" Sally had the necklace around her neck. She raised her arms artistically above her head, in the fifth position, minced forward, and placed their slender wreath around Grorley's neck. As she hung on him, sacklike, he felt that she saw them both, a tender picture, in some lurking pier glass of her mind.

The door opened, and Eunice came in. She shut it behind her with a "not before the servants" air, and stood looking at him. Her face was blurred at the edges; she hadn't decked herself out for anybody. She looked the way a tired, pretty woman, of a certain age and responsibilities, might look at the hour before dinner, at the moment when age and prettiness tussle for her face, and age momentarily has won.

"Look what I got!" Georgie brandished the knife.

"And mine!" Sally undulated herself. "Mums! Doesn't it just *go!*" She stopped, looking from father to mother, her face hesitant, but shrewd.

"Open yours, Mums. Go on."

"Later," said Eunice. "Right now I think Mrs. Lederer wants you both to help with the chestnuts."

"No fair, no fair," said Georgie. "You saw ours."

"Do what your mother says," said Grorley. The paternal phrase, how it steadied him, was almost a hearthstone under his feet.

"Oh, well," said Eunice, wilting toward the children, as she invariably did when he was stern with them. Opening the package he indicated, she drew out the bauble. Georgie rushed to look at it, awarded it a quick, classifying disinterest, and returned to his knife.

"Oo – I know how to work those! Margie's sister has one," said Sally. She worked it. "If that isn't corny!" she gurgled. Eunice's head was bent over the gift. Sally straightened up, gave her and Grorley a swift, amending glance. "But cute!" she said. She flushed. Then, with one of the lightning changes that were the bane of her thirteen years, she began to cry. "Honestly, it's sweet!" she said.

Grorley looped an arm around her, gave her a squeeze and a kiss. "Now, shoo," he said. "Both of you."

When he turned back to the room, Eunice was looking out the window, chin up, her face not quite averted. Recognizing the posture, he quailed. It was the stance of the possessor of the stellar role – of the nightingale with her heart against the thorn. It was the stance of the woman who demands her scene.

He sighed, rat-tatted his fingers on a table top. "Well," he said. "Guess this is the season the corn grows tall."

A small movement of her shoulder. The back of her head to him. Now protocol demanded that he talk, into her silence, dredging his self-abasement until he hit upon some remark which made it possible for her to turn, to rend it, to show it up for the heartless, illogical, tawdry remark that it was. He could repeat a list of the game birds of North America, or a passage from the Congressional Record. The effect would be the same.

"Go on," he said, "get it over with. I deserve it. I just want you to know...mentally, I'm out of the Village."

She turned, head up, nostrils dilated. Her mouth opened. "Get it ov − !" Breath failed her. But not for long.

MUCH LATER, they linked arms in front of the same window. Supper had been eaten, the turkey had been trussed, the children at last persuaded into their beds. That was the consolatory side of family life, Grorley thought − the long, Olympian codas of the emotions were cut short by the niggling detail. Women thought otherwise, of course. In the past, he had himself.

Eunice began clearing off the bed. "What's in those two? Father's and Mother's?"

"Oh Lord. I forgot Father."

"Never mind. I'll look in the white-elephant box." The household phrase − how comfortably it rang. She looked up. "What's in these then?"

"For Mother and Mrs. Lederer. Those leather satchel-things. Pinseal."

"Both the same, I'll bet."

He nodded.

Eunice began to laugh. "Oh, Lord. How they'll hate it." She continued to laugh, fondly, until Grorley smirked response. This, too, was familiar. Masculine gifts: the inappropriateness thereof.

But Eunice continued to laugh, steadily, hysterically, clutching her stomach, collapsing into a chair. "It's that hat," she said. "It's that s-specimen of a hat!"

Grorley's hat lay on the bed, where he had flung it. Brazenly dirty, limp denizen of bars, it reared sideways on a crest of tissue paper, one curling red whorl around its crown. "L-like something out of Hogarth," she said. "The R-rounder's Return."

Grorley forced a smile. "You can buy me another."

"Mmmm...for Christmas." She stopped laughing. "You know... I think that's what convinced me − your coming back tonight. Knowing you − that complex of yours. Suppose I felt if you meant to stand us through the holidays, you meant to stand us for good."

Grorley coughed, bent to stuff some paper into the wastebasket. In fancy, he was stuffing in a picture too, portrait of Vida, woman of imagination, outdistanced forever by the value of a woman who had none.

Eunice yawned. "Oh…I forgot to turn out the tree."

"I'll go down."

"Here, take this along." She piled his arms with crushed paper. In grinning afterthought, she clapped the hat on his head.

HE WENT to the kitchen and emptied his arms in the bin. The kitchen was in chaos, the cookery methods of *alt Wien* demanding that each meal rise like a phœnix, from a flaming muddle below-stairs. Tomorrow, as Mrs. Lederer mellowed with wine, they would hear once again of her grandfather's house, where the coffee was not even *roasted* until the guests' carriages appeared in the driveway.

In the dining room, the table was set in state, from damask to silver nut dishes. Father would sit here. He was teetotal, but anecdotalism signs no pledge. His jousts as purchasing agent for the city of his birth now left both narrator and listener with the impression that he had built it as well. They would hear from Mother too. It was unfortunate that her bit of glory — her grandfather had once attended Grover Cleveland — should have crystallized itself in that one sentence so shifty for false teeth — "Yes, my father was a physician, you know."

Grorley sighed, and walked into the living room. He looked out, across the flowing blackness of the river. There to the south, somewhere in that jittering corona of yellow lights, was the apartment. He shuddered pleasurably, thinking of all the waifs in the world tonight. His own safety was too new for altruism; it was only by a paring of luck as thin as this pane of glass that he was safely here — on the inside, looking out.

Behind him, the tree shone — that *trompe-l'oeil* triumphant — yearly symbol of how eternally people had to use the spurious to catch at the real. If there was an angel at the top, then here was the devil at its base — that, at this season, anybody who opened his eyes and ears too wide caught the poor fools, caught himself, hard at it.

Home is where the heart...the best things in life are...spin it and it says I. L. O. V. E. U.

Grorley reached up absently and took off his hat. This is middle age, he thought. Stand still and hear the sound of it, bonging like carillons, the gathering sound of all the platitudes, sternly coming true.

He looked down at the hat in his hand. It was an able hat; not every hat could cock a snook like that one. From now on, he'd need every ally he could muster. Holding it, he bent down and switched off the tree. He was out of the living room and halfway up the stairs, still holding it, before he turned back. Now the house was entirely dark, but he needed no light other than the last red sputter of rebellion in his heart. He crept down, felt along the wall, clasped a remembered hook. Firmly, he hung his hat in the hall. Then he turned, and went back up the stairs.

Elaine Marcus Starkman

ANNIVERSARY

W E'VE GROWN SO ALIKE standing before our bedroom mirror this morning. Today, our fifteenth wedding anniversary. Even our reflections look alike. Two full faces, steady hazel eyes hidden beneath silver-rimmed glasses, sensitive lips, he, balding, I with the color of my hair gone drab.

Wordless he shaves, black stubble from his electric razor falling into our double-bowl vanity, onto our white carpet. Hum of his razor and my toothbrush droning under harsh fluorescent light.

He pulls out the plug, stuffs razor into our toothpaste-smudged drawer, that drawer like all our dresser drawers. Cluttered with indispensable litter that ties us together. Inside: notes, change, mismatched socks, graying underwear. Outside: surgical journals, poems, math tests, tennis shoes.

He throws his pajamas into the old straw laundry basket and dresses, clothes unstylish and conservative as the day we met. Dark suit, narrow lapels. Reluctantly pulls on blue-flowered shirt I gave him for his birthday.

Banging of bathroom door, burnt toast, bitter coffee, frantic search for jackets and lunch money fade into morning routine. House silent. Only whirring of washer and dryer. When did I start them?

An ordinary morning. Hair unclipped, terrycloth robe stained.

Yet different. Fifteenth anniversary, and I find his face among towels. How he rushed in late last night, high beneficent forehead pink with chill, glasses steamy.

"Sorry, got stuck again. Just a standard procedure. Nothing interesting. Maybe we could go to a movie tomorrow. The one by that woman film director is playing in Berkeley."

"*Swept Away*? I thought you said it was too violent."

"It's the old taming of the shrew updated, isn't it?"

"Yes. You won't like it."

"Probably not, but you said it was important to see. Ingmar Bergman's got a new film out. Maybe I'll come home early. We can go to either one."

What sudden extravagance, when has he ever cared about films? Has he remembered our anniversary this year? The year of my migraines, his weight gain, our son's running away, our daughter's school failure? The summer we fought on the Santa Cruz beach in front of a crowd of strangers, I screaming, "Doctor, doctor, doctor," he slapping me across the cheek, voice seething, "Shut up; I'm sick of you. From now on I'll do what *I* want." We drove home from his day off, the children shocked into silence. Those endless hot months, no classes, no poems to sustain me, only family responsibility. I hated what I'd once loved. Maury, a doctor before he was born. He *had* to be. And I his wife.

Throw wet towels into the dryer. What would I do in my spare time without laundry? Golf, shop, drive to the city, join the hospital auxiliary?

Brush my hair and dress. Our wedding portrait. How voguish I look. Blonde teased pageboy. Squinting through my contact lenses. A tiny pearl crown on my head. My mother sighing with relief: *A doctor she's marrying, thank God; she's nearly twenty-three.* Except for his baldness, he hasn't changed a bit. Same soft eyes, same earnest smile, same uncompromising values, same rabbinical look. In those days I'd look away modestly and say, "I love you." Even when he cut short our three-day honeymoon to return to his residency. How understanding I was.

How quickly we fell into routine. The long weekends of his final year, endless hours in the emergency room, his exhaustion, my posing with a huge belly in the St. Louis snow. After lovemaking he'd stand awkwardly in the hall in his white gown almost afraid to say those words: "I have to go now, Nina. I'll be back tomorrow night."

"All right," I lied.

"Maybe you should phone your mother so you won't be lonely."

"No, no, everything's fine. I'd rather be alone."

"Then why are you crying? You knew it would be this way."

"It's okay. Go on." Listen to footsteps resound in the dark hallway of our apartment building.

Five years and we never quarreled. *Nina, my friend needs a loan. But Maury, we haven't gone anywhere for so long. I've got to lend him some money. All right, Maury. Time to visit my family. Can't we skip this Friday night? You don't have to say anything. Just sit with them. Listen, let's invite them here next week. Maury, you know I can't cook anything your mother does. Make something simple; it doesn't matter.*

How grateful I was. His family called me lucky. What could I do to please such a giving man? Only conceive and that I managed despite our obstetrician-friend's prognosis: *her pelvis is small.* But they came anyway, three births in five years, the miracle of our children's lives escaping us, distracting us from our own goals. They ran through the town house shrieking, crying, tumbling down the stairs, biting each other, demanding love and attention. He loved them; they bewildered him. "Why are they so wild?" he scratched his head.

"Because they're spoiled. Didn't your mother spoil you?"

"She didn't have time. She always worked in the grocery to save money for our schooling."

"Why don't you humor them? Why are you so strict?"

"Because I love them, because I want them to know right from wrong."

How problematic they were — Joey repeating first grade, Amy moody and withdrawn, Rachel with her temper tantrums. Every year we were unprepared for their growing pains. And our own as well. Every year he said, *the medical profession's got to change. No, Maury, you've got to adapt to it. What you want is impossible.* Six times we moved chasing impossibilities. All the time our parents hovering in the background: *Tell him medicine is a business; his income depends on that.*

Our final move to the west coast nearly destroyed us. Here away from friends and family among capricious San Francisco temperaments, Rachel crawls out of diapers and into kindergarten. "I'm sick of your ideals. Sick of being called 'doctor's wife.' I'm going after mine now," I rant.

"What are you going to do?"

"I don't know, but I'll find out."

"Do what you want. Have I ever stopped you from doing what you want?"

"Your very presence stops me. Your — "

"That's your fault, not mine. I could never please you anyway. Just don't ask *me* to change; just leave me alone."

I don't ask. I sit in the kitchen of our new California-style house late at night writing poems. For the first time in years. Those poems, that passion, born of my guts, my joy alone, not his, *mine.* Published in an obscure feminist university journal. I'm a feminist, liberated. Suburban mother of three, I howl with delight. Dance with the children, drive to the top of Mt. Diablo, shout from its peaks: *Mamma's gone mad.*

With that madness 1970 breaks, and I'm transformed. Nina the Iconoclast. Chipping away at his pedestal. He's rigid, unathletic, boring, *too moral.* I'll leave. Go to live in a women's commune in Berkeley, fly to Israel and build the desert, make up for lost time. Drown myself in Bergman, look for the young Chicano I met in the poetry stacks. But I watch him say *Kaddish* for the death of his patient, listen to the sound of his Danish rocker and favorite Oistrakh, look into his deep hazel eyes that refuse to see the sense-lessness of our lives, and bound off to the laundry room like a hurt puppy. There in that familiar maze of underwear, old texts and paperbacks, I announce, "I'm starting school again."

"Good idea, but don't become too compulsive about it."

How well he knows my compulsiveness. School's not so easy now. My forehead tingles, my stomach cramps. Rachel asks why I'm not room-mother. "Because I have to study," I snap, a dragon at dinner hour. Course after course. Women and Madness, La Raza Studies, Seminar in Faulkner, Tai Chi, the Yiddish Novel.

The children's diapers are replaced by braces, lessons, tutors, car pools, conferences, puberty. They alone grow. We merely age, I studying at night toward some unknown pursuit, Maury reading journals and Middle East news reports.

"Ten o'clock. I'm on call. I've got to get some rest."

"Go ahead. I'm studying."

"Why do you play this game every night?"

"What game?"

"All right, study. Study until you beg me to touch you. I'm fed up. You and your games."

"I'm not playing games. I just have no desire."

"Then why don't you leave? It's fashionable for women to leave men these days. I'll give you anything you want. Just go so I can have some peace."

"Don't be ridiculous; you think I'd leave you and the children?"

"Why not? You probably have a lover anyway."

"Are you mad? Are you *absolutely* mad?"

"Then why do you act like this?"

"Like what?"

"Your lack of desire, your inability to manage the kids. Why don't you go for help?"

"Because I'm trying to change? Because I'm trying to do something for myself? You're the one who should go. You've lost touch with reality."

"Go in the kitchen and study. You don't respect anything I believe in. You want something I can't give you. I'm just a small man."

The yellow wallpaper rages in silence. All these years — wasted. He with his kindness has made me afraid of the world, he with his selflessness has made me nothing, and I've let it happen. What am I next to him?

The phone rings. He dresses and leaves. I close my text and creep into our bedroom, lie by the telephone on his side of the bed. Browse in a new novel. What reckless heroines, what cads the men are. Why can't we be like that?

He's gone an hour now. The rage dissolves into a whimper. The wind bangs at the patio windows, dogs bark, children moan, the faucet drips. What if Maury dies? Would I mourn him for years? Would I ever take a lover?

Phone again. A woman I met at school.

"One partner in fourteen years? This is the Age of Aquarius."

"For him it isn't."

"And for you?"

"Me? I don't know."

"You're still hung up because he's a doctor."

"It's not that. It's the kind of person he is."

"You mean *you are*. You'll change, you'll see. By the end of the year you'll change."

"Not in *that* way. You know I still have some traditional values."

"You and he are just alike, killing yourselves with an outmoded moral code. You have to move with the times."

"I know, I know."

"No you don't. Otherwise you'd forget your fantasies or admit you still care for him."

"I can't."

At 2:00 A.M. he comes in, face sallow, tired, blood on his under-shorts. "A terrible case, Nina, a young man. Motorcycle accident. He'll be dead by morning. Let me hold you. I can't do my work without you."

A winter moon floods our bedroom. Succumb but don't surrender. Don't share his act of love. Separate mind, nourish it with illusions of young men in my classes. He falls asleep immediately, not waking to wash. Listen to his snoring. Anesthetic on his fingers, spittle on his lip. How could I ever leave? He'd work himself to death. I'm the small one, not he. If only I'd let go of my anger, if only I'd stop blaming him for my failures. Sleep, morning, obligation, make lunch, the children —

We wake, shut off from one another, two strangers. Wordless, he shaves, runs off to the hospital. Phones me at ten. A sudden joy in his voice. "Nina, he's going to *live*. There *must* be a God, do you hear? When I told that to the men, they laughed. Nina, say something."

I can't. He waits for my silence to end. "Listen, I know this has been a hard month. One of the men told me about a place in Mexico. Maybe we could drive down with the kids when they're on spring vacation."

"I don't think they'll want to go. Last time we took them with us it was a disaster. You hollered at Joey the whole time, and Amy's complaints drove me crazy."

"We could leave them with Mrs. Larsen."

"Rachel hates Mrs. Larsen."

"How about Mrs. Bertoli?"

"Too expensive."

"Well, I just wanted to check before I take extra call this month. This malpractice insurance will either kill me or make me retire."

"Take the call, Maury; we'll stay at home."

"You're sure?"

"I'm sure; you're not ready to retire. Maury — I'm glad about your patient."

"Don't be glad for me, be glad for him."

He didn't even mention our anniversary; he didn't remember. Every year he forgets. Yes, we'll stay home this time as we have all the other times. And yet there's something different this year as I sort the towels. His key in the door, breakfast dishes unwashed. He's home so soon flipping on the news.

"It's too early for lunch."

"I know." Hands me a single rose, kisses my neck. "Happy Anniversary." Looks so helpless I want to reach out but don't. My eyes wet. "Come on. I'll make you lunch. What time do you have to be back?"

"I don't; the anesthesiologist is on strike. No work."

He changes into his gardening pants. When did he let his sideburns grow? They're nearly gray. How he loves watering the garden. Always has been more nurturing than I. Awkward eating without the children. What to say to each other — just two of us alone. A new phase we're entering this fifteenth year.

"The salad's great. You know, we should become vegetarians," he suddenly laughs.

"Can you see Joey existing without his sloppy joes and hot dogs?"

"Give him five more years, he will. He get off okay this morning? He was mumbling about some science project."

"Fine, he's even turning into a decent kid. Decent but different from us."

"He's growing up in such different times; it's hard on him. Good to be home. After seeing that patient this morning I promised myself not to worry about anything. Are you angry at me?"

"Why do you ask?"

"You seemed upset this morning."

"I was angry at myself."

"What for?"

"Because I've let myself become too much like you."

"Why do you say that? We have our separate friends, interests — "

"Even Bob Stoller said we're getting to look alike."

He grins. "Only our noses. Did you know that Stoller and his wife broke up last week?"

"Nothing surprises me these days. How come you didn't tell me?"

"What's the use of telling bad news? Nina, let's sell the house; let's go live in the country. I'm sick and tired of everything. I'm going to look at a place this weekend."

"Are you kidding?"

"I'm not. Let's finish lunch and talk about it in bed."

"But Rachel comes home at two, and I've got to finish a poem."

"Forget the poem. If you work too hard, you'll become a poet. Then what would I do?"

"Maury, you're a chauvinist!"

"No, I'm not, just jealous."

"*You're* jealous of *me?*"

"You've more time to think, to be yourself."

"I suppose I do."

"More time to do what you want."

"Oh, come on now."

"Well, I can't do what I want either. People like us have too many responsibilities. We live limited lives."

He stands there in his underwear, his pale skin covered with black down. The veins in his neck pulsate like the days in our old St. Louis apartment when we were first married. March twenty-first, 1960. First day of spring. *I still care, I still care.* I didn't know that I did, but I do.

Willa Cather

THE SENTIMENTALITY

OF WILLIAM TAVENER

IT TAKES A STRONG WOMAN to make any sort of success of living in the West, and Hester undoubtedly was that. When people spoke of William Tavener as the most prosperous farmer in McPherson County, they usually added that his wife was a "good manager." She was an executive woman, quick of tongue and something of an imperatrix.* The only reason her husband did not consult her about his business was that she did not wait to be consulted.

It would have been quite impossible for one man, within the limited sphere of human action, to follow all Hester's advice, but in the end William usually acted upon some of her suggestions. When she incessantly denounced the "shiftlessness" of letting a new threshing machine stand unprotected in the open, he eventually built a shed for it. When she sniffed contemptuously at his notion of fencing a hog corral with sod walls, he made a spiritless beginning on the structure — merely to "show his temper," as she put it — but in the end he went off quietly to town and bought enough barbed wire to complete the fence. When the first heavy rains came on, and the pigs rooted down the sod wall and made little paths all over it to facilitate their ascent, he heard his wife relate with relish the story of the little pig that built a mud house, to the minister at the dinner table, and William's gravity never relaxed for an instant.

* *Imperatrix*: female emperor.

Silence, indeed, was William's refuge and his strength.

William set his boys a wholesome example to respect their mother. People who knew him very well suspected that he even admired her. He was a hard man toward his neighbors, and even toward his sons: grasping, determined and ambitious.

There was an occasional blue day about the house when William went over the store bills, but he never objected to any items relating to his wife's gowns or bonnets. So it came about that many of the foolish, unnecessary little things that Hester bought for her boys, she had charged to her personal account.

One spring night Hester sat in a rocking chair by the sitting room window, darning socks. She rocked violently and sent her long needle vigorously back and forth over her gourd, and it took only a very casual glance to see that she was wrought up over something. William sat on the other side of the table reading his farm paper. If he had noticed his wife's agitation, his calm, clean-shaven face betrayed no sign of concern. He must have noticed the sarcastic turn of her remarks at the supper table, and he must have noticed the moody silence of the older boys as they ate. When supper was but half over little Billy, the youngest, had suddenly pushed back his plate and slipped away from the table, manfully trying to swallow a sob. But William Tavener never heeded ominous forecasts in the domestic horizon, and he never looked for a storm until it broke.

After supper the boys had gone to the pond under the willows in the big cattle corral, to get rid of the dust of plowing. Hester could hear an occasional splash and a laugh ringing clear through the stillness of the night, as she sat by the open window. She sat silent for almost an hour reviewing in her mind many plans of attack. But she was too vigorous a woman to be much of a strategist, and she usually came to her point with directness. At last she cut her thread and suddenly put her darning down, saying emphatically:

"William, I don't think it would hurt you to let the boys go to that circus in town tomorrow."

William continued to read his farm paper, but it was not Hester's custom to wait for an answer. She usually divined his arguments and assailed them one by one before he uttered them.

"You've been short of hands all summer, and you've worked the boys hard, and a man ought use his own flesh and blood as well as he does his hired hands. We're plenty able to afford it, and it's little enough our boys ever spend. I don't see how you can expect 'em to be steady and hard workin', unless you encourage 'em a little. I never could see much harm in circuses, and our boys have never been to one. Oh, I know Jim Howley's boys get drunk an' carry on when they go, but our boys ain't that sort, an' you know it, William. The animals are real instructive, an' our boys don't get to see much out here on the prairie. It was different where we were raised, but the boys have got no advantages here, an' if you don't take care, they'll grow up to be greenhorns."

Hester paused a moment, and William folded up his paper, but vouchsafed no remark. His sisters in Virginia had often said that only a quiet man like William could ever have lived with Hester Perkins. Secretly, William was rather proud of his wife's "gift of speech," and of the fact that she could talk in prayer meeting as fluently as a man. He confined his own efforts in that line to a brief prayer at Covenant meetings.

Hester shook out another sock and went on.

"Nobody was ever hurt by goin' to a circus. Why, law me! I remember I went to one myself once, when I was little. I had most forgot about it. It was over at Pewtown, an' I remember how I had set my heart on going. I don't think I'd ever forgiven my father if he hadn't taken me, though that red clay road was in a frightful way after the rain. I mind they had an elephant and six poll parrots, an' a Rocky Mountain lion, an' a cage of monkeys, an' two camels. My! but they were a sight to me then!"

Hester dropped the black sock and shook her head and smiled at the recollection. She was not expecting anything from William yet, and she was fairly startled when he said gravely, in much the same tone in which he announced the hymns in prayer meeting:

"No, there was only one camel. The other was a dromedary."

She peered around the lamp and looked at him keenly.

"Why, William, how come you to know?"

William folded his paper and answered with some hesitation, "I was there, too."

Hester's interest flashed up. "Well, I never, William! To think of my finding it out after all these years! Why, you couldn't have been much bigger'n our Billy then. It seems queer I never saw you when you was little, to remember about you. But then you Back Creek folks never have anything to do with us Gap people. But how come you to go? Your father was stricter with you than you are with your boys."

"I reckon I shouldn't 'a gone," he said slowly, "but boys will do foolish things. I had done a good deal of fox hunting the winter before, and Father let me keep the bounty money. I hired Tom Smith's Tap to weed the corn for me, an' I slipped off unbeknownst to Father an' went to the show."

Hester spoke up warmly: "Nonsense, William! It didn't do you no harm, I guess. You was always worked hard enough. It must have been a big sight for a little fellow. That clown must have just tickled you to death."

William crossed his knees and leaned back in his chair.

"I reckon I could tell all that fool's jokes now. Sometimes I can't help thinkin' about 'em in meetin' when the sermon's long. I mind I had on a pair of new boots that hurt me like the mischief, but I forgot all about 'em when that fellow rode the donkey. I recall I had to take them boots off as soon as I got out of sight o' town, and walked home in the mud barefoot."

"O poor little fellow!" Hester ejaculated, drawing her chair nearer and leaning her elbows on the table. "What cruel shoes they did use to make for children. I remember I went up to Back Creek to see the circus wagons go by. They came down from Romney, you know. The circus men stopped at the creek to water the animals, an' the elephant got stubborn an' broke a big limb off the yellow willow tree that grew there by the toll house porch, an' the Scribners were 'fraid as death he'd pull the house down. But this much I saw him do; he waded in the creek an' filled his trunk with water and squirted it in at the window and nearly ruined Ellen Scribner's pink lawn dress that she had just ironed an' laid out on the bed ready to wear to the circus."

"I reckon that must have been a trial to Ellen," chuckled William, "for she was mighty prim in them days."

Hester drew her chair still nearer William's. Since the children had begun growing up, her conversation with her husband had been almost wholly confined to questions of economy and expense. Their relationship had become purely a business one, like that between landlord and tenant. In her desire to indulge her boys she had unconsciously assumed a defensive and almost hostile attitude toward her husband. No debtor ever haggled with his usurer more doggedly than did Hester with her husband in behalf of her sons. The strategic contest had gone on so long that it had almost crowded out the memory of a closer relationship. This exchange of confidences tonight, when common recollections took them unawares and opened their hearts, had all the miracle of romance. They talked on and on; of old neighbors, of old familiar faces in the valley where they had grown up, of long forgotten incidents of their youth — weddings, picnics, sleighing parties and baptizings. For years they had talked of nothing else but butter and eggs and the prices of things, and now they had as much to say to each other as people who meet after a long separation.

When the clock struck ten, William rose and went over to his walnut secretary and unlocked it. From his red leather wallet he took out a ten-dollar bill and laid it on the table beside Hester.

"Tell the boys not to stay late, an' not to drive the horses hard," he said quietly, and went off to bed.

Hester blew out the lamp and sat still in the dark a long time. She left the bill lying on the table where William had placed it. She had a painful sense of having missed something, or lost something; she felt that somehow the years had cheated her.

The little locust trees that grew by the fence were white with blossoms. Their heavy odor floated in to her on the night wind and recalled a night long ago, when the first whippoorwill of the spring was heard, and the rough, buxom girls of Hawkins Gap had held her laughing and struggling under the locust trees, and searched in her bosom for a lock of her sweetheart's hair, which is supposed to be on every girl's breast when the first whippoorwill sings. Two of those same girls had been her bridesmaids. Hester had been a very happy bride. She rose and went softly into the room where William lay. He was sleeping heavily, but occasionally moved his hand before his face to ward off the flies. Hester went into the parlor and took the piece of mosquito net from the basket of wax apples and pears that her sister had made before she died. One of the boys had brought it all the way from Virginia, packed in a tin pail, since Hester would not risk shipping so precious an ornament by freight. She went back to the bedroom and spread the net over William's head. Then she sat down by the bed and listened to his deep, regular breathing until she heard the boys returning. She went out to meet them and warn them not to waken their father.

"I'll be up early to get your breakfast, boys. Your father says you can go to the show." As she handed the money to the eldest, she felt a sudden throb of allegiance to her husband and said sharply, "And you be careful of that, an' don't waste it. Your father works hard for his money."

The boys looked at each other in astonishment and felt that they had lost a powerful ally.

Mothers

&

Daughters

A mother's hardest to forgive.
Life is the fruit she longs to hand you,
Ripe on a plate. And while you live,
Relentlessly she understands you.

PHYLLIS McGINLEY

INTRODUCTION

THE RELATIONSHIP between mother and daughter is a primary one in women's lives. This bond is particularly strong because mothers and daughters spend much time together sharing common activities. Also, daughters imitate and identify with their mothers, while mothers invariably see reflections of their younger selves in their daughters. Mothers tend to be invested in the lives of their daughters, since they expect their daughters to experience joys and sorrows similar to their own and often seek to fulfill their unrealized dreams through their daughters' opportunities. Moreover, since females are taught to be sensitive to others' needs and feelings and are encouraged to be nurturing and verbal, mothers and daughters are often "tuned in" to one another, even during an argument. When a mother and daughter interact, the mother's behavior often bears the stamp of her relationship with her own mother. Over and over again, we see in mother-daughter literature the importance of the three-generation connection among the women in a family.

The powerful mother-daughter bond is characterized by ambivalence. Deep affection fuses with bitter resentment as mothers and daughters take care of one another, focus on their mutual expectations, and struggle to clarify boundaries.

One of the most common difficulties faced by a mother and

daughter is their inability to view themselves as two separate individuals. This difficulty becomes particularly apparent during the
daughter's teen years, and the ambivalence experienced by both
mother and daughter is often heightened during this period. Needing independence and a sense of herself as a unique individual, the
teenaged daughter struggles to find paths leading away from
mother's sphere of influence, while still wanting maternal support
and protection. At this time, a mother faces dilemmas of her own,
since, in her role as supportive parent, she is expected to affirm her
daughter in the face of what are often vehement criticisms and
powerful signs of rejection. In addition, the mother of a growing
daughter is torn between anxiously guarding the innocence of her
daughter and encouraging her to be a self-sufficient young
woman.

What further complicates the mother-daughter relationship at
any given time is the fact that despite their deep, often intuitive,
understanding of one another, mothers and daughters will always
be at different stages of the life cycle, tackling a distinct set of personal challenges. Thus, for example, an adolescent daughter experiencing an identity crisis and a mother approaching menopause
will be preoccupied with two separate sets of developmental issues.
Or a daughter caught up in the first fantasies of romantic love will
be miles apart from a mother preoccupied with the disillusion-
ments of an unfulfilling marriage.

Taken together, the stories within this section capture the com-
plexities of the generation gap and explore mother-daughter interactions through the presentation of the mother's as well as the
daughter's point of view. In each story, the daughter finds her own
way to establish a distinct identity. While some keep secrets,
others align themselves with father or ridicule mother's tastes and
beliefs. Counteracting the motifs of conflict and separation in
these stories is the presence of both the mother's and daughter's
desire to protect and nurture one another.

Bowen's "Coming Home" and Colette's "The Sempstress"
complement one another, for both stories are about a young
daughter's loss of innocence and distancing from mother, but
while the first focuses on the daughter's ambivalence, the second
highlights the mother's dismay.

With its unusually lengthy time span, Bentley's "Mother and

Daughter" provides us with a unique perspective on the mother-daughter relationship, for we are privy to the thoughts and feelings of a seventeen-year-old daughter who in turn becomes the mother of her own teenaged daughter in the story's second section. In fact, Bentley's story actually presents four generations of women in one family and provides clues as to how patterns repeat themselves within families and how fathers affect the separation process between mothers and daughters.

Portnoy's "Loving Strangers" also provides a multi-generational view of the mother-daughter bond, since it highlights an afternoon conversation between a mother and a young adult daughter just learning how to parent her own baby girl. Through their sharing of common roles, the two women in this last story, unlike those in Bentley's tale, achieve a new level of understanding.   G.C.

Elizabeth Bowen

COMING HOME

Aᴌʟ ᴛʜᴇ ᴡᴀʏ ʜᴏᴍᴇ from school Rosalind's cheeks burnt, she felt something throbbing in her ears. It was sometimes terrible to live so far away. Before her body had turned the first corner her mind had many times wrenched open their gate, many times rushed up their path through the damp smells of the garden, waving the essay-book, and seen Darlingest coming to the window. Nothing like this had ever happened before to either her or Darlingest; it was the supreme moment that all these years they had been approaching, of which those dim, improbable future years would be spent in retrospect.

Rosalind's essay had been read aloud and everybody had praised it. Everybody had been there, the big girls sitting along the sides of the room had turned and looked at her, raising their eyebrows and smiling. For an infinity of time the room had held nothing but the rising and falling of Miss Wilfred's beautiful voice doing the service of Rosalind's brain. When the voice dropped to silence and the room was once more unbearably crowded, Rosalind had looked at the clock and seen that her essay had taken four and a half minutes to read. She found that her mouth was dry and her eyes ached from staring at a small fixed spot in the heart of whirling circles, and her knotted hands were damp and trembling. Somebody behind her gently poked the small of her back. Everybody in the room was thinking about Rosalind; she felt their admiration and attention lapping up against her in small waves. A long way off somebody spoke her name repeatedly, she stood up stupidly and everybody laughed. Miss Wilfred was trying to pass her back the red exercise book. Rosalind sat down thinking to herself how dazed she was, dazed with glory. She was beginning already to feel about for words for Darlingest.

She had understood some time ago that nothing became real for her until she had had time to live it over again. An actual occurrence was nothing but the blankness of a shock, then the knowledge that something had happened; afterwards one could creep back and look into one's mind and find new things in it, clear and solid. It was like waiting outside the hen-house till the hen came off the nest and then going in to look for the egg. She would not touch this egg until she was with Darlingest, then they would go and look for it together. Suddenly and vividly this afternoon would be real for her. "I won't think about it yet," she said, "for fear I'd spoil it."

The houses grew scarcer and the roads greener, and Rosalind relaxed a little; she was nearly home. She looked at the syringa bushes by the gate, and it was as if a cold wind had brushed against her. Supposing Darlingest were out…?

She slowed down her running steps to a walk. From here she would be able to call to Darlingest. But if she didn't answer there would be still a tortuous hope; she might be at the back of the house. She decided to pretend it didn't matter, one way or the other; she had done this before, and it rather took the wind out of Somebody's sails, she felt. She hitched up her essay-book under her arm, approached the gate, turned carefully to shut it, and walked slowly up the path looking carefully down at her feet, not up at all at the drawing-room window. Darlingest would think she was playing a game. Why didn't she hear her tapping on the glass with her thimble?

As soon as she entered the hall she knew that the house was empty. Clocks ticked very loudly; upstairs and downstairs the doors were a little open, letting through pale strips of light. Only the kitchen door was shut, down the end of the passage, and she could hear Emma moving about behind it. There was a spectral shimmer of light in the white panelling. On the table was a bowl of primroses, Darlingest must have put them there that morning. The hall was chilly; she could not think why the primroses gave her such a feeling of horror, then she remembered the wreath of primroses, and the scent of it, lying on the raw new earth of that grave....The pair of grey gloves were gone from the bowl of visiting-cards. Darlingest had spent the morning doing those deathly primroses, and then taken up her grey gloves and gone out, at the end of the afternoon, just when she knew her little girl would be coming in. A quarter-past four. It was unforgivable of Darlingest: she had been a mother for more than twelve years, the mother exclusively of Rosalind, and still, it seemed, she knew no better than to do a thing like that. Other people's mothers had terrible little babies: they ran quickly in and out to go to them, or they had smoky husbands who came in and sat, with big feet. There was something distracted about other people's mothers. But Darlingest, so exclusively one's own....

Darlingest could never have really believed in her. She could never have really believed that Rosalind would do anything wonderful at school, or she would have been more careful to be in to hear about it. Rosalind flung herself into the drawing-room; it was honey-coloured and lovely in the pale spring light, another little clock was ticking in the corner, there were more bowls of primroses and black-eyed, lowering anemones. The tarnished mirror on the wall distorted and reproved her angry face in its mild mauveness. Tea was spread on the table by the window, tea for two that the two might never....Her work and an open book lay on the tumbled cushions of the window-seat. All the afternoon she had sat there waiting and working, and now — poor little Darlingest, perhaps she had gone out because she was lonely.

People who went out sometimes never came back again. Here she was, being angry with Darlingest, and all the time....Well, she had drawn on those grey gloves and gone out wandering along the roads, vague and beautiful, because she was lonely, and then?

Ask Emma? No, she wouldn't; fancy having to ask *her!*

"Yes, your mother'll be in soon, Miss Rosie. Now run and get your things off, there's a good girl — " Oh no, intolerable.

The whole house was full of the scent and horror of the primroses. Rosalind dropped the exercise-book on the floor, looked at it, hesitated, and putting her hands over her mouth, went upstairs, choking back her sobs. She heard the handle of the kitchen door turn; Emma was coming out. O God! Now she was on the floor by Darlingest's bed, with the branches swaying and brushing outside the window, smothering her face in the eiderdown, smelling and tasting the wet satin. Down in the hall she heard Emma call her, mutter something, and slam back into the kitchen.

How could she ever have left Darlingest? She might have known, she might have known. The sense of insecurity had been growing on her year by year. A person might be part of you, almost part of your body, and yet once you went away from them they might utterly cease to be. That sea of horror ebbing and flowing around the edges of the world, whose tides were charted in the newspapers, might sweep out a long wave over them and they would be gone. There was no security. Safety and happiness were a game that grown-up people played with children to keep them from understanding, possibly to keep themselves from thinking. But they did think, that was what made grown-up people — queer. Anything might happen, there was no security. And now Darlingest —

This was her dressing-table, with the long beads straggling over it, the little coloured glass barrels and bottles had bright flames in the centre. In front of the looking-glass, filmed faintly over with a cloud of powder, Darlingest had put her hat on — for the last time. Supposing all that had ever been reflected in it were imprisoned somewhere in the back of a looking-glass. The blue hat with the drooping brim was hanging over the corner of a chair. Rosalind had never been kind about that blue hat, she didn't think it was becoming. And Darlingest had loved it so. She must have gone out wearing the brown one; Rosalind went over to the wardrobe and stood on tiptoe to look on the top shelf. Yes, the brown hat was gone. She would never see Darlingest again, in the brown hat, coming down the road to meet her and not seeing her because she was thinking about something else. Peau d'Espagne crept faintly from among the folds of the dresses; the blue, the gold, the soft furred edges of the tea-gown dripping out of the wardrobe. She heard herself making a high, whining noise at the back of her throat, like a puppy, felt her swollen face distorted by another paroxysm.

"I can't bear it, I can't bear it. What have I done? I did love her, I did so awfully love her.

"Perhaps she was all right when I came in; coming home smiling. Then I stopped loving her, I hated her and was angry. And it happened. She was crossing a road and something happened to her. I was angry and she died. I killed her.

"I don't know that she's dead. I'd better get used to believing it, it will hurt less afterwards. Supposing she does come back this time; it's only for a little. I shall never be able to keep her; now I've found out about this I shall never be happy. Life's nothing but waiting for awfulness to happen and trying to think about something else.

"If she could come back just this once – Darlingest."

Emma came half-way upstairs; Rosalind flattened herself behind the door.

"Will you begin your tea, Miss Rosie?"

"No. Where's Mother?"

"I didn't hear her go out. I have the kettle boiling – will I make your tea?"

"No. *No*."

Rosalind slammed the door on the angry mutterings, and heard with a sense of desolation Emma go downstairs. The silver clock by Darlingest's bed ticked; it was five o'clock. They had tea at a quarter-past four; Darlingest was never, never late. When they came to tell her about *It*, men would come, and they would tell Emma, and Emma would come up with a frightened, triumphant face and tell her.

She saw the grey-gloved hands spread out in the dust.

A sound at the gate. "I can't bear it, I can't bear it. Oh, save me, God!"

Steps on the gravel.

Darlingest.

She was at the window, pressing her speechless lips together.

Darlingest came slowly up the path with the long ends of her veil, untied, hanging over her shoulders. A paper parcel was pressed between her arm and her side. She paused, stood smiling down at the daffodils. Then she looked up with a start at the windows, as though she heard somebody calling. Rosalind drew back into the room.

She heard her mother's footsteps cross the stone floor of the hall, hesitate at the door of the drawing-room, and come over to the foot of the stairs. The voice was calling "Lindie! Lindie, duckie!" She was coming upstairs.

Rosalind leaned the weight of her body against the dressing-table and dabbed her face with the big powder-puff; the powder clung in paste to her wet lashes and in patches over her nose and cheeks. She was not happy, she was not relieved, she felt no particular feeling about Darlingest, did not even want to see her. Something had slackened down inside her, leaving her a little sick.

"Oh, you're *there*," said Darlingest from outside, hearing her movements. "Where did, where were — ?"

She was standing in the doorway. Nothing had been for the last time, after all. She had come back. One could never explain to her how wrong she had been. She was holding out her arms; something drew one towards them.

"But, my little *Clown*," said Darlingest, wiping off the powder. "But, oh — " She scanned the glazed, blurred face. "Tell me why," she said.

"You were late."

"Yes, it was horrid of me; did you mind?...But that was silly, Rosalind; I can't always be in."

"But you're my mother."

Darlingest was amused; little trickles of laughter and gratification ran out of her. "You weren't *frightened*, Silly Billy." Her tone changed to distress. "Oh, Rosalind, don't be cross."

"I'm not," said Rosalind coldly.

"Then come — "

"I was wanting my tea."

"Rosalind, *don't* be — "

Rosalind walked past her to the door. She was hurting Darlingest, beautifully hurting her. She would never tell her about that essay. Everybody would be talking about it, and when Darlingest heard and asked her about it she would say: "Oh, that? I didn't think you'd be interested." That would hurt. She went down into the drawing-room, past the primroses. The grey gloves were back on the table. This was the mauve and golden room that Darlingest had come back to, from under the Shadow of Death, expecting to find her little daughter....They would have sat together on the window-seat while Rosalind read the essay aloud, leaning their heads together as the room grew darker.

That was all spoilt.

Poor Darlingest, up there alone in the bedroom, puzzled, hurt, disappointed, taking off her hat. She hadn't known she was going to be hurt like this when she stood out there on the gravel, smiling at the daffodils. The red essay-book lay spread open on the carpet. There was the paper bag she had been carrying, lying on a table by the door; macaroons, all squashy from being carried the wrong way, disgorging, through a tear in the paper, a little trickle of crumbs.

The pathos of the forgotten macaroons, the silent pain! Rosalind ran upstairs to the bedroom.

Darlingest did not hear her; she had forgotten. She was standing in the middle of the room with her face turned towards the window, looking at something a long way away, smiling and singing to herself and rolling up her veil.

Colette

THE SEMPTRESS

D O YOU MEAN to say your daughter is nine years old," said a
friend, "and she doesn't know how to sew? She really must
learn to sew. In bad weather sewing is a better occupation for a
child of that age than reading story books."

"Nine years old? And she can't sew?" said another friend.
"When she was eight, my daughter embroidered this tray cloth
for me, look at it....Oh! I don't say it's fine needlework, but it's
nicely done all the same. Nowadays my daughter cuts out her own
underclothes. I can't bear anyone in my house to mend holes with
pins!"

I meekly poured all this domestic wisdom over Bel-Gazou.

"You're nine years old and you don't know how to sew? You
really must learn to sew...."

Flouting truth, I even added:

"When I was eight years old, I remember I embroidered a tray
cloth....Oh! It wasn't fine needlework, I dare say....And then, in
bad weather...."

She has therefore learned to sew. And although — with one bare
sunburnt leg tucked beneath her, and her body at ease in its bathing
suit — she looks more like a fisherboy mending a net than an indus-
trious little girl, she seems to experience no boyish repugnance.
Her hands, stained the colour of tobacco-juice by sun and sea, hem

in a way that seems against nature; their version of the simple running stitch resembles the zigzag dotted lines of a road map, but she
buttonholes and scallops with elegance and is severely critical of
the embroidery of others.

She sews and kindly keeps me company if rain blurs the horizon
of the sea. She also sews during the torrid hour when the spindle
bushes gather their circles of shadow directly under them.
Moreover, it sometimes happens that a quarter of an hour before
dinner, black in her white dress – "Bel-Gazou! your hands and
frock are clean, and don't forget it!" – she sits solemnly down
with a square of material between her fingers. Then my friends
applaud: "Just look at her! Isn't she good? That's right! Your
mother must be pleased!"

Her mother says nothing – great joys must be controlled. But
ought one to feign them? I shall speak the truth: I don't much like
my daughter sewing.

When she reads, she returns all bewildered and with flaming
cheeks, from the island where the chest full of precious stones is
hidden, from the dismal castle where a fair-haired orphan child is
persecuted. She is soaking up a tested and time-honoured poison,
whose effects have long been familiar. If she draws, or colours pictures, a semi-articulate song issues from her, unceasing as the
hum of bees round the privet. It is the same as the buzzing of flies
as they work, the slow waltz of the house-painter, the refrain of
the spinner at her wheel. But Bel-Gazou is silent when she sews,
silent for hours on end, with her mouth firmly closed, concealing
her large, new-cut incisors that bite into the moist heart of a fruit
like little saw-edged blades. She is silent, and she – why not write
down the word that frightens me – she is thinking.

A new evil? A torment that I had not foreseen? Sitting in a grassy
dell, or half buried in hot sand and gazing out to sea, she is thinking, as well I know. She thinks rapidly when she is listening, with
a well-bred pretence of discretion, to remarks imprudently exchanged above her head. But it would seem that with this needle-
play she has discovered the perfect means of adventuring, stitch
by stitch, point by point, along a road of risks and temptations.
Silence…the hand armed with the steel dart moves back and forth.
Nothing will stop the unchecked little explorer. At what moment
must I utter the "Halt!" that will brutally arrest her in full flight?

Oh, for those young embroiderers of bygone days, sitting on a hard little stool in the shelter of their mother's ample skirts! Maternal authority kept them there for years and years, never rising except to change the skein of silk, or to elope with a stranger. Think of Philomène de Watteville and her canvas on which she embroidered the loss and the despair of Albert Savarus....

"What are you thinking about, Bel-Gazou?"

"Nothing, mother. I'm counting my stitches."

Silence. The needle pierces the material. A coarse trail of chain-stitch follows very unevenly in its wake. Silence....

"Mother?"

"Darling?"

"Is it only when people are married that a man can put his arm round a lady's waist?"

"Yes....No....It depends. If they are very good friends and have know each other a long time, you understand... As I said before: it depends. Why do you want to know?"

"For no particular reason, mother."

Two stitches, ten misshapen chain-stitches.

"Mother? Is Madame X married?"

"She has been. She is divorced."

"I see. And Monsieur F, is he married?"

"Why, of course he is; you know that."

"Oh! Yes....Then it's all right if one of the two is married?"

"What is all right?"

"To depend."

"One doesn't say: 'To depend.'"

"But you said just now that it depended."

"But what has it got to do with you? Is it any concern of yours?"

"No, mother."

I let it drop. I feel inadequate, self-conscious, displeased with myself. I should have answered differently and I could not think what to say.

Bel-Gazou also drops the subject; she sews. But she pays little attention to her sewing, overlaying it with pictures, associations of names and people, all the results of patient observation. A little later will come other curiosities, other questions, and especially other silences. Would to God that Bel-Gazou were the bewildered and simple child who questions crudely, open-eyed! But she is too near the truth, and too natural not to know as a birthright, that all nature hesitates before that most majestic and most disturbing of instincts, and that it is wise to tremble, to be silent and to lie when one draws near to it.

Phyllis Bentley

MOTHER AND DAUGHTER

I

IT WAS A TUESDAY IN the first quarter of the twentieth century.

The mother and the daughter sat together over the family mending. Upstairs the grandmother dozed in her rocking-chair after the toil of being dressed. In the kitchen the cook was baking, in the pantry the housemaid cleaned the silver. The daughter had just left an expensive boarding-school "for good."

The mother frowned, and rippled her needle over and under the strands of wool in her husband's sock with angry impatience.

The mind of the daughter, Dorothy, was filled with fear and hate. In her mother's appearance and behaviour this morning — the flushed cheek, the angry sparkle of the eye, the quick breathing, the vehement gestures of the hands — she recognised the storm signals; an explosion of temper threatened. The daughter's prayer was that it might by some means be postponed; that it should be averted altogether was too much to hope. She glanced at the clock; in half an hour her father would return for the midday meal. She hoped with all her heart that the storm would be deferred till after his arrival, so that she should not have to bear its brunt alone — but then immediately reproached herself. Did she really wish her beloved father to suffer the thunders and lightnings of his wife's anger? It was a sight she hated more than anything else in the world. Before her brothers' marriages the storms had been as it were divided between them all, so that the share of each was diminished by the others' presence; now her father and herself received the whole force about their defenceless heads.

Yes, defenceless, thought the daughter, sick with fear; and the worst of it was, this state of suspense, of fear, of tension, would last as long as the grandmother stayed in the house. The mother was always intolerable during the grandmother's periodic visits. She had just come downstairs now from dressing the grandmother. As the invalid old lady was slightly deaf, all communication with her had to be shouted, so that it was heard all over the house. The daughter had quivered with shame and indignation as she heard the sharp, unkind, disrespectful utterances of her mother to the grandmother. True, in all things material her mother served the grandmother well. The fire in her room was always glowing, the bed warmly furnished, the meals suitable and agreeably served. But what was the use of material comfort if one was unhappy? The daughter would rather starve and freeze amid kindness and love, she told herself fiercely, than eat a Lucullan feast surrounded by sharpness and ill-temper. (It gave her some satisfaction to realise that her mother would not know the meaning of the word Lucullan.)

"How are you getting on with those gloves?" enquired the mother, turning a sock inside out with swift impatient efficiency.

The daughter timidly extended her handiwork for inspection.

"That isn't what I wanted at all!" cried the mother in impatient disgust. "They're just dusting gloves. I wanted them cobbled roughly together. I thought you could at least do that for me, Dorothy. Really I seem to be surrounded by imbeciles! What with one and another of you, it's almost more than a woman can bear. Well," she concluded with an air of resignation as the front door latch sounded: "Here's your father. Go up and sit with your grandmother for a while."

Thankfully the daughter slipped from the room. In the hall her slender, handsome father, so distinguished-looking with his fine fastidious profile and iron-grey hair, was removing his thick winter overcoat with the velvet collar. Dorothy bounded across to him and hung up the coat, then flung her arms round him and kissed him. Her father, his brown eyes aglow, responded with quiet fervour.

"Walter!" called her mother's voice.

"Coming, Maud!" murmured her father.

Dorothy skipped away up the stairs and entered her grandmother's room.

Clad in the correct attire for an old lady of the period — black silk dress, white silk shawl, lace cap, gold chain — old Mrs. Binns made an impressive figure as she rocked slowly to and fro. (Binns, thought Dorothy; what a hideous name! Fancy being called Maud Binns!) In spite of her great age Mrs. Binns was still a personality; her heavy body did not lack dignity and though her plump face had crumpled, her jaw was still firm.

The daughter sat down beside the hearth, facing her grandmother, and leaning forward so that her voice should carry better, began to shout conventional enquiries as to the grandmother's health and welfare. Nothing of interest was said. The two were kept apart by an immutable barrier, a barrier of loyalty to the generation between them. Much though the daughter hated her mother, she also loved her, and could not complain of her or receive complaints of her — except perhaps amongst her chosen friends, the Radcliffes.

"What have you been doing this morning, then?" asked the grandmother at length.

"Helping mother with the mending."

"Ah, your mother!" said the grandmother in what might have been thought a slightly sardonic tone. "She was always one to kick against the pricks, was Maud."

The daughter said nothing, and the grandmother rocked in silence for a few moments. Her faded eyes were downcast and she seemed to be lost in thought. At last, touching her solid bosom uncertainly with her wrinkled hand, as if in some way seeking reassurance, she remarked:

"It's my wedding day today."

"Really, grandmother?" exclaimed the daughter, filled at once with shame that this anniversary had not been commemorated, and with anger that her mother had not remembered it.

"It's a long time ago now," said the grandmother with a slightly surprised air. "It was a great match for me, you know. Binns and Binns. I travelled in a hat with two feathers."

At this moment the bell which stood in the hall was rung by the housemaid for the midday meal.

At table the father, without speaking, carved the joint with his usual judicious skill, giving fair shares to all the household. The daughter from her place between her parents watched this happen every day, noted her mother's slight frown as the maids' plates were filled with plentiful helpings, admired her father's calm justice and despised her mother's illiberal autocracy.

"Haven't either of you anything to say for yourselves?" enquired the mother impatiently.

The daughter resented this on behalf of her father and herself. She had sat mending all the morning and could have nothing of interest to report. Her father, on the other hand, as head of the great manufacturing firm of Binns and Binns, might naturally be weighed down by innumerable cares, preoccupied. Besides, her father was naturally sparing of speech, and quiet and moderate and polite when he gave utterance. The daughter liked to believe that she resembled him in this as in other matters.

"How was Rowland today?" pressed the mother.

"As usual. The baby's cut a tooth, I believe," replied the father quietly with a smile.

The afternoon dragged wearily along. Six hours had to be got through somehow before the daughter would be happy, out of the house and away from her mother and enjoying herself with her friends.

After the meal there was a precious time of solitude. The father and mother sat together downstairs, the daughter wrapped in a coat read in her cold bedroom one of the books which the Radcliffes had lent her. Then her father left for the mill. The daughter reluctantly put her book away — it could not be left about lest her mother saw it — and went downstairs to practise, for she was taking singing lessons. She had no faith in her own voice, but did her best from a sense of duty. She sang her scales, her exercises, and proceeded to her new ballad.

"I have no crown to give thee, love, save love," she sang fervently, enjoying this idealistic sentiment, so different from the mother's material views.

"And mother says that is not any use!" sang the mother, laughing heartily as she suddenly entered the room. "Come along now, Dorothy — we'll go to town." She pushed the daughter playfully ahead of her.

The daughter felt sick with outrage. It was as though her mother had dug out her most intimate being with a knife and exposed it to derision. She dressed to go out in silence. The mother came into her room as was her habit; it was an invasion of her privacy which the daughter resented with all her heart.

"I think it's cold enough for me to wear my fur, don't you?"

The fur in question was a stole and muff of black fox, elaborate with heads and tails, the recent gift of the father. The daughter despised the excessive fondness for dress which she thought the mother displayed, and answered with an indifference meant to be a snub.

"I've no idea."

"You won't be pleasant about it, will you?" said the mother crossly. "We might call at the mill — your father would like to see the fur in wear. If it's cold enough," she added, stepping to the window to examine the September day. "There's a good deal of sun," she concluded doubtfully.

"But the breeze is cool," urged the daughter, responsive to the idea of her father's pleasure.

The mother's face brightened. She donned the fur, and the pair set off together in a reasonably cheerful mood. They called at the mill. Rowland's wife had had the same idea. The baby was charming, and Rowland's wife a pretty woman. The daughter had reason to believe that the mother disliked Rowland's wife. As they left the mill she thought to win approbation, therefore, by commenting adversely on her sister-in-law's manners and dress.

"She's got herself a man, however," snapped the mother, "which is more than you'll ever do, Dorothy, if you don't cheer up. You stand drooping in the corner and saying nothing, you look like a dying duck in a thunderstorm. No man will bother with you unless you bestir yourself."

The sharpness of this sudden onslaught brought tears to the daughter's eyes.

"For heaven's sake!" exclaimed the mother in exasperation.

"Surely you don't mean to make a fool of yourself, Dorothy, by crying in the street!"

The daughter fought down her tears, and was proud of herself for being able presently to remark in a normal tone, as they passed a flower shop, that she wished to go in to buy some flowers for her grandmother.

"It's her wedding day."

The mother coloured.

"I don't know why your grandmother didn't mention it to me, I'm sure," she said.

She seemed, observed the daughter with surprise, genuinely hurt and vexed. She entered into plans for presents for the grandmother energetically, helped the daughter to choose flowers, bought on her own behalf some expensive lace and mauve velvet ribbon for a new cap. Though the grandmother received the gifts with her customary reserve, she was clearly pleased. This shared activity united the mother and the daughter, and the daughter withdrew to her room to dress for the evening in a more cheerful mood. After all, in an hour she would be with her friends.

It was then that the blow fell. The mother came into the daughter's room. The curtains were not drawn, for the daughter, who enjoyed the spectacle of the soft September dusk with the yellow lights springing up one by one, had asked the housemaid to leave them open. The mother drew them vigorously, then seemed to pause.

"It's no good you putting on your best blouse, Dorothy," she said at length. "Your father doesn't want you to go to the Radcliffes' tonight."

"Father doesn't want me to go to the Radcliffes'!" exclaimed the daughter, astounded. "Why not?"

"They're not the right kind of people for you, Dorothy," said the mother in an almost pleading tone. "All that Socialism and those other silly ideas. Who made the wealth of England that they're living on, I should like to know? And those disgusting outspoken books! And smoking cigarettes! I'd rather see my daughter dead than smoking cigarettes!"

The daughter's heart pounded with fear, for it seemed as if her mother's keen eye would surely penetrate to where, between layers of woollen underclothes, lay a treasured packet of cigarettes. Oh!

If only she could live away from home, earn her own living, buy what she chose! Her economic dependence was a prison wall.

"Why do you want to mix yourself up with such people? It's an insult to your father, really."

"It isn't father who's forbidding me to go to the Radcliffes'," said the daughter, choking with fear and rage. "It's you, mother."

"Well, whoever it is," said the mother, her voice hardening: "You're not going, Dorothy, and that's flat. Is this what we sent you away to that expensive school for? To mix with such vulgar people! Not a penny they can call their own!"

"Money! Money! That's all anyone ever thinks about in this house!" cried the daughter.

"That's not true of your father, anyway," said the mother angrily. "Understand me, Dorothy, you're not going to the Radcliffes' any more. I won't have you mixed up with such disgraceful ideas."

She waited a moment for a reply, but the daughter gave her none. After a pause she flounced from the room.

The daughter's resentment was so powerful and massive that its upward surge obliterated her fear and her obedience and drove her into a determination to resist. She drew the curtains back with a violent hand, merely because her mother had closed them. Darkness had fallen; her lighted room exposed her to the derisive glance of neighbours passing in the road. On an impulse she turned out the lights and seated herself beside the window. The bell rang for the evening meal; she did not stir. It was dark, cold and comfortless sitting there; nevertheless she enjoyed it. Presently the housemaid came upstairs, knocked timidly on her door, and announced that the meal was on the table.

"I am not coming down," said the daughter.

The girl exclaimed and withdrew. The daughter felt sorry for her; she pitied anyone who had to deliver such a message to her mother. She felt more sorry for herself when at last, after a long half-hour, she heard her mother's quick footsteps on the stairs. Her heart beat full and fast with fear.

Her mother burst into the bedroom with her usual impatient directness, then stopped abruptly, evidently taken aback by the darkness. There was a pause.

"Now, Dorothy," said her mother in a pleading, almost wheedling tone: "Don't be like this, dear. Don't be sulky now that you've come home. We've been without you so long, we've been so looking forward to having you at home. Don't disappoint us." She paused again. The daughter made no reply. "Think of your father, Dorothy," urged the mother with real feeling.

At this the daughter was almost suffocated by emotion. She realised the force of her mother's latest plea, for her serious and honourable father would be deeply distressed by any rift between those he held dear. But she bit her lip and clenched her fists; even for her father's sake she would not surrender. She remained silent; it was the hardest, the most courageous action of her life. Across the dark room there was a silent battle of wills. Just when the daughter felt she could not hold out a moment longer, the mother gave a deep sigh and withdrew.

The daughter, released, trembled from the effort of the struggle, and the too-ready tears flowed down her cheeks. She rose and in a kind of despairing resignation pulled close the curtains. This proved a fortunate action, for she had her back to the door when her mother re-entered the room. Switching on the light, the mother cried in shrill pretended joyousness:

"Your father says you can go to the Radcliffes' after all!"

It was all a lie, the daughter angrily reflected: her father had neither withheld nor granted permission; he had been bullied into complying with the refusal and had accepted only too eagerly the chance to withdraw. But what was the use of saying so now? She had won the permission, and that was what mattered. In any case she felt too exhausted to struggle any more.

"Why not wear your green crêpe, Dorothy?" cried the mother, extracting this garment from the wardrobe with an appearance of zest.

The daughter detested the green crêpe. It was a present from her mother; she had found it lying on her bed awaiting her on her return from school. Her bedroom, too, had been re-decorated in welcome. The daughter was disappointed and resentful; she had hoped to choose her own clothes and her own surroundings; she had forced herself dutifully to utter thanks, but her gratitude lacked enthusiasm. The green crêpe, irritatingly enough, suited her; but it was too bright, too highly decorated, too expensive, in a word too bourgeois, to please the daughter's progressive modern taste.

For a quiet evening at the Radcliffes', devoted to talk and music, it was altogether wrong. However....

"Let me give your hair a good brush, Dorothy," said the mother eagerly. She pushed the daughter down to a chair and attacked her straight brown hair with determination. "I can't think why you wanted to have it bobbed. It's left you with no dignity."

With hair flattened to her skull so that she resembled a frightened rabbit, the green crêpe with its embroideries and panels hanging uneasily on her still childish figure, the daughter at length was pronounced ready for the evening's visit.

"You've a little too much powder on the side of your nose, dear," said the mother finally. "Just let me — "

She put out a finger and delicately flicked at the daughter's cheek.

"Doesn't she *see* how she destroys my self-confidence!" raged the daughter inwardly.

"Go in and say goodbye to your father before you go," commanded the mother as they descended the stairs together. "Now, Dorothy, be nice to him."

"*You* tell *me* to be nice to *father!*" thought the daughter in a fury.

Her father was sitting behind an evening newspaper beside the fire. He lowered the paper as she came in and gave her a searching look; his handsome, lined face looked troubled and unhappy. She stooped to kiss him; he returned her embrace warmly. They were both perfectly aware of the mother's strategical defeat and face-saving tactics, reflected the daughter; but such matters could not be spoken of openly in families.

"Don't be too late, Dorothy," said the mother anxiously.

At last the daughter was safely out of the house. She walked sedately down the front path and along the road and turned the corner.

Now she was out of sight of her parents' home. Now she was no longer merely her parents' daughter, but an individual personality, Dorothy Greaves. She tore off the hat which middle-class convention then demanded, and fluffed up her hair with energetic fingers. She ran eagerly towards the Radcliffes' house.

Dorothy was the last guest to arrive. As she was admitted to the hall by the slatternly but cheerful little maid she could hear that conversation had already started. She threw aside her coat with a hasty hand, and a moment later, sitting on the floor — the Radcliffes' floors were apt to be rather dusty and the apple-green crêpe, thought Dorothy rejoicing, might well suffer damage — amid a group of six or seven whose ages fitted closely round her own, had entered the paradise of free discussion. It was enthralling! They talked about world peace, condemning strongly the treaty of Versailles; they talked about the need for open agreements openly arrived at between the nations; about economic justice, re-distribution of the nation's wealth, better material conditions for all, the abolition of capital punishment, the works of Freud and far more education for far more people. The eldest Radcliffe boy, who had proceeded by scholarships to Oxford University and was therefore held in great esteem, also threw off lightly a few theories about the probable results of women's recent emancipation, and mentioned his support for marriage in a registrar's office as opposed to the obsolete rituals of the church, and for cremation as opposed to earth-burial, on the grounds of its greater decency and cleanliness. Somehow this word earth-burial tickled the assembly, and they laughed.

"A mere literal description of fact," said the eldest Radcliffe boy loftily. "One speaks of Etruscan urn-burial, so I don't see why — "

"Charles Lambert, you're drawing again," interrupted the youngest Radcliffe girl, Dorothy's especial friend.

(Almost the only fault Dorothy could discern in the Radcliffes was their habit of thus skipping from topic to topic, without ever finishing one thoroughly.)

All eyes turned upon Charles, whom Dorothy had not seen before. He was tall and fair, not exactly handsome but strong-featured and distinguished-looking, with sparkling grey eyes and a very full, finely chiselled mouth which often smiled. From the youngest Radcliffe girl's proprietary tone it seemed that he belonged, or was about to belong, to her. It also seemed that he worked in the office of Mr. Radcliffe senior, who was an architect. The youngest Radcliffe girl seized the small block on which he had been drawing, and passed it round. Murmurs of laughing admiration arose. He had certainly caught the eldest Radcliffe boy to the life: the broad forehead, the quiff of hair, the left eye half-closed in discriminating observation, the look of mingled power and pomposity, were all there, gleefully satirised.

"Draw us all, Charles!" exclaimed the youngest Radcliffe girl.

Charles laughed, frowned, shrugged, pouted. It was not easy to know whether he wished to draw or not; perhaps he did not know himself. But he could hardly refuse his hostess's request, after all. With easy good-nature he began to draw. One after the other, amusing likenesses of all the company fell from his ready pencil, till there remained only Dorothy undelineated. At this point Charles slipped his block and pencil into his pocket.

"You haven't drawn me!" exclaimed Dorothy, hurt.

Charles gave an embarrassed laugh, coloured and looked aside. He was clearly unwilling to draw Dorothy, and as Mrs. Radcliffe came in at the moment to invite her children's guests to the other room for supper, he had an excuse for not doing so. But Dorothy insisted.

"Draw *me!*" she said.

Charles, raising his fair eyebrows and twisting his handsome lips into an impish grin, sketched rapidly, and handed the result to Dorothy. She exclaimed, and tears rushed to her eyes. All her weakness and timidity showed in the pictured face, and, even without its crude colouring, the loathsome apple-green crêpe displayed its jejune and bourgeois quality, while her hair stuck out at all angles. The drawing was an insult. In a confused turmoil of rage and pain, Dorothy felt that if she accepted this without revolt, she would accept anything, and all her spirit was against such a cowardly surrender. It was too much. Her temper flew.

"You draw me like this because you despise me!" she cried. "What right have you to despise me? You know nothing about me! Perhaps you think that because I wear this silly dress I've given in?"

To give in was a phrase much employed at this time by the Radcliffe circle; to say of a girl: "She's given in," meant that she had decided to conform, to become conventional, to accept the stupid, narrow, petty and altogether antediluvian prejudices of her parents. Charles Lambert presumably understood the phrase in this sense. He said nothing, but gazed down at Dorothy, smiling joyously. (His eyelashes, Dorothy observed, like his eyebrows were very thick and smooth and fair.) Dorothy tore the sketch neatly in half. She then put the halves neatly together, and with a confused sense that to halve them was altogether too mild to express her feeling towards Charles Lambert, she tore them into three parts. The paper was thick and resistant, but no paper could withstand Dorothy's rage on this occasion. She extended the scraps towards Charles Lambert. He did not take them. She dropped them contemptuously on the floor and stalked out of the room. Her cheeks burned, indeed her whole body burned, with painful feeling; at the same time she had a remarkable sense of liberation.

She went through the rest of the evening preoccupied with her own sensations. At times she put on a factitious gaiety and participated in the various games of intelligence favoured by the Radcliffes with feverish excitement; at other times she could hardly restrain herself from tears and was obliged to be morose and withdrawn in order to conceal her emotion. At length the evening, so long anticipated with so much hope of enjoyment, in the event so disappointing, came to an end. A laughing group left the house, and split off presently in various directions. Dorothy turned angrily towards her home. She had taken some dozen steps when she discovered that Charles Lambert was at her side, and that they were alone.

At once a most exquisite sensation filled her whole body, spreading even to her finger-ends, even to her toes. She said nothing, and they walked along in silence.

"I don't think the sketch was as bad as you made out, you know," said Charles Lambert at last in a dreamy, considering tone. "But you're such a spitfire, aren't you?"

"Me?" said Dorothy, astonished. (It was her mother who was the spitfire, the vehement one.) "No!"

"Well — very emotional, anyhow."

"Not in the least," said Dorothy. She added diffidently: "I'm really very meek and mild."

Charles Lambert laughed. Dorothy turned furiously on him. She saw at once, however, that the laugh was a kindly one; his very agreeable grey eyes sparkled with friendly fun. After a moment she too began to laugh.

"Spitfire," said Charles Lambert, taking her in his arms.

It was half an hour later when he left her at the gate. There were lights in the hall and in the front room, showing round the curtain, and Dorothy rather thought she saw a movement of one curtain, as though someone were looking out. She rang the bell — for of course she had no latchkey — and was admitted by a sleepy-looking maid, who as soon as she had closed the door scurried off upstairs to bed.

"Dorothy!" called her mother's voice.

Her mother was sitting alone in the front room, playing patience — her father was probably out at the club. Dorothy entered the room and seated herself beside her mother, smiling cheerfully; she was ready to babble about the evening's events — some of them at least — with a good deal of confidence and warmth. She might even go so far, she reflected, as to mention the sketch. Her mother, however, continued to play patience, slowly and thoughtfully; her eyes were bent upon the cards; after one quick glance she did not look at her daughter. Slowly Dorothy's confidence evaporated, her heart chilled; she became again only the daughter.

At last — but it was too late — as, the game over, the mother slowly shuffled the cards, she turned her attention to her daughter.

"Well? What sort of an evening have you had?"

"It was lovely," replied the daughter.

"What do you *do* at the Radcliffes' that's so attractive?" said the mother impatiently.

"We talk."

"What *about?*"

"Oh — everything."

"But what does it *lead* to? What's the *point?*"

"You wouldn't understand, mother," said the daughter, rising.

"Put these cards away in the bureau drawer," said the mother, handing her the box. As the daughter turned away on this errand, the mother said quickly: "Who was that young man who brought you home?"

"Charles Lambert," said the daughter, affecting a nonchalant tone.

"Who is he?" asked the mother anxiously. "He doesn't belong to those Ashworth Lamberts, does he?"

"I don't know. I daresay. He's in Mr. Radcliffe's office, I believe."

"Oh, Dorothy! He *is* one of those Ashworth Lamberts," said the mother with reproachful conviction. "I've heard of him. They've bad blood in the family, all those Lamberts. They used to have a big mill, the biggest in Ashworth, but they've thrown all their money away. The father died an undischarged bankrupt and the uncle disappeared and was seen driving a tramcar in Bradford. This Charles has been taken into Mr. Radcliffe's office out of pity – he'll never work hard enough to be an architect. What is he like? Attractive, I dare say. These ne'er-do-wells always are."

"He draws rather well," said the daughter, again striving for an indifferent air.

"I've been told the youngest Radcliffe girl is rather smitten with him," said the mother, watching her.

"Really?"

"But he isn't minded to tie himself down yet; he flirts around," said the mother. "Or so I hear. If he leaves one, he'll leave another, you know."

These vulgar and obvious hints were very distasteful to the daughter.

"Really, mother!" she said.

"You're like your father, Dorothy," said the mother with some bitterness. "Noble ideals and lofty artistic thoughts and all that sort of thing, and never standing up for your own. But somebody in the house has to be practical, as you'll discover."

"Goodnight, mother," said the daughter coldly.

"Goodnight, dear," said the mother, kissing her.

II

It was a Tuesday evening in the third quarter of the twentieth century.

Dorothy Lambert was standing over the newly installed automatic dishwasher, stacking china, when her daughter Carol entered the kitchen. Slouched into the kitchen would be a more accurate description, reflected Dorothy, giving Carol a worried glance.

She always felt an especial responsibility, almost an especial guilt, certainly an especially fierce protective love towards this youngest child of hers, because Carol had been brought into the world as the price of a reconciliation with Dorothy's husband, Charles. And just at present she was especially anxious about Carol. The child was rising seventeen, so that the next few years were the most important years of Carol's life, the years when her future destiny was being settled. Everything possible had been done for Carol so far. Her health had been scrupulously tended – how many nights had Dorothy not sat up with her, a delicate and vulnerable child. Her mind and body had been well educated – not without cost; money saved from Dorothy's own expenses, or wrung out of Charles at the price of an angry row, had paid for the dancing slippers, the extra coaching. Amusements for Carol had been liberally provided; again, not without sacrifices. But that had all been straightforward; clearly needed, obvious, simple. Now Dorothy felt confused and puzzled about her daughter. These people she went about with, this slick little job she held in such casual but tenacious fashion: were these really the right ones for her? Weren't they unworthy? Wasn't the child making all the wrong choices, ruining her chances of future stability and happiness? Dorothy greatly feared so. She felt uneasy and perplexed.

Carol came slowly towards her and lounged against the kitchen table.

"When will supper be ready, mummy?" she said impatiently.

Dorothy sighed. Carol was handsome, like her father. She was tall and well formed, and her fair sulky face had all the charm of Charles Lambert's strong features, chiselled away into a more incisive profile, more feminine lines. Was her nature like her father's too, wondered Dorothy in momentary alarm? For Charles was a man given to sensual pleasures.

Her whole life had been moulded by that fact. She lived it all through in a moment: the excitement of her secret courtship by Charles Lambert – secret because he was in truth half-committed to Mary Radcliffe at the time; the thrill of their furtive meetings, the feelings of guilt and disloyalty swept away in the great flood-tide of joyous ecstasy Charles could arouse in her when he made love. (Even the naïve and innocent young Dorothy Greaves, remembered Dorothy Lambert, had felt a vague surprise at the skill with which Charles made love – it seemed to argue a certain degree of experience, but that of course, thought the young Dorothy, could not be so. She soon learned differently.) She lived through again now the actual incidents of her seduction – which had taken place, incredibly, in Mr. Radcliffe's office when everyone else happened to be out; the physical ecstasy, the fierce rejoicing that in spite of her mother's care she had achieved this ultimate experience of womanhood; the sickening anguish of the weeks which followed when she began to suspect she was with child; the maddening difficulties in the way of getting a safe moment alone with Charles in which to tell him.

"Oh, *no!*" exclaimed Charles, when told. "Dorothy, really!"

He made a sardonic *moue* and gazed at Dorothy expectantly. Dorothy's temper flew.

"If you're waiting for me to ask you to marry me, Charles Lambert," she said fiercely, "you'll have to wait a long time, for I never shall."

"Spitfire," said Charles, laughing, and took her in his arms.

They married; but Dorothy was never quite sure whether this would have happened in time to give their eldest child a respectable birth had they not that day, on leaving the office, encountered Mr. Radcliffe on the stairs. He gave them a grave look, and passed by without a word.

"We shall have to go through with it now," said Charles.

"Why?"

"He'll tell your father."

"Oh, no!" exclaimed Dorothy vehemently. "No, Charles! It would break father's heart. Please don't let that happen."

Charles, who could never bear to see a woman in distress, agreed hastily to ask for Dorothy's hand that very afternoon. Indeed he went off to the premises of Messrs. Binns and Binns at once, in a cab. For Charles was not cold and callous; on the contrary he was warm-hearted and loving; it was just his misfortune that he was also careless and indolent, disinclined to put himself to trouble. And given, of course, to sensual pleasure. He could not help flirting with any pretty woman who crossed his path. Luckily their two sons resembled Dorothy, both in appearance and character, more than they did their father; they lacked Charles's talent, but were shrewd and sensible, well able to look after themselves. But Carol? Dorothy wondered. Looking at Carol's fair pouting face, listening to her slow warm drawl, she greatly wondered.

But no, no! reflected Dorothy with relief, giving her daughter another glance. Carol surely could not have the desire to attract the opposite sex which was a basic element in her father's character, for she showed continual carelessness about her appearance. Indeed she went altogether too far in this direction; she totally neglected sexual glamour. The dirty jeans, the sloppy mended sweater, the tousled hair — why, oh why, reflected Dorothy sadly, must her daughter handicap herself thus in the struggle of existence?

"There's a clean pair of jeans in your wardrobe drawer," she proffered.

Carol scowled.

"I don't want a clean pair," she said.

"Oh? I thought you were going round to the club tonight?"

"I am."

(Keep it light and witty, Dorothy admonished herself.)

"Well, of course if you want to hide the colour under the dirt, your present pair is completely successful."

Carol turned away. Her blonde head, seen from this angle, resembled a dusty and dishevelled bird-nest, thought Dorothy.

"There's a tube of that new hair-cream on my dressing-table, if you like to use it," she suggested.

"I don't, thanks."

"Just hand me those plates and things from that tray, Carol," said Dorothy, pointing.

Carol scowled and tossed her head, but obeyed.

"Shall you be going to — " Dorothy paused, but finally forced out the silly nickname — "that pub, the *Dirty Duck* or whatever you call it, tonight?"

"I daresay."

"Carol," said Dorothy warmly, "I do wish you wouldn't. Your father dislikes it so much."

"Daddy goes to pubs himself, even if you don't," pointed out Carol.

Dorothy winced.

For there had been a period in Charles's life when he had gone altogether too much to pubs. It was during their quarrel, when they were living apart. Dorothy kept hearing rumours that Charles was frequenting the Black Swan, but was too angry with her husband on other counts to pay much attention to them. Then came the day when their respective lawyers arranged a meeting between Charles and Dorothy to discuss the details of their proposed legal separation. Dorothy was punctual to the time appointed, as always. Charles was late. The lawyers' patience was wearing thin, pencils were being tapped and lips bitten, when at last Charles burst into the room. He looked plump and flushed, and his grey suit was unpressed.

"I should like a word with my husband alone," said Dorothy at once.

"Is that wise, Mrs. Lambert?" warned her lawyer.

Dorothy rebuked him with a look; the lawyer sighed and withdrew with his colleague.

"You're drunk, Charles," said Dorothy.

"Well, what of it?" said Charles irritably. "I've no encouragement to be otherwise."

Dorothy's heart overflowed with pity and love.

"Look at your suit, all creased. You'd better come back to me, Charles dear," she said.

"I like that!" fumed Charles. "Whose fault is it we're apart? I should never have left you if you hadn't made such a fuss."

"Will you come back?" said Dorothy, weeping.

"All right. But I won't be nagged," said Charles.

They were reconciled, and Carol (somewhat to Charles's irritation) was the result. The scandal of Charles's drinking ceased, but for some years the fear that it might be resumed was a nagging worry in Dorothy's heart. Clearly it was one of his temptations. Gradually, however, his need for whisky seemed to subside into a moderate liking, and by the time their sons were grown and in need of guidance he was quite reliable on this point. But the thought of Carol, so strongly Charles's daughter, exposed to temptation in the bar of the Black Swan was hateful to Dorothy.

"Daddy's going to pubs is quite different, Carol dear," said Dorothy aloud. "You're a young girl, under age."

"I only drink soft drinks."

"Then why go there at all? What's the attraction?"

"We talk," said Carol with her mutinous look.

"You could talk at home, just as well."

"Oh, *no!*" said Carol with emphasis.

"We talked a great deal when I was young, you know," said Dorothy. "But of course not in a pub. And our talk had so much more point, so much more sense, in those days. We had definite aims for the world."

"You didn't get very far with them," said Carol scornfully.

"Yes, we *did*. Who made the Welfare State, I should like to know? It was our generation."

"And atom bombs, and flame-throwers," said Carol.

"You won't get rid of atom bombs by the sort of whining recrimination and self-pity which forms the talk of your generation," said Dorothy hotly. "This attack on everything – it's so aimless, it's so negative, it's so pointless. Why can't you formulate some positive plan? Decide on something you want instead of merely rejecting everything? What's the good of this flailing about in all directions?"

"You wouldn't understand, mummy," said Carol wearily. "We're a ginger group. Against the Establishment, naturally."

Dorothy, exasperated but touched by the quotation of these naïve clichés, said nothing, but busied herself in closing the lid of the dishwasher.

"There are these to go in," said Carol, proffering forks and spoons.

"Oh, Carol! Why didn't you give me them before? You know they go at the bottom," said Dorothy, vexed. She raised the lid and began carefully to lift out the top trays. "You might try to concentrate on what you're doing a little more, dear," she said.

"You didn't mention the silver," muttered Carol.

"Oh well, never mind," said Dorothy soothingly.

There was a pause.

"Mummy?" began Carol.

"Yes, dear," said Dorothy.

She smiled hopefully. Perhaps the child would at last say something to reveal what she was really thinking about life.

"Could you lend me a pound till Friday?"

Two scenes leaped at once into Dorothy's mind. She saw herself at a post-office counter sending a telegram to her brother Rowland – it was shortly after their marriage, when Charles had first taken a job in London; Mr. Radcliffe had thrown Charles out of his office as soon as he decently could having regard to his daughter's pride. The telegram read: *Please send seventeen pounds for rent at once Dorothy.*

In the other scene she was pacing slowly up and down the Hudley railway station with her father, who was already at that time looking an ailing man.

"I can't do it again, Dorothy," her father was saying in his quiet careful way. "Charles *must* make a success of it this time, for I can't do it again. It's only fair to warn you. And I shall have to take it off what I leave you, you know — it wouldn't be fair to your brothers, otherwise."

"Charles doesn't *mean* to do anything wrong, father," said Dorothy in a trembling voice.

"No, no, my dear," agreed her father soothingly. "He's just careless and happy-go-lucky, that's all."

"I wish you'd try to be a little more careful about money, Carol," said Dorothy anxiously.

"If you don't want to lend it to me, I can manage without," said Carol in a huff. "There's always such a fuss about money in this house."

"Of course I'll lend it to you, dear," said Dorothy. "Fetch my handbag — it's in the hall."

The bag was fetched and the pound note changed hands.

"Thanks," said Carol ungraciously. "I'll pay you back on Friday night."

"I hope so," said Dorothy. (Charles had never repaid any money in his life.)

"Daddy!" cried Carol joyfully.

She leaped to the doorway, where Charles had appeared, and hugged him heartily. Charles responded with gusto.

"Hullo, my little daughter!" he said, lifting her up with his arms round her waist. "Not so little nowadays, either," he added, giving her a squeeze.

A pang of jealousy stabbed Dorothy's heart. Yes, it was a pang of jealousy, she admitted it frankly; but whether the jealousy was of her husband's affection or her daughter's, she really did not know. She was past being jealous of Charles by this time, surely? After all his infidelities, bodily and spiritual, major and minor?

Their honeymoon was not a week old before she had come upon him kissing the chambermaid in the hotel. To Dorothy, brought up in the austere Binns-Greaves nonconformist atmosphere, this seemed almost an obscenity. She retired to their room and sat awaiting him, her cheeks deep crimson, with hanging head. Charles came in presently, whistling in a dreamy but cheerful way, as was his habit. He stopped dead when he saw her and gazed at her in alarm.

"What's the matter, Dolly? Are you ill?"

"I saw you," murmured Dorothy.

Charles seemed not to understand; he gazed around, perplexed.

"With the maid."

"Oh! That! You didn't mind that, surely, did you?" said Charles.

"Of course I minded."

Charles seemed genuinely surprised. "Well — perhaps it was rather silly of me," said he, with the air of one making a great concession. "Little puritan!" he added fondly, kissing her.

Nothing in Dorothy's sheltered life had prepared her for this and she had not the least idea how to handle it. Accordingly she did not handle it; she remained silent, and her cheeks remained crimson, for an hour, but that was all.

She did not wish to recall the various incidents — the contradictions in Charles's alibis, the remarks, innocent or intended, of friends, the actual confrontations, the tell-tale changes in Charles's demeanour — by which she gradually came to learn that her husband was an inveterate womaniser, but by the time she was pregnant with her third child she knew it all. It was then that the rows began. Hitherto Dorothy's pregnancies had been straightforward and normal; now for some reason she was uncomfortable and sickly, and Charles had to go to social functions without her. This left Charles altogether too free a hand; he came home late, glowing and cheerful, and gave evasive answers to his wife's questions. One evening at last she broke out:

"Don't trouble to lie to me. You've been making love to some woman."

"Can't I show a little politeness to a pretty girl without you bringing these accusations, Dolly?" said Charles in a virtuous tone.

"Who was the pretty girl this time?" demanded his wife.

Charles muttered a name.

"It's difficult to keep up with them, really," remarked Dorothy sarcastically. "Does she know that, I wonder? Somebody ought to tell her. It would really be a kindness, Charles."

Charles stormed out of the room and banged the door.

The deterioration in their relations was halted for this time by the trouble over Dorothy's confinement. The birth was premature and everything went wrong; the child was a tiny waxen doll who had no hold on life. For some months afterwards Dorothy was so low in spirit and weak in body that she really did not care whether Charles was unfaithful to her or not; physical intercourse was forbidden to her and again she did not care. It was when she had made the enormous effort necessary to resume ordinary life that trouble between them began again. She felt cross and tired, and in need of admiring appreciation for her efforts; now Charles did not like a cross, tired wife. He liked women to be glamorous and bent on pleasing.

What made a woman glamorous? Dorothy had often wondered. She knew she did not possess this quality herself, but tried to analyse it sincerely, with objectivity. At one time she decided contemptuously that the habit of thinking about sex all the time conferred glamour; but this, she found by experience, was not so, though it contributed. Nor was beauty the whole answer. Whatever glamour was, Muriel Tilley had it. She was dark, with blue eyes and a wonderful clear delicate complexion; she had a langorous drawl and a handsome though heavy figure. She was the wife of a wealthy man, and used his wealth to clothe herself with admirable elegance; the husband was rather a stick, and Dorothy suspected that Charles was not her only or her first lover. The husband was a client of Charles's firm, which gave them a great many opportunities; indeed, reflected Dorothy angrily, it was a situation quite Galsworthian. But what she resented most of all was Muriel Tilley's intelligence; the woman read widely, attended concerts and art exhibitions and spoke of them with discrimination. This invasion of Dorothy's own special territory was intolerable. This time she was deeply hurt, her self-confidence irrevocably shaken. She could not bring herself at first to mention the matter directly to Charles, but continually nagged and hinted. The climax came when, returning home one afternoon bringing the two little boys from school, she met Charles and Muriel Tilley emerging from her own house. A rendezvous in the family home was really not bearable. The quarrel that followed was deep and lasting; Charles left his family and remained five years absent.

After all this, surely it was impossible for Dorothy to feel jealousy of her husband? Surely that feeling had worn out long ago? But no. Even after all these mutual disappointments and miseries, Charles and she were still man and wife, inextricably intermingled.

Besides, there were worse husbands than Charles. She remembered the unfailing rapture of their physical intimacy; when she withdrew from Charles's bed because of Muriel Tilley, she had punished herself probably more than she punished him. She remembered, too, many other instances of Charles's tender warmth. He brought her the most delicious flowers — sometimes wildly expensive, sometimes preposterous but beautiful oddities picked up from a barrow for sixpence. (They proved messy about the house and soon died, but undeniably gave pleasure on their first arrival.) When she was ill he was bad-tempered from sheer misery. He did not, it was true, ever change her pillow, but he gave her the most sensitive sympathy. As regards the children: he never wanted any of them to be born, regarding them jealously as competitors for his wife's affection; but when they had arrived he became a very loving, if unwise, parent. He brought them odd little toys which they adored, and played with them charmingly — when he was not stamping with fury at their noise and general inconvenience. When poor little Johnny, the premature third baby, died, he was quite heartbroken — tears stood in his eyes. No husband could have been sweeter to Dorothy, then.

Oh, no! When all was said, nobody meant more to her than Charles. Charles was her life and she could not bear to be supplanted in his affections even by their daughter.

Still, some of the jealous pang was on Carol's account, thought Dorothy; pain throbbed at the thought that this innocent young girl, her daughter whom she had borne, and nursed, and washed and dressed and taught, and made heartrending sacrifices for, day by day through many years, should now prefer the careless, light-hearted father who had not wished for her and who would never have troubled to earn a living to maintain her if his wife had not continually pressed him into doing so. Charles knew nothing of Carol's needs. He did not even know that she was worried about her height, reflected Dorothy with scorn. However — Freud had a word for all this, thought Dorothy, turning the dishwasher switch.

"You're late, Charles," said Dorothy sharply. (Surely he was not beginning to philander again? Let him see that she would be aware of it immediately.)

"Don't *scold* him so, mummy," said Carol reprovingly.

Dorothy smiled to herself. Everything that Carol had — her

clothes, her food, her roof, her long-playing records, her tennis racquet — existed because Dorothy had scolded Charles in the past for his own good. She had *made* him pass his architectural examinations; she had driven him to work, she had nagged him every evening until for the sake of peace and quiet in sheer desperation he had sat down to his books. Of course Charles always had plenty of original ideas, lots of talent; but if he were now a highly respected partner in a highly successful firm of architects (and a reputable Sunday painter to boot), it was because Dorothy had scolded him every night for some four years. Some of Dorothy's soft-heartedness and mild temper had been lost in the process, she admitted; but it was for a good end.

"Your father understands me, Carol," said Dorothy.

She offered her cheek to her husband, who kissed it. There was no great enthusiasm in the kiss, but there was all their life together.

The telephone rang. Carol flew to answer it. Charles perched himself on a table and crunched a lump of sugar. Dorothy continued to attend to the routine of the dishwasher. Through the various sounds of gushing water she could not distinguish the actual words which Carol spoke, but she heard their tone and the brevity of Carol's responses, and knew that the girl was disturbed.

"She's shy, as I used to be, and when she's shy she's abrupt and farouche, as I used to be," thought Dorothy with pity. How crude, how naïve, how morbid she herself had been in her girlhood, she thought, looking back. What slights she had experienced in consequence! She could not bear to think of Carol experiencing such slights.

Carol put her head round the kitchen door. An angry colour warmed her cheeks.

"I'm going out now, mummy," she said abruptly.

"No supper, dear?" said Dorothy anxiously. "Is anything wrong?"

"Of course not, mummy," snapped Carol, her colour deepening. "The arrangements have been changed, that's all."

"Why not change into a dress, dear?" suggested Dorothy. (When vexed, or about to enter a hostile company, it was always best to put on one's most becoming clothes.)

Carol scowled.

"Oh, mummy!" she said irritably, and closed the door.

The evening passed outwardly in calm domesticity. Dorothy prepared supper, served and cleared it. Charles had brought some work home from the office and stood at his drawing-board for an hour or so. From time to time they exchanged a word on family affairs – their two sons, one now at the university, one working with his father and married; Charles's disreputable uncle, still alive and causing trouble; the estate of Dorothy's mother, long widowed and lately deceased. Presently Charles went out to his club, and Dorothy switched on the television set. But beneath this calm domestic surface, as is so often the case with calm domestic surfaces, reflected Dorothy, seethed trouble; she could not rid herself of her concern for her young daughter. What had gone wrong over the telephone? What had distressed Carol? Why did she need money? She worried.

It was late when Dorothy at last caught the sound of voices in the drive and heard the click of Carol's latchkey in the door.

The moment the girl entered the room Dorothy knew that Carol had been making love. She bore all the signs: the glowing eyes, the lovely carmine in her cheeks, the heaving breast. At once Dorothy's pain sprang from a dull ache to a burning anguish. She is in love, she thought; and with whom, with whom? What fate is preparing for her, what will be her life? She could not bear to think of Carol suffering as she herself had suffered. The anguish, the worry, the love betrayed but ever painfully renewed, the financial harassment, the hardening of the heart, the gradual inevitable suppression of the generous impulse, the slow corrosion of ideals. No, no! Carol should not suffer that. Dorothy would fight tooth and nail to prevent such suffering from touching Carol. But you must be clever about it, she admonished herself. Take it easy. Don't press for confidences. Let the child come out with it in her own way and her own time. She smiled up at her daughter, but said nothing till the television serial episode ended.

"Turn it off, dear," she then said comfortably. Carol complied but did not speak, so Dorothy was obliged to open the conversation.

"Well, what kind of an evening have you had?" she said, forcing herself to use a brisk, cheerful tone.

"It was lovely," replied Carol dreamily.

"What did you do, then?"

"Oh — just talked."

Dorothy sighed.

"Who was that I heard in the garden with you?"

"Derek."

"Do I know him?" pressed on Dorothy, trying to sound casual.

"He was here last week."

"Was he the dark one with the crimson pullover and the guitar?" said Dorothy in sudden alarm.

"I daresay."

"Oh, Carol!" exclaimed Dorothy reproachfully.

The lad in question was, she had thought, the most coarse, selfish and graceless of all the young people who used her house with such careless condescension. How *could* Carol, brought up as she had been in a house which, after all and in spite of all, had a certain cultural atmosphere, a certain fastidiousness of taste, like such a young man, who took the rock-and-roll craze seriously and looked as if he hadn't washed for a week? Besides, Dorothy had seen him with her own eyes, pinching the bottom of a girl in an emerald skirt....

"Who is he, Carol?" fretted Dorothy. "I can't say I was taken with him."

"I didn't expect you would be. He's no money and he's a red-brick man."

"Those weren't quite my reasons," began Dorothy, vexed.

"But Grannie once told me that Grandpapa was just that kind of person when she first fell in love with him," said Carol in a hurry. "So really I don't see why — just a boy in the office, she said — that kind of idea is out of date now in any case. Hopelessly."

"You mean my father was an office boy when my mother first met him?" said Dorothy, amazed.

"Yes. In the great firm of Binns and Binns. There was no end of a doodah about it, I imagine," said Carol sardonically.

"She never told *me* that," reflected Dorothy.

"No? But then, you never got on with Grannie very well, did you?" said Carol.

Her voice held a reproach and a rebuke, and Dorothy was oddly reminded of her own indignant shame when she had had to listen to her own mother's sharp handling of her grandmother. It was almost as though the situation was the same between Dorothy and her daughter as between Dorothy's mother and Dorothy....

But good heavens, exclaimed Dorothy to herself, the situation *was* the same! The outward circumstances had changed with the changing times of course, but in all essentials the situation was exactly the same. In each case the daughter stood on the threshold of life, yearning for liberty to enter alone, while the mother sought anxiously to guide her through what she had found to be a dangerous jungle. In each case the exchanges between mother and daughter had the same motivation: the mother wanting always to protect, the daughter wanting always to be free.

Yes! Amusing, ironic, tragic, whichever you liked to consider it, such, thought Dorothy with a wry smile, was the fact. Every phrase Dorothy had uttered to her daughter tonight had been uttered by Dorothy's mother to Dorothy in her youth.

How different they sounded, however, when one uttered them, from when one heard them! Heard, they sounded hard, domineering, reactionary, unsympathetic. (Poor Carol!) Spoken, they throbbed with anxious protective love.

What could be done about it? Very little. It was part of the eternal strife of the generations, without which no progress could be made. All one could do was to try to extend understanding and compassion in both directions, up and down the family tree.

The trouble was, one could only know the *whole* truth about *one* side of these dialogues between the generations — the side on which one happened to be standing at the time. Take her own utterances to Carol tonight, for instance. They sprang from the most profound experiences of Dorothy's life, of which Carol would always inevitably remain ignorant.

It occurred to Dorothy for the first time to wonder — sharply, poignantly, achingly, for it was too late now ever to have an answer — what troubles her mother had had, with mother, husband, children, life, death, love, which had caused her to speak so to her daughter.

Marsha Portnoy

LOVING STRANGERS

MOTHER HAS INVITED ME to lunch. I am sitting at the small maple table in her immaculate kitchen, watching while she fusses over our salads. I know she would have preferred to take me to her favorite restaurant, The Arbor, where we could have reposed in cool wicker chairs amid feathery palms and dripping ivy. But I am still nursing Louise, and an infant would not be graciously welcomed there.

Mother moves crisply and efficiently, even in this late summer heat, gliding from refrigerator to sink to counter, talking on and on about a former neighbor of whom she recently had news. The tone of her voice, deliberately airy and pleasant, is one she usually reserves for company. I try to appear interested, although I can hardly concentrate on anything except how frumpy and uncomfortable I feel in my jeans and smock top. None of my clothes fit any more.

I look around the room. The surfaces all gleam familiarly, but something has changed. I realize it is the wallpaper, a pattern of paired white dots, like tiny eyes, on a background of apple green.

"That's new," I say, pointing. "Nice."

"Thank you, Marianne." She is pleased that I noticed. Mother has excellent taste. All her friends know this and have often sought her advice. She has spent many afternoons lunching at The Arbor, with one or another of them. After they ate their sole bonne femme and strawberry mousse, they would fly off in search of fabrics, prowl antique shops, wade through carpet showrooms. Mother always returned irritable and exhausted, confirming my belief that the entire enterprise had been a waste of energy.

"Will you have wine?" she asks.

"No, milk, if you don't mind."

"Of course I don't mind." She pours some into a stemmed glass. "Let's eat in the dining room. It will be cooler in there."

"Let's just stay in here."

She nods her assent, unwilling to argue the point. Mother's most prized possession is her dining-room table. When I lived here, I would often see her sitting there alone, drinking tea from a delicate china cup, stopping occasionally to polish out a smudge on the table with her handkerchief. If she is disappointed in missing this opportunity to show it off, she gives no sign.

Our lunch looks like a magazine picture, a colorful blend of pink shrimp and green onions and creamy-white mayonnaise surrounded by thin slices of avocado. She carries a basket of hot rolls and a bowl of melon wedges to the table and sits down.

"This is lovely," I tell her, shaking out my linen napkin. "But you shouldn't have bothered just for me."

"I don't consider this any bother. Besides, I think every new mother needs to be pampered a little."

Mother sits erect in her chair. I used to think of her as a tall woman, but she is of only average height. Though she is nearly fifty, she is as lithe as a girl, a remarkable contrast to my own plumpness from my recent pregnancy. I have trouble imagining her as she must have looked when she was carrying me. She has often told me the story of how, when she was in her ninth month and living in a two-room apartment in the city, she decided to fix up a nursery for me in an alcove next to her bedroom. My father was stationed in Korea then, and she was alone. She lumbered up and down the stepladder herself, cleaning, painting, papering until she had created a niche of brightness in that gloomy place. In a second-hand store she found a crib and a chest of drawers that she scrubbed and sanded clean and then painted white. She went into labor soon after she finished. She always said she was glad I had sense enough to wait until she was done.

"Is something wrong, Marianne? You're staring at me."

"I was just trying to imagine how you looked when you were pregnant."

She smiles and closes her eyes. "I was a sight you wouldn't believe. I'm glad your father didn't have to see me like that."

I nibble thoughtfully at my roll. If Jack had not been there to hold my hand and breathe with me, I don't think I could have survived Louise's birth. He would like to share the responsibility for taking care of her, but it hasn't worked out. He has been working long hours, and by the time he comes home I have already bathed and fed the baby and put her to bed.

Several silent minutes pass. I swallow a mouthful of salad, think of the laundry lying all over the bathroom floor at home, wonder how many minutes I have until Louise wakes up and I can leave.

Mother looks up suddenly, fork poised in mid-air. "I forgot to tell you. Daddy has given me permission to redo his study."

"After all these years?"

"Yes. I can hardly believe it."

This is surprising news. Daddy has always made it clear we were never to disturb the jumbled room he calls his study. It is the only room in this house that Mother has not transformed in the ten years since his public-relations business became successful.

"I suppose this calls for a toast or something," I say, and we clink our glasses together in mock solemnity.

"It's rather a small victory, though. I think he just got tired of arguing about it." Mother takes a sip of wine. "Speaking of decorating, dear, have you decided yet what you're going to do with your house?"

She asks this as though it were an innocent question. Mother hates my house. "How could I possibly find the time to worry about my dumb old house?" I say, not even trying to keep irritation out of my voice.

"You don't have to do it all at once, Marianne." Her tone is patronizing. Louise is fretting in her carriage, and I rush to pick her up.

Mother reaches for her wine again and stares into the glass. I have wounded her with my sharp words. I kiss Louise's clenched face, cradling her in my arm while she arches hungrily for my breast. I lift my blouse and place the nipple in her mouth. Soon the familiar tug releases all the tension.

"She looks like you, she really does," Mother says. It is a peace offering that I accept.

"Funny-looking, isn't she?"

"You were, too, when you were newborn. You looked like a raspberry, all curled up and red. But soon enough you began to look human. Actually, you were a pretty little girl, and you grew up to be an attractive young woman."

"Really, Mother—"

"I mean it. Of course, you never were one for makeup or clothes, but you have nice features, good skin." She looks at me critically, like a plumber estimating a repair job.

"Maybe, when you finish making over Daddy's study, you could start on me."

She smiles, catching the humor in my tone.

When we have finished our lunch, I put the baby on my shoulder and burp her while Mother clears the table. She scrapes the plates and stacks them in the dishwasher. In a few minutes all traces of our repast are gone.

"Well," she says, wiping her hands on a tea towel, "shall we take a walk?"

I am feeling heavy, sleepy. Though I had planned to leave right after lunch, I decide to stay a while longer. I ask if she would mind taking Louise while I lie down. We put the baby in her carriage, and Mother guides her out the door.

Instinctively, I go up to my old room but stop at the threshold. Mother has converted it into her sitting room. My bed is gone, replaced by a fragile-looking French Provincial writing table, and, on the wall where I used to tape pictures of my favorite rock stars, there is now a group of still lifes.

I go into my parents' room and stretch out on the bed, surveying through half-closed eyes the ice-blue walls and carpet. The spread beneath me is also blue, overprinted with a pattern of geometric designs that look to me like snowflakes. At the window, white curtains billow like cumulus clouds. I cannot imagine anyone making love in such a cold, cold room.

THE CLOCK TELLS ME I have slept for over an hour. I sit up in a panic, listening for Louise, until I remember that Mother is watching her. I get up and see out the window that they are resting in the shade of the maple tree. Mother is rocking Louise and singing to her in a picture of such familial bliss that it causes me a momentary pang of jealousy. I wish I could afford such unhurried repose with my daughter.

I study my face in the bathroom mirror. It is puffy, and there are dark smudges under my eyes. Jack and I had an argument yesterday over something trivial, and I spent the night wakeful and fretting. Since the baby, I feel ugly, and my moods are unpredictable, even to me. I wonder if Jack still loves me. Sometimes, I worry about how the baby and I would survive if he ever left us.

My skin feels sticky, and my hair needs washing. I pull off my clothes and step into the shower, lathering myself with Mother's fragrant soap. Later, when I have dressed and tied my hair back, I make iced tea and carry the pitcher and glasses out to the garden.

"You look quite refreshed, Marianne," Mother says. "You must have needed the rest."

"I did. Was the baby any trouble?"

"No, not at all. We've had a lovely time, haven't we, sweetheart?" She rubs her finger under Louise's chin. "She was wet, but I changed her."

"Thanks."

I pick up Louise, and Mother hands me a glass of tea. "Did you see the colors I chose for the study?" she asks.

"The ones on your sitting-room table? Yes."

"Do you think Daddy will approve?"

"I guess so, but why ask me? I'm not very good at decorating."

She juggles the ice cubes in her glass. "It's just that you two were always so close. I remember how you used to kid each other and joke, always telling secrets and keeping them from me. So I simply figured you might know Daddy's tastes better than I."

Mother's version of life with my father is different from my own. I feel I hardly know him. For all the years I was growing up, he was like a benevolent stranger who frequently shared our suppers and occasionally took us on an outing to the lake or the zoo. But Daddy was often away — or sequestered in his study.

"I think you should ask him what he'd like," I say.

She continues to sip her tea, avoiding my eyes. Louise is fussing in my arms, and I put her back in the carriage to nap. "You're right, I should ask him," Mother continues. "But whenever I bring the subject up, he seems so preoccupied, as if what I have to say couldn't be of less importance."

She looks up momentarily, and in that instant I see a cloud of pain muddy her light-brown eyes. I know what she means. I have sometimes gotten the same treatment from Jack, though I don't tell her so. "I'm sure he'll like what you've chosen," I say.

"Yes, I hope so." She makes light of it all with a half-smile and a little shrug. A breeze blows up, rustling the thick leaves. We recline in our chairs, enjoying the temporary respite from the heat. Louise is still whimpering. I pick her up and settle her in my lap to nurse. The strength of her tiny rosebud mouth still surprises me, makes me wince.

Mother watches Louise, then looks at me and without prelude asks, "Is it difficult for you, Marianne?"

I hesitate, not knowing what to say. I would like to tell her that we are managing well, that Jack and I are full of the inexpressible joy of parenthood. But there is little truth in that. Finally, I confess that it is probably no harder for me than it was for her. She smiles ruefully. "I think it was worse for me. Your father didn't come home until you were nearly eighteen months old, and he was never much help."

"Jack's not much help, either."

Her face becomes quickly serious, and she leans toward me as if to convey a secret. "Don't shut him out, Marianne. Give him every opportunity to be the best father he can." She sits back, then laughs softly. "Oh, dear, when I think of it, the mistakes I made."

This suprises me. I never expected Mother to admit to a mistake. "What would you have done differently?"

"Well — listen more, perhaps. Expect less. I don't know. Sometimes I think it's better not to look back."

MOTHER HOLDS LOUISE while I gather up my purse and the diaper bag and carriage. Before I leave, she asks me to look at something in the garage. I open the garage door, inhaling the cool, damp air. It takes a moment for my eyes to adjust to the dim light, so I do not immediately recognize the object under the sheet Mother has just pulled away. When I do, I am amazed. It is the little chest of drawers she fixed up for me before I was born. I never guessed she had kept it all these years.

"I thought you might have use for this, for Louise's room."

It is a homely piece of furniture, too tall for its width, too narrow to be of much use for anything but baby clothes. I bend down and open the drawers one by one, rubbing my fingers over the glossy white paint and the tiny flowers stenciled on the drawers. The carefully applied paint and cheerful flowers distract from the ugliness. It is a perfect example of the triumph of style over substance, and it makes me realize, perhaps not for the first time, that it is emblematic of Mother's entire married existence. Though she is the envy of her friends, she has had her disappointments. I know I am not the ideal daughter, and my father has not turned out to be the knight in shining armor she may have dreamed of marrying. Who knows how many other failed dreams and broken promises she has collected, stored like the Royal Doulton teacups she has locked away in the Sheraton cabinets? I think back and wonder how much sadness she has managed to conceal inside her beautiful, beautiful house.

"It only needs a little cleaning up, some fresh paper for the drawers." She looks at me expectantly, waiting for my reply.

"Yes, it will be perfect for Louise's room."

Mother smiles. "I hoped you would say that."

We walk to my car. While I stash the carriage in the trunk, she places Louise in her car seat and gives her a last, tender kiss. Turning to me, she says, "Marianne, I — well, what I want to say is, let's not be strangers."

We embrace each other, a little stiffly at first. Then I feel her fingers in my hair, and I press my face into her neck.

"Will you come next week?" she asks as I climb into my car.

"Yes, I'd like that."

We agree on a picnic lunch if the weather is good. She plans to have the chest of drawers ready by then. And who knows? In 20 or 30 years that fragile little construction of wood and glue, paint and hope, may still be usable for my own grandchildren.

As I ease the car down the driveway and wave good-bye to my mother, I try to remember if Jack knows the story behind my baby furniture. No, I don't think I've ever told him, but it will make something interesting to share with him tonight at supper.

Fathers

&

Daughters

INTRODUCTION

IN BOTH A positive and negative sense, fathers have significant impact on their daughters' self-image, personal happiness, and career development. Fathers mentor their daughters in two primary ways — by sending cogent messages, both spoken and unspoken, regarding what kinds of feminine behavior will win male approval and by modeling ways to behave in the world outside the family circle. Although a daughter identifies with her father, her identification often takes the form of empathy and loyalty to his ideas and opinions, when she realizes she cannot grow up to become just like him. A father also may identify with his daughter, viewing her proudly as an extension of himself, yet at the same time responding to her as the embodiment of all those female characteristics he has been taught to avoid.

To his daughters, a father typically represents adventure and the vast world of opportunities beyond the borders of home. Since a father is usually not as involved as a mother in child care and domestic activities, he tends to be a more distant figure on his daughter's horizon. Moreover, fathers establish distance by defining themselves primarily as protectors and providers and not as emotional mediators. According to most fathers, the domain of feelings belongs to mother. While a father tends to affirm and even adore a daughter's cuteness and charm, he typically does not encourage his daughter to reveal the needy part of herself. Furthermore, in struggling to be a successful provider, a father often expends a great deal of energy at work. A daughter thus learns that she shouldn't expect too much of her father's time and attention. Moreover, as a daughter starts maturing, her father may retreat, withholding affection or approval because he is uncomfortable with his daughter's emerging sexuality. This paternal response to a deeply ingrained incest taboo complicates the daughter's development, frustrating her desire to flirt and win affirmation of her femininity.

A young girl tends to idealize her father because of his powerful presence as the mysterious Other in her life. A father is flattered by this adoration and usually finds it difficult to descend from his pedestal and reveal human weaknesses. However, as a daughter grows up, her early image of father as the inaccessible knight-like figure is replaced by a more complex portrait of a human being complete with faults as well as strengths. With the tarnishing of her father's hero image, the daughter characteristically experiences conflict between her desire to continue winning father's approval and her need to transcend the "daddy's little girl" stage.

In the stories that follow, we will see how daughters either obtain or fail to win their father's approval of their femininity and individuality. We will see how a sense of mystery separates fathers and daughters, creating reticence on both sides, and how a daughter's idealization of her father develops into a more mature understanding. We will also have the opportunity to explore some ways in which a mother's presence or absence affects the father-daughter bond.

Clearly in the idealization stage, the daughter in Narell's "Papa's Tea" strives to win her father's approval, primarily by compensating for her mother's shortcomings. As this young heroine aligns with her father, her ambivalence toward her mother emerges quite clearly.

We move from a daughter's adoration to a father's glow of pride when we read Updike's "Man and Daughter in the Cold." In Updike's story, the father's affirmation of his accomplished adolescent daughter is complicated by his growing sense of his own mortality. Thus, Updike's story highlights one way in which the specific life stages of father and daughter can affect their relationship.

In Gibbs's "Father Was a Wit" and Anderson's "Unlighted Lamps," the drama of the father-daughter connection is intensified by the absence of mother and by the fact that both daughters in these stories are young women about to enter the adult world. In Gibbs's story, an introspective daughter recognizes the profound effect her father has on her sense of self and her behavior with teachers and peers. As we read this story, we become spectators at a psychological battle between this daughter's thirst for paternal approval and her desire to nurture that part of herself lacking in her father. Like Gibbs's heroine, the motherless daughter in "Unlighted Lamps" reflects back on her relationship with her father and learns to view him as a complex human being with shortcomings as well as strengths. Both daughters in these stories crave a warmth they have never received from their unapproachable fathers; however, in Anderson's story, we are privy to the father's as well as the daughter's inner thoughts and thus can appreciate how the struggle to connect takes place on both sides.   G.C.

Irena Narell

PAPA'S TEA

PAPA LIKED HIS TEA strong and piping hot. He would come into the kitchen, his dignified, fastidious figure in utter contrast to the disorder that reigned all over the room. With a helpless glance at the large kitchen table on which, as usual, lay an infinite variety of objects of non-culinary character, he would ask:

"Well, where is Mama? I'd like some tea."

Where was Mama? Where was the wind, he could just as well have asked. She had flown off an hour, maybe two hours ago, no one knew precisely when. Where was she off to? The bakery maybe or the dry goods store? She was going to look at that piece of blue wool for my sister Bessie's new coat, so maybe that's where she went…

"Max, where did Mama go?"

"I don't know," came a disgruntled reply from my brother. "Don't bother me."

"Oh, for a glass of tea," sighed my father. "One glass, what am I saying? I could drink a dozen glasses."

What was the matter with Mama? She never could remember the time Papa was due home. Even if she did, she was sure to find some errand that couldn't wait and forget all about him.

Not that there was anything personal she had against Papa. Oh, no. Didn't she often forget when we were supposed to come home from school for a quick, half-hour lunch, and didn't we end up crying in the street dozens of times until some neighbor would feel sorry for us and let us in? And when we would berate her afterwards, she would say:

"I know, I know. I only went shopping for a short while. So why couldn't you wait five minutes?"

That was Mama. You couldn't change her and you couldn't make her understand certain simple facts of life, I thought, as I went into the kitchen, determined to take care of Papa. One just had to accept Mama as she was. And she was wonderful in so many ways! When she sang near the open window, it was as if all the sound and glory of a spring morning in the country had found its way into our Bronx apartment. The neighbors would hang their heads out of the windows to listen and comment:

"Mrs. Siegel, how you can sing! Like a regular opera star."

And Mama was always smiling. Sometimes there really wasn't anything to be cheerful about, but Mama invariably found some little thing to make her happy. Maybe it was a concert in the park, or a ticket to the opera, or the neighbor's fat new baby, or the pretty dress she had just made for me with her beautiful, clear stitches. I often wondered how a person so untidy in her household could sew so perfectly and be so painstakingly neat in this work. And she never, never hit us.

Her mind was always on beautiful things. And how she loved pretty clothes! Next to music, I guess she loved clothes just about the best. When the tailor got through making her a handsome new suit, Mama would go out and buy a twenty-dollar silk blouse to wear with it.

We all thought she looked simply stunning. She was a little thing with a lovely head of brown hair, an elfish face, and a good figure, despite her lack of height. She carried her clothes well. But what happened to these clothes when she took them off!

Papa was fond of saying:

"Mama needs nice clothes so she can keep them under the kitchen sink."

And he wasn't far from wrong. Her things were everywhere except in the closet where they should have been. Once she got it into her head that she wanted a mink stole. Papa only said:

"Mama wants a mink stole so she can keep it underneath the washtub." And that was the end of that.

IN THE KITCHEN, I put my arms around Papa's neck.

"How is my Lily today?" he said, and smiled in that special way he reserved only for me. Even though there were four of us children, Papa's preference for me was acknowledged by the whole family and most resented by my brother Max.

"Papa's darling!" he would jeer at me when he got good and mad.

"Go in the living room, Papa," I said. "I'll make you some tea."

"Thank you, Lily dear, that would be very nice," Papa answered and he walked out.

The kitchen table was a real mess! There was the fabric for my skirt, and the pieces for Bessie's new hat, and two pots from last night's supper, and seven dirty spoons and forks, and the cookie jar, and the pot of jam from breakfast, and last Sunday's paper! The disarray was not exactly out of the ordinary. Only the items changed from time to time. Even when Mama happened to be home the table was so piled up with bundles that there was barely enough room for a plate or two.

I took off the two pots and put them in the sink and began moving the other things, one by one. For once Papa would have a completely clear table to drink his tea!

I found a pretty plate with rose clusters to put under the glass, and a white napkin. Where was there a clean spoon? I got the kettle going and prepared the tea. I took Mama's bundle of fabrics to her bedroom, the "dump" room. This was where we hastily dumped everything that lay all week long on chairs and couches and the floor, when a visitor was announced. Why did the house always have to be so disorderly? It would look exactly the same when we came back from school as when we had left it in the morning.

"But Mama, I'm ashamed to even bring a friend home," I would complain.

"If you don't like it, stay home and do it yourself. I got too many other things to do."

"But you know I have to go to school, Mama."

"So, is that my fault?"

What could you say?

The kettle was whistling. I ran back to the kitchen. What was that Papa had said?

"I could drink a dozen glasses." That was it.

He shall have a dozen glasses then! My heart was bursting with love for Papa who was good and kind. I knew how determined he was that we, his children, should have a better life than he himself had led, and how hard he labored to make it come true.

Papa's father was an innkeeper in a Russian town. His first wife, Papa's mother, came from a wealthy family and stayed with him just long enough to bear him two sons. Then she divorced him and married the town mayor. My grandfather promptly married a widow with two little girls. One of those girls was Mama! Grandfather was of sturdy stock and proceeded to outlive this wife of his, and then married twice more, each time outliving his much younger wives. Finally there were seventeen children in the house, and Papa, as the oldest, bore most of the responsibility for them. Mama was a very determined little girl even then. As Papa told it:

"When we were children, Mama decided that we would get married some day. As far as I was concerned, I could have stayed single all of my life!"

Mama had a good voice and wanted to go on the stage but instead was apprenticed to a dressmaker. Still, she managed to sneak out every now and then and sing in cabarets, until her stepfather would find out and drag her home virtually by the hair. But did this stop her? No. At the very next opportunity she was out, like a spark of flame, dancing, singing, enjoying herself. Life beckoned to Mama with irresistible force.

Papa felt responsible for her even then. For her, and the whole brood of children, until he was drafted into the czar's army. This was a calamity and Mama was in despair. She saved money from her earnings as a seamstress and it was arranged, over Papa's protests, to have him smuggled over the border the first time he came home on leave. Mama took care of getting him a passport and a change of clothes, bribing whomever was necessary, but Papa resisted to the very last. It wasn't legal, he said. It was not the proper way of doing things and Papa was a very proper person. Well, they got him over the border somehow and then onto a boat bound for England where an uncle lived.

There Papa who wanted to be an artist became a house painter so that he could earn a living. As soon as he had mastered the trade he was shipped off to America with a letter of recommendation to a "lantzman" on the Lower East Side of Manhattan. He worked and saved and sent for Mama. She too moved into a "lantzman's" railroad flat and went to work, sewing in a factory.

They didn't get married right away. How could they afford it, with so many brothers and sisters back home to send for? First, there was Aunt Esther. As soon as she came she fell in love with a cousin and the foursome worked to bring more relatives to America. Next came my Aunt Minnie. But that was after Mama and Papa got married and moved uptown to a five-room apartment. Aunt Esther and Uncle Abe also moved in with them, and when Minnie came, naturally, she moved in as well.

Papa said to Minnie:

"Now it's your turn to go to work and send for your sisters."

But my Aunt Minnie wasn't that altruistic. Besides, she hated to work.

"I should work for them?" she said. "To hell with that!" Aunt Minnie didn't mince words.

"But Minnie, how can you behave like that?" Papa said. "Didn't we send for you?"

"So what!" was her answer. "I don't feel like it."

"Well, if that's the case, then maybe we'll let your sisters stay back in the old country," said Papa.

Aunt Minnie finally went to work for about a year but hated it so much that as soon as Uncle Sam proposed to her, she married him, although she was only sixteen and he over twenty-five. From that moment on, she wiped her hands of her family in Russia. It took years for Papa to save enough money to try to bring more of them over, what with his own growing family to support.

By that time it was very difficult to locate them. They were scattered all over what was now the Soviet Union and had families and roots of their own. Besides, the government made it impossible for them to leave the country. Papa never saw them again.

I was rummaging in Mama's cupboard, trying to find twelve clean glasses. Then I tiptoed to the living room to steal a look at what Papa was doing. I didn't want him to discover my surprise a moment too soon!

Papa was sitting with his dictionary and a pad, writing down his daily quota of words. Papa read a lot, mostly Jewish books and Jewish newspapers. But he also made it a point to study Webster's dictionary, increasing his vocabulary by at least three words each day. He would write the definitions painstakingly on a little pad and never forget them.

"Why aren't you a businessman like Uncle Hymie, Papa?" I remember asking him once. Uncle Hymie lived in Brooklyn and had a fancy car.

"You really are so clever, Papa. You could make a lot of money, I'm sure!"

"Because, Lily darling, I'm just not made to be a businessman. A businessman, he has to be a little bit crooked. Don't let anybody tell you it isn't so. You can't make money in business being a hundred percent honest. But your uncle Hymie, he is made to be a businessman. Even when we were children together in Russia, I knew he would be a businessman one day."

"Why, Papa?"

"Well, I'll tell you. On Saturdays when our father would go to shule, your uncle Hymie would set up a little business of his own. There was a window at the inn that went out onto a side street. And under this window was a high, long table. Your uncle Hymie would have a show right under that window, on top of that table, and he would charge money for it. A kopeck apiece to all the children in our town, and they could see the show from outside. And business was good! Sometimes he would make a whole ruble on a Saturday!"

"But how, Papa?"

"Well, he would just pull down his pants and show his behind to the other children for a kopeck, that's how!"

"No, Papa!" I collapsed, convulsed with laughter.

"So, you see, Lily, that's how I knew he would be a businessman," Papa concluded triumphantly.

HERE WERE THE GLASSES at last. I counted an even dozen. Some of them didn't look any too clean, so I took them down from the shelf and reached under the sink for soap. I pulled out Mama's skirt instead, the one with the front pleat. She had only had it a month! Oh, well, the soap must be around somewhere. There was Bessie's slipper that she'd been looking for all week! Here was the soap, finally. I washed the glasses with care, making them shine for Papa. Where could Mama be all this time? I bet she went to the movies. There was a new musical at the Prospect, that's where she must be! Mama and her movies!

I smiled at the memory of all the movies she and we had seen together. We, the children, I mean. You see, Papa works very hard and during the week he likes to be in bed early. Nine o'clock and he is snoring away. But not Mama. Night does things to her. Her eyes begin to shine, her little feet begin to dance with impatience. She must be off and going somewhere. Sometimes I think that only with the advent of night does Mama really begin to realize fully her fierce joy of living. And it is not until the early hours of the morning that she begins to lose her nocturnal sparkle and makes ready to surrender herself to death-simulating sleep.

Well, the four of us children have to be put to bed. That is, four of us since a year and a half ago, when Claire was born. Until then there was just Max, Bessie, and I. Papa needs his rest and Mama must go out to see a movie. Since we children make a lot of noise all alone by ourselves, Mama worked out a perfect compromise. She'd take us along!

As soon as Papa was asleep Mama would dress us all, including Claire, the baby, and off we would be, to the movies. We would settle ourselves as comfortably as we could, for we were good for the night. Mama had to see the picture several times over and often we would not go home until the movie house shut down for the night. Mama watched the movie and we slept until it was time to go home. She even got these nightly excursions down to a science. We would be wearing our pajamas underneath our clothes so that we could jump right into bed when we got home. Mama would open the door as quietly as she could, and would warn us when we staggered into bed:

"Shh! Don't wake Papa!"

It was nearly three years before Papa caught onto the fact that his whole family was missing, night after night. Claire at that point had been going with us for over a year. It seems that he had an attack of indigestion and got up at about 11 p.m., looked for Mama, then took a peek into our rooms. Nobody home. Well!

When we tiptoed in that night who should be sitting in the kitchen but Papa! What a rumpus there was! I have never seen Papa so mad. He took a plate and broke it right before our eyes! We all hid but we could hear his roaring.

"The children have to go to school! What do you mean by keeping them out so late? And a baby, too!"

He went on like this, fuming and shouting for quite a long time. Mama just sat there.

Finally she said, calm as calm could be:

"You're finished?"

"Yes, I'm finished!" Papa roared.

"What do you expect me to do? I'm not going to stay home night after night. If you want, I'll leave them home."

And that's just what she did. From then on our nightly escapades were over. All went well until one night Claire had a fit. She demanded Mama's presence and Papa couldn't calm her down. Finally, exasperated and worn to a frazzle, he gave her a good spanking. The next day, sheepishly, he said to Mama:

"From now on, you take *her* along." So Claire was now the only one of us children qualified to be a movie critic.

I HAD the gleaming glasses neatly arranged on the table. An even dozen! I brought over the sugar bowl, a little lemon. That's how Papa like it. The tea smelled delicious. I poured it carefully, and didn't spill a drop.

"Papa, your tea is ready!" I called.

As he came into the kitchen, I pointed proudly.

"A dozen glasses, just like you wanted."

Papa looked surprised.

"But Lily, darling, I didn't really mean..."

He reached for his eyeglasses, and his handkerchief, and wiped them. Then he took me around and began to laugh. It was a happy kind of laughter, and I was relieved, because for a moment I thought he was going to cry. I guess he was pleased with his tea. But instead of drinking it, Papa kept laughing and laughing. I don't remember when I had heard Papa laugh like that before.

My, it was good to hear Papa laugh!

John Updike

MAN AND DAUGHTER IN THE COLD

L OOK AT THAT GIRL ski!" The exclamation arose at Ethan's side as if, in the disconnecting cold, a rib of his had cried out; but it was his friend, friend and fellow-teacher, an inferior teacher but superior skier, Matt Langley, admiring Becky, Ethan's own daughter. It took an effort, in this air like slices of transparent metal interposed everywhere, to make these connections and to relate the young girl, her round face red with windburn as she skimmed down the run-out slope, to himself. She was his daughter, age thirteen. Ethan had twin sons, two years younger, and his attention had always been focused on their skiing, on the irksome comedy of their double needs — the four boots to lace, the four mittens to find — and then their cute yet grim competition as now one and now the other gained the edge in the expertise of geländesprungs and slalom form. On their trips north into the mountains, Becky had come along for the ride. "Look how solid she is," Matt went on. "She doesn't cheat on it like your boys — those feet are absolutely together." The girl, grinning as if she could hear herself praised, wiggle-waggled to a flashy stop that sprayed snow over the men's ski tips.

"Where's Mommy?" she asked.

Ethan answered, "She went with the boys into the lodge. They couldn't take it." Their sinewy little male bodies had no insulation;

weeping and shivering, they had begged to go in after a single T-bar run.

"What sissies," Becky said.

Matt said, "This wind is wicked. And it's picking up. You should have been here at nine; Lord, it was lovely. All that fresh powder, and not a stir of wind."

Becky told him, "Dumb Tommy couldn't find his mittens, we spent an *hour* looking, and then Daddy got the jeep stuck." Ethan, alerted now for signs of the wonderful in his daughter, was struck by the strange fact that she was making conversation. Unafraid, she was talking to Matt without her father's intercession.

"Mr. Langley was saying how nicely you were skiing."

"You're Olympic material, Becky."

The girl perhaps blushed; but her cheeks could get no redder. Her eyes, which, were she a child, she would have instantly averted, remained a second on Matt's face, as if to estimate how much he meant it. "It's easy down here," Becky said. "It's babyish."

Ethan asked, "Do you want to go up to the top?" He was freezing standing still, and the gondola would be sheltered from the wind.

Her eyes shifted to his, with another unconsciously thoughtful hesitation. "Sure, if you want to."

"Come along, Matt?"

"Thanks, no. It's too rough for me; I've had enough runs. This is the trouble with January — once it stops snowing, the wind comes up. I'll keep Elaine company in the lodge." Matt himself had no wife, no children. At thirty-eight, he was as free as his students, as light on his skis and as full of brave know-how. "In case of frostbite," he shouted after them, "rub snow on it."

Becky effortlessly skated ahead to the lift shed. The encumbered motion of walking on skis, not natural to him, made Ethan feel asthmatic: a fish out of water. He touched his parka pocket, to check that the inhalator was there. As a child he had imagined death as something attacking from outside, but now he saw that it was carried within; we nurse it for years, and it grows. The clock on the lodge wall said a quarter to noon. The giant thermometer read two degrees above zero. The racks outside were dense as hedges with idle skis. Crowds, any sensation of crowding or delay, quickened his asthma; as therapy he imagined the emptiness, the blue freedom, at the top of the mountain. The clatter of machinery inside the shed was comforting, and enough teenage boys were boarding gondolas to make the ascent seem normal and safe. Ethan's breathing eased. Becky proficiently handed her poles to the loader points up; her father was always caught by surprise, and often as not fumbled the little maneuver of letting his skis be taken from him. Until, five years ago, he had become an assistant professor at a New Hampshire college an hour to the south, he had never skied; he had lived in those Middle Atlantic cities where snow, its moment of virgin beauty by, is only an encumbering nuisance, a threat of suffocation. Whereas his children had grown up on skis.

Alone with his daughter in the rumbling isolation of the gondola, he wanted to explore her, and found her strange — strange in her uninquisitive child's silence, her accustomed poise in this ascending egg of metal. A dark figure with spreading legs veered out of control beneath them, fell forward, and vanished. Ethan cried out, astonished, scandalized; he imagined the man had buried himself alive. Becky was barely amused, and looked away before the dark spots struggling in the drift were lost from sight. As if she might know, Ethan asked, "Who was that?"

"Some kid." Kids, her tone suggested, were in plentiful supply; one could be spared.

He offered to dramatize the adventure ahead of them: "Do you think we'll freeze at the top?"

"Not exactly."

"What do you think it'll be like?"

"Miserable."

"Why are we doing this, do you think?"

"Because we paid the money for the all-day lift ticket."

"Becky, you think you're pretty smart, don't you?"

"Not really."

The gondola rumbled and lurched into the shed at the top; an attendant opened the door, and there was a howling mixed of wind and of boys whooping to keep warm. He was roughly handed two pairs of skis, and the handler, muffled to the eyes with a scarf, stared as if amazed that Ethan was so old. All the others struggling into skis in the lee of the shed were adolescent boys. Students: after fifteen years of teaching, Ethan tended to flinch from youth — its harsh noises, its cheerful rapacity, its cruel onward flow as one class replaced another, ate a year of his life, and was replaced by another.

Away from the shelter of the shed, the wind was a high monotonous pitch of pain. His cheeks instantly ached, and the hinges linking the elements of his face seemed exposed. His septum tingled like glass – the rim of a glass being rubbed by a moist finger to produce a note. Drifts ribbed the trail, obscuring Becky's ski tracks seconds after she made them, and at each push through the heaped snow his scope of breathing narrowed. By the time he reached the first steep section, the left half of his back hurt as it did only in the panic of a full asthmatic attack, and his skis, ignored, too heavy to manage, spread and swept him toward a snowbank at the side of the trail. He was bent far forward but kept his balance; the snow kissed his face lightly, instantly, all over; he straightened up, refreshed by the shock, thankful not to have lost a ski. Down the slope Becky had halted and was staring upward at him, worried. A huge blowing feather, a partition of snow, came between them. The cold, unprecedented in his experience, shone through his clothes like furious light, and as he rummaged through his parka for the inhalator he seemed to be searching glass shelves backed by a black wall. He found it, its icy plastic the touch of life, a clumsy key to his insides. Gasping, he exhaled, put it into his mouth, and inhaled; the isoproterenol spray, chilled into drops, opened his lungs enough for him to call to his daughter, "Keep moving! I'll catch up!"

Solid on her skis, she swung down among the moguls and windbared ice, and became small, and again waited. The moderate slope seemed a cliff; if he fell and sprained anything, he would freeze. His entire body would become locked tight against air and light and thought. His legs trembled; his breath moved in and out of a narrow slot beneath the pain in his back. The cold and blowing snow all around him constituted an immense crowding, but there was no way out of this white cave but to slide downward toward the dark spot that was his daughter. He had forgotten all his lessons. Leaning backward in an infant's tense snowplow, he floundered through alternating powder and ice.

"You O.K., Daddy?" Her stare was wide, its fright underlined by a pale patch on her cheek.

He used the inhalator again and gave himself breath to tell her, "I'm fine. Let's get down."

In this way, in steps of her leading and waiting, they worked down the mountain, out of the worst wind, into the lower trail that ran between birches and hemlocks. The cold had the quality not of absence but of force: an inverted burning. The last time Becky stopped and waited, the colorless crescent on her scarlet cheek disturbed him, reminded him of some injunction, but he could find in his brain, whittled to a dim determination to persist, only the advice to keep going, toward shelter and warmth. She told him, at a division of trails, "This is the easier way."

"Let's go the quicker way," he said, and in this last descent recovered the rhythm — knees together, shoulders facing the valley, weight forward as if in the moment of release from a diving board — not a resistance but a joyous acceptance of falling. They reached the base lodge, and with unfeeling hands removed their skis. Pushing into the cafeteria, Ethan saw in the momentary mirror of the door window that his face was a spectre's; chin, nose, and eyebrows had retained the snow from that near-fall near the top. "Becky, look," he said, turning in the crowded warmth and clatter inside the door. "I'm a monster."

"I know, your face was absolutely white, I didn't know whether to tell you or not. I thought it might scare you."

He touched the pale patch on her cheek. "Feel anything?"

"No."

"Damn. I should have rubbed snow on it."

Matt and Elaine and the twins, flushed and stripped of their parkas, had eaten lunch; shouting and laughing with a strange guilty shrillness, they said that there had been repeated loudspeaker announcements not to go up to the top without face masks, because of frostbite. They had expected Ethan and Becky to come back down on the gondola, as others had, after tasting the top. "It never occurred to us," Ethan said. He took the blame upon himself by adding, "I wanted to see the girl ski."

THEIR COMMON ADVENTURE, and the guilt of his having given her frostbite, bound Becky and Ethan together in complicity for the rest of the day. They arrived home as sun was leaving even the tips of the hills; Elaine had invited Matt to supper, and while the windows of the house burned golden Ethan shoveled out the jeep.

The house was a typical New Hampshire farmhouse, less than two miles from the college, on the side of a hill, overlooking what had been a pasture, with the usual capacious porch running around three sides, cluttered with cordwood and last summer's lawn furniture. The woodsy sheltered scent of these porches, the sense of rural waste space, never failed to please Ethan, who had been raised in a Newark half-house, then a West Side apartment, and just before college a row house in Baltimore, with his grandparents. The wind had been left behind in the mountains. The air was as still as the stars. Shoveling the light dry snow became a lazy dance. But when he bent suddenly, his knees creaked, and his breathing shortened so that he paused. A sudden rectangle of light was flung from the shadows of the porch. Becky came out into the cold with him. She was carrying a lawn rake.

He asked her, "Should you be out again? How's your frostbite?" Though she was a distance away, there was no need, in the immaculate air, to raise his voice.

"It's O.K. It kind of tingles. And under my chin. Mommy made me put on a scarf."

"What's the lawn rake for?"

"It's a way you can make a path. It really works."

"O.K., you make a path to the garage and after I get my breath I'll see if I can get the jeep back in."

"Are you having asthma?"

"A little."

"We were reading about it in biology. Dad, see, it's kind of a tree inside you, and every branch has a little ring of muscle around it, and they tighten." From her gestures in the dark she was demonstrating, with mittens on.

What she described, of course, was classic unalloyed asthma, whereas his was shading into emphysema, which could only worsen. But he liked being lectured to — preferred it, indeed, to lecturing — and as the minutes of companionable silence with his daughter passed he took inward notes on the bright quick impressions flowing over him like a continuous voice. The silent cold. The stars. Orion behind an elm. Minute scintillæ in the snow at his feet. His daughter's strange black bulk against the white; the solid grace that had stolen upon her. The conspiracy of love. His father and he shoveling the car free from a sudden unwelcome storm in

Newark, instantly gray with soot, the undercurrent of desperation, his father a salesman and must get to Camden. Got to get to Camden, boy, get to Camden or bust. Dead of a heart attack at forty-seven. Ethan tossed a shovelful into the air so the scintillæ flashed in the steady golden chord from the house windows. Elaine and Matt sitting flushed at the lodge table, parkas off, in deshabille, as if sitting up in bed. Matt's way of turning a half circle on the top of a mogul, light as a diver. The cancerous unwieldiness of Ethan's own skis. His jealousy of his students, the many-headed immortality of their annual renewal. The flawless tall cruelty of the stars. Orion intertwined with the silhouetted elm. A black tree inside him. His daughter, busily sweeping with the rake, childish yet lithe, so curiously demonstrating this preference for his company. Feminine of her to forgive him her frostbite. Perhaps, flattered on skis, felt the cold her element. Her womanhood soon enough to be smothered in warmth. A plow a mile away painstakingly scraped. He was missing the point of the lecture. The point was unstated: an absence. He was looking upon his daughter as a woman but without lust. The music around him was being produced, in the zero air, like a finger on crystal, by this hollowness, this generosity of negation. Without lust, without jealousy. Space seemed love, bestowed to be free in, and coldness the price. He felt joined to the great dead whose words it was his duty to teach.

The jeep came up unprotestingly from the fluffy snow. It looked happy to be penned in the garage with Elaine's station wagon, and the skis, and the oiled chain saw, and the power mower dreamlessly waiting for spring. Ethan was happy, precariously so, so that rather than break he uttered a sound: "Becky?"

"Yeah?"

"You want to know what else Mr. Langley said?"

"What?" They trudged toward the porch, up the path the gentle rake had cleared.

"He said you ski better than the boys."

"I bet," she said, and raced to the porch, and in the precipitate way, evasive and female and pleased, that she flung herself to the top step he glimpsed something generic and joyous, a pageant that would leave him behind.

Angelica Gibbs

FATHER WAS A WIT

BECAUSE SHE WAS a senior and because – she knew perfectly well – she was going to win a prize, they had assigned her a seat in the front row in the study hall. By turning her head a little Helena could see the open double doors through which the parents and faculty were strolling now, chattering and laughing and rustling their programs, the fathers pompous and self-conscious, the mothers smiling too graciously as they teetered on high heels or waddled on low ones, looking, she thought with a burst of rage, for all the world like a collection of barnyard animals. It would be fun to leap up and hurry them along; to drive Mrs. Dunbar, clucking like a chicken, to her place on the platform, and to switch Miss Black, mooing gently, into one of the stiff-backed chairs lined up facing the school; to climb up and wrench the hands of the clock around so that it would be time for the doors to swing shut. Almost anything would be better than sitting here with the sweat starting out on the palms of her hands.

She still had five minutes to wait, while her mind went darting like a rabbit into its familiar burrows. If Father caught the two o'clock from New York he couldn't possibly get here on time. The train would reach Cavendish at three-fifteen. Allow ten minutes for a taxi, five to find the way to the study hall. No, if they closed the doors now he would be too late, and would have to fidget in the dark little parlor downstairs, with only the white marble bust of the Founder for company. Once the doors were closed, no one could come in. She went limp with relief, letting her hands drop on the desk in front of her, seeing her father so tall and spare pacing the parlor with quick jerky steps while the Mission magazines blinked up at him from the black oak table in the center.

Without warning, fear was pricking her again. He had said nothing about coming by train. Perhaps he had borrowed a car and might wander in even now, smiling vaguely, taking the one remaining empty seat beside Mrs. Gordon, who would tell him how much she enjoyed his drawings, never recognizing the amusement in his eyes when he answered her. He would be polite enough when he met them all, she knew; he had beautiful manners, even for the people like Miss Evans, who writhed around when she talked and who used such awful expressions.

"Your daughter has a gift, all righty, Mr. Phillips, but it's a delicate one. We're proud of her here, but when she gets out in the great world she'll have to be careful not to fall in with sophisticates. Yes, siree."

If Miss Evans said things like that to Father she could not bear it. Her arms and legs were cold underneath the pinpoints that stabbed at them. Her cheeks were hot with hate for these people lined up so stiff and prim in their chairs. It was like coming face to face with one of Father's cartoons. She detested Mrs. Dunbar's chitting chatter and Mrs. Black's bovine calm, the constant motion of Miss Evans's hands, and Mrs. Gordon's suburban clothes. Oh, she would write a marvelous poem about them, a satire, and the critics would dust off their best adjectives for her…"merciless, unfogged by trivia, an unsparing commentator on our times"…the words that had been Father's for years.

She sat up stiffly, she was regal, triumphant. The applause of the critics died away, leaving her suspended in quietness. For an instant there was no sound at all, then a long whispering rustle, dragged her back into the room and the hard study hall chair, and she knew that behind her all the girls were straightening up at their desks. Some one had closed the double doors. They were about to begin and Father would be left outside.

Up on the platform Mrs. Dunbar fussed with the packages stacked on the table before her, waiting for the last murmurs to fade away, for the parents to lean back in their chairs, their faces taking on a look of bright strained expectancy. Her hands fluttered among the flat, white-wrapped prizes, arranging them in neat piles and then shifting them into others. Her lips moved without sound to form the speech which always prefaced the prize giving. The speech was a school classic now. In ten years it had varied by scarcely a word, and Helena could do it to perfection. Last year, after commencement, she had gone over it for Father word for word even to the quick jerk of the head and the spasmodic titter at the end of each sentence. It was marvelous – he had said.

"Next year, darling, when you graduate I'll come to hear the original, if it's the last thing I do."

Made a little drunk by success, she had answered, "I doubt if you do, the way you are about getting anywhere."

He had looked at her sharply, jamming his half-smoked cigarette onto an ash tray until the paper flew open and the brown grains of tobacco swirled out and were blown across the table.

"Do you think Mrs. Dunbar would...approve of me?" he had asked. "I'm not exactly her type, you know."

She had nothing to say to that, knowing how bored he was by people like Mrs. Dunbar, how restless they made him. He often accepted their invitations, it was true, but as the time drew near for him to go his uneasiness would grow, until he was really ill; then he would shut himself in his studio, a blanket about his knees, and work with savage concentration at his drawings while the train pulled out without him. That probably was why he had not come today.

Now the doors were shut, and Mrs. Dunbar's sharp, high-pitched words were dropping unevenly into the silence of the room. "At the end of another Cavendish year we members of the faculty are very very glad to have you all with us. Of course you have heard quite a bit about just how hard your girls have been studying...."

The parents laughed politely and glances arch, scornful, resigned, amused, flew between the teachers.

Helena did not listen. Unleashed by the familiar voice, her mind had leaped away to the memory of the night before when she had run shaking and cold down the dark corridor between her room and the principal's and had knocked on the door. They had needed few words then, although it was midnight and unthinkable that a student should waken Mrs. Dunbar from her sleep.

"What's the matter, Helena?"

"I'm afraid."

"Afraid to go home?"

"To leave here, I think."

Mrs. Dunbar had taken her into bed then, holding her until the trembling stopped and she fell asleep. They had awakened early in the morning with the sun stabbing at their eyes, and Father would have laughed to have seen the two of them trailing down the hall to Helena's room, past the closed doors of the rooms where all the other girls were lying, Mrs. Dunbar's well-worn felt slippers flapping as she walked and a Japanese kimono, with a red dragon curling across the back of it, draped tight around her. The chicken woman, Father called her.

The speech quavered to its appointed end and for the second time a rustle swept over the study hall. The mothers leaned forward in their chairs, clutching their possessions tensely, knowing that, until the exercises were really under way, the slither and crash of a dropped pocketbook, or an absurdly muffled sneeze might easily set off the wildfire of giggles that always smouldered among the younger girls.

"To Jane Gordon," said Mrs. Dunbar, "goes the award for excellence and achievement in history."

Jane bounced up to the platform, her behind jiggling as she walked, and took the prize in capable hands. It was undoubtedly a book, a biography or a collection of essays, but how logical and unsurprising it would have been if the red ribbon had untied itself, the paper had flown open and out had come yards and yards of tape covered with neatly written dates, all the numbers that Jane had been digging so industriously from one book after another during the past months.

Miss Black, who taught history, smiled at Jane's mother placidly, triumphantly, and Mrs. Gordon smiled back, her face shining and her hat askew. It was as if a page had been turned for Helena in an album to a familiar picture, making her warm and secure, setting before her the holidays she had spent in Mrs. Gordon's house these last three years. Christmas, Thanksgiving, Easter, they were all blurred by time into one holiday, surrounding her so completely that she ludicrously could smell the brussels sprouts that Mrs. Gordon had always ordered for her benefit ("poor motherless child, so far from home, let's have everything she likes") and that tinged every room in the house for hours after the meal had clattered to a close.

This is ridiculous, she told herself, wanting to laugh or to cry, this is nothing but sob stuff, the kind of slop that Father most despises.

"From self-pity and all stupid abuses of the mind," he would say, "Good Lord deliver us!"

For what were these holidays after all but a certain number of hours spent in a small cluttered house in a town that no one had ever heard of? She was afraid to look at them too clearly, taking them out like playing cards and laying them on the table of her mind, setting them beside the weekends she had spent with Father now in this apartment, now in that (for he could not bear to be tied by a lease) where the food was never whisked in about one's shoulders, where the conversation was always good and the people, endlessly coming and going, were so swiftly self-possessed, that although she could seldom remember their names or what they did she knew instinctively and with awe that they were of importance.

These were the weekends she flourished before her friends, casually, expertly, so that they never dreamed of peering behind the veil of words to the harsh, inescapable hours during which she was either a spectator of a play half understood and wholly envied or a somewhat shaky actress, horrible and second-rate, she told herself, digging her nails into the desk before her, feeling sick with shame, doing her chicken woman act for Father's friends while he watched her with that anxious, proud intensity in his eyes.

Oh, to be certain of oneself, never to pause or stumble, never to blurt out words that echoed mockingly in one's ears for hours after they were spoken, surely these were the most desirable things in the world, and the things that Father admired most! Never to have the memory of times when one had grown hot and then cold with sheer horror; of that weekend, for instance, so long past and so indelibly imprinted, when Father had her do Mrs. Dunbar for his friend, Craig, the artist, whom he liked most among his friends. She could never forget how, at the end, with Father laughing, looking restlessly from her to Craig, there had been an awful, eternal pause, how Craig had never even smiled. "She'll have as bad a time as you've had, if you let her think it's so important to be clever," he said.

When he had left, Father had taken her out to dinner, for the first time in months, and they had been very gay. He had done sketches of Craig for her on the tablecloth, "Craig the critic," "Craig the pompous ass," "Craig on Olympus." But even now, she did not like to remember it.

Anyhow Father would like Eva Luce, she almost said out loud, pressing her back hard against the chair to remind herself that she was in the study hall. He should be here now to see her drifting so casually up to Mrs. Dunbar's desk to take the French prize, with her head bowed to show the fine line of her neck, and her dress, so much more graceful than anyone else's, swirling around her hips as she walked. No one but Eva could manage the thing that well, the shy smile as she passed Mademoiselle, who was crying bravo and rattling her bracelets, the half curtsy at the foot of the platform and the serene return to her own desk, her step as firm as though she were not well aware of the hatred beneath the applause that bore her up.

It was easy, of course, for Eva to be oblivious of hatred. She had so much to carry her along; she could remember exciting places and expensive schools where she had been before her family lost their money, and a thousand other things of which she never spoke but which lingered with quiet arrogance in every move she made. She had not even needed to study for her prize, but had spent hours on the river bank instead gabbling wildly with Mademoiselle about the lycée in Paris and the vacations in Switzerland, while her classmates toiled over their verbs.

It would be fine to be like Eva, to be thoroughly disliked and not to care. She was as hard and as shining as steel and because of this she would always get exactly what she wanted. She was like the women at Father's parties, despising the second-rate and dull, demolishing the nondescripts with a stare. When she left school she would waste no time remembering the people here, in wishing they had liked her, or detesting them because they didn't. She would simply forget them five minutes after she had closed the door. There were no dramatics on Eva's part because her parents were not here today. Last evening Helena had found her lying on her bed, smoking a forbidden cigarette, and staring with dead eyes at the wall of her room.

"When are your family coming?" she had asked. "I'd like to meet them. They sound so grand."

Eva looked at her without a flicker of expression on her face. "I doubt if they'll bother to scrape up the fare," she said evenly, "to get to a grubby place like this."

If I were like Eva, Helena thought, Father would have come to-day. It is because he always feels me dragging at him that he veers away. She pressed her eyelids down tight against the tears. In the darkness Father's dark clever face began wavering before her, she could hear him say, "Aren't you being a little emotional, darling? Don't get like your friend Jane, that sort of crumpled girl."

That was a very funny description of Jane, "that sort of crumpled girl." It was a magnifying glass held up to the wrinkles in her clothes and the untidiness of her hair. Since Father had said that, it had been hard not to be impatient and restless with Jane, not to slash at the bonds between them with a witty phrase or a laugh, turning away quickly from the bewilderment on her face. Once she and Jane had made plans together for next summer, for the winter after, for years ahead. They had arranged each other's weddings (how silly they'd been) and had named their children after each other. They never mentioned these things any more.

It was strange to be sitting here now between Jane and Eva, alone in spite of all the other girls and their parents and the faculty, alone in a room that suddenly seemed to stretch out enormously, to grow cold and a little dark. It would be good to reach out her hand and touch Jane, or to turn her head and smile at Eva. But it would be no use. She would always be like this, taking comfort from Jane and then running from her, hating herself for it but not being able to help it, trying to catch up with Eva who would never really want her.

The double doors were moving, buckling against a gust of wind that rushed up the outside stairs. It was foolish to look toward the doors. No one would open them now. If she stared long enough at the faces of the people in front of her, if she listened for all the small creaks and rustles in the room, and pressed her palms hard against the wood of the desk perhaps she could forget what she was waiting for. There was really nothing to wait for, to dread, except perhaps a telegram from Father like the one he had sent the last time he had promised to come. "Oops darling got all mixed up stop try again soon stop love father."

Jane had read it over her shoulder.

"What does that mean?" she asked.

"It's funny. All Father's friends send telegrams like that."

"If it's as funny as that," Jane said, "you'd better stop bawling over it," and she had stamped out to play hockey.

Only one prize, glistening in its white wrapping remained in front of Mrs. Dunbar. That, Helena knew and had known for weeks, would be hers. In a minute she would have to get up from her desk and go across those acres of polished floor to the platform. Suppose she should slip and fall, spraining her ankle, and be carried in groaning ignominy to the infirmary, would Father hear about it? Would people notice the trembling of her hand as she reached for the package and laugh and tell him later on?

It was too late to run, to hide, Mrs. Dunbar had begun to speak again, and this time the words caught and held her beyond recall. *The award for English composition.* How terrible that sounded. Here's the girl who won the award for English composition, just what *is* English composition anyhow, Father's friends would say, while all the words she had written wilted on the paper and trailed foolishly into nothing. *This year, we feel, goes to work of especial merit.* That meant her poem, the one that had sounded so fine when Miss Evans read it out in class. She could tear it up, thank heaven, before he saw it. She had not let them print it in the Year Book. *To Helena Phillips. . . .* Well, there it was. She would have to go now. The applause broke out all around her. She got up from her desk as blindly as a swimmer pushing his way from the surf to the dry beach beyond. The applause slowed and steadied, the girls began drumming their heels on the floor.

Why, this was not hard at all. It was like walking to music! Time stretched out for her so that as she went past the rows of parents and faculty she could see each face clearly and separately, the image driven home by the beat of her own footsteps. Miss Black and Miss Evans, Mademoiselle, Mrs. Gordon, and all the rest — they were smiling at her. They were no longer grotesque or foolish, the lines of their faces had softened into beauty.

Marvelously light and unafraid, she stopped at the foot of the platform, close enough to smell the oversweet carnation scent that Mrs. Dunbar used, to watch the tightening of the sinews as her fingers closed over the prize. The package wavered in the air, but it was Mrs. Dunbar's hand that trembled and not her own. For an endless instant before she turned away Helena lifted her head and faced her — ugly, tired, and superb, safe in a world that Father could never touch.

She had courage now to go back to her own desk. Buoyed up by the thrum of heels and the clapping of hands, she could still feel and hear with that strange sharpened intensity. Her eyes were open at last to the things about her. She was able to look out over the study hall without resenting the stares of the other girls. The room was very bright. The sun struck in through the high old-fashioned windows and stained the floor with yellow bands, splashed itself on the desks. There was a breeze too, straight from the warm, weed-spiced surface of the river.

Often this spring on evenings when she had begun to be afraid she had gone to the path that paralleled the river and had started running, slowly at first, gathering reassurance from the firmly packed earth under her feet, then faster until the water on one side and the trees on the other dimmed and wavered crazily. Her feet had that same lightness now, not because of fear, but because for the first time in so long she was free from it.

It would be grand to have Father here, watching her. If he could see that these people at least liked her and were glad she had won the prize perhaps he would not hate them so savagely. Hearing the applause they were giving her he might forget for a few minutes to search their faces for the lines that betrayed them and that leaped so viciously into life under his pencil. Later, of course, they would bore and frighten him, but in the excitement of this moment he might realize that they, like her poem, were the best she had, that he must not destroy them before she was able to go on to something else.

But he wasn't here. She had better not think about him at all, for, back at her desk, trembling as if she had run a long way she knew that without motion she was lost, given up to her thoughts. Huddled there she could feel the coldness creeping around her, the pulse throbbing in her wrist, the walls of the room closing in.

He had not come this afternoon after all. Caught in his own panic and restlessness he had probably sent another telegram for her to explain to her friends. Another funny telegram to show them. She went dizzy with anger. Oh, if they feel sorry for me I shall die. I can laugh this off, I know how swell he really is, that he would have come if he had been able. But if they pity me when I explain, I'll hate them the rest of my life.

She stared sullenly at Mrs. Dunbar who thought, catching Helena's eye, how stupid the child looks, how incredibly stupid for one who's just walked away with a prize.

Sherwood Anderson

UNLIGHTED LAMPS

MARY COCHRAN WENT OUT of the rooms where she lived with her father, Doctor Lester Cochran, at seven o'clock on a Sunday evening. It was June of the year nineteen hundred and eight and Mary was eighteen years old. She walked along Tremont to Main Street and across the railroad tracks to Upper Main, lined with small shops and shoddy houses, a rather quiet cheerless place on Sundays when there were few people about. She had told her father she was going to church but did not intend doing anything of the kind. She did not know what she wanted to do. "I'll get off by myself and think," she told herself as she walked slowly along. The night she thought promised to be too fine to be spent sitting in a stuffy church and hearing a man talk of things that had apparently nothing to do with her own problem. Her own affairs were approaching a crisis and it was time for her to begin thinking seriously of her future.

The thoughtful serious state of mind in which Mary found herself had been induced in her by a conversation had with her father on the evening before. Without any preliminary talk and quite suddenly and abruptly he had told her that he was a victim of heart disease and might die at any moment. He had made the announcement as they stood together in the doctor's office, back of which were the rooms in which the father and daughter lived.

It was growing dark outside when she came into the office and found him sitting alone. The office and living rooms were on the second floor of an old frame building in the town of Huntersburg, Illinois, and as the doctor talked he stood beside his daughter near one of the windows that looked down into Tremont Street. The hushed murmur of the town's Saturday night life went on in Main Street just around a corner, and the evening train, bound to Chicago fifty miles to the east, had just passed. The hotel bus came rattling out of Lincoln Street and went through Tremont toward the hotel on Lower Main. A cloud of dust kicked up by the horses' hoofs floated on the quiet air. A straggling group of people followed the bus and the row of hitching posts on Tremont Street was already lined with buggies in which farmers and their wives had driven into town for the evening of shopping and gossip.

After the station bus had passed three or four more buggies were driven into the street. From one of them a young man helped his sweetheart to alight. He took hold of her arm with a certain air of tenderness, and a hunger to be touched thus tenderly by a man's hand, that had come to Mary many times before, returned at almost the same moment her father made the announcement of his approaching death.

As the doctor began to speak Barney Smithfield, who owned a livery barn that opened into Tremont Street directly opposite the building in which the Cochrans lived, came back to his place of business from his evening meal. He stopped to tell a story to a group of men gathered before the barn door and a shout of laughter arose. One of the loungers in the street, a strongly built young man in a checkered suit, stepped away from the others and stood before the liveryman. Having seen Mary he was trying to attract her attention. He also began to tell a story and as he talked he gesticulated, waved his arms and from time to time looked over his shoulder to see if the girl still stood by the window and if she were watching.

Doctor Cochran had told his daughter of his approaching death in a cold quiet voice. To the girl it had seemed that everything concerning her father must be cold and quiet. "I have a disease of the heart," he said flatly, "have long suspected there was something of the sort the matter with me and on Thursday when I went into Chicago I had myself examined. The truth is I may die at any moment.

I would not tell you but for one reason — I will leave little money and you must be making plans for the future."

The doctor stepped nearer the window where his daughter stood with her hand on the frame. The announcement had made her a little pale and her hand trembled. In spite of his apparent coldness he was touched and wanted to reassure her. "There now," he said hesitatingly, "it'll likely be all right after all. Don't worry. I haven't been a doctor for thirty years without knowing there's a great deal of nonsense about these pronouncements on the part of experts. In a matter like this, that is to say when a man has a disease of the heart, he may putter about for years." He laughed uncomfortably. "I've even heard it said that the best way to insure a long life is to contract a disease of the heart."

With these words the doctor had turned and walked out of his office, going down a wooden stairway to the street. He had wanted to put his arm about his daughter's shoulders as he talked to her, but never having shown any feeling in his relations with her could not sufficiently release some tight thing in himself.

Mary had stood for a long time looking down into the street. The young man in the checkered suit, whose name was Duke Yetter, had finished telling his tale and a shout of laughter arose. She turned to look toward the door through which her father had passed and dread took possession of her. In all her life there had never been anything warm and close. She shivered although the night was warm and with a quick girlish gesture passed her hand over her eyes.

The gesture was but an expression of a desire to brush away the cloud of fear that had settled down upon her but it was misinterpreted by Duke Yetter who now stood a little apart from the other men before the livery barn. When he saw Mary's hand go up he smiled and turning quickly to be sure he was unobserved began jerking his head and making motions with his hand as a sign that he wished her to come down into the street where he would have an opportunity to join her.

ON THE SUNDAY EVENING Mary, having walked through Upper Main, turned into Wilmott, a street of workmen's houses. During that year the first sign of the march of factories westward from

Chicago into the prairie towns had come to Huntersburg. A Chicago manufacturer of furniture had built a plant in the sleepy little farming town, hoping thus to escape the labor organizations that had begun to give him trouble in the city. At the upper end of town, in Wilmott, Swift, Harrison and Chestnut Streets and in cheap, badly constructed frame houses, most of the factory workers lived. On the warm summer evening they were gathered on the porches at the front of the houses and a mob of children played in the dusty streets. Red-faced men in white shirts and without collars and coats slept in chairs or lay sprawled on strips of grass or on the hard earth before the doors of the houses.

The laborers' wives had gathered in groups and stood gossiping by the fences that separated the yards. Occasionally the voice of one of the women arose sharp and distinct above the steady flow of voices that ran like a murmuring river through the hot little streets.

In the roadway two children had got into a fight. A thick-shouldered red-haired boy struck another boy who had a pale sharp-featured face, a blow on the shoulder. Other children came running. The mother of the red-haired boy brought the promised fight to an end. "Stop it Johnny, I tell you to stop it. I'll break your neck if you don't," the woman screamed.

The pale boy turned and walked away from his antagonist. As he went slinking along the sidewalk past Mary Cochran his sharp little eyes, burning with hatred, looked up at her.

Mary went quickly along. The strange new part of her native town with the hubbub of life always stirring and asserting itself had a strong fascination for her. There was something dark and resentful in her own nature that made her feel at home in the crowded place where life carried itself off darkly, with a blow and an oath. The habitual silence of her father and the mystery concerning the unhappy married life of her father and mother, that had affected the attitude toward her of the people of the town, had made her own life a lonely one and had encouraged in her a rather dogged determination to in some way think her own way through the things of life she could not understand.

And back of Mary's thinking there was an intense curiosity and a courageous determination toward adventure. She was like a little animal of the forest that has been robbed of its mother by the gun of a sportsman and has been driven by hunger to go forth and seek food. Twenty times during the year she had walked alone at evening in the new and fast growing factory district of her town. She was eighteen and had begun to look like a woman, and she felt that other girls of the town of her own age would not have dared to walk in such a place alone. The feeling made her somewhat proud and as she went along she looked boldly about.

Among the workers in Wilmott Street, men and women who had been brought to town by the furniture manufacturer, were many who spoke in foreign tongues. Mary walked among them and liked the sound of the strange voices. To be in the street made her feel that she had gone out of her town and on a voyage into a strange land. In Lower Main Street or in the residence streets in the eastern part of town where lived the young men and women she had always known and where lived also the merchants, the clerks, the lawyers and the more well-to-do American workmen of Huntersburg, she felt always a secret antagonism to herself. The antagonism was not due to anything in her own character. She was sure of that. She had kept so much to herself that she was in fact but little known. "It is because I am the daughter of my mother," she told herself and did not walk often in the part of town where other girls of her class lived.

Mary had been so often in Wilmott Street that many of the people had begun to feel acquainted with her. "She is the daughter of some farmer and has got into the habit of walking into town," they said. A red-haired, broad-hipped woman who came out at the front door of one of the houses nodded to her. On a narrow strip of grass beside another house sat a young man with his back against a tree. He was smoking a pipe, but when he looked up and saw her he took the pipe from his mouth. She decided he must be an Italian, his hair and eyes were so black. "Ne bella! si fai un onore a passare di qua," he called waving his hand and smiling.

Mary went to the end of Wilmott Street and came out upon a country road. It seemed to her that a long time must have passed since she left her father's presence although the walk had in fact occupied but a few minutes. By the side of the road and on top of a small hill there was a ruined barn, and before the barn a great hole filled with the charred timbers of what had once been a farmhouse. A pile of stones lay beside the hole and these were covered with creeping vines. Between the site of the house and the barn there was an old orchard in which grew a mass of tangled weeds.

Pushing her way in among the weeds, many of which were covered with blossoms, Mary found herself a seat on a rock that had been rolled against the trunk of an old apple tree. The weeds half concealed her and from the road only her head was visible. Buried away thus in the weeds she looked like a quail that runs in the tall grass and that on hearing some unusual sound, stops, throws up its head and looks sharply about.

The doctor's daughter had been to the decayed old orchard many times before. At the foot of the hill on which it stood the streets of the town began, and as she sat on the rock she could hear faint shouts and cries coming out of Wilmott Street. A hedge separated the orchard from the fields on the hillside. Mary intended to sit by the tree until darkness came creeping over the land and to try to think out some plan regarding her future. The notion that her father was soon to die seemed both true and untrue, but her mind was unable to take hold of the thought of him as physically dead. For the moment death in relation to her father did not take the form of a cold inanimate body that was to be buried in the ground, instead it seemed to her that her father was not to die but to go away somewhere on a journey. Long ago her mother had done that. There was a strange hesitating sense of relief in the thought. "Well," she told herself, "when the time comes I also shall be setting out, I shall get out of here and into the world." On several occasions Mary had gone to spend a day with her father in Chicago and she was fascinated by the thought that soon she might be going there to live. Before her mind's eye floated a vision of long streets filled with thousands of people all strangers to herself. To go into such streets and to live her life among strangers would be like coming out of a waterless desert and into a cool forest carpeted with tender young grass.

In Huntersburg she had always lived under a cloud and now she was becoming a woman and the close stuffy atmosphere she had always breathed was becoming constantly more and more oppressive. It was true no direct question had ever been raised touching her own standing in the community life, but she felt that a kind of prejudice against her existed. While she was still a baby there had been a scandal involving her father and mother. The town of Huntersburg had rocked with it and when she was a child people had sometimes looked at her with mocking sympathetic eyes. "Poor child! It's too bad," they said. Once, on a cloudy summer evening when her father had driven off to the country and she sat alone in the darkness by his office window, she heard a man and woman in the street mention her name. The couple stumbled along in the darkness on the sidewalk below the office window. "That daughter of Doc Cochran's a nice girl," said the man. The woman laughed. "She's growing up and attracting men's attention now. Better keep your eyes in your head. She'll turn out bad. Like mother, like daughter," the woman replied.

For ten or fifteen minutes Mary sat on the stone beneath the tree in the orchard and thought of the attitude of the town toward herself and her father. "It should have drawn us together," she told herself, and wondered if the approach of death would do what the cloud that had for years hung over them had not done. It did not at the moment seem to her cruel that the figure of death was soon to visit her father. In a way Death had become for her and for the time a lovely and gracious figure intent upon good. The hand of death was to open the door out of her father's house and into life. With the cruelty of youth she thought first of the adventurous possibilities of the new life.

Mary sat very still. In the long weeds the insects that had been disturbed in their evening song began to sing again. A robin flew into the tree beneath which she sat and struck a clear sharp note of alarm. The voices of people in the town's new factory district came softly up the hillside. They were like bells of distant cathedrals calling people to worship. Something within the girl's breast seemed to break and putting her head into her hands she rocked slowly back and forth. Tears came accompanied by a warm tender impulse toward the living men and women of Huntersburg.

And then from the road came a call. "Hello there kid," shouted a voice, and Mary sprang quickly to her feet. Her mellow mood passed like a puff of wind and in its place hot anger came.

In the road stood Duke Yetter who from his loafing place before the livery barn had seen her set out for the Sunday evening walk and had followed. When she went through Upper Main

Street and into the new factory district he was sure of his conquest. "She doesn't want to be seen walking with me," he had told himself, "that's all right. She knows well enough I'll follow but doesn't want me to put in an appearance until she is well out of sight of her friends. She's a little stuck up and needs to be brought down a peg, but what do I care? She's gone out of her way to give me this chance and maybe she's only afraid of her dad."

Duke climbed the little incline out of the road and came into the orchard, but when he reached the pile of stones covered by vines he stumbled and fell. He arose and laughed. Mary had not waited for him to reach her but had started toward him, and when his laugh broke the silence that lay over the orchard she sprang forward and with her open hand struck him a sharp blow on the cheek. Then she turned and as he stood with his feet tangled in the vines ran out to the road. "If you follow or speak to me I'll get someone to kill you," she shouted.

Mary walked along the road and down the hill toward Wilmott Street. Broken bits of the story concerning her mother that had for years circulated in town had reached her ears. Her mother, it was said, had disappeared on a summer night long ago and a young town rough, who had been in the habit of loitering before Barney Smithfield's Livery Barn, had gone away with her. Now another young rough was trying to make up to her. The thought made her furious.

Her mind groped about striving to lay hold of some weapon with which she could strike a more telling blow at Duke Yetter. In desperation it lit upon the figure of her father already broken in health and now about to die. "My father just wants the chance to kill some such fellow as you," she shouted, turning to face the young man, who having got clear of the mass of vines in the orchard, had followed her into the road. "My father just wants to kill someone because of the lies that have been told in this town about Mother."

Having given way to the impulse to threaten Duke Yetter Mary was instantly ashamed of her outburst and walked rapidly along, the tears running from her eyes. With hanging head Duke walked at her heels. "I didn't mean no harm, Miss Cochran," he pleaded. "I didn't mean no harm. Don't tell your father. I was only funning with you. I tell you I didn't mean no harm."

THE LIGHT of the summer evening had begun to fall and the faces of the people made soft little ovals of light as they stood grouped under the dark porches or by the fences in Wilmott Street. The voices of the children had become subdued and they also stood in groups. They became silent as Mary passed and stood with upturned faces and staring eyes. "The lady doesn't live very far. She must be almost a neighbor," she heard a woman's voice saying in English. When she turned her head she saw only a crowd of dark-skinned men standing before a house. From within the house came the sound of a woman's voice singing a child to sleep.

The young Italian, who had called to her earlier in the evening and who was now apparently setting out on his own Sunday evening's adventures, came along the sidewalk and walked quickly away into the darkness. He had dressed himself in his Sunday clothes and had put on a black derby hat and a stiff white collar, set off by a red necktie. The shining whiteness of the collar made his brown skin look almost black. He smiled boyishly and raised his hat awkwardly but did not speak.

Mary kept looking back along the street to be sure Duke Yetter had not followed but in the dim light could see nothing of him. Her angry excited mood went away.

She did not want to go home and decided it was too late to go to church. From Upper Main Street there was a short street that ran eastward and fell rather sharply down a hillside to a creek and a bridge that marked the end of the town's growth in that direction. She went down along the street to the bridge and stood in the failing light watching two boys who were fishing in the creek.

A broad-shouldered man dressed in rough clothes came down along the street and stopping on the bridge spoke to her. It was the first time she had ever heard a citizen of her home town speak with feeling of her father. "You are Doctor Cochran's daughter?" he asked hesitatingly. "I guess you don't know who I am but your father does." He pointed toward the two boys who sat with fishpoles in their hands on the weed-grown bank of the creek. "Those are my boys and I have four other children," he explained. "There

is another boy and I have three girls. One of my daughters has a
job in a store. She is as old as yourself." The man explained his relations with Doctor Cochran. He had been a farm laborer, he said,
and had but recently moved to town to work in the furniture factory. During the previous winter he had been ill for a long time
and had no money. While he lay in bed one of his boys fell out of
a barn loft and there was a terrible cut in his head.

"Your father came every day to see us and he sewed up my
Tom's head." The laborer turned away from Mary and stood with
his cap in his hand looking toward the boys. "I was down and out
and your father not only took care of me and the boys but he gave
my old woman money to buy the things we had to have from the
stores in town here, groceries and medicines." The man spoke in
such low tones that Mary had to lean forward to hear his words.
Her face almost touched the laborer's shoulder. "Your father is a
good man and I don't think he is very happy," he went on. "The
boy and I got well and I got work here in town but he wouldn't take
any money from me. 'You know how to live with your children
and your wife. You know how to make them happy. Keep your
money and spend it on them,' that's what he said to me."

The laborer went on across the bridge and along the creek bank
toward the spot where his two sons sat fishing and Mary leaned
on the railing of the bridge and looked at the slow moving water. It
was almost black in the shadows under the bridge and she thought
that it was thus her father's life had been lived. "It has been like a
stream running always in shadows and never coming out into the
sunlight," she thought, and fear that her own life would run on in
darkness gripped her. A great new love for her father swept over
her and in fancy she felt his arms about her. As a child she had continually dreamed of caresses received at her father's hands and
now the dream came back. For a long time she stood looking at
the stream and she resolved that the night should not pass without
an effort on her part to make the old dream come true. When she
again looked up the laborer had built a little fire of sticks at the
edge of the stream. "We catch bullheads here," he called. "The
light of the fire draws them close to the shore. If you want to come
and try your hand at fishing the boys will lend you one of the
poles."

"Oh, I thank you, I won't do it tonight," Mary said, and then fearing she might suddenly begin weeping and that if the man spoke to her again she would find herself unable to answer, she hurried away. "Good-by!" shouted the man and the two boys. The words came quite spontaneously out of the three throats and created a sharp trumpet-like effect that rang like a glad cry across the heaviness of her mood.

WHEN HIS DAUGHTER Mary went out for her evening walk Doctor Cochran sat for an hour alone in his office. It began to grow dark and the men who all afternoon had been sitting on chairs and boxes before the livery barn across the street went home for the evening meal. The noise of voices grew faint and sometimes for five or ten minutes there was silence. Then from some distant street came a child's cry. Presently church bells began to ring.

The doctor was not a very neat man and sometimes for several days he forgot to shave. With a long lean hand he stroked his half-grown beard. His illness had struck deeper than he had admitted even to himself and his mind had an inclination to float out of his body. Often when he sat thus his hands lay in his lap and he looked at them with a child's absorption. It seemed to him they must belong to someone else. He grew philosophic. "It's an odd thing about my body. Here I've lived in it all these years and how little use I have had of it. Now it's going to die and decay never having been used. I wonder why it did not get another tenant." He smiled sadly over his fancy but went on with it. "Well I've had thoughts enough concerning people and I've had the use of these lips and a tongue but I've let them lie idle. When my Ellen was here living with me I let her think me cold and unfeeling while something within me was straining and straining trying to tear itself loose."

He remembered how often, as a young man, he had sat in the evening in silence beside his wife in this same office and how his hands had ached to reach across the narrow space that separated them and touch her hands, her face, her hair.

Well, everyone in town had predicted his marriage would turn out badly! His wife had been an actress with a company that came to Huntersburg and got stranded there. At the same time the girl became ill and had no money to pay for her room at the hotel. The young doctor had attended to that and when the girl was convalescent took her to ride about the country in his buggy. Her life had been a hard one and the notion of leading a quiet existence in the little town appealed to her.

And then after the marriage and after the child was born she had suddenly found herself unable to go on living with the silent cold man. There had been a story of her having run away with a young sport, the son of a saloon keeper who had disappeared from town at the same time, but the story was untrue. Lester Cochran had himself taken her to Chicago where she got work with a company going into the far western states. Then he had taken her to the door of her hotel, had put money into her hands and in silence and without even a farewell kiss had turned and walked away.

The doctor sat in his office living over the moment and other intense moments when he had been deeply stirred and had been on the surface so cool and quiet. He wondered if the woman had known. How many times he had asked himself that question. After he left her that night at the hotel door she never wrote. "Perhaps she is dead," he thought for the thousandth time.

A thing happened that had been happening at odd moments for more than a year. In Doctor Cochran's mind the remembered figure of his wife became confused with the figure of his daughter. When at such moments he tried to separate the two figures, to make them stand out distinct from each other, he was unsuccessful. Turning his head slightly he imagined he saw a white girlish figure coming through a door out of the rooms in which he and his daughter lived. The door was painted white and swung slowly in a light breeze that came in at an open window. The wind ran softly and quietly through the room and played over some papers lying on a desk in a corner. There was a soft swishing sound as of a woman's skirts. The doctor arose and stood trembling. "Which is it? Is it you Mary or is it Ellen?"

On the stairway leading up from the street there was the sound of heavy feet and the outer door opened. The doctor's weak heart fluttered and he dropped heavily back into his chair.

A man came into his room. He was a farmer, one of the doctor's patients, and coming to the center of the room he struck a match, held it above his head and shouted. "Hello!" he called. When the doctor arose from his chair and answered he was so startled that the match fell from his hand and lay burning faintly at his feet.

The young farmer had sturdy legs that were like two pillars of stone supporting a heavy building, and the little flame of the match that burned and fluttered in the light breeze on the floor between his feet threw dancing shadows along the walls of the room. The doctor's confused mind refused to clear itself of his fancies that now began to feed upon this new situation.

He forgot the presence of the farmer and his mind raced back over his life as a married man. The flickering light on the wall recalled another dancing light. One afternoon in the summer during the first year after his marriage his wife Ellen had driven with him into the country. They were then furnishing their rooms and at a farmer's house Ellen had seen an old mirror, no longer in use, standing against a wall in a shed. Because of something quaint in the design the mirror had taken her fancy and the farmer's wife had given it to her. On the drive home the young wife had told her husband of her pregnancy and the doctor had been stirred as never before. He sat holding the mirror on his knees while his wife drove and when she announced the coming of the child she looked away across the fields.

How deeply etched, that scene in the sick man's mind! The sun was going down over young corn and oat fields beside the road. The prairie land was black and occasionally the road ran through the short lanes of trees that also looked black in the waning light.

The mirror on his knees caught the rays of the departing sun and sent a great ball of golden light dancing across the fields and among the branches of trees. Now as he stood in the presence of the farmer and as the little light from the burning match on the floor recalled that other evening of dancing lights, he thought he understood the failure of his marriage and of his life. On that evening long ago when Ellen had told him of the coming of the great adventure of their marriage he had remained silent because he had thought no words he could utter would express what he felt. There had been a defense for himself built up. "I told myself she should have understood without words and I've all my life been telling myself the same thing about Mary. I've been a fool and a coward. I've always been silent because I've been afraid of expressing myself — like a blundering fool. I've been a proud man and a coward.

"Tonight I'll do it. If it kills me I'll make myself talk to the girl," he said aloud, his mind coming back to the figure of his daughter.

"Hey! What's that?" asked the farmer who stood with his hat in his hand waiting to tell of his mission.

The doctor got his horse from Barney Smithfield's livery and drove off to the country to attend the farmer's wife who was about to give birth to her first child. She was a slender narrow-hipped woman and the child was large, but the doctor was feverishly strong. He worked desperately and the woman, who was frightened, groaned and struggled. Her husband kept coming in and going out of the room and two neighbor women appeared and stood silently about waiting to be of service. It was past ten o'clock when everything was done and the doctor was ready to depart for town.

The farmer hitched his horse and brought it to the door and the doctor drove off feeling strangely weak and at the same time strong. How simple now seemed the thing he had yet to do. Perhaps when he got home his daughter would have gone to bed but he would ask her to get up and come into the office. Then he would tell the whole story of his marriage and its failure sparing himself no humiliation. "There was something very dear and beautiful in my Ellen and I must make Mary understand that. It will help her to be a beautiful woman," he thought, full of confidence in the strength of his resolution.

He got to the door of the livery barn at eleven o'clock and Barney Smithfield with young Duke Yetter and two other men sat talking there. The liveryman took his horse away into the darkness of the barn and the doctor stood for a moment leaning against the wall of the building. The town's night watchman stood with the group by the barn door and a quarrel broke out between him and Duke Yetter, but the doctor did not hear the hot words that flew back and forth or Duke's loud laughter at the night watchman's anger. A queer hesitating mood had taken possession of him. There was something he passionately desired to do but could not remember. Did it have to do with his wife Ellen or Mary his daughter? The figures of the two women were again confused in his mind and to add to the confusion there was a third figure, that of the woman he had just assisted through childbirth. Everything was confusion. He started across the street toward the entrance of the stairway leading to his office and then stopped in the road and stared about. Barney Smithfield having returned from putting his horse in the stall shut the door of the barn and a hanging lantern over the door swung back and forth. It threw grotesque dancing shadows down over the faces and forms of the men standing and quarreling beside the wall of the barn.

MARY SAT by a window in the doctor's office awaiting his return. So absorbed was she in her own thoughts that she was unconscious of the voice of Duke Yetter talking with the men in the street.

When Duke had come into the street the hot anger of the early part of the evening had returned and she again saw him advancing toward her in the orchard with the look of arrogant male confidence in his eyes but presently she forgot him and thought only of her father. An incident of her childhood returned to haunt her. One afternoon in the month of May when she was fifteen her father had asked her to accompany him on an evening drive into the country. The doctor went to visit a sick woman at a farmhouse five miles from town and as there had been a great deal of rain the roads were heavy. It was dark when they reached the farmer's house and they went into the kitchen and ate cold food off a kitchen table. For some reason her father had, on that evening, appeared boyish and almost gay. On the road he had talked a little. Even at that early age Mary had grown tall and her figure was becoming womanly. After the cold supper in the farm kitchen he walked with her around the house and she sat on a narrow porch. For a moment her father stood before her. He put his hands into his trouser pockets and throwing back his head laughed almost heartily. "It seems strange to think you will soon be a woman," he said. "When you do become a woman what do you suppose is going to happen, eh? What kind of life will you lead? What will happen to you?"

The doctor sat on the porch beside the child and for a moment she had thought he was about to put his arm around her. Then he jumped up and went into the house leaving her to sit alone in the darkness.

As she remembered the incident Mary remembered also that on that evening of her childhood she had met her father's advances in silence. It seemed to her that she, not her father, was to blame for the life they had led together. The farm laborer she had met on the bridge had not felt her father's coldness. That was because he had himself been warm and generous in his attitude toward the man who had cared for him in his hour of sickness and misfortune. Her father had said that the laborer knew how to be a father and Mary remembered with what warmth the two boys fishing by the creek had called to her as she went away into the darkness. "Their father has known how to be a father because his children have known how to give themselves," she thought guiltily. She also would give herself. Before the night had passed she would do that. On that evening long ago and as she rode home beside her father he had made another unsuccessful effort to break through the wall that separated them. The heavy rains had swollen the streams they had to cross and when they had almost reached town he had stopped the horse on a wooden bridge. The horse danced nervously about and her father held the reins firmly and occasionally spoke to him. Beneath the bridge the swollen stream made a great roaring sound and beside the road in a long flat field there was a lake of flood water. At that moment the moon had come out from behind the clouds and the wind that blew across the water made little waves. The lake of flood water was covered with dancing lights. "I'm going to tell you about your mother and myself," her father said huskily, but at that moment the timbers of the bridge began to crack dangerously and the horse plunged forward. When her father had regained control of the frightened beast they were in the streets of the town and his diffident silent nature had reasserted itself.

Mary sat in the darkness by the office window and saw her father drive into the street. When his horse had been put away he did not, as was his custom, come at once up the stairway to the office but lingered in the darkness before the barn door. Once he started to cross the street and then returned into the darkness.

Among the men who for two hours had been sitting and talking quietly a quarrel broke out. Jack Fisher the town night watchman had been telling the others the story of a battle in which he had fought during the Civil War and Duke Yetter had begun bantering him. The night watchman grew angry. Grasping his nightstick he limped up and down. The loud voice of Duke Yetter cut across the shrill angry voice of the victim of his wit. "You ought to a flanked the fellow, I tell you Jack. Yes sir'ee, you ought to a flanked that reb and then when you got him flanked you ought to a knocked the stuffings out of the cuss. That's what I would a done," Duke shouted, laughing boisterously. "You would a raised hell, you would," the night watchman answered, filled with ineffectual wrath.

The old soldier went off along the street followed by the laughter of Duke and his companions and Barney Smithfield, having put the doctor's horse away, came out and closed the barn door. A lantern hanging above the door swung back and forth. Doctor Cochran again started across the steet and when he had reached the foot of the stairway turned and shouted to the men. "Good night," he called cheerfully. A strand of hair was blown by the light summer breeze across Mary's cheek and she jumped to her feet as though she had been touched by a hand reached out to her from the darkness. A hundred times she had seen her father return from drives in the evening but never before had he said anything at all to the loiterers by the barn door. She became half convinced that not her father but some other man was now coming up the stairway.

The heavy dragging footsteps rang loudly on the wooden stairs and Mary heard her father set down the little square medicine case he always carried. The strange cheerful hearty mood of the man continued but his mind was in a confused riot. Mary imagined she could see his dark form in the doorway. "The woman has had a baby," said the hearty voice from the landing outside the door. "Who did that happen to? Was it Ellen or that other woman or my little Mary?"

A stream of words, a protest came from the man's lips. "Who's been having a baby? I want to know. Who's been having a baby? Life doesn't work out. Why are babies always being born?" he asked.

A laugh broke from the doctor's lips and his daughter leaned forward and gripped the arms of her chair. "A babe has been born," he said again. "It's strange, eh, that my hands should have helped a baby be born while all the time death stood at my elbow?"

Doctor Cochran stamped upon the floor of the landing. "My feet are cold and numb from waiting for life to come out of life," he said heavily. "The woman struggled and now I must struggle."

Silence followed the stamping of feet and the tired heavy declaration from the sick man's lips. From the street below came another loud shout of laughter from Duke Yetter.

And then Doctor Cochran fell backward down the narrow stairs to the street. There was no cry from him, just the clatter of his shoes upon the stairs and the terrible subdued sound of the body falling.

Mary did not move from her chair. With closed eyes she waited. Her heart pounded. A weakness complete and overmastering had possession of her and from feet to head ran little waves of feeling as though tiny creatures with soft hair-like feet were playing upon her body.

It was Duke Yetter who carried the dead man up the stairs and laid him on a bed in one of the rooms back of the office. One of the men who had been sitting with him before the door of the barn followed lifting his hands and dropping them nervously. Between his fingers he held a forgotten cigarette, the light from which danced up and down in the darkness.

Fathers

&

Sons

INTRODUCTION

SOCIAL MORES GOVERNING masculine behavior along with a father's traditional role as breadwinner profoundly affect the father-son relationship. In teaching their sons to be strong, competitive, and tough in a "man's world," fathers tend to hide their own vulnerability while discouraging what they see as "feminine" behavior in their sons. Spending so much of their time and energy outside the home, fathers are often seen by their sons as inaccessible strangers. Therefore, in developing a sense of themselves as males, sons identify more with aspects of a father's role than with a person they intimately know as an individual. This already distant image of father is often filtered through the judgments and emotions of the mother. Thus, a son often gets a second-hand image of the person with whom he is expected to identify.

The emotional and physical distance separating sons from fathers is further magnified by the elimination in our modern world of both the apprenticeship system, whereby sons learned a trade from their fathers, and the ritualized initiation rites whereby sons entered the world of their fathers. This loss has created a vacuum in today's father-son relationship.

Despite their lack of intimacy, both father and son want to get close to one another and often discover indirect ways to do so. A son may try to connect with his father by attempting to imitate him or excel in an activity that carries the paternal stamp of approval. In his quest for his father's responsiveness, a son is often forced to read between the lines to receive a message of caring, for many fathers demonstrate their love not by words or physical displays of affection but by participating in sports activities or by completing projects with their sons.

Besides craving more intimacy, sons also want their fathers to accept their uniqueness as individuals. Like daughters with their mothers, sons need to individuate from their same-sex parent. This desire often runs counter to the father's expectations that his son follow in his footsteps, emulating his life choices or realizing his own unfulfilled dreams. A typical scenario between a father and son involves a father's efforts to woo his son into the family business. By sharing his life's work in this way, a father hopes not only to narrow the gap between himself and his son but also to gain a greater sense of his place within the continuity of the generations. However, a father's efforts to impose his own dreams on his son often lead to rebellion on the son's part, thus increasing the distance between the two generations of males.

From the four stories in this section, it is obvious that fathers and sons are crucial figures to one another, despite displays of resentment and a dearth of emotional response on both sides. The feelings that are expressed usually surprise both father and son because they are so unexpected. Across a barrier of reserve, the sons in these stories closely scrutinize their fathers in order to unlock the key to their own masculine development, while the fathers silently seek affirmation of their life choices in the behavior of their sons.

Shaw's "In High Country" introduces us to a sixteen-year-old son on a backpacking expedition with his recently divorced father. While their joint participation in this activity creates a new bond, both father and son find it very difficult to reveal their fears or communicate their sadness and love.

In Eunson's "The Hero's Son," the thoughts of a mother occupy center stage, as she mediates conflict between her husband and their nineteen-year-old son. To a lesser extent, we are also privy to the thoughts of the father who is very invested in his son's future success. Locked in conflict with a son whose decisions contradict his own expectations, this father submerges his tender feelings under layers of critical response and expressions of disappointment.

Disappointment typifies the adult son's reaction in this section's next story, "The Blue Winged Teal." As in the previous stories, the mixed feelings of both father and son are evident here. The father's poolroom existence represents a masculine world that both attracts and repels this son in Stegner's story. While he perceives his father's choices as a betrayal of both himself and his recently deceased mother, Stegner's hero desperately wants to win his father's approval. Driven to leave his father's world, the son is puzzled by his reluctance to say goodbye.

From the pool hall, we move to the world of the baseball diamond in Cheever's "The National Pastime." In this story, the adult son recounts details of his father's life and his own rather tenuous place within that life. Forced to grow up without the blessing of paternal acceptance, the son in Cheever's tale struggles to assume his place in a masculine arena.   G.C.

Janet Beeler Shaw

IN HIGH COUNTRY

U NSPOILED." Bill's dad spread the map out on the dining room floor, moving his coffee mug to lay it out flat. His heavy hands with fine dark fur sprouting down from his wrists smoothed the folds. "Virgin territory, these mountains."

Bill felt like laughing and crying at the same time. It was a comedy: two city slickers from the North Shore enter virgin territory! But against his will he felt some excitement. Delivering groceries for the last grocery in Wilmette that took phone orders didn't seem like much of a summer, even if he had finally got his driver's license. *"We're* going to camp in virgin territory?"

"Why not? Why the hell not? We can learn. Never too old to learn." He bent over the map, traced the ridge line of the range. "The watershed," he announced, as though he'd discovered it on foot.

His dad's face seemed another kind of map to Bill: dark prints traced beneath his eyes, skin tight over his cheekbones, his chin shadowed by his evening beard, lips thinned by fatigue. Bill prodded an edge of the terrain map with his thumb. It crackled, some kind of waterproof paper — the real thing. "I don't see how we can, that's all."

His dad laid both hands down on the map, fingers outspread.

He'd taken off his wedding band and that finger was pale, seemed swollen, injured. He leaned forward, his heavy head wagging as he spoke. "So what's to stop us? What?"

Bill looked away. They hadn't talked about the divorce.

He saw his mom twice a week when she picked him up after track practice and took him for supper at Scottie's. Even though he thought he shouldn't show too much interest, he always ran when he saw her pull up in her VW, the late sun catching her auburn hair. Since she'd left she seemed as mysterious and as remote as the high country his dad described — each time he saw her now he examined her for changes. When he jumped into her car she touched his arm, shyly. "Hey, old Billy," she said.

At Scottie's she drew her finger down the list of sandwiches as though she might choose something other than tuna on rye; she was on a diet now, that was new. He always ordered double cheeseburgers, and a chocolate shake. He was hungry, but mostly he knew it pleased her to see him eat.

Their talk was the same. "How's school? Track going okay, sweetie?" she'd ask, dipping her tea bag into her cup, her gray eyes watching him as he ate.

He'd stayed with his dad because he hadn't wanted to change schools now, his junior year. At least that's why he thought he'd stayed. He also thought maybe she'd come back. She had sublet a tiny apartment in Winnetka; it didn't look permanent to him. "Track's fine."

She leaned toward him, holding her cup in both hands as though she were warming herself. "Are your shin splints better?"

"Some. Everybody's got them. How's business, Mom?"

She sold real estate. Usually she described recent customers to him, making the encounters into dramatic little episodes. On the way to a movie one night, peering out of the back seat of a car filled with a gang of guys, he'd caught a glimpse of her in a pale dress going into Henrici's with a tall man, her arm laced through his. Could he have bought a house from her? Bill didn't want to ask. There was a lot it was better not to know. He stuck to school and business for conversation. And he hadn't told her that Dad was talking about backpacking, although he suspected his dad wanted him to. Frankly, he hadn't believed it would ever happen — his dad wasn't one to take risks.

But apparently they were going. The evidence was all around him. Besides the trail maps, his dad had bought tarps, insulated socks, fold-up plates with knives and forks that snapped on. The confusion of objects made Bill's head ache. It was too much. "Listen, dad, what do you say I fix us some supper and we work on this after?"

His dad sat back on his haunches, his hands on his knees. "Yeah, I've got to slow down. You can't master a map in an hour. And I want to understand it. Not just learn what to do, but why. Do you see what I mean?" He looked up at Bill from under his unruly gray eyebrows.

"You want to get it right?"

"That's it!" He slapped his thigh, then rose, brushing off his knees. Neither of them had talked about housekeeping yet. "I want to get a grip on this whole thing."

THE INTERSTATE was crowded with trucks and Bill wished they had a CB; he and his dad didn't talk much. When Bill drove, his dad either studied his maps, lists, and manuals, or dozed, his thick legs splayed out, one stockinged foot resting on the other. He wore his hiking boots, breaking them in, he said. But when he napped he pulled them off and they sat by his feet, lined up, the waxed laces as crisp as fencing wire. Bill's boots were still in the box. They were stiff and awkward; his feet felt trapped.

When his dad drove, Bill let his forehead rest against the cool window, his eyes slit almost shut against the June sun, a copper shadow on the glass — he had his mom's hair. The plains opened away around them, rectangles of pale green or black patchworking all the way to the horizon on every side. Mostly he watched the sky. Once he saw a storm pass, far away and silently, like a film track with no sound. Finally the first line of mountains appeared like a weather front moving in, a line of blue that gradually became the color of a bruise.

"The Rockies," his dad said. So he'd been watching, too. "We'll make Denver tonight and cross the divide tomorrow. From there we go up into high country."

Bill nodded. Until he'd seen the mountains he'd thought only of what he was leaving behind; now they were on their way.

WHAT SURPRISED HIM most about the mountains was the quality of light, air so clear that details far away were magnified. Sun dazzled off the granite at the road edge and boulders seemed lit from within, like street lights.

When his dad pulled the station wagon over to cool it down, Bill walked to the guardrail for a better look. Cliffs rose sharply above them and fell away below. He wondered if his mom had ever been to the mountains. She could barely force herself to walk along the bluff over Lake Michigan. He'd asked her once if she was afraid of heights. "I'm scared I might throw myself right over. Maybe that's the same," she whispered. He pressed his knees against the guardrail and leaned out into the wind, the clean, pitchy gusts rising through the pines, rinsing over him like chill water. His chest was tight with excitement that was almost like joy: mountains! Had his dad guessed *this?* He was in the car studying his map.

The town his dad had picked to start up from, Telluride, wasn't much — a trash of abandoned shacks left from gold rush times, small gray houses separated by empty lots scattered between them like gaps in a kid's teeth. Behind some of them aproned women worked in their kitchen gardens, early lettuce coming up, bean poles set in. Outside the hotel a tethered cow mooed in the early evening, waiting to be milked. It was like a foreign country.

They got their supper at the diner next to the hotel: pork chops and applesauce, a crater of gravy centered in the mashed potatoes. Bill ordered two glasses of milk. "The condemned men eat a hearty meal," he said.

"Hey," his dad said. "So far it's been all right. Something we've never done before. Admit that much."

"I admit that." He passed him the plate of bread. "Do we get a guide here?"

"Guide? Why do you think I've been memorizing the maps? Some things you've got to do on your own, Billy. There comes a time in a man's life when he's got to take hold and *do* it, not think about it anymore. Do *something.*" He wiped up his gravy with a piece of bread, rhythmically, drawing circles on the white plate. "Are you game to try?"

"I'm here, aren't I?" It was the best he could do.

"I found a guy with a jeep who'll take us to the top of the range.

We can hike down along the south slopes. Three nights of camping should do for a start."

Bill pushed his hair out of his eyes with the back of his hand. "Listen, Dad, would you call me Bill instead of Billy? In front of the guy with the jeep and all."

His dad nodded sternly. "Right, Bill." He nodded again to confirm the agreement, then signaled to the waitress for more coffee.

BUT IN THE MORNING nothing went as smoothly as Bill had expected from all the planning. By the time they got the packs loaded his was so heavy he had to lean against the wall. His dad grunted, shouldering his, and slipped it off. "We've got to cut them by half. I didn't figure right. The altitude."

They repacked. The pickax went, half the food. They kept the sterno, left the stove. Tent, sleeping bags stayed, but no extra clothing. They took the snakebite kit, left the paperback books. When they finished the second time Bill's pack weighed in at thirty-five pounds on the "Your Weight and Your Fortune" scales in the hotel lobby. His fortune card read, "Your social life will improve."

His dad's pack weighed forty-four pounds. "That's the best we can do," he said, handing the fortune card to Bill. "Don't tell me if it's bad news."

"It says, 'Rethink your investment plans.'"

His dad shook his head; he was wearing his old army fatigue hat and army jacket with his name on the pocket: Hoornstra. "I don't want to think about anything for a while. Let's get out of here."

They stored their extra gear in the car, locked it, and by the time they met the jeep driver at the gas station it was almost noon.

The jeep road led upward through pine woods, then through open fields to a mining village, the buildings caved in, a graveyard with wooden markers tumbled down like broken fence posts. The treeline ended at the edge of the village and the switchbacks on the narrow road were sharper. The jeep driver had to back up to make the turns. Finally he backed and hauled around the final switchback and pulled up on the highest rise, a ridge about fifteen feet across. A faintly marked trail led away to the south like a line down a cat's spine, the mountain yellow and tawny with streaks of iron. Scattering rock chips, the jeep backed around. The driver waved, "Luck, fellas!"

They were alone. They had a quick snack of peanut butter and crackers while his dad gave the map a final look. On all sides the mountain fell away from them. Scrub pine and piñon were gray shadows in the upland valleys far below. The insect sounds that had scoured the noon fields they had come through were gone. There was only the wind. Bill studied the narrow trail. His mom would faint if she could see that stone face sheered away on both sides, he thought. He focused on the height, trying to form an idea of what such space might mean to her. She would leap, she couldn't help herself, she would be killed! He imagined his mother plummeting through the drafts where a hawk hung below them, sailing in and out of the shadows. For the first time he thought of her not just as his mom, but as a person with deep fears, and he was afraid for her. "I bet women don't hike up here," he blurted, but his dad had the map spread out on a slab of rock and didn't answer.

Hiking was harder than Bill had guessed. Within half an hour his heels began to ache and sting. He should have broken his boots in; he knew better. His pack slipped until he got the straps right, and then he felt as though he were carrying a boulder. His dad led the way, shoulders hunched, feet sliding on loose rock. After less than an hour he stopped, slipped off his pack, laid himself spread-eagled beside the trail.

Bill lay down beside him, gasping. "Slow down?"

"Right." His voice was hard to hear in the wind.

When they started again they went very slowly and by the time they stopped to set up their tent they were still far above the highest timber. The last sun was no warmer than light glancing off ice. Around them tiny tundra blooms were confetti specks of orange and red, the rocks coated with lichen.

Bill ate what his dad spooned onto his tin dish — something that tasted of tomato paste. They had some chocolate, and after they wiped off their plates they had cocoa. It was dark by eight-thirty and they crawled into their sleeping bags, feet pointing downhill.

"Any bears up here?" Bill asked.

"The ranger said not."

"When did you talk to a ranger?"

"At the gas station. You were in the can. He lives in one of these upland valleys. Says there's a lot of deer and elk poaching around here. But no bears."

His dad's breath smelled of chocolate. Only a moment had gone by before Bill heard him snore. He closed his eyes, feeling an edge of stone against his ribs. The wind howled in their tent and he imagined wolves. It wouldn't be good to think about home, he knew that. Then he felt himself hurtling backward into sleep as though he were falling from the side of the gorge into the space wind had hollowed out below him, his arms and legs jerking wildly with fatigue.

When he woke in the morning it was hard to move. He watched from his sleeping bag as his dad crept around their campsite, piling bits of dried moss onto the fire. His thick, gray hair was matted — he'd been in the same position each time Bill woke during the night: knees drawn up, face buried inside his bag.

Around them the mountains loomed bronze and dense. "Christ!" Bill whispered.

"Hey," his dad said.

"You know what I mean." Bill raised his arm to trace the horizon line of sharp-edged peaks.

"It's a lot," his dad said: his gift.

That day was better. They paced themselves, urging each other to stop, to rest. They had a snack of nuts or dried fruit every hour or so. Bill took off his windbreaker and tied it to his pack, and by the time they reached the first fork in the trail his dad's sides were dark with sweat. A stream ran beside the new trail. The rushing water smelled of clean stones, of rain, and small trout leaped next to the bank. Bill swung along behind his dad, whistling. Maybe they would become outdoorsmen, after all. Who knew what was possible?

That night they camped in a meadow by the stream. There was soft grass under their tent and the wind had died down. His dad fixed beef and noodles. After, they built the fire up and sang a few songs, mostly ones that Bill remembered from Y camp. He hugged his knees, feeling the fire on his face like a comforting hand. An owl circled low over the meadow; after mice, Bill guessed. The moon had come up and it gazed down like a white eye. At home he had never paid much attention to the moon.

In his sleeping bag, Bill was restless. "You know any stories?" he asked.

His dad grunted no.

"I wish I had a book."

"Too heavy." He was falling asleep, his voice deepening.

"I just want something to do. It's only nine."

"Long day, Bill." There was an emphasis on the single syllable of his name — his dad was keeping his word.

"I know."

"So go on to sleep."

"Mind if I sing some more?"

No answer.

So he sang. He started in on "Rock and roll is here to stay," moved on to "Blueberry Hill," and then went way back in time for "One little, two little, three little Indians."

"That's the first song Mom taught me," he said, not especially talking to his dad.

Silence.

Then from inside his sleeping bag his dad said, "Wrong. 'Baby's bed is like a boat,' that was her song for you."

"I forgot that one."

Startled, he heard his father's voice start up, low and muzzy with fatigue.

> Baby's bed is like a boat,
> Sailing out to sea.
> When morning comes then baby's boat
> Comes sailing back to me.

After the first verse there was silence again.

Bill turned on his side, curling himself around his jacket. He felt a painful but not unwelcome ache of consciousness: after all, he loved his dad, no matter that he was clumsy or misjudged what he could do, no matter even that somehow he'd let Mom leave, hadn't been able to stop her, persuade her, love her enough, whatever it was he couldn't do or couldn't be. "We've hiked a long way up here," he said by way of thank you, but his dad was asleep.

IN THE MORNING they followed the trail through the high mea-dow grass, birds flying up around them. After lunch the pines and aspen closed over the trail and the light was dappled; if there were deer moving Bill couldn't see them. At the side of the stream the trail forked. "Which way?" Bill called. He was leading.

His dad slipped off his pack and pulled the map from his hip pocket, opened it, rubbed his two-day beard with his knuckles while he studied it. "This doesn't show any fork here."

Bill chucked a stone into the stream. The trail beside the water was rocky but looked more direct than the one that crossed over and into the woods again. "So what do we do?"

His dad looked up, brow furrowed, eyebrows almost meeting. "Don't know."

"Is there a wrong choice?"

His dad looked down at the map again as if the answer to Bill's question might be there. "Don't know that, either."

Bill shifted his weight, impatient. "We got a lot to learn."

His dad pulled on his pack but didn't answer. Overhead, birds settled back into the pines. The stream sounded like leaves rustling.

"Well?"

His dad was looking down into the stream; he looked up, star-tled, and shrugged. Moving ahead of Bill he started down the trail beside the stream.

After the first quarter-mile the trail grew suddenly steeper. He motioned Bill to go ahead of him. "Something's wrong," he said as Bill inched past.

"We'll get down quicker, that's all." But he was anxious; he had to concentrate on each step, set his feet in sideways, grasp at sap-lings where the stones were slick and wet underfoot. It was like climbing down a broken ladder and no end in sight. They climbed like that an hour, two. Dark came on earlier under the thick pines. "Should we camp here?" he asked, his heart crashing with fatigue — no matter how he dug in at each step the rocks slid from beneath his boots.

"A little farther. Let's get the hell out of here."

Bill turned to see his dad leaning on a pine branch that was thrust out ahead of him like the cane of a blind man. So Bill pushed on, tasting the sweat that ran onto his lips. When his dad fell he heard, rather than saw, the fall — the wild scattering of rocks, birds beating up, the thud of a man's body careening into stones as he slid. The cry was Bill's, "No!"

He ripped off his pack and half-stumbled, half-climbed back up the steep trail. His dad lay on his side, his head on the trail, legs in the stream, his pack torn open and foil packets and cookware scattered around him. His face was as pale as the stones that pillowed him. "My goddamn knee," he moaned as Bill crouched by him. "Oh, god! My knee!"

Bill felt as though all his blood had suddenly been forced into the valves of his heart. It was like the stories he'd read of parents lifting cars off their children: he could pick up his father and carry him on his back as easily as he could his pack. "I'll take you!"

"Just get me out of the water. Then go on down and find that ranger." He held up his arms to Bill.

When Bill bent to pull, his feet slipping in the stream, his strength left him as quickly as it had come. His dad's foot was wedged. When he tugged to pull him free his dad screamed, a long scream that grew in size and weight and then dropped off sharply. The trail grew dark as though the light had been drained away by the cry. Bill closed his eyes a moment and when he opened them he could see again. Lifting more than pulling, he got his dad up on the trail.

"How far to the ranger?"

No answer. His dad dragged his sleeping bag out of the torn pack, wrapped in it. "Hurry," he said without moving his lips, the word an exhalation. Bill began to run, skidding and sliding.

Around the second bend the trail abruptly joined a fire road that ran parallel to the stream. They'd been beside a road all the time! Directly below, Bill spotted a thin line of smoke: the ranger's cabin. For all their climbing they'd never been far away at all.

The ranger had a jeep. In less than an hour they had his dad in to see the doctor. Nothing broken, bruises, a sprain. The doctor gave Bill's dad an envelope of pills for the pain. "Don't worry," he said. "Nothing serious." He'd turned from them before they reached the office door.

"I'll put you up with me for the night." The ranger was tanned already and wore a red ski cap pushed jauntily over one ear.

"Caused you enough trouble," his dad said.

"It's my job." He stroked his yellow mustache. "But I'd sure like company."

His dad turned his hands palms up, asking Bill to decide.

"Thanks. That would be great." Bill's voice was too loud in the small waiting room.

"I'd like a drink," his dad said. He didn't look up.

"You got it," the ranger said.

AT THE RANGER'S CABIN the whiskey bottle was already out on the counter beside the dish detergent. The ranger rinsed a jelly glass, poured some whiskey straight up, and handed it to Bill's dad at the table where he sat, foot propped up on an extra chair. "Take it easy with those pills. I'll fix chow."

Bill brought in their packs, took off his boots, then his dad's, set them by the door to clean in the morning. He laid out forks and knives, paper napkins. The delicious, dizzying aroma of onions and potatoes frying in bacon drippings made his stomach moan with hunger. The ranger poured a beer for himself and a glass of milk for Bill. They ate without talking, his dad working on the whiskey as well as the fried eggs, fried potatoes, slices of ham.

After supper Bill cleared the table and washed up. Behind him the two men talked. His dad had his hiking map spread out on the table, the crackle sounding like a fire. Bill went at the dishes slowly, the warm water making him lazy.

"You started on the right trail, no doubt about that. See, there? You started off just right." After each sentence the ranger paused to suck on his pipe.

"And this fork?"

"Right there, too."

"I studied it." His dad's voice was blurred with the pain medicine and the whiskey. "I studied so hard."

"You were going right."

"But somewhere things went wrong."

"Let's have another look."

Bill glanced back to see the ranger, still in his ski hat, bent over the map, head close to his dad's. "You were doing fine here at the meadows."

His dad shook his head. "It's different. I mean, on a map it's all so clear. When you're *in* it things aren't the same. You don't know until it's too late."

The ranger turned the map toward him, then back again. He tapped the stem of his pipe against his teeth. "The fact is you got onto the goat path. You weren't on any hiking trail at all. You must have seen that," he said gently.

It was hard for Bill to hear his dad. "I thought maybe that's how hiking trails were."

The ranger slapped the table with his open hand. "But how the hell would you know? I mean, you hadn't done it before! You were trying something new."

Bill put the last plate in the drainer and took the coffeepot to the table. He poured an inch into his dad's cup, although it was still almost full. The ranger held his empty cup out for more.

His dad bent his head and rested it on his arms. "I got it wrong, it's just that simple. Dead wrong."

"Hey, man, what did you lose? You're here. You ain't hurt bad." The ranger rocked back in his chair. "Nothing's broke that can't be fixed or bought new!" he laughed, winking at Bill.

His dad didn't raise his head.

THERE WERE two wooden bunks in the spare room. The lantern lit the rough pine walls, the calendar with a picture of a girl smiling over a basket of apples, her breasts full at the basket rim. There were no curtains at the window. The moon rose high above the pines, outdistancing the branches, its light a second lantern in the dim room.

Bill helped his dad unbutton his flannel shirt, ease his trousers over his bruised knee. There were a couple of inches of whiskey in the tumbler, and his dad set it close to the bunk on the floor where he could reach it.

Bill turned down the lantern wick and climbed into the upper bunk. The pillow prickled and smelled of mold. His bunk was on a level with the upper window and a square of moonlight lay on his blanket.

From below his dad asked, "Want to sing?"

"No, Dad. Go on to sleep."

"I feel like singing."

"Dad, you're kind of smashed. Get some sleep."

"My goddamn leg hurts."

Bill climbed down and put his pillow under his dad's knee to take the pressure off. "Better?"

"Better." He didn't open his eyes.

Bill bundled his jacket into a pillow. It smelled of pine and smoke. "Night, Dad."

There was silence for a while, and then his dad began to sing — a broken, atonal line. "Five foot two, eyes of blue, and oh what those blue eyes can do…" His voice trailed off.

Bill drew his knees up to his chest. His longing for home left him as alert as if he'd just awakened. He was sure he would not sleep at all; he would watch the moon until it set, wishing for home the way it used to be, his mother there.

Long after Bill thought he must have fallen asleep, his dad whispered up to him. "Billy? Awake?"

"Yeah."

"Listen. I got to ask you something. A promise. Don't *tell*, okay? When you see her again, don't *tell*."

There was the terrible sound of his father trying not to cry.

Bill turned his face against his jacket. His mouth was dry with panic, as though his dad's sorrow and shame had entered him like a fever and become his own. Like his dad, he would never again have what he needed. He clenched his teeth, biting down until his head ached with effort. When he heard his father's breathing steady into sleep he opened his eyes. The patch of moonlight had crept up to his chest like a small animal and nestled there. Over the dark pines the owl circled in wide, descending spirals through the cloudless night.

Dale Eunson

THE HERO'S SON

D ON'T LET IT spoil your trip," Ann said as the *No Smoking* sign blinked off.

"It's your trip too," John said.

"I didn't mean it that way."

"Well, that's the way it sounded."

The bloated 747 leveled off and cruised over floating-island clouds that smeared the Mojave 35,000 feet below. John unsnapped his seat belt and tried to attract the stewardess taking drink orders.

"I could use one too," Ann said. Her tentative smile coaxed no response from him. "Can't we not think about it for a while?"

"I wasn't thinking about it," John said. "I was wondering if he'd remember to give Scotty his Digitoxin."

"Darling," Ann said, "Little John is nineteen years old. You don't have to remind him of everything."

"That, as my old man used to say, is a moot point." He frowned. "What do you have to do to get that idiot girl to look at you?"

"For openers," Ann said, "you might try pinching her behind as she passes."

John glanced at Ann and readjusted the grim set of his features into something resembling a smile. "I'm sorry," he said. "It's just that whenever I think about that dumb kid...ah, Miss, how about a couple of very dry martinis?"

They ate lunch high above the Wasatch Mountains of Utah. As they passed over Wyoming and the Dakotas, John sat hooked up to the sound track of the movie, hoping Woody Allen could divert his mind from the problem that had come to a head yesterday. Come to a head *again,* rather, because it was always there. But this time it had been worse, and Ann finally cried out, "Stop it, both of you!" And then for the first time in her life she had resorted to emotional blackmail. "Do you love me?" she asked her son.

"Why, yeah, sure, Mom," the boy answered. "So what?"

"Then do me a favor. Listen to your father."

"I've been listening."

"Not with your mind. It's clamped shut. Maybe you're right, but it's possible your father's right too. He's lived a lot longer than you have. He might have learned something in all those years."

"But he talks to me like I'm a ten-year-old."

"And by God, that's giving you the benefit of a few years!" John said, whirling on his son.

"John! Please please please!" Ann put her hand on her son's arm. "Nothing can be settled today. I want you to promise me to remain in college till we come home. Stay here and take care of things — the house, Scotty, the plants — and then — "

"But, Mom," the boy said, "they need me now. This is the only meaningful thing I've ever wanted to do."

"Oh, Lord!" John groaned. "Meaningful. Can't you kids think up another word this year? And spare me *relevant.* I'm up to here with relevant too."

"Please, can we skip the lecture on semantics?" Ann turned back to Little John. "Nothing very significant will be lost if you postpone joining the campaign for a month, will it?"

"He needs all the help he can get, man," Little John said.

John winced; then, in the same sarcastic tone, said, "No doubt he does, man. But you may be losing your hold on pure, indigenous wisdom. Nineteen…why, you're old enough to vote, God help us every one!"

"I can't talk to him, Mom," Little John said.

The boy stole a furtive glance at his father, who was staring at him with all the puzzled fascination of a scientist attempting to identify a rare specimen under his microscope. The specimen lowered its head, long hair completely concealing the face. "I'll tell ya, man," it mumbled, "it's like, well, he knows where it's at."

"I see," John said slowly. "And you — out of vast experience acquired in the sandbox — are an authority on politics and politicians, is that it?"

"Ya see, Mom?" the boy said shrugging shoulders that seemed already set in a permanent shrug.

"John," Ann said hopelessly. She turned and stared out the library window at Scotty who had treed a cat and was barking for his family to come share his triumph.

"Go on. I'm waiting," she heard John say to their son.

"I mean — well — you wouldn't have to keep on giving me an allowance while I was campaigning for the senator."

Which was not what the boy meant to say at all, Ann suspected, but why did he have to let such a stupid thing come out of his mouth?

"Did you hear that, Ann?" John asked. "We wouldn't need to support the senator's brain trust. I knew if we kept up these round-the-clock bargaining sessions we'd win some valuable concessions." He turned to the boy. "I'll tell you what, Mr. Meany. Your mother and I want very much to go to England for a few weeks. You stay here and take care of the house while we're gone, and I'll pay you a hundred dollars. And when we come home you may pack up your mind-blasting rock records, rip out your stereo, sweep up your beads and hair ribbons, load them all on your horrible Honda and present them — and yourself — as a campaign gift to the senator of your choice!"...

"If you look down to your left at ten o'clock," the pilot's voice was saying, "that's Winnipeg coming up on the Red River."

Ann looked out the window of the plane, but she did not see Winnipeg. What she saw was John's dear young face, blurred by the anesthetic they had given her. His eyes were red, and he was telling her that the baby had not lived. A boy, it had been. Perfect in every way. It just had not lived, that was all.

Three years later Little John, as they called him, was born. He was handsome and normal — and he had lived! And few children have known such love.

They would shield him, John swore fervently, from all the things his own tender psyche had been exposed to (and somehow survived). He was to be nourished at prescribed intervals, sleep according to the schedule recommended by Dr. Spock, be spared the unconscious chauvinism of military toys and exposed to the virus of television only enough to immunize him. Any talent that might bubble to the surface would be coddled and fertilized. And when Little John reached the age of six, Big John was already weighing the merits of one college against another.

Yet all this protection and love did not produce the child John had anticipated. Little John's capacity to learn was only average. His lack of physical coordination made him indifferent at competitive sports. As he approached adolescence, he seemed deliberately unresponsive — negativistic was the child psychiatrist's term for it. "Most children," this authority assured the Hastingses, "pass through a similar phase. It is assertion of ego, a perfectly normal rebellion against authority and direction."

"But the boy has nothing to rebel against," John told him. "Nothing but our love for him."

"That may be the trouble," the doctor told them. "He's got to rebel against something. Most of us have palpable grievances as children. Plenty of our parents *are* stupid, unfair, selfish — not at all the omnipotent gods we think they are when we are toddlers. In the case of your boy, I suspect he has translated your love and concern into a fence. Lower the fence. Make it easy for him to climb over — and come back across."

"That is a lot of bull," John said as he and Ann drove home to their puzzling 13-year-old. "He admitted he had no kids of his own. You're damn right he hasn't!"

"Let's just try to ignore what Little John does and says," Ann said. "Try not to keep at him about studying for a while."

"Then he'll never crack a book."

"Let him. He'll have to take the consequences. Not you."

"But he's my son!" John cried.

And so everything and anything became an issue. There was the matter of his posture, his long scraggly hair, the shattering rock music and the beat-up motorcycle that he bought with his allowance, took apart and wired together regularly once a week.

Ann tried to act as buffer between father and son, but John interpreted this as defense of the boy's inadequacies: to the boy it was interference in his resistance to what he maddeningly termed his father's square life-style.

"Don't you see, Mom?" he once said in a rare moment of closeness between them. "It's not how you look — or what you say or do — it's what you are inside."

But what was the boy inside? Ann wondered. And why didn't how he looked, or what he said or did, give them a clue? He did not even fall in love at 16 or 17 or if so, he kept it secret.

"What girl would be foolish enough to go for our pride and joy?" John said. "You don't suppose he's working up to being a queer, do you?"

"They all look like that these days," Ann said.

"Mine won't, if he continues to live in my house!" John said darkly.

Ann had hoped that going off to college would not only mature the boy but that the absence of daily friction between father and son would begin to heal scar tissue. But Little John did not go away. His grades were too low for him to be accepted at any of the first-rate universities, and John could see no point in shelling out what it would take to board him at some distant state college when a duplicate local branch lay within five miles of home.

The sight of Little John taking off for a day at State was, Ann had to admit, ludicrous. To his father, it was closer to agony than humor. When he kicked the Honda into life and rocketed off, wearing run-over cowboy boots, skintight jeans, beads, a torn sweat shirt impregnated with a photograph of W. C. Fields, long hair tied at the back with a psychedelic ribbon, Little John was not precisely his father's notion of a clean-cut American boy entering the halls of Academe.

Watching him disappear around the corner, John said, "If he's trying for Mr. Repulsive, he's a smash."

"John, you sound as if you hate him."

John thought this over, then he said, "No. I'm just appalled. My God, the kid's going out in the world one of these days. It's rough. Who'd give him a job? If his grades don't pick up soon, he'll even get kicked out of State. And that's not easy, man!"

DARKNESS CAME SWIFTLY as the 747 droned eastward. Only four hours after sunset the northeast horizon crimsoned, and presently the plane settled into the bumpy veil of clouds below, and then suddenly, there was England with her clean little row houses, the gentle, intimate green landscape dotted with sheep and cattle, a well-behaved river meandering between manicured meadows. "That's the Thames," John said. "Brother! Was that a sight for sore eyes when we finally made it back from the Continent! Look, there's Windsor! Our base was only a few miles to the north."

Peter Proctor was at Heathrow to meet them. It was difficult for Ann to reconcile this middle-aged Londoner — settled, inclining slightly to paunch, hair graying (what was left of it), neat pin-striped suit — with the crazy American youngster John had told her about. They'd been quite a pair, those two. John the P-38 squadron leader and Pete, his buddy and constant concern.

"I daresay Johnny has regaled you with tales of my sticky dere-lictions," Peter said to Ann as he drove them toward London.

"A few hair-raising highlights," Ann admitted.

"All gross libels," Peter said. "Substitute Johnny's name for mine, and you'll approximate the truth."

John laughed. It was the first time Ann had heard the sound since the crisis. "Listen to Pomona Pete. He's turned into a Limey."

Peter Proctor's love affair with England had begun when he read the legends of King Arthur, and it had been intensified by the romantic notion that he was something of a knight himself, com-ing to the rescue of prostrate Britannia in 1943. It was inevitable that he should fall in love with an English girl, and he had. She was a fashion model, and her name was Sarah Calvert. After the war Peter married her. He promptly got a job in the London branch of Hamilton Assurance, Ltd., and was now assistant man-ager.

The Proctors lived in a pleasant, airy flat two blocks off Hyde Park in Kensington. John and Ann were to occupy the room that had been their son's before Gerald married.

Sarah Proctor, while still pretty, no longer possessed the figure of a model. "All that Devonshire cream," Pete said, patting her fanny.

After dinner that evening Gerald, now 24, and Ellen, his very pregnant young wife, came by to pay their respects to their fa-ther's old friends. They seemed to be smudgy carbon copies of many American young people — long-haired, healthy, rumpled, relaxed. "Gerald," Sarah explained, "does something tedious about recording the prenatal mewlings of fetuses."

"That's why I got Ellen pregnant," Gerald explained. "It beats getting picked up for approaching strange women in Piccadilly," he said, laughing.

"It's cold — having a microphone strapped to your belly," Ellen said.

"Do you mean to say that you're going to market these — ah — recordings? You are putting us on, aren't you?" John asked.

"Not at all, old man," Peter said. "Gerald's got a firm contract for twenty-five thousand first pressings."

"You see, Mr. Hastings," the young man said, peering at John through his bangs, "we amplify those sounds five thousand times, and it comes out like — like Genesis. And the birth is Exodus."

"Beautiful!" Ellen sighed. "The way God would have wanted you to hear it if he'd thought of four-track stereo."

It had been, both John and Ann agreed when they were finally alone, an unsettling evening, to say the least. Maybe, Ann said, they were merely victims of jet lag, and it had not really happened; it seemed impossible that nice, average parents like Peter and Sarah could casually accept — even seem to love and admire — such a far-out son and daughter-in-law.

During the next few days the Hastingses visited St. Paul's and the Tower and Parliament; they paid their respects to Sherlock Holmes and Dr. Watson in Baker Street, to Leslie Howard in Berkeley Square and to Sir Winston Churchill at 10 Downing Street.

On Sunday morning the *Times* assured them that skies would clear by noon. Sarah packed a lunch, and the four of them drove to a peaceful meadow that, almost three decades ago, had been home base for Lt. John Hastings' squadron of the P-38 wing of the U.S. Army Air Corps.

The government had chosen, wisely, to reclaim the land for a park, to plant trees and shrubs and create a man-made lake around which flowers and children blossomed, to set up tables and benches and yet leave space for the ubiquitous cricket fields, now dotted with slim figures in white. Nothing remained of the military installation, nothing was there of what had been except two middle-aged men who presently strolled across the field, watched the cricket players and noisy children and peaceful picnickers, and frequently paused and seemed to cock their ears (for the drone of a plane that would never come back?). As they returned to Ann and Sarah, they were speaking softly as one does on the steps of a church after a funeral.

"It was so long, so long ago," John was saying.

"God...a lifetime," Peter said, and bent to kiss Sarah.

"If it hadn't been for the war we'd never have had each other," Sarah said, as though John and Ann were not there.

"And Gerald would never have been born."

"The *ifs* of life," Sarah mused, and turned to Ann. "Can you imagine your life if you'd never met Lieutenant John Hastings?"

Ann stared at John. "It wouldn't have been life," she said simply, and then tried for a lighter tone. "The uniform — that's what got me."

"So you have the Air Corps uniform to thank for your kid," Peter said. And after a moment, "What's with your boy, Johnny?"

John turned away, focused on a child chasing a purple balloon. "Well — we've had our problems," he finally said.

"We all have," Sarah said.

"As long as you haven't killed each other, there's hope." Peter laughed.

"It's the damnedest thing," John said, and jammed his fist into the spongy English earth. "All these years — not caring a damn for anything but his own selfish comfort. And now — now after he finally gets into the only college that will have him — now he wants to drop out and promote the election of some senator. You'd think if he didn't, the world would come to an end."

"That's a healthy sign," Sarah said quietly.

"Healthy sign of what?" John asked, trying to suppress his anger.

"I don't know anything about your senator," Sarah replied, "but at least your son finally believes in something enough to do something about it."

"But *I* think the senator's an idiot," John exploded.

Sarah and Peter did not comment on what John had just said. No comment was needed. Presently Peter spoke. "When we were having our last hit-and-run rhubarb with Gerald, I felt I had to have help. We went to a shrink — "

John snorted. "Psychiatrists!"

"Yes, I know, I know. Maybe we were just lucky and found a sensible man," Peter continued amiably. "What he said was, playing father isn't always the hero part in the play. We get fouled up in a self-admiration society and — how did he put it, Sarah?"

"He said a father seldom loves a son as a separate entity. He loves his own image in his son. And if the son grows up and doesn't turn out to be you at all, you — I mean the father — either want to chain him to the nest or kick him out. Something like that."

Peter nodded. "When the only thing to do is to let him go. And pray a lot."

John got to his feet and brushed the grass off his trousers. "It's not that at all," he said. "It's — I know what the kid's going to be up against. I want what's best for him — that's all."

Peter stood beside his old friend. "Johnny, I wanted what was best for Gerald too, but he didn't give a damn about that, still doesn't....How old is — young John?"

John seemed not to hear the question. "Nineteen," Ann finally said.

"Just our age when you were my all-wise squadron leader," Peter observed.

John turned and stared at him, then looked out across the park. In his mind's eye he saw the base as it was 28 years ago — the bleak barracks and hangars, the control tower and, right where the lake was now, the runway. It was cloudy as always — like today — and then breaking through the clouds came the wobbly, stricken wreck of a twin-fuselaged plane, a grinning grasshopper impudently appliquéd on one nose. The pilot was bringing her home, hanging onto the controls with naked nerve endings, letting her down — by some miracle — right on the runway. And then he must have blacked out because the plane suddenly went into a dive and crashed — about *there* — beneath that flaming laburnum tree flaunting its gaudy yellow clusters....

And *there* — right there among the stark-white cricketeers — was young Lt. Hastings, strapped beneath the bubble of his own P-38, waiting to be flagged off once the rubbish of Hoppy's plane and body could be scraped off the runway. What was he thinking? *God,*

I don't remember! How did I have the guts — or was it plain stupidity! — to gun my plane when I finally got the flag? Didn't I have any imagination at nineteen? Nineteen...I was only nineteen. Little John's age!

"But we were men!" There was anguish in John's voice when he finally spoke.

"We sure as hell were," Peter said. "And if we didn't get into the fight the world would come to an end." He shrugged. "Maybe it has anyhow, but we gave it all we had because we believed. We believed we could do something about it, damn it!"

When they got back to the flat in Kensington there was a cable under the door and the telephone was ringing. Sarah picked up the cablegram and hurried to the phone. It was Gerald. Ellen was in labor and would like Sarah to go to the hospital with her. Gerald had all that sound equipment to lug.

"I'll be right there!" Sarah cried, hung up the phone and reported that she was about to be made a grandmother. She pecked Peter's cheek and rushed out the door only to return a second later and hand John the cablegram. "Silly me," she said. "This is for you."

The cable was from Dr. Patterson. Little John had been in an accident and was in the hospital. The doctor did not want to alarm them unduly, but for the boy's peace of mind he felt they ought to come home at once.

Two hours later they were on a plane headed for Los Angeles.

DR. PATTERSON'S CABLE had really told them nothing. Not how the accident had happened or how seriously Little John was injured. Was he maimed? Would he be a cripple? Blinded? His brain damaged? Both of his parents immediately assumed that his head had been injured in a crash of that damned motorcycle. It had to be that, didn't it?

Once John took Ann's hand in his and closed his eyes. She hoped he could doze for a few minutes, but his eyes were closed by acute distress, not sleep. "And I told him to pack his junk and get out," he muttered.

"I know," Ann said. "But he knew you were provoked. People say things they don't mean when they're — "

"I meant it at the time," John said, punishing himself. "I wonder now...am I so all-fired anxious to get home and make him well again? Or is it mixed up with my wanting to make sure he's forgiven me — in case — "

"Don't say it!" Ann said sharply.

John seemed not to hear her. "Little John....Who said it first?"

"I don't remember....Does it matter?"

"Me, probably. Right away I tried to make him a pint-size version of the old man."

"Hush," Ann said. She lifted her hand and turned his troubled face to hers. "It'll be all right," she murmured. "Everything will be all right, you'll see," and she knew as she said it that there was no reason in God's world — if indeed it was, or ever had been, God's world — to suppose that anything would be all right again.

They went straight to the hospital from the airport, and it was still only nine that same evening. It was insane. Ellen probably had her baby by now, and no doubt its mother's every moan and its first gasp for breath had been lovingly taped for the record's soaring climax. Exodus indeed!

"What room is John Hastings in?" Ann asked.

"Four-sixty-five," the young woman at the reception desk said. "But visiting hours are over."

Then he's not dead, Ann thought, and leaned against the wall for support. "We're his parents," John was saying.

The door to 465 was ajar. John pushed it open and held it for Ann to enter. A dim night-light burned. A black boy, his leg in a cast, occupied the first bed. A white boy lay in the bed near the window, but he was obviously not Little John. He was asleep, or seemed to be.

"You lookin' for somebody?" the black boy asked.

"Yes, but we must be in the wrong room," Ann said.

The figure in the other bed spoke. "That you, Mom?"

ANN CAUGHT HER BREATH, hurried around the black boy's bed and leaned over her son. "Darling, darling," she said, kissing him lightly on the cheek, then drew back and looked at him. His head was bandaged, the long hair gone. Without the wild, scraggly hair, his face looked different. She realized that it had changed. It hadn't really matured, but it was no longer the pimply, baby face of an adolescent.

"Baby, what happened?"

"A car hit me," he said.

"I was sure of that," Ann said. "Knocked you off your motor-cycle?"

"No. I knew you'd think that."

"It doesn't matter. I'm sorry I said it."

"It wasn't my fault. Honest. I was just standing there by the curb, waiting for Scotty to lift his leg on the hydrant, and this car comes highballing around the corner and can't quite make the turn. Man, next thing I know I'm on the ground and Scotty's lick-ing my face."

"But what happened? I mean, how were you hurt? How badly?"

"Compound fracture — back here," the boy said, indicating the back of his skull. "I get dizzy. Sometimes I don't see so good either."

"He's gonna be okay," the black boy volunteered. "His doc says he just needs to stay flat on his back for a spell. So don't go show-ing off trying to scare your folks, whitey."

"My *folks?*" Little John murmured. "You mean Dad came home too?"

"Why, of course," Ann said. "Whatever made you think…?"

"Well, I don't know. I just — "

John came forward and took the boy's hand in his own.

"I'm sorry I fouled up your trip," the boy said.

"Don't — don't," John said. He leaned over, fearful lest the ges-ture he ached for would be rebuffed. Closer, closer, then he put out his arms, and, after a long moment, the boy's arms reached out and went around his father, and they clung to each other and felt the other's heartbeat and breath and warmth. And finally John drew back and looked down into the face that was undeniably the spit and image of Lt. John Hastings, P-38 squadron leader, age 19.

"Listen, Dad," the boy said.

"I'm listening." *And keep me listening.*

"Well — I'm kinda mixed up. Maybe it's this" — he tapped the bandage at the base of his skull — "but — I don't know. Maybe I shouldn't drop out when I get well and go off campaigning for the senator if you're so dead set against it."

"But I want you to," John cried out, and was shocked to hear his own voice saying it, because he had not consciously thought it before.

"You want me to?"

"I mean — you mustn't let me talk you out of anything you really believe in," John said. "You're a man now — your own man. You do what you've got to do — and I'm with you."

The boy looked from his father to his mother, his brow furrowed. "I don't get it," he said. "You're treating me as if I'm going to die. I'm not."

"I'm treating you as if you're going to live — your own life," John said.

Ann could see their son think this over, weigh it, test the sudden burden of it.

"But maybe I won't want to go — "

"That's up to you," John said. "It'll be your decision."

The man and the young man stared at each other for a long, long moment. Something was happening to them, between them, a current beginning to alternate that had been short-circuited somewhere, somehow, a long while ago. It was coming on too fast, too strong, too sudden to be coped with. John looked away.

"They had to cut my hair," the boy said with a grin. "Close enough for you this time, Dad?"

"Too close," John whispered. "Too close."

Wallace Stegner

THE BLUE-WINGED TEAL

STILL IN WADERS, with the string of ducks across his shoulder, he stood hesitating on the sidewalk in the cold November wind. His knees were stiff from being cramped up all day in the blind, and his feet were cold. Today, all day, he had been alive; now he was back ready to be dead again.

Lights were on all up and down the street, and there was a rush of traffic and a hurrying of people past and around him, yet the town was not his town, the people passing were strangers, the sounds of evening in this place were no sounds that carried warmth or familiarity. Though he had spent most of his twenty years in the town, knew hundreds of its people, could draw maps of its streets from memory, he wanted to admit familiarity with none of it. He had shut himself off.

Then what was he doing here, in front of this poolhall, loaded down with nine dead ducks? What had possessed him in the first place to borrow gun and waders and car from his father and go hunting? If he had wanted to breathe freely for a change, why hadn't he kept right on going? What was there in this place to draw him back? A hunter had to have a lodge to bring his meat to and people who would be glad of his skill. He had this poolhall and his father, John Lederer, Prop.

He stepped out of a woman's path and leaned against the door.

Downstairs, in addition to his father, he would find old Max Schmeckebier, who ran a cheap blackjack game in the room under the sidewalk. He would find Giuseppe Sciutti, the Sicilian barber, closing his shop or tidying up the rack of *Artists and Models* and *The Nudist* with which he lured trade. He would probably find Billy Hammond, the night clerk from the Windsor hotel, having his sandwich and beer and pie, or moving alone around a pool table, whistling abstractedly, practicing shots. If the afternoon blackjack game had broken up, there would be Navy Edwards, dealer and bouncer for Schmeckebier. At this time of evening there might be a few counter customers and a cop collecting his tribute of a beer or that other tribute that Schmeckebier paid to keep the cardroom open.

And he would find sour contrast with the bright sky and the wind of the tule marshes, the cavelike room with its back corners in darkness, would smell that smell compounded of steam heat and cue-chalk dust, of sodden butts in cuspidors, of coffee and meat and beer smells from the counter, of cigarette smoke so un-aired that it darkened the walls. From anywhere back of the mid-dle tables there would be the pervasive reek of toilet disinfectant. Back of the lunch counter his father would be presiding, throwing the poolhall light switch to save a few cents when the place was empty, flipping it on to give an air of brilliant and successful use when feet came down the stairs past Sciutti's shop.

The hunter moved his shoulder under the weight of the ducks, his mind full for a moment with the image of his father's face, dark-ly pale, fallen in on its bones, and the pouched, restless, suspicious eyes that seemed always looking for someone. Over that image came the image of his mother, dead now and six weeks buried. His teeth clicked at the thought of how she had held the old man up for thirty years, kept him at a respectable job, kept him from slip-ping back into the poolroom Johnny he had been when she mar-ried him. Within ten days of her death he had hunted up this old failure of a poolhall.

In anger the hunter turned, thinking of the hotel room he shared with his father. But he had to eat. Broke as he was, a student yanked from his studies, he had no choice but to eat on the old man. Besides, there were the ducks. He felt somehow that the thing would be incomplete unless he brought his game back for his father to see.

His knees unwilling in the stiff waders, he went down the steps, descending into the light shining through Joe Sciutti's door, and into the momentary layer of clean bay-rum smell, talcum smell, hair-tonic smell, that rose past the still revolving barber pole in the angle of the stairs.

Joe Sciutti was sweeping wads of hair from his tile floor, and hunched over the counter beyond, their backs to the door, were Schmeckebier, Navy Edwards, Billy Hammond, and an unknown customer. John Lederer was behind the counter, mopping alertly with a rag. The poolroom lights were up bright, but when Lederer saw who was coming he flipped the switch and dropped the big room back into dusk.

As the hunter came to the end of the counter their heads turned toward him. "Well I'm a son of a bee," Navy Edwards said, and scrambled off his stool. Next to him Billy Hammond half stood up so that his pale yellow hair took a halo from the backbar lights. "Say!" Max Schmeckebier said. "Say, dot's goot, dot's pooty goot, Henry!"

But Henry was watching his father so intently he did not turn to them. He slid the string of ducks off his shoulder and swung them up onto the wide walnut bar. They landed solidly – offering or tribute or ransom or whatever they were. For a moment it was as if this little act were private between the two of them. He felt queerly moved, his stomach tightened in suspense or triumph. Then the old man's pouchy eyes slipped from his and the old man came quickly forward along the counter and laid hands on the ducks.

He handled them as if he were petting kittens, his big white hands stringing the heads one by one from the wire.

"Two spoonbill," he said, more to himself than to the others crowding around. "Shovel ducks. Don't see many of those any more. And two, no, three, hen mallards and one drake. Those make good eating."

Schmeckebier jutted his enormous lower lip. Knowing him for a stingy, crooked, suspicious little man, Henry almost laughed at the air he could put on, the air of a man of probity about to make an honest judgment in a dispute between neighbors. "I take a budderball," he said thickly. "A liddle budderball, dot is vot eats goot."

An arm fell across Henry's shoulders, and he turned his head to see the hand with red hairs rising from its pores, the wristband of a gray silk shirt with four pearl buttons. Navy Edwards's red face was close to his. "Come clean now," Navy said. "You shot 'em all sitting, didn't you, Henry?"

"I just waited till they stuck their heads out of their holes and let them have it," Henry said.

Navy walloped him on the back and convulsed himself laughing. Then his face got serious again, and he bore down on Henry's shoulder. "By God, you could've fooled me," he said. "If I'd been makin' book on what you'd bring in I'd've lost my shirt."

"Such a pretty shirt, too," Billy Hammond said.

Across the counter John Lederer cradled a little drab duck in his hand. Its neck, stretched from the carrier, hung far down, but its body was neat and plump and its feet were waxy. Watching the sallow face of his father, Henry thought it looked oddly soft.

"Ain't that a beauty, though?" the old man said. "There ain't a prettier duck made than a blue-winged teal. You can have all your wood ducks and redheads, all the flashy ones." He spread a wing until the hidden band of bright blue showed. "Pretty?" he said, and shook his head and laughed suddenly, as if he had not expected to. When he laid the duck down beside the others his eyes were bright with sentimental moisture.

So now, Henry thought, you're right in your element. You always did want to be one of the boys from the poolroom pouring out to see the elk on somebody's running board, or leaning on a bar with a schooner of beer talking baseball or telling the boys about the big German Brown someone brought in in a cake of ice. We haven't any elk or German Browns right now, but we've got some nice ducks, a fine display along five feet of counter. And who brought them in? The student, the alien son. It must gravel you.

He drew himself a beer. Several other men had come in, and he saw three more stooping to look in the door beyond Sciutti's. Then they too came in. Three tables were going; his father had started to hustle, filling orders. After a few minutes Schmeckebier and Navy went into the cardroom with four men. The poolroom lights were up bright again, there was an ivory click of balls, a rumble of talk. The smoke-filled air was full of movement.

Still more people dropped in, kids in high school athletic sweaters and bums from the fringes of skid road. They all stopped to look at the ducks, and Henry saw glances at his waders, heard questions and answers. John Lederer's boy. Some of them spoke to him, deriving importance from contact with him. A fellowship was promoted by the ducks strung out along the counter. Henry felt it himself. He was so mellowed by the way they spoke to him that when the players at the first table thumped with their cues, he got off his stool to rack them up and collect their nickels. It occurred to him that he ought to go to the room and get into a bath, but he didn't want to leave yet. Instead he came back to the counter and slid the nickels toward his father and drew himself another beer.

"Pretty good night tonight," he said. The old man nodded and slapped his rag on the counter, his eyes already past Henry and fixed on two youths coming in, his mouth fixing itself for the greeting and the "Well, boys, what'll it be?"

Billy Hammond wandered by, stopped beside Henry a moment. "Well, time for my nightly wrestle with temptation."

"I was just going to challenge you to a game of call-shot."

"Maybe tomorrow," Billy said, and let himself out carefully as if afraid a noise would disturb someone – a mild, gentle, golden-haired boy who looked as if he ought to be in some prep school learning to say "Sir" to grownups instead of clerking in a girlie hotel. He was the only one of the poolroom crowd that Henry half liked. He thought he understood Billy Hammond a little.

He turned back to the counter to hear his father talking with Max Schmeckebier. "I don't see how we could on this rig. That's the hell of it, we need a regular oven."

"In my room in back," Schmeckebier said. "Dot old electric range."

"Does it work?"

"Sure. Vy not? I tink so."

"By God," John Lederer said. "Nine ducks, that ought to give us a real old-fashioned feed." He mopped the counter, refilled a coffee cup, came back to the end and pinched the breast of a duck, pulled out a wing and looked at the band of blue hidden among the drab feathers. "Just like old times, for a change," he said, and his eyes touched Henry's in a look that might have meant anything from a challenge to an apology.

Henry had no desire to ease the strain that had been between them for months. He did not forgive his father the poolhall, or forget the way the old man had sprung back into the old pattern, as if his wife had been a jailer and he was now released. He neither forgot nor forgave the red-haired woman who sometimes came to the poolhall late at night and waited on a bar stool while the old man closed up. Yet now when his father remarked that the ducks ought to be drawn and plucked right away, Henry stood up.

"I could do ten while you were doing one," his father said.

The blood spread hotter in Henry's face, but he bit off what he might have said. "All right," he said. "You do them and I'll take over the counter for you."

So here he was, in the poolhall he had passionately sworn he would never do a lick of work in, dispensing Mrs. Morrison's meat pies and tamales smothered in chile, clumping behind the counter in the waders which had been the sign of his temporary freedom. Leaning back between orders, watching the Saturday night activity of the place, he half understood why he had gone hunting, and why it had seemed to him essential that he bring his trophies back here.

That somewhat disconcerted understanding was still troubling him when his father came back. The old man had put on a clean apron and brushed his hair. His pouched eyes, brighter and less houndlike than usual, darted along the bar, counting, and darted across the bright tables, counting again. His eyes met Henry's, and both half smiled. Both of them, Henry thought, were a little astonished.

LATER, PROPPED in bed in the hotel room, he put down the magazine he had been reading and stared at the drawn blinds, the sleazy drapes, and asked himself why he was here. The story he had told others, and himself, that his mother's death had interrupted his school term and he was waiting for the new term before going back, he knew to be an evasion. He was staying because he couldn't get away, or wouldn't. He hated his father, hated the poolhall, hated the people he was thrown with. He made no move to hobnob with them, or hadn't until tonight, and yet he deliberately avoided seeing any of the people who had been his friends for years. Why?

He could force his mind to the barrier, but not across it. Within a half minute he found himself reading again, diving deep, and when he made himself look up from the page he stared for a long time at his father's bed, his father's shoes under the bed, his father's soiled shirts hanging in the open closet. All the home he had any more was this little room. He could not pretend that as long as he stayed here the fragments of his home and family were held together. He couldn't fool himself that he had any function in his father's life any more, or his father in his, unless his own hatred and his father's uneasy suspicion were functions. He ought to get out and get a job until he could go back to school. But he didn't.

Thinking made him sleepy, and he knew what that was, too. Sleep was another evasion, like the torpor and monotony of his life. But he let drowsiness drift over him, and drowsily he thought of his father behind the counter tonight, vigorous and jovial, Mine Host, and he saw that the usual fretful petulance had gone from his face.

He snapped off the bed light and dropped the magazine on the floor. Then he heard the rain, the swish and hiss of traffic in the wet street. He felt sad and alone, and he disliked the coldness of his own isolation. Again he thought of his father, of the failing body that had once been tireless and bull-strong, of the face before it had sagged and grown dewlaps of flesh on the square jaws. He thought of the many failures, the jobs that never quite worked out, the schemes that never quite paid off, and of the eyes that could not quite meet, not quite hold, the eyes of his cold son.

Thinking of this, and remembering when they had been a family and when his mother had been alive to hold them together, he felt pity, and he cried.

His father's entrance awakened him. He heard the fumbling at the door, the creak, the quiet click, the footsteps that groped in darkness, the body that bumped into something and halted, getting its bearings. He heard the sighing weight of his father's body on the other bed, his father's sighing breath as he bent to untie his shoes. Feigning sleep, he lay unmoving, breathing deeply and steadily, but an anguish of fury had leaped in him as sharp and sudden as a sudden fear, for he smelled the smells his father brought with him: wet wool, stale tobacco, liquor; and above all, more penetrating than any, spreading through the room and polluting everything there, the echo of cheap musky perfume.

The control Henry imposed upon his body was like an ecstasy. He raged at himself for the weak sympathy that had troubled him all evening. One good night, he said to himself now, staring furiously upward. One lively Saturday night in the joint and he can't contain himself, he has to go top off the evening with his girl friend. And how? A drink in her room? A walk over to some illegal afterhours bar on Rum Alley? Maybe just a trip to bed, blunt and immediate?

His jaws ached from the tight clamping of his teeth, but his orderly breathing went in and out, in and out, while the old man sighed into bed and creaked a little, rolling over, and lay still. The taint of perfume seemed even stronger now. The sow must slop it on by the cupful. And so cuddly. Such a sugar baby. How's my old sweetie tonight? It's been too long since you came to see your baby. I should be real mad at you. The cheek against the lapel, the unreal hair against the collar, the perfume like some gaseous poison tainting the clothes it touched.

The picture of his mother's bureau drawers came to him, the careless simple collection of handkerchiefs and gloves and lace collars and cuffs, and he saw the dusty blue sachet packets and smelled the faint fragrance. That was all the scent she had ever used.

My God, he said, how can he stand himself?

After a time his father began to breathe heavily, then to snore. In the little prison of the room his breathing was obscene — loose and bubbling, undisciplined, animal. Henry with an effort relaxed his tense arms and legs, let himself sink. He tried to concentrate on his own breathing, but the other dominated him, burst out and died and whiffled and sighed again. By now he had a resolution in him like an iron bar. Tomorrow, for sure, for good, he would break out of his self-imposed isolation and see Frank, see Welby. They would lend him enough to get to the coast. Not another day in this hateful relationship. Not another night in this room.

He yawned. It must be late, two or three o'clock. He ought to get to sleep. But he lay uneasily, his mind tainted with hatred as the room was tainted with perfume. He tried cunningly to elude his mind, to get to sleep before it could notice, but no matter how he composed himself for blankness and shut his eyes and breathed deeply, his mind was out again in a half minute, bright-eyed, lively as a weasel, and he was helplessly hunted again from hiding place to hiding place.

Eventually he fell back upon his old device.

He went into a big dark room in his mind, a room shadowy with great half-seen tables. He groped and found a string above him and pulled, and light fell suddenly in a bright cone from the darker cone of the shade. Below the light lay an expanse of dark green cloth, and this was the only lighted thing in all that darkness. Carefully he gathered bright balls into a wooden triangle, pushing them forward until the apex lay over a round spot on the cloth. Quietly and thoroughly he chalked a cue: the inlaid handle and the smooth taper of the shaft were very real to his eyes and hands. He lined up the cue ball, aimed, drew the cue back and forth in smooth motions over the bridge of his left hand. He saw the balls run from the spinning shock of the break, and carom, and come to rest, and he hunted up the yellow 1-ball and got a shot at it between two others. He had to cut it very fine, but he saw the shot go true, the 1 angle off cleanly into the side pocket. He saw the cue ball rebound and kiss and stop, and he shot the 2 in a straight shot for the left corner pocket, putting drawers on the cue ball to get shape for the 3.

Yellow and blue and red, spotted and striped, he shot pool balls into pockets as deep and black and silent as the cellars of his consciousness. He was not now quarry that his mind chased, but an actor, a willer, a doer, a man in command. By an act of will or of flight he focused his whole awareness on the game he played. His mind undertook it with intent concentration. He took pride in little two-cushion banks, little triumphs of accuracy, small successes of foresight. When he had finished one game and the green cloth was bare he dug the balls from the bin under the end of the table and racked them and began another.

Eventually, he knew, nothing would remain in his mind but the clean green cloth traced with running color and bounced by simple problems, and sometime in the middle of an intricately planned combination shot he would pale off into sleep.

At noon, after the rain, the sun seemed very bright. It poured down from a clearing sky, glittered on wet roofs, gleamed in reflection from pavements and sidewalks. On the peaks beyond the city there was a purity of snow.

Coming down the hill, Henry noticed the excessive brightness and could not tell whether it was really as it seemed, or whether his plunge out of the dark and isolated hole of his life had restored a lost capacity to see. A slavery, or a paralysis, was ended; he had been for three hours in the company of a friend; he had been eyed with concern; he had been warmed by solicitude and generosity. In his pocket he had fifty dollars, enough to get him to the coast and let him renew his life. It seemed to him incredible that he had alternated between dismal hotel and dismal poolroom so long. He could not understand why he had not before this moved his legs in the direction of the hill. He perceived that he had been sullen and morbid, and he concluded with some surprise that even Schmeckebier and Edwards and the rest might have found him a difficult companion.

His father, too. The fury of the night before had passed, but he knew he would not bend again toward companionship. That antipathy was too deep. He would never think of his father again without getting the whiff of that perfume. Let him have it; it was what he wanted, let him have it. They could part without an open quarrel, maybe, but they would part without love. They could part right now, within an hour.

Two grimy stairways led down into the cellar from the alley he turned into. One went to the furnace room, the other to the poolhall. The iron rail was blockaded with filled ashcans. Descent into Avernus, he said to himself, and went down the left-hand stair.

The door was locked. He knocked, and after some time knocked again. Finally someone pulled on the door from inside. It stuck, and was yanked irritably inward. His father stood there in his shirt sleeves, a cigar in his mouth.

"Oh," he said. "I was wondering what had become of you."

The basement air was foul and heavy, dense with the reek from the toilets. Henry saw as he stepped inside that at the far end only the night light behind the bar was on, but that light was coming from Schmeckebier's door at this end too, the two weak illuminations diffusing in the shadowy poolroom, leaving the middle in almost absolute dark. It was the appropriate time, the appropriate place, the stink of his prison appropriately concentrated. He drew his lungs full of it with a kind of passion, and he said, "I just came down to..."

"Who is dot?" Schmeckebier called out. He came to his door, wrapped to the armpits in a bar apron, with a spoon in his hand, and he bent, peering out into the dusk like a disturbed dwarf in an underhill cave. "John? Who? Oh, Henry. Shust in time, shust in time. It is not long now." His lower lip waggled, and he pulled it up, apparently with an effort.

Henry said, "What's not long?"

"Vot?" Schmeckebier said, and thrust his big head far out. "You forgot about it?"

"I must have," Henry said.

"The duck feed," his father said impatiently.

They stood staring at one another in the dusk. The right moment was gone. With a little twitch of the shoulder Henry let it go. He would wait a while, pick his time. When Schmeckebier went back to his cooking, Henry saw through the doorway the lumpy bed, the big chair with a blanket folded over it, the rolltop desk littered with pots and pans, the green and white enamel of the range. A rich smell of roasting came out and mingled oddly with the chemical stink of toilet disinfectant.

"Are we going to eat in here?" he asked.

His father snorted. "How could we eat in there? Old Maxie lived in the ghetto too damn long. By God, I never saw such a boar's nest."

"Vot's duh matter? Vot's duh matter?" Schmeckebier said. His big lip thrust out, he stooped to look into the oven, and John Lederer went shaking his head up between the tables to the counter. Henry followed him, intending to make the break when he got the old man alone. But he saw the three plates set up on the bar, the three glasses of tomato juice, the platter of olives and celery, and he hesitated. His father reached with a salt shaker and shook a little salt into each glass of tomato juice.

"All the fixings," he said. "Soon as Max gets those birds out of the oven we can take her on."

Now it was easy to say, "As soon as the feed's over I'll be shoving off." Henry opened his mouth to say it, but was interrupted this time by a light tapping at the glass door beyond Sciutti's shop. He swung around angrily and saw duskily beyond the glass the smooth blond hair, the even smile.

"It's Billy," he said. "Shall I let him in."

"Sure," the old man said. "Tell him to come in and have a duck with us."

But Billy Hammond shook his head when Henry asked him. He was shaking his head almost as he came through the door. "No thanks, I just ate. I'm full of chow mein. This is a family dinner anyway. You go on ahead."

"Got plenty," John Lederer said, and made a motion as if to set a fourth place at the counter.

"Who is dot?" Schmeckebier bawled from the back. "Who come in? Is dot Billy Hammond? Set him up a blate."

"By God, his nose sticks as far into things as his lip," Lederer said. Still holding the plate, he roared back, "Catch up with the parade, for Christ sake, or else tend to your cooking." He looked at Henry and Billy and chuckled.

Schmeckebier had disappeared, but now his squat figure blotted the lighted doorway again. "Vot? Vot you say?"

"Vot?" John Lederer said. "Vot, vot, vot? Vot does it matter vot I said? Get the hell back to your kitchen."

He was, Henry saw, in a high humor. The effect of last night was still with him. He was playing Mine Host. He looked at the two of them and laughed so naturally that Henry almost joined him. "I think old Maxie's head is full of duck dressing," he said, and leaned on the counter. "I ever tell you about the time we came back from Reno together? We stopped off in the desert to look at a mine, and got lost on a little dirt road so we had to camp. I was trying to figure out where we were, and started looking for stars, but it was clouded over, hard to locate anything. So I ask old Maxie if he can see the Big Dipper anywhere. He thinks about that maybe ten minutes with his lip stuck out and then he says, 'I t'ink it's in duh water bucket.'"

He did the grating gutturals of Schmeckebier's speech so accurately that Henry smiled in spite of himself. His old man made another motion with the plate at Billy Hammond. "Better let me set you up a place."

"Thanks," Billy said. His voice was as polite and soft as his face, and his eyes had the ingenuous liquid softness of a girl's. "Thanks, I really just ate. You go on, I'll shoot a little pool if it's all right."

Now came Schmeckebier with a big platter held in both hands. He bore it smoking through the gloom of the poolhall and up the steps to the counter, and John Lederer took it from him there and with a flourish speared one after another three tight-skinned brown ducks and slid them onto the plates set side by side for the feast. The one frugal light from the backbar shone on them as they sat down. Henry looked over his shoulder to see Billy Hammond pull the cord and flood a table with a sharp-edged cone of brilliance. Deliberately, already absorbed, he chalked a cue. His lips pursed, and he whistled, and whistling, bent to take aim.

Lined up in a row, they were not placed for conversation, but John Lederer kept attempting it, leaning forward over his plate to see Schmeckebier or Henry. He filled his mouth with duck and dressing and chewed, shaking his head with pleasure, and snapped off a bite of celery with a crack like a breaking stick. When his mouth was clear he leaned and said to Schmeckebier, "Ah, das schmeckt gut, hey, Maxie?"

"Ja," Schmeckebier said, and sucked grease off his lip and only then turned in surprise. "Say, you speak German?"

"Sure I speak German," Lederer said. "I worked three weeks once with an old squarehead brick mason that taught me the whole language. He taught me about sehr gut and nicht wahr and besser I bleiben right hier, and he always had his frau make me up a lunch full of kalter aufschnitt and gemixte pickeln. I know all about German."

Schmeckebier stared a moment, grunted, and went back to his eating. He had already stripped the meat from the bones and was gnawing the carcass.

"Anyway," John Lederer said, "es schmeckt God damn good." He got up and went around the counter and drew a mug of coffee from the urn. "Coffee?" he said to Henry.

"Please."

His father drew another mug and set it before him. "Maxie?"

Schmeckebier shook his head, his mouth too full for talk. For a minute, after he had set out two little jugs of cream, Lederer stood as if thinking. He was watching Billy Hammond move quietly around the one lighted table, whistling. "Look at that sucker," Lederer said. "I bet he doesn't even know where he is."

By the time he got around to his stool he was back at the German. *"Schmeckebier,"* he said. "What's that mean?"

"Uh?"

"What's your name mean? Tastes beer? Likes beer?"

Schmeckebier rolled his shoulders. The sounds he made eating were like sounds from a sty. Henry was half sickened, sitting next to him, and he wished the old man would let the conversation drop. But apparently it had to be a feast, and a feast called for chatter.

"That's a hell of a name, you know it?" Lederer said, and already he was up again and around the end of the counter. "You couldn't get into any church with a name like that." His eyes fastened on the big drooping greasy lip, and he grinned.

"Schmeckeduck, that ought to be your name," he said. "What's German for duck? Vogel? Old Max Schmeckevogel. How about number two?"

Schmeckebier pushed his plate forward and Lederer forked a duck out of the steam table. Henry did not have a second.

"You ought to have one," his father told him. "You don't get grub like this every day."

"One's my limit," Henry said.

For a while they worked at their plates. Back of him Henry heard the clack of balls hitting, and a moment later the rumble as a ball rolled down the chute from a pocket. The thin, abstracted whistling of Billy Hammond broke off, became words:

"Now Annie doesn't live here any more.
  So you're the guy that she's been waiting for?
  She told me that I'd know you by the blue of your eyes..."

"Talk about one being your limit," his father said. "When we lived in Nebraska we used to put on some feeds. You remember anything about Nebraska at all?"

"A little," Henry said. He was irritated at being dragged into reminiscences, and he did not want to hear how many ducks the town hog could eat at a sitting.

"We'd go out, a whole bunch of us," John Lederer said. "The

sloughs were black with ducks in those days. We'd come back with a buggyful, and the womenfolks'd really put us on a feed. Fifteen, twenty, thirty people. Take a hundred ducks to fill 'em up." He was silent a moment, staring across the counter, chewing. Henry noticed that he had tacked two wings of a teal up on the frame of the backbar mirror, small, strong bows with a band of bright blue half hidden in them. The old man's eyes slanted over, caught Henry's looking at the wings.

"Doesn't seem as if we'd had a duck feed since we left there," he said. His forehead wrinkled; he rubbed his neck, leaning forward over his plate, and his eyes met Henry's in the backbar mirror. He spoke to the mirror, ignoring the gobbling image of Schmeckebier between his own reflection and Henry's.

"You remember that set of china your mother used to have? The one she painted herself? Just the plain white china with the one design on each plate?"

Henry sat stiffly, angry that his mother's name should even be mentioned between them in this murky hole, and what had passed. Gabble, gabble, gabble, he said to himself. If you can't think of anything else to gabble about, gabble about your dead wife. Drag her through the poolroom too. Aloud he said, "No, I guess I don't."

"Blue-wing teal," his father said, and nodded at the wings tacked to the mirror frame. "Just the wings, like that. Awful pretty. She thought a teal was about the prettiest duck there was."

His vaguely rubbing hand came around from the back of his neck and rubbed along the cheek, pulling the slack flesh and distorting the mouth. Henry said nothing, watching the pouched hound eyes in the mirror.

It was a cold, skin-tightening shock to realize that the hound eyes were cloudy with tears. The rubbing hand went over them, shaded them like a hatbrim, but the mouth below remained distorted. With a plunging movement his father was off the stool.

"Oh, God damn!" he said in a strangling voice, and went past Henry on hard, heavy feet, down the steps and past Billy Hammond, who neither looked up nor broke the sad thin whistling.

Schmeckebier had swung around. "Vot's duh matter? Now vot's duh matter?"

With a short shake of the head, Henry turned away from him,

staring after his father down the dark poolhall. He felt as if orderly things were breaking and flying apart in his mind; he had a moment of white blind terror that this whole scene upon whose reality he counted was really only a dream, something conjured up out of the bottom of his consciousness where he was accustomed to comfort himself into total sleep. His mind was still full of the anguished look his father had hurled at the mirror before he ran.

The hell with you, the look had said. The hell with you, Schmeckebier, and you, my son Henry. The hell with your ignorance, whether you're stupid or whether you just don't know all you think you know. You don't know enough to kick dirt down a hole. You know nothing at all, you know less than nothing because you know things wrong.

He heard Billy's soft whistling, saw him move around his one lighted table — a well-brought up boy from some suburban town, a polite soft gentle boy lost and wandering among pimps and prostitutes, burying himself for some reason among people who never even touched his surface. Did he shoot pool in his bed at night, tempting sleep, as Henry did? Did his mind run carefully to angles and banks and englishes, making a reflecting mirror of them to keep from looking through them at other things?

Almost in terror he looked out across the sullen cave, past where the light came down in an intense isolated cone above Billy's table, and heard the lugubrious whistling that went on without intention of audience, a recurrent and deadening and only half-conscious sound. He looked toward the back, where his father had disappeared in the gloom, and wondered if in his bed before sleeping the old man worked through a routine of little jobs: cleaning the steam table, ordering a hundred pounds of coffee, jacking up the janitor about the mess in the hall. He wondered if it was possible to wash yourself to sleep with restaurant crockery, work yourself to sleep with chores, add yourself to sleep with columns of figures, as you could play yourself to sleep with a pool cue and a green table and fifteen colored balls. For a moment, in the sad old light with the wreckage of the duck feast at his elbow, he wondered if there was anything more to his life, or his father's life, or Billy Hammond's life, or anyone's life, than playing the careful games that deadened you into sleep.

Schmeckebier, beside him, was still groping in the fog of his mind for an explanation of what had happened. "Vere'd he go?" he said, and nudged Henry fiercely. "Vot's duh matter?"

Henry shook him off irritably, watching Billy Hammond's oblivious bent head under the light. He heard Schmeckebier's big lip flop and heard him sucking his teeth.

"I tell you," the guttural voice said. "I got somet'ing dot fixes him if he feels bum."

He too went down the stairs past the lighted table and into the gloom at the back. The light went on in his room, and after a minute or two his voice was shouting, "John! Say, come here, uh? Say, John!"

Eventually John Lederer came out of the toilet and they walked together between the tables. In his fist Schmeckebier was clutching a square bottle. He waved it in front of Henry's face as they passed, but Henry was watching his father. He saw the crumpled face, oddly rigid, like the face of a man in the grip of a barely controlled rage, but his father avoided his eyes.

"Kümmel," Schmeckebier said. He set four ice cream dishes on the counter and poured three about a third full of clear liquor. His squinted eyes lifted and peered toward Billy Hammond, but Henry said, on an impulse, "Let him alone. He's walking in his sleep."

So there were only the three. They stood together a moment and raised their glasses. "Happy days," John Lederer said automatically. They drank.

Schmeckebier smacked his lips, looked at them one after another, shook his head in admiration of the quality of his kümmel, and waddled back toward his room with the bottle. John Lederer was already drawing hot water to wash the dishes.

In the core of the quiet which even the clatter of crockery and the whistling of Billy Hammond did not break into, Henry said what he had to say, "I'll be leaving," he said. "Probably tonight."

But he did not say it in anger, or with the cold command of himself that he had imagined in advance. He said it like a cry, and with the feeling he might have had on letting go the hand of a friend too weak and too exhausted to cling any longer to their inadequate shared driftwood in a wide cold sea.

John Cheever

THE NATIONAL PASTIME

To be an American and unable to play baseball is comparable to being a Polynesian and unable to swim. It's an impossible situation. This will be apparent to everyone, and it was to me, a country boy brought up on a farm — or, to be precise, in a country house — just outside the village of St. Botolph's, in Massachusetts. The place is called West Farm. My ancestors had lived in that village and in that house since the seventeenth century, and they had distinguished themselves as sailors and athletes. Leander, my father (his brothers were named Orpheus and Hamlet), had played shortstop for the St. Botolph's Hose Company. Although the hose-company games sometimes figured in his recollections, his memories were usually of a different order. He was nearly sixty when I was born, and he could remember the last days of St. Botolph's as a port. My grandfather had been a ship's master, and when I was a boy, our house was partly furnished with things that he had brought back from Ceylon and China. The maritime past that my father glimpsed had been glorious, full of gold and silver, full of Samoan beauties and tests of courage. Then — so he told me — boxwood had grown in our garden, and the paths had been covered once a year with pebbles that were brought from a cove near West Travertine where the stones were as round and white as pearls. In the rear wing of our house, there was a peculiar, clean smell that was supposed to have been left there by my grandfather's Chinese servants. My father liked to recall this period of splendor, but he liked even better to recall his success as a partner in the gold-bead factory that had been built in St. Botolph's when its maritime prosperity was ended. He had gone to work as an office boy, and his rise had been brilliant and swift. He had business acumen, and he was convivial. He took an intense pleasure in having the factory whistle blown. He had it blown for all our birthdays and for his wedding anniversary, and when my mother had guests for lunch, the whistle usually blew as the ladies sat down.

In the twenties, the gold-bead factory was mortgaged and converted to the manufacture of table silver, and presently my father and his partner were ruined. My father felt that he was an old man who had spent all his energy and all his money on things that were unredeemable and vulgar, and he was inconsolable. He went away, and my mother called my two sisters and me to her room and told us that she was afraid he had killed himself. He had left a note hinting at this, and he had taken a pistol with him. I was nine years old then, and my sisters were fourteen and fifteen. Suicide may have been my father's intention, but he returned a few days later and began to support the family by selling the valuables that had come to him from the shipmaster. I had decided to become a professional baseball player. I had bought a Louisville Slugger, a ball, and a first baseman's mitt. I asked my father to play catch with me one Sunday afternoon, but he refused. My mother must have overheard this conversation, because she called him to her room, where they quarreled. In a little while, he came out to the garden and asked me to throw the ball to him. What happened then was ridiculous and ugly. I threw the ball clumsily once or twice and missed the catches he threw to me. Then I turned my head to see something — a boat on the river. He threw the ball, and it got me in the nape of the neck and stretched me out unconscious in my grandfather's ruined garden. When I came to, my nose was bleeding and my mouth was full of blood. I felt that I was being drowned. My father was standing over me. "Don't tell your mother about this," he said. When I sat up and he saw that I was all right, he went down through the garden toward the barn and the river.

My mother called me to her room that night after supper. She had become an invalid and she seldom left her bed. All the furniture in her room was white, and the rugs were white, and there was a picture of "Jesus the Shepherd" on the wall beside her bed. The room was getting dark, I remember, and I felt, from the tone of her voice, that we were approaching a kind of emotional darkness I had noticed before in our family affairs. "You must try to understand your father," she said, putting down her Bible and reaching for my hand. "He is old. He is spoiled." Then, although I don't think he was in the house, she lowered her voice to a whisper, so that we could not be overheard. "You see, some years ago his cousin Lucy Hartshorn left him a great deal of money, in trust. She was a meddlesome old lady. I guess you don't remember her. She was an antivivisectionist, and wanted to abolish the celebration of Christmas. She liked to order your father around, and she felt the family was petering out. We had Grace and Vikery then, and she left your father the money on condition that he not have any more children. He was very upset when he found out that I was *enceinte*. I wouldn't want you to know what went on. He had planned a luxurious old age — he wanted to raise pigeons and have a sailboat — and I think he sometimes sees in you the difference between what he had planned and what he has been reduced to. You'll have to try and understand." Her words made almost no impression on me at the time. I remember counting the larches outside her window while she talked to me, and looking beyond them to the faded lettering on the wall of the barn — "Boston Store: Rock Bottom Prices" — and to some pines ringed with darkness beyond the barn. The little that I knew of our family history was made up of revokable trusts, purloined wills, and dark human secrets, and since I had never seen Lucy Hartshorn, this new secret seemed to have no more to do with me than the others did.

The school I went to was an old frame building in the village, and every morning I walked two miles upriver to get there. Two of the spinster teachers were cousins of mine, and the man who taught manual training and coached athletics was the son of our garbage collector. My parents had helped him through normal school. The New England spring was in force, and one fine morning we left the gymnasium for the ball field. The instructor was carrying some baseball equipment, and as soon as I saw it, the sweet, salty taste of blood came into my mouth. My heart began to pound, my legs felt weak, and while I thought, from these symptoms, that I must be sick, I knew instinctively how to cure myself. On the way to the field, we passed an old field house that stood on some concrete posts, concealed by a scrim of rotten lattice. I began to walk slowly, and when the rest of the class had passed the field house, I got down on my hands and knees and crawled through a broken place in the lattice and underneath the building. There was hardly room for me to lie there between the dirt and the sills that were covered with cobwebs. Someone had stuffed an old sneaker and a rusted watering can under the building, confident that they would never be seen again. I could hear from the field the voices of my friends choosing sides, and I felt the horror of having expelled myself from the light of a fine day, but I also felt, lying in the dirt, that the taste of blood was beginning to leave my mouth, that my heart was beginning to regulate its beating, and that the strength was returning to my legs. I lay in the dirt until the game ended and I could see, through the lattice, the players returning to school.

I felt that the fault was Leander's, and that if I could bring myself to approach him again, when he was in a better humor, he would respond humanely. The feeling that I could not assume my responsibilities as a baseball player without some help from him was deep, as if parental love and baseball were both national pastimes. One afternoon, I got my ball and mitt and went into the library, where he was taking books down from the shelves and tying them up in bundles of ten, to be taken into Boston and sold. He had been a handsome man, I think. I had heard my relations speak of how he had aged, and so I suppose that his looks had begun to deteriorate. He would have been taken for a Yankee anywhere, and he seemed to feel that his alliance to the sea was by blood as well as tradition. When he went into an oyster bar and found people who were patently not American-born eating oysters, he would be stirred. He ate quantities of fish, swam daily in the salt river, and washed himself each morning with a sea sponge, so he always smelled faintly of brine and iodine, as if he had only recently come dripping out of the Atlantic. The brilliant blue of his eyes had not faded, and the boyish character of his face — its lightness and ovalness — was intact. He had not understood the economic fragility of his world, his wife's invalidism seemed to be a manifest rebuke for the confusion of his affairs, and his mind must have been thronged with feelings of being unwanted and also feelings of guilt. The books he was preparing to sell were his father's and his grandfather's; he would rail about this later, feeling that if histrionics would not redeem him, they would at least recapture for a minute his sense of identity and pride. If I had looked closely, I might have seen a face harried with anxiety and the weaknesses of old age, but I expected him, for my sake, to regain his youth and to appear like the paternal images I had seen on calendars and in magazine advertisements.

"Will you please play catch with me, Poppa?" I asked.

"How can you ask me to play baseball when I will be dead in another month!" he said. He sighed and then said, "I won't live through the summer. Your mother has been complaining all morning. She has nothing to say to me unless she has a complaint to make. She's complaining now of pains in her feet. She can't leave her bed because of the pains in her feet. She's trying to make me more unhappy than I already am, but I have some facts to fall back on. Here, let me show you." He took down one of the many volumes in which he had recorded his life, and searched through the pages until he found what he wanted. "Your mother wore custom-made shoes from 1904 until 1908, when Mr. Schultz died. He made her six, twelve, fourteen — he made her seventeen pairs of shoes in four years. Then she began buying her shoes at Nettleton's." He wet his finger and turned a page. "She never paid less than twelve dollars a pair there, and in 1908 she bought four pairs of shoes and two pairs of canvas pumps. In 1910, she bought four pairs of shoes at Nettleton's and a pair of evening slippers at Stetson's. She said the slippers pinched her feet, but we couldn't take them back because she'd worn them. In 1911, she bought three pairs of shoes at Stetson's and two at Nettleton's. In 1912, she had Henderson make her a pair of walking shoes. They cost eighteen dollars. She paid twenty-four dollars for a pair of gold pumps at Stetson's. In 1913, she bought another pair of canvas pumps, two pairs of suède shoes, golf shoes, and some beaded shoes." He looked to me for some confirmation of the unreasonableness of my mother's illness, but I hung my head and went out of the library.

The next time the class went out for baseball, I hid in a building closer to the school, where rakes and rollers and other grounds equipment were stored. This place was also dark, but there was room to stand and move and enjoy an illusion of freedom, although the light of day and the voices on the field from which I was hidden seemed like the lights and the sounds of life. I had been there only a few minutes when I heard someone approach and open the door. I had thought it would be the old grounds keeper, but it was a classmate of mine, who recognized, a second after he saw me, what I was doing, and seemed — since he was doing the same thing — delighted to have a conspirator. I disliked him and his friends, but I couldn't have disliked him more than I disliked the symptoms of my own panic, for I didn't leave the building. After this I had to hide not only from the ball game but from my classmate. He continued to hide in the tool shed and I hid near the playing field, in some woods behind the backstop, and chewed pieces of grass until the period ended.

That fall, I went out for football, and I had always liked winter sports, but in the spring, when the garbage man's son took the balls and bats out of the chest near the door of the gymnasium, the taste of blood in my mouth, the beating of my heart, and the weakness in my legs were keener than ever, and I found myself stuffed in the dirt under the track house again, with the old tennis sneaker and the watering can, horrified that I should have chosen or should have been made to lie in this filth when I could be walking freely over a green field. As the season progressed, I began to find new hiding places and to invent new ailments that would excuse me from having to play baseball, and the feeling that Leander had the cure to my cowardice returned, although I could not bring myself to approach him again. He still seemed to preserve, well on the dark side of his mind, some hard feelings about my being responsible for the revocation of Lucy Hartshorn's trust. Several times when I went to a movie or a dance, he locked the house up so tight that I couldn't find any way to get in, and had to sleep in the barn. Once, I returned in the daytime and found the house locked. I heard him moving inside and I rang the bell. He opened the door long enough to say, "Whatever it is you're selling, I don't want any." Then he slammed the door in my face. A minute later, he opened the door again. "I'm sorry, Eben," he said. "I didn't realize it was you."

My mother died when I was in my third year of high school. When I graduated the following year, Leander claimed to be too infirm to come to the ceremony, and when I looked down from the platform into a gathering where there were no near relatives of mine, it occurred to me — without pleasure or guilt — that I had probably not been up to bat more than three times.

My Cousin Juliana put up the money to send me to college, and I entered college feeling that my troubles with Leander and baseball were over. Both my sisters had married by then, and gone to live in the West, and I dutifully spent part of my Christmas holiday at West Farm and planned to spend all my Easter vacation there. On the morning that college closed for the spring recess, I drove with my two roommates over to Mount Holyoke, where we picked up three girls. We were planning to have a picnic somewhere along the river. When we stopped for lunch, one of my roommates went around to the back of the car and got out his camera to take a picture of the girls. Glancing into the luggage compartment, I noticed a baseball and a bat. Everyone was around in front of the car. I couldn't be seen. The ground was loose, and with my hands I dug a hole nearly a foot deep. Then I dropped the baseball into this hole and buried it.

It was late when we got into Boston, and I took the last train to St. Botolph's. I had written Leander that I was coming, in the hope that he would not lock the house up, but when I reached there, after midnight, all the doors and windows were secured. I didn't feel like spending the night in the barn, and I broke a windowpane in the dining room and climbed in. I could hear Leander moving around upstairs, and because I felt irritated, I didn't call out to him. A few seconds later, there was an explosion in the room. Somebody had shot off a pistol and I thought I had been killed. I got to a switch and turned on the lights and saw, with a wild, crazy uprush of joy that I was alive and unharmed. Then I saw Leander standing in the doorway with the pistol in his hand. He dropped it to the floor and, stumbling toward me, laid his head on my shoulder and wept. "Oh, Eben! Eben! Eben!" he sobbed. "I thought it was a prowler! I heard someone trying to get in! I heard the breaking glass. Forgive me, forgive me."

I remember that he was wearing a fez, and some kind of ragged and outrageous robe over his shoulders. He had, up until that year, always dressed with great simplicity and care, feeling that a sensible regard for appearances facilitated human relationships. He had always put on a dark coat for dinner, and he would never consider as acquaintances or as business associates men with grease in their hair, men with curls, men who wore pointed shoes or diamond cuff links or who put pheasant feathers in their colored hats. Age seemed to have revised these principles, and during the Easter holidays he appeared in many brilliant costumes, many of them the robes and surplices of a fraternal order that had been disbanded in the twenties. Once when I stepped into the bathroom, I found him before the full-length mirror in the ostrich-plumed hat, the cross-ribbon heavy with orders, and the ornate sword of a Poor Knight of Christ and the Temple and a Guardian of the Gates of Gaza. He often quoted from Shakespeare.

THE FIRST JOB I got after leaving college was at Chatfield Academy. The school was in New Hampshire — in the mountains — and I went north in the fall. I liked teaching, and the place itself seemed oddly detached and peaceful. Chimes rang at the quarter hour, the buildings were old or copied old forms, the leaves fell past the classroom windows for a month, the nights smelled of smoke, and, leaving my classroom one evening in December, I found the air full of a swift, dry snow. The school was conservative, and at its helm was old Dr. Wareham. Robust on the playing field, tearful in chapel, bull-necked and vigorous in spite of his advanced age, he was that kind of monolithic father image that used to be thought a necessity for the education of youth. After the Easter recess, I signed a contract for the following year and arranged to teach summer school. In April, I got a notice that faculty participation in the annual meeting of the board of trustees was mandatory. I asked a man at supper one night what this meant.

"Well, they come up on Friday," my colleague said, "and Wareham gives them a dinner. Then they have their annual meeting. We have demonstration classes on Saturday and they snoop around, but they're mostly intelligent and they don't make trouble. Then Saturday noon, the old troll barbecues a side of beef and we have lunch with them. After this, there's a ball game between the trustees and the faculty members. The new members are always expected to play, and you'd better be good. The old troll feels that men get to know one another best on the playing field, and he doesn't miss a trick. We had a frail art teacher here a couple of years ago who claimed to have a headache, but Wareham got him out of bed and made him play third base. He made three errors and Wareham fired him. Then, after that, there's a cocktail party at Wareham's house, with good sour-mash bourbon for the brass and sherry for the rest of us. Then they go home."

The old taste of blood came into my mouth. My appetite for the meat and potatoes I had heaped onto my plate was gone. I nevertheless gorged myself, for I seemed to have been put into a position where my only recourse was to overlook my feelings or to conceal them where this was not possible. I knew by then that a thorough inspection of the history of the problem would not alter the facts, and that the best I could bring to the situation was a kind of hollow good cheer. I told myself that the game was inconsequential, and presently I seemed to feel this. There was some gossip the next day about Dr. Wareham's seriousness about the game. The piano teacher — a tall man named Bacon — had refused to play, and somebody said that he would be fired. But I was occupied with my classwork and I nearly forgot about the annual meeting until leaving my classroom on a Friday afternoon, I saw a large car driven by a chauffeur go around the quadrangle and stop at Dr. Wareham's house. The trustees were beginning to arrive.

After supper I corrected papers until about eleven, when I went to bed. Something woke me at three in the morning, and I went to the open window and I looked out at the night for signs of rain before I realized that this was an old habit of childhood. Rain had meant that I would be free, for a day, of hiding under the field house or in the woods behind the backstop. And now, still half asleep, I turned my ear to the window, listening with the purest anxiety, colored by a kind of pleading, for the stir of rain beginning or the heavier sound of a settled storm. A single drop of water would have sounded like music. I knew from which quarter the rain wind might rise; I knew how cumbrously the wind would blow, how it would smell of wetness, how the storm, as it came west through the village, would make a distant roar, how the first drops would sound on the elm trees in the yard and the shrubs against the wall, how the rain would drum in the grass, how it would swell, how it would wet the kindling at the barbecue pit and disintegrate the paper bags that contained the charcoal, how it would confine the trustees to Dr. Wareham's house and prevail on one or two of them to leave before the cocktail party, and how it would first fill in the slight indentation around second base and then spread slowly toward first and third, until the whole field was flooded....But I saw only a starry and a windless night. I got back into bed and, settling for the best I had — a kind of hollow good cheer — fell asleep.

THE MORNING was the best kind of spring weather; even I saw this. The demonstration classes satisfied everyone, and at noon we went over to the barbecue pit to have our lunch with the trustees. The food seemed to stick in my throat, but this may have been the fault of the barbecue itself, because the meat was raw and the cooking arrangements were a disappointment all around. I was still eating my dessert when the Doctor gave the rallying cry, "Into your uniforms, men!" I put down my plate and started for the field house, with the arm of a French instructor thrown warmly over my shoulder and in a cheerful, friendly crowd that seemed blamelessly on their way to recapturing, or at least to reënacting, the secure pleasures of youth. But since the hour they returned to was one that I had never possessed, I felt the falseness of my position. I was handed a uniform — a gesture that seemed unalterably to be one of parting. But it was the too large shoes, wrapped with friction tape, that, when I bent over to lace them, gave me the worst spasm of despair. I picked a glove out of a box near the door and jogged out to the field.

The bleachers were full of students and faculty wives, and Dr. Wareham was walking up and down, leading them in singing to the band. The faculty members were first up, facing a formidable concentration of power and wealth in the field. The first batter got a line drive that was missed by the bank president on first and was good for a double. The second man up struck out, but the third man reached first, and the industrialist who was pitching walked the fourth batter. I gave a yank to my cap and stepped up to the plate, working my mouth and swallowing to clean it, if I could, of the salty taste of blood. I kept my eye on the ball, and when the first pitch seemed to be coming straight over the plate, I chopped at it with all my might. I heard the crack, I felt the vibration up my forearm, and, telling myself that a baseball diamond, like most things, must operate on a clockwise principle, I sprinted for third and knocked down the runner who was coming in to score. I knocked him flat, and, bending over to see if he was all right, I heard Dr. Wareham roaring at me, "Get off the field! Get out of my sight!"

I walked back to the field house alone. The soberness of my feeling seemed almost to verge on romantic love — it seemed to make the air I walked through heavy — as if I were sick at heart for some gorgeous raven-haired woman who had been separated from me by a convulsion of nature. I took off my uniform and stood for a long time in the shower. Then I dressed and walked back across the quadrangle, where I could hear, from the open windows of the music building, Bacon playing the Chopin preludes. The music — swept with rains, with ruins, with unrequited and autumnal loves, with here and there a passage of the purest narcissism — seemed to outrage my senses, and I wanted to stop my ears. It took me an hour or so to pack, and when I carried my bags downstairs, I could still hear the cheering from the field. I drove into the village and had the tank filled with gas. At the edge of town, I wondered what direction to take, and then I turned south, for the farm.

IT WAS SIX or seven when I got to St. Botolph's, and I took the precaution of calling Leander before I drove out to the house. "Hello, hello, hello!" the old man shouted. "You must have the wrong number. Oh, hello, Eben…" When I got to the house, I left my bags in the hall and went upstairs. Leander was in his room. "Welcome home, Eben," he said. "I was reading a little Shakespeare to the cat."

When I sat down, the arm of my chair crashed to the floor, and I let it lie there. On his thick white hair Leander still wore his fez. For clothing, he had drawn from his store of old-fashioned bathing suits one with a striped skirt. It must have been stolen, since there were some numerals stenciled on the back. He had decided some time before that the most comfortable shoes he had were some old riding boots, and he was wearing these. Pictures of lost sailboats, lost cottages, dead friends and dogs gazed down at him from the wall. He had tied a length of string between the four wooden pineapples of his high poster bed and had hung his wash there to dry. The cat and his copy of Shakespeare were on his lap. "What are your plans?" he asked.

"I've been fired," I said. "I thought I'd leave some clothes here. I think I'll go for a swim now."

"Have you any clothes I can wear?"

"You're welcome to anything I have. The bags are downstairs."

"I still swim every day," Leander said. "Every day, that is, until the first of October. Last year I went swimming through the fifteenth — the fifteenth or the sixteenth. If you'll wait a minute, I'll make sure." He got up from his chair, and, stooping a little, so the tassel of his fez hung over his brow, he walked to his journal. After consulting it, he said, "I went swimming on the fifteenth last year. I went swimming on the twenty-fifth the year before that. Of course, that was nothing to what I could do when I was younger. I went swimming on the fourth of December, the eighth of January, the second of March. I went swimming on Christmas Day, New Year's Day, the twelfth of January, and the tenth of February…"

After I left him to go out to the river, he went downstairs to where my bags were. An old pair of riding pants took his eye. He managed to get his legs well into them before he realized they were too small. He tried to remove the pants and couldn't, because his legs had begun to swell. And when he tried to stand, the pants knifed him in the tendons at the back of his knees and brought him to the floor. Halfway out in the river, I could hear him roaring for help, and I swam back to shore and ran up to the house and found him moving slowly and painfully toward the kitchen, where he hoped to find a knife and cut himself free. I cut the riding breeches off him, and we drank some whiskey together, but I left in the morning for New York.

It was a good thing that I did leave, because I got a job the day I reached the city, and sailed three days later for Basra, to work for an oil company. I took the long voyage out on one of the company ships; it was five weeks after leaving New York that we stopped at Aden and another four days before we docked at Basra. It was hot. The flat volcanic ruins trembled in the heat, and the car that took me across the city to the oil-company settlement traveled through a maze of foul-smelling streets. The dormitory where I was to be quartered was like an army barracks, and when I reached it, in midafternoon, there was no one there but some Arabs, who helped me with my bags and told me the other men would be in after four, when the offices closed. When the men I shared the barracks with came in, they seemed pleased to see anyone newly arrived from the States, and they were full of practical information about how to make a life in Basra. "We practice baseball two or three nights a week," one of them said, "and then on Sundays we play Shell or Standard Oil. We only have eleven men on the squad now, so if you could play outfield? We call ourselves the Infidels...."

IT WAS NOT until long after my return from Basra, long after my marriage, that Leander died, one summer afternoon, sitting in the rose garden, with a copy of "Primitive Sexual Mores" on his lap. The housekeeper found him there, and the local undertaker sent me a wire in New York. I did not feel any grief when I got the news. Alice and I had three children by then, and my life would not in any way be affected by Leander's death. I telephoned my sisters, in Denver, but neither of them felt that they could come East. The next day, I drove to St. Botolph's, and found that the undertaker had made all the arrangements. The services were to be at two. Three old cousins came out from Boston, to my surprise, and we were the only mourners. It was the kind of weather that we used to call haying weather when I lived in the valley. The fields of timothy and sweet grass had been cut, the cemetery smelled of cut hay, and while the minister was praying, I heard the sound of distant thunder and saw the daylight dim, the way the lights dim in a farmhouse during a storm. After the ceremony, I returned to the house, feeling that there would be a lot there to occupy me, but it turned out that there was not much to do. It had begun to rain. I wandered through the rooms to see if there was anything left in them. I found some whiskey. The bird cages, the three-legged tables, and the cracked soup tureens must have been refused by the junkman. I thought that there must be a will, and I went reluctantly — disconsolately, at any rate — up to Leander's room and sat uneasily in his chair. His papers were copious and bizarre, and it took me nearly two hours to find the will. He left the house and the land to my older sister. To my other sister he left the jewelry, but this was immaterial, since all the jewelry had been sold. I was mentioned. "To my changeling son, Eben," he wrote, "the author of all my misfortunes, I leave my copy of Shakespeare, a hacking cough…" The list was long and wicked, and although he had written it ten years earlier and although I had buried him that afternoon, I couldn't help feeling, for a minute, that the piece of paper was evidence of my own defeat. It was dark then, and it was still raining. The whiskey bottle was empty and the unshaded electric light was baneful. The old house, which had always seemed to have an extensive life of its own, was creaking and stirring under the slender weight of the storm. The feeling that in burying Leander I had resolved a sad story seemed farcical, and if my reaction to his will was evidence, the old fool had pierced the rites and ceremonies of death. I thought desperately of my family in New York, and of the rooms where my return was waited with anxiety and love, but I had never been able to build any kind of bridge from Leander's world to the worlds where I lived, and I failed now in my efforts to remember New York. I went downstairs to telephone my wife, but the telephone was dead, and for all I knew it might have been disconnected years ago. I packed my bag, turned out the lights, threw the house key into the river, and started home.

IN THE YEARS that followed, I thought now and then about Leander and the farm, and although I had resolved to break with these memories, they both continued to enjoy the perfect freedom of my dreams; the bare halls of the house, the massive granite stoop, the rain dripping from the wooden gutters, and the mass of weeds in the garden often surrounded me while I slept. My participation in baseball continued to be painful. I drove a ball through my mother-in-law's parlor window — and the rest of the family, who were intimidated, didn't understand why I should feel so happy — but it was not enough to lay Leander's ghost, and I still didn't like old men with white hair to be at the helm of the ships I traveled on. Some years later — my oldest son was nine — I took all five boys uptown to Yankee Stadium to see their first game. It was one of the hottest days of the year. I bought my sons food, eyeshades, pennants, score cards, pencils, and souvenir pins, and I took the youngest two to the bathroom several times. Mantle was up in the sixth, with a count of three and two. He fouled three balls into the netting above the backstop and fouled the fourth straight toward where we were sitting — a little high. It was coming like a shot, but I made the catch — one-handed, barehanded — and although I thought the impact had broken some bones in my hand, the pain was followed swiftly by a sense of perfect joy. The old man and the old house seemed at last to fall from the company and the places of my dreams, and I smelled the timothy and the sweet grass again, and saw a gravedigger hidden behind a marble angel, and the smoky, the grainy light of a thunderstorm, when the clearness of the green world — the emblazoned fields — reminds us briefly of a great freedom of body and mind. Then the boys began to argue for possession of the ball, and I gave it to the oldest one, hoping that I wouldn't have any more use for it. It would have troubled Leander to think that he would be buried in any place as distant from West Farm as Yankee Stadium, but that is where his bones were laid to rest.

Mothers

&

Sons

INTRODUCTION

WHILE SOME TEND to deny or minimize the depth of the bond between mothers and sons, the mother-son connection is both powerful and lasting. Yet, like the other family relationships, the mother-son bond is marked by ambivalence.

Sons struggle between their profound attachment to mother and their need to function as brave, self-reliant individuals. A young son's passionate longing for mother goes beyond sexual craving despite Freud's emphasis on the erotic aspects of this bond. The young son identifies with his mother, for she is usually his primary source of nurturing and comfort; yet as he grows, he struggles to deny his dependency on her and to distance himself from what she as a woman represents, in order to define himself as masculine. In spite of this separating process, sons do learn much from their mothers about values and relationships and are likely to acquire many of their mother's traits and habits, since it is natural to resemble people with whom we spend a great deal of time. A mother's powerful influence over her son is often graphically illustrated in her son's possessive behavior. A young son, in particular, tends to be possessive of his mother's attentions and affections and may resent the adult male figure in his mother's life, whether it be father, stepfather, or lover.

Despite an underlying desire to hold on to mother's love, a son learns to avoid the humiliating label of "mamma's boy." In his attempts to resolve or deny his childhood longing for mother, a son may either look for his mother's image in other women or find women totally different from his mother. Also, he may submerge his emotional side, that part of himself viewed as mother's domain, and may adopt a contemptuous, critical attitude toward his mother's lifestyle, roles, and values. Yet, even while a son is learning to disdain what he sees as his mother's weakness, he is, more than likely, continuing to rely on her for comfort and support.

In raising sons, mothers experience a common dilemma. While most mothers want sons who embody their ideal of a male who is both strong and caring, they often hesitate to reinforce the gentle side of their boy children because they fear society's ostracism of the "sissy." While they want sons who are empathetic and cooperative, they often feel compelled to foster competitiveness and discourage displays of emotion in their sons. Largely because of societal injunctions, mothers encourage sons more than daughters to be self-sufficient and to fight for themselves at a very early age.

Having a son and caring for him opens up feelings in a mother about being a woman in relation to males. A mother's feelings toward her son stem at least in part from living in a society where males are more valued than females; thus while a woman may derive a sense of personal prestige and power from her son, she may also, on some level, resent the superior status of her male offspring. Since women have been taught not to be selfish, particularly in relating to men, they often cater to their sons' needs and feel guilty if they put their own self-interest ahead of their sons' welfare. However, they may bitterly regret their actions and become angry when their sons begin expecting to be served. A mother's hostility toward a demanding son tends to be complicated by her fear of losing his love, and a son recognizes quite early in his life the power he wields when he withholds his affections.

As her son's protector and as a parent very invested in her son's well-being and success, a mother wants to stay involved in her son's life as long as she can, yet feels compelled to help prepare him for his place in the world.

The powerful struggle between letting go and holding on is one facing sons as well as mothers in the stories to follow. The absence of fathers in the household intensifies the mother-son interactions in all four stories and causes both mother and son to feel the burden of their responsibility for one another. Apparent in these stories is the presence of an underlying connectedness that is threatened by either the mother's efforts to "masculinize" her son or the son's attempts to deny his dependency. Also threaded through these stories are the themes of possessiveness, jealousy, and guilt.

In Berriault's "Houses of the City," the familiar Oedipal triangle emerges, as we experience a ten-year-old son's jealousy and confusion when he encounters a male rival for his mother's attention. In this story, as in the one following it by Gaines, we also see how a son's attachment to his mother takes the form of protectiveness. In "The Sky is Gray," Gaines invites us to empathize with a young son's responses to a mother who knows she must teach survival skills in a world of poverty and hardship. In rising to his mother's expectations that he be strong and unemotional, this son repeatedly denies his childlike self.

In the last two stories, O'Connor's "Everything That Rises Must Converge" and Purdy's "Encore," a young adult son's emotional withdrawal and a mother's desire to maintain contact are prominent features. The son in both these stories actively distances himself from his mother through fault-finding, yet experiences a gnawing sense of half-recognized guilt. O'Connor's and Purdy's stories can be read as counterpoints to one another, since the former captures the son's view while the latter focuses on the mother's reactions. While the former seethes with the son's bitterness and hyperbolic attempts to sever emotional ties with his mother, the latter traces the mother's anguish and desperate attempts to retain influence over her son's life.   G.C.

Gina Berriault

THE HOUSES OF THE CITY

ON SOME DAYS he longed to be with his mother before the hour of her return to their rooms, and in the afternoon he would seek her out at whatever house she was cleaning that day, even though the place was halfway across the city, up in the heights where the big houses stood apart like rich merchants' wives watching their husbands' ships entering the bay below. In his small body was the quality of the pointer dog. He walked slightly stooped, pushing forward, his feet going down in a plodding way.

It was late in his tenth year when he began this practice. He would be in the midst of a scuffle after school, along a sidewalk somewhere, and suddenly he would think of her and at that moment offer nothing further to the struggle. This silent urgency was more effective in breaking his opponent's grip than was his fierce, animal strength. Always in the morning she told him where she would be that day, so that if anything happened to him at school his teacher could call her right away. He felt that it was impossible for anything to harm him; but anything could harm her.

She was alarmed the first time she opened a door to him. He was not sick, he told her. But he had no other reason to give. Of his fear of her dying he could not tell, because to give words to this fear was like pronouncing sentence upon her. If he kept it to himself, the fear might prove groundless. After the first time they said nothing on his arrival. He made no demands upon her, and sat in the chair she pointed to, his hands folded obviously away from the lure of knickknacks and magazines. He listened to the sounds of her cleaning in other rooms, and was not restless.

Certain women were fascinated by him, as if, in his silent clinging to one chair, he were a large moth, its intentions unknown. Once, as he sat in a glass-enclosed sunporch, a large-leafed plant growing from a blue, glazed bowl on the carpet fingered his cheek, touched his elbow each time he fidgeted, but he did not move to another chair, hypnotized by the plant and its curiosity as if it were the lady of the house. Then one afternoon he was sitting in the hallway of an upstairs apartment, facing in a dutiful way the opposite wall and taking a small liberty in examining minutely the oval piece of wood that hung on the wall, a yellow horse painted on it, the long, white tail of the horse touching the green grass sprouting up. Aside from the sounds of his mother at her tasks, he heard another person astir in the bedroom beyond the oval picture. He heard the sluggish movement of a person turning under blankets, then the sound of slippers scraped along the floor. He heard a man talking to himself with the voice that is acquired while the body is lying down: a voice pocketed deep in the throat, granular, caressing, complaining.

From the half-open bedroom door came a young man, not much older than a high school boy. His hair was red and stood up in curls, as if startled in advance, and he paused there in the doorway, staring in exaggerated surprise at the boy in the hallway chair. He was tying the tasseled belt of his bathrobe, which was a jewel-green silk, and one end of the belt he held in surprise across the palm of his right hand.

"Fran!" he called. "Who is this you let in?" His voice was cajoling and demanding; he listened to his own voice like a violin pupil listens to the music he makes. "Do you want to see me?" he asked, dropping his head in a pointing way. "If you have any business with me, speak up! If it's a debt I owe, let me congratulate you on getting past the door. Most of my creditors sit on the steps outside. Well, how much do I owe you? Whatever it is, I can't pay it."

Now he placed his hands on the arms of the chair, leaning over the boy, and the boy turned his face away, embarrassed, from the corners of his eyes meeting the young man's eyes.

"I can't pay you for this reason," explained the young man. "Do you see this house, how clean it is? Well, you should have seen it before that woman took a mop and vacuum to it." His close face was sleepily plump, and his hair, so near, was something to be puzzled out, something with an answer to it, its curls were so many and entwined. "If anyone is going to be paid," he said, "it's her, and you'll have to wait your turn. She works like a dog and stands for a lot of abuse from her employers, and she's constantly worrying all the time about that son of hers. She's got to keep him decently clothed, you know, and fed." Their eyes met again, forced by the young man's eyes to a mutual comprehension of her plight. "But I'll tell you," he said, laying his hand on the boy's shoulders, "come into the kitchen with me and settle for a cup of chocolate."

Under the spell the boy slid off the chair so abruptly that his head hit the young man in the chest. With the nape of his neck in his host's hand, the boy was marched down the hallway. In the kitchen his mother was seated on a high stool, polishing silverware at the sink, a scarf of many faded colors wrapped around her head. She glanced over her shoulder at them, an absentness in her eyes as if she watched a dog or a cat, a household pet, saunter into the kitchen. Afraid suddenly that his presence jeopardized her job and that she was not going to recognize him, he stumbled as the young man pressed him down into a chair. For a moment he did not know who he should be, her son or the bill collector.

From the refrigerator, the host drew out a bottle of milk and poured some into a pan. Then he stirred in several teaspoons of cocoa and several of sugar, in this process spilling some of both on the waxed linoleum, and his leather slippers made a sticky, rasping sound as, uncaring, unhearing, he walked about.

"He don't need no chocolate," she said.

Up went the young man's spoon in a gesture of disbelief and dismay. The young man was startled by this rudeness. "Is that the way to talk to a guest of mine?"

The boy laughed out loud because he was sure now of who he was, and he shifted in his chair, granted a freedom of movement in the chairs of this house.

"For that," said the young man to her, "you can't have any. She can't can she?" he asked, but he asked it of her, bringing his face close to hers, delicately close, the two profiles, presented to the boy in the chair, reminding him of the approach and ascent of butterflies, touching and yet not touching. At once he was left out of the game. He had thought the game was for him and he learned that it was played only to accentuate some knowledge between his mother and the young man. And the boy was caught in the midst of his laughter, his elbows lifted eccentrically behind him like wings going up.

They had hot chocolate together, the young man and he, the host sitting with his legs apart, his robe falling away from his bare thighs, not at all embarrassed that a woman could see so much of his body. The young man drank in a hungry, nervous way, bobbing his head down impatiently to meet the cup on its way up. It was when he was lifting his head, swallowing elaborately in his haste to continue what he was saying, that he spoke the boy's name: "Matt," he said, "you've got catchall ears. Listen to this," and went on with his story. But the boy glanced up at his mother, unbelievingly. She had told his name to the young man, but of the young man the boy had been told not a thing.

When the host said, "Well, come along," Matt followed him up the hallway and into the bedroom. The curtains were closed, and the young man switched on the lamp by the bed, got down on his knee, and rummaged through a pile of magazines that lay under the bed. This room hadn't been cleaned yet. It smelled of cigarette smoke, of night perspiration, and upon the lamp's table were strewn a number of little things: theater tickets, manicure scissors, a red glass ashtray, a man's handkerchief, a lifesaver candy, a dime and four pennies. Was the young man an actor? he wondered, for he had heard that actors slept all day. There was something dramatic in the young man's bowed back, covered with the slick green robe, and in the leg, stretched out behind the bent knee, with its white knot of calf and its quivering heel. Rising, the young man placed in the boy's hand a thick magazine, a photograph of a Dalmatian dog on its cover, and gently prodded him to turn around; and the boy, lifting his head so that he could find his way out through the dimness beyond the lamp, saw his mother's black coat thrown over the back of a rocker, and on the seat of the rocker lay her small red hat.

Again he sat in the hallway, turning the pages of the sports magazine, while in the bedroom the young man poked about, getting dressed. The magazine had pictures of men in hip boots, fishing, of dogs carrying ducks from reedy water, of horses; and the smell of the paper was clean, strong as lacquer, the pages satin smooth and weighted in his hands. He turned up the palm of his right hand to see if it were dirty and would soil the white luster. Usually, he thought, she left her coat and hat in the kitchen. Once, in another house, when it was time for them to go, she had brought her coat from the back porch, where a late afternoon rain had flicked it through the screen; it was too shabby, she had said, to hang in the hall closet, because, if a guest came, he would not want to hang his coat next to hers. But in this house her coat was lying on a chair in a bedroom. His right hand was again on the magazine, but he still could not say whether his hands were clean or grimy. Lifting his hand again, he decided that it was not clean enough, and he closed the magazine, placing it on the floor beside his chair.

Closely, he listened to the sound of her in the kitchen, his hands clasped in his lap. By such devout observance of her presence he was proving to her that he was a more loving son than the young man could ever be, no matter how hard the other tried.

THEY WOULD RIDE HOME together in the evening, boarding a trolley or a cable car, depending upon which neighborhood she was working in, and something in the waning day and in sitting beside her, watching the tall, narrow houses slip by like boards in one long fence, caused him to become tired of premonition. With the onset of evening's soft glamor, she would become for him quite alive and everlasting. On their journey home that evening, he sat beside her in the trolley, clasping between his knees her shopping bag, and each time she laid her hand on his knee, the love and shame of the betrayed wrinkled across his face. If he was unduly frightened by the way her hands were turning translucent, by the way her veins were rising along her forearms, if she was, after all, not going to die, there was, he thought another way she could be lost. When they climbed down from the trolley and walked along the street to their apartment house, he swung the shopping bag in his left hand so that the bag separated her and himself. But when the bag, light as it was, scraped against her ankle, his heart contracted with remorse as if he had deliberately hit her.

When she unlocked the door, he slipped in before her and lay directly down on the couch. Since their kitchen had no window, she switched on its ceiling light, and gradually as the street grew darker, as the sun, shining eastward down the street, withdrew its flame from the lamp at the corner, leaving a dark gray smudge in the globe, the panes of the bow window in which he lay became black mirrors and he saw in the one that was near to his face the reflection of the kitchen doorway and his mother by the stove. The picture was miniature, unreal, and when she spoke to him he answered her by speaking to the reflection, but this disturbed him and he turned his face to the rooms.

She came from the kitchen carrying plates, but instead of placing them on the table she continued to hold them in her hands while she faced him, pressing her hip against the edge of the table. Her face and down the front of her were obscured by the darkness of the room, but the sides of her thin body and some outer strands of her short hair were lit by the light from the kitchen behind her. She laughed a bit, in a wry way that did not change the set of her head.

"What do you want to follow me for?"

He put his hands over his ears.

When she had set the table, she came and stood over him. Into this room whose cold was not yet dispelled by the warm air from the kitchen, she brought in her body the heat from the stove and on her skin the steam.

"Well?" And, hearing no answer, "Come, sit down and eat."

Obediently he sat up, but as he got to his feet she put her hands against his chest, pushing him down again; before he knew it, she was lying beside him and they were holding each other so closely that to breathe he had to turn his face upward.

"What do you want to follow me for?"

With his arms around her, he found himself listening to her body and heard her listening to his, and it was comical, almost, like two persons staring at each other through the same keyhole. It was not the possibility of her dying that troubled him, but something else he had picked up just an hour ago. The young man was pretending to be her son, and she did not object. This disloyalty of hers became so loud in their bodies that she had to let go of him and sit up.

"How did he know my name?"

"I told him," she said. "Can't I talk about my own son?"

"But you never told me you told him my name."

"Do I have to tell you about everybody I tell about my son?"

Was it something he had exaggerated all along, he wondered, their alliance against the persons she worked for? Although she came home bringing stories about them, describing them and their visitors jabbingly, vindictively, had he believed mistakenly that with these stories she bound herself and him together?

"Come now," she said. "Get up and eat."

But he made no effort to rise. She was standing away from him, weary of her own guilt, but he knew she was uncertain over which side she was on, his or the young man's with the crudely bared thighs.

Ernest J. Gaines

THE SKY IS GRAY

GO'N BE COMING in a few minutes. Coming 'round that bend down there full speed. And I'm go'n get out my hankercher and I'm go'n wave it down, and us go'n get on it and go.

I keep on looking for it, but Mama don't look that way no more. She looking down the road where us just came from. It's a long old road, and far's you can see you don't see nothing but gravel. You got dry weeds on both sides, and you got trees on both sides, and fences on both sides, too. And you got cows in the pastures and they standing close together. And when us was coming out yer to catch the bus I seen the smoke coming out o' the cow's nose.

I look at my mama and I know what she thinking. I been with Mama so much, jest me and her, I know what she thinking all the time. Right now it's home — Auntie and them. She thinking if they got 'nough wood — if she left 'nough there to keep 'em warm till us get back. She thinking if it go'n rain and if any of 'em go'n leave to go out in the rain. She thinking 'bout the hog — if he go'n get out, and if Ty and Val be able to get him back in. She always worry too much if she leave me there with the smaller ones 'cause she knows I'm go'n look after 'em and look after Auntie and everything else. I'm the oldest and she say I'm the man.

I look at my mama and I love my mama. She wearing that black coat and that black hat and she looking sad. I love my mama and I want put my arm 'round her and tell her. But I'm not s'pose to do that. She say that's weakness and that's crybaby stuff, and she don't want no crybaby 'round her. She don't want you to be scared neither. 'Cause Ty scared of ghosts and she always whipping him. I'm scared of the dark, too. But I make 'tend I ain't. I make 'tend I ain't 'cause I'm the oldest, and I got to set a good sample for the rest. I can't ever be scared and I can't ever cry. And that's the reason I didn't never say nothing 'bout my teef. It been hurting me and hurting me close to a month now. But I didn't say it. I didn't say it 'cause I didn't want act like no crybaby, and 'cause I know us didn't have 'nough money to have it pulled. But, Lord, it been hurting me. And look like it won't start till at night when you trying to get little sleep. Then soon's you shet your eyes — umm-umm, Lord, look like it go right down to your heartstring.

"Hurting, hanh?" Ty'd say.

I'd shake my head, but I wouldn't open my mouth for nothing. You open your mouth and let that wind in, and it almost kill you.

I'd jest lay there and listen to 'em snore. Ty, there, right 'side me, and Auntie and Val over by the fireplace. Val younger 'an me and Ty, and he sleep with Auntie. Mama sleep 'round the other side with Louis and Walker.

I'd jest lay there and listen to 'em, and listen to that wind out there, and listen to that fire in the fireplace. Sometime it'd stop long enough to let me get little rest. Sometimes it jest hurt, hurt, hurt. Lord, have mercy.

II

AUNTIE KNOWED it was hurting me. I didn't tell nobody but Ty, 'cause us buddies and he ain't go'n tell nobody. But some kind o' way Auntie found out. When she asked me, I told her no, nothing was wrong. But she knowed it all the time. She told me to mash up a piece o' aspirin and wrap it in some cotton and jug it down in that hole. I did it, but it didn't do no good. It stopped for a little while, and started right back again. She wanted to tell Mama, but I told her Uh-uh. 'Cause I knowed Mama didn't have no money, and it jest was go'n make her mad again. So she told Monsieur Bayonne, and Monsieur Bayonne came to the house and told me to kneel down 'side him on the fireplace. He put his finger in my mouth and made the Sign of the Cross on my jaw. The tip of Monsieur Bayonne finger is some hard, 'cause he always playing on that guitar. If us sit outside at night us can always hear Monsieur Bayonne playing on his guitar. Sometime us leave him out there playing on the guitar.

He made the Sign of the Cross over and over on my jaw, but that didn't do no good. Even when he prayed and told me to pray some too, that teef still hurt.

"How you feeling?" he say.

"Same," I say.

He kept on praying and making the Sign of the Cross and I kept on praying, too.

"Still hurting?" he say.

"Yes, sir."

Monsieur Bayonne mashed harder and harder on my jaw. He mashed so hard he almost pushed me on Ty. But then he stopped.

"What kind o' prayers you praying, boy?" he say.

"Baptist," I say.

"Then you better start saying it."

"Yes, sir."

He started mashing again, and I could hear him praying at the same time. And, sure 'nough, afterwhile it stopped.

Me and Ty went outside where Monsieur Bayonne two hounds was, and us started playing with 'em. "Let's go hunting," Ty say. "All right," I say; and us went on back in the pasture. Soon the hounds got on a trail, and me and Ty followed 'em all 'cross the pasture and then back in the woods, too. And then they cornered this little old rabbit and killed him, and me and Ty made 'em get back, and us picked up the rabbit and started on back home. But it had started hurting me again. It was hurting me plenty now, but I wouldn't tell Monsieur Bayonne. That night I didn't sleep a bit, and first thing in the morning Auntie told me to go back and let Monsieur Bayonne pray over me some more. Monsieur Bayonne was in his kitchen making coffee when I got there. Soon's he seen me, he knowed what was wrong.

"All right, kneel down there 'side that stove," he say. "And this time pray Catholic. I don't know nothing 'bout Baptist, and don't want know nothing 'bout him."

III

LAST NIGHT Mama say: "Tomorrow us going to town."

"It ain't hurting me no more," I say. "I can eat anything on it."

"Tomorrow us going to town," she say.

And after she finished eating, she got up and went to bed. She always go to bed early now. 'Fore Daddy went in the Army, she used to stay up late. All o' us sitting out on the gallery or 'round the fire. But now, look like soon's she finish eating she go to bed.

This morning when I woke up, her and Auntie was standing 'fore the fireplace. She say: "'Nough to get there and back. Dollar and a half to have it pulled. Twenty-five for me to go, twenty-five for him. Twenty-five for me to come back, twenty-five for him. Fifty cents left. Guess I get a little piece o' salt meat with that."

"Sure can use a piece," Auntie say. "White beans and no salt meat ain't white beans."

"I do the best I can," Mama say.

They was quiet after that, and I made 'tend I was still sleep.

"James, hit the floor," Auntie say.

I still made 'tend I was sleep. I didn't want 'em to know I was listening.

"All right," Auntie say, shaking me by the shoulder. "Come on. Today's the day."

I pushed the cover down to get out, and Ty grabbed it and pulled it back.

"You too, Ty," Auntie say.

"I ain't getting no teef pulled," Ty say.

"Don't mean it ain't time to get up," Auntie say. "Hit it, Ty."

Ty got up grumbling.

"James, you hurry up and get in your clothes and eat your food," Auntie say. "What time y'all coming back?" she say to Mama.

"That 'leven o'clock bus," Mama say. "Got to get back that field this evening."

"Get a move on you, James," Auntie say.

I went in the kitchen and washed my face, then I ate my breakfast. I was having bread and syrup. The bread was warm and hard and tasted good. And I tried to make it last a long time.

Ty came back there, grumbling, and mad at me.

"Got to get up," he say. "I ain't having no teef pulled. What I got to be getting up for?"

Ty poured some syrup in his pan and got a piece of bread. He didn't wash his hands, neither his face, and I could see that white stuff in his eyes.

"You the one getting a teef pulled," he say. "What I got to get up for. I bet you if I was getting a teef pulled, you wouldn't be getting up. Shucks; syrup again. I'm getting tired of this old syrup. Syrup, syrup, syrup. I want me some bacon sometime."

"Go out in the field and work and you can have bacon," Auntie say, "but I know where you go'n be hot, you keep that grumbling up. James, get a move on you; your mama waiting."

I ate my last piece of bread and went in the front room. Mama was standing 'fore the fireplace warming her hands. I put on my coat and my cap, and us left the house.

IV

I LOOK DOWN there again, but it still ain't coming. I almost say, "It ain't coming, yet," but I keep my mouth shet. 'Cause that's something else she don't like. She don't like for you to say something for nothing. She can see it ain't coming. I can see it ain't coming, so why say it ain't coming. I don't say it, and I turn and look at the river that's back o' us. It so cold the smoke jest rising up from the water. I see a bunch of pull-doos not too far out — jest on the other side the lilies. I'm wondering if you can eat pull-doos. I ain't too sure, 'cause I ain't never ate some. But I done ate owls and blackbirds, and I done ate red birds, too. I didn't want kill the red birds, but she made me kill 'em. They had two of 'em back there. One in my trap, one in Ty trap. Me and Ty was go'n play with 'em and let 'em go. But she made me kill 'em 'cause we needed the food.

"I can't," I say. "I can't."

"Here," she say. "Take it."

"I can't," I say. "I can't. I can't kill him, Mama. Please."

"Here," she say. "Take this fork, James."

"Please, Mama, I can't kill him," I say.

I could tell she was go'n hit me. And I jecked back, but I didn't jeck back soon enough.

"Take it," she say.

I took it and reached in for him, but he kept hopping to the back.

"I can't, Mama," I say. The water jest kept running down my face. "I can't."

"Get him out o' there," she say.

I reached in for him and he kept hopping to the back. Then I reached in farther, and he pecked me on the hand.

"I can't, Mama," I say.

She slapped me again.

I reached in again, but he kept hopping out my way. Then he hopped to one side, and I reached there. The fork got him on the leg and I heard his leg pop. I pulled my hand out 'cause I had hurt him.

"Give it here," she say, and jecked the fork out my hand.

She reached and got the little bird right in the neck. I heard the fork go in his neck, and I heard it go in the ground. She brought him out and helt him right in front o' me.

"That's one," she say. She shook him off and gived me the fork. "Get the other one."

"I can't, Mama. I do anything. But I can't do that."

She went to the corner o' the fence and broke the biggest switch over there. I knelt 'side the trap crying.

"Get him out o' there," she say.

"I can't, Mama."

She started hitting me cross the back. I went down on the ground crying.

"Get him," she say.

"Octavia," Auntie say, "explain to him. Explain to him. Jest don't beat him. Explain to him."

But she hit me and hit me and hit me.

I'm still young. I ain't no more 'an eight. But I know now. I know why I had to. (They was so little, though. They was so little. I 'member how I picked the feathers off 'em and cleaned 'em and helt 'em over the fire. Then us all ate 'em. Ain't had but little bitty piece, but us all little bitty piece, and ever'body jest looked at me, 'cause they was so proud.) S'pose she had to go away? That's why I had to do it. S'pose she had to go away like Daddy went away? Then who was go'n look after us? They had to be somebody left to carry on. I didn't know it then, but I know it now. Auntie and Monsieur Bayonne talked to me and made me see.

V

TIME I SEE IT, I get out my hankercher and start waving. It still 'way down there, but I keep waving anyhow. Then it came closer and stop and me and Mama get on. Mama tell me go sit in the back while she pay. I do like she say, and the people look at me. When I pass the little sign that say White and Colored, I start looking for a seat. I jest see one of 'em back there, but I don't take it, 'cause I want my mama to sit down herself. She come in the back and sit down, and I lean on the seat. They got seats in the front, but I know I can't sit there, 'cause I have to sit back o' the sign. Anyhow, I don't want sit there if my mama go'n sit back here.

They got a lady sitting 'side my mama and she look at me and grin little bit. I grin back, but I don't open my mouth, 'cause the wind'll get in and make that teef hurt. The lady take out a pack o' gum and reach me a slice, but I shake my head. She reach Mama a slice, and Mama shake her head. The lady jest can't understand why a little boy'll turn down gum, and she reached me a slice again. This time I point to my jaw. The lady understand and grin little bit, and I grin little bit, but I don't open my mouth, though.

They got a girl sitting 'cross from me. She got on a red overcoat, and her hair plaited in one big plait. First, I make 'tend I don't even see her. But then I start looking at her little bit. She make 'tend she don't see me neither, but I catch her looking that way. She got a cold, and ever' now and then she hist that little hankercher to her nose. She ought to blow it, but she don't. Must think she too much a lady or something.

Ever' time she hist that little hankercher, the lady 'side her say something in her yer. She shake her head and lay her hands in her lap again. Then I catch her kind o' looking where I'm at. I grin at her. But think she'll grin back? No. She turn up her little old nose like I got some snot on my face or something. Well, I show her both o' us can turn us head. I turn mine, too, and look out at the river.

The river is gray. The sky is gray. They have pull-doos on the water. The water is wavy, and the pull-doos go up and down. The bus go 'round a turn, and you got plenty trees hiding the river. Then the bus go 'round another turn, and I can see the river again.

I look to the front where all the white people sitting. Then I look at that little old gal again. I don't look right at her, 'cause I don't want all them people to know I love her. I jest look at her little bit, like I'm looking out that window over there. But she know I'm looking out that way, and she kind o' look at me, too. The lady sitting 'side her catch her this time, and she lean over and say something in her yer.

"I don't love him nothing," that little old gal say out loud.

Ever'body back there yer her mouth, and all of 'em look at us and laugh.

"I don't love you, neither," I say. "So you don't have to turn up your nose, miss."

"You the one looking," she say.

"I wasn't looking at you," I say. "I was looking out that window, there."

"Out that window, my foot," she say. "I seen you. Ever'time I turn 'round you look at me."

"You must o' been looking yourself if you seen me all them times," I say.

"Shucks," she say, "I got me all kind o' boyfriends."

"I got girlfriends, too," I say.

"Well, I just don't want you to get your hopes up," she say.

I don't say no more to that little old gal, 'cause I don't want have to bust her in the mouth. I lean on the seat where Mama sitting, and I don't even look that way no more. When us get to Bayonne, she jug her little old tongue out at me. I make 'tend I'm go'n hit her, and she duck down side her mama. And all the people laugh at us again.

VI

ME AND MAMA get off and start walking in town. Bayonne is a little bitty town. Baton Rouge is a hundred times bigger 'an Bayonne. I went to Baton Rouge once – me, Ty, Mama, and Daddy. But that was 'way back yonder – 'fore he went in the Army. I wonder when us go'n see him again. I wonder when. Look like he ain't ever coming home....Even the pavement all cracked in Bayonne. Look like it colder 'an it is home. The wind blow in my face, and I feel that stuff running down my nose. I sniff. Mama say use that hankercher. I blow my nose and put it back.

Us pass a school and I see them white children playing in the yard. Big old red school, and them children jest running and playing. Then us pass a cafe, and I see a bunch of 'em in there eating. I wish I was in there, 'cause I'm cold. Mama tell me keep my eyes in front where they blonks.

Us pass stores that got dummies, and us pass another cafe, and then us pass a shoe shop, and that baldhead man in there fixing on a shoe. I look at him and I butt into that white lady, and Mama jeck me in front and tell me stay there.

Us come to the courthouse, and I see the flag waving there. This one yer ain't like the one us got at school. This one yer ain't got but a handful of stars. One at school got a big pile of stars – one for ever' state. Us pass it and us turn and there it is – the dentist office. Me and Mama go in, and they got people sitting ever'where you look. They even got a little boy in there younger 'an me.

Me and Mama sit on that bench, and a white lady come in there and ask me what my name. Mama tell her, and the white lady go back. Then I yer somebody hollering in there. And soon's that little boy hear him hollering, he start hollering too. His mama pat him and pat him, trying to make him hush up, but he ain't thinking 'bout her.

The man that was hollering in there comes out holding his jaw.

"Got it, hanh?" another man say.

The man shake his head.

"Man, I thought they was killing you in there," the other man say. "Hollering like a pig under a gate."

The man don't say nothing. He jest head for the door, and the other man follow him.

"John Lee," the white lady say. "John Lee Williams."

The little boy jug his head down in his mama lap and holler more now. His mama tell him go with the nurse, but he ain't thinking 'bout her. His mama tell him again, but he don't even yer.

His mama pick him up and take him in there, and even when the white lady shet the door I can still hear him hollering.

"I often wonder why the Lord let a child like that suffer," a lady say to my mama. The lady's sitting right in front o' us on another bench. She got on a white dress and a black sweater. She must be a nurse or something herself, I reckoned.

"Not us to question," a man say.

"Sometimes I don't know if we shouldn't," the lady say.

"I know definitely we shouldn't," the man say. The man look like a preacher. He big and fat and he got on a black suit. He got a gold chain, too.

"Why?" the lady say.

"Why anything?" the preacher say.

"Yes," the lady say. "Why anything?"

"Not us to question," the preacher say.

The lady look at the preacher a little while and look at Mama again.

"And look like it's the poor who do most the suffering," she say. "I don't understand it."

"Best not to even try," the preacher say. "He works in mysterious ways. Wonders to perform."

Right then Little John Lee bust out hollering, and ever'body turn their head.

"He's not a good dentist," the lady say. "Dr. Robillard is much better. But more expensive. That's why most of the colored people come here. The white people go to Dr. Robillard. Y'all from Bayonne?"

"Down the river," my mama say. And that's all she go'n say, 'cause she don't talk much. But the lady keep on looking at her, and so she say: "Near Morgan."

"I see," the lady say.

VII

"THAT'S THE TROUBLE with the black people in this country today," somebody else say. This one yer sitting on the same side me and Mama sitting, and he kind o' sitting in front of that preacher. He look like a teacher or somebody that go to college. He got on a suit, and he got a book that he been reading. "We don't question is exactly the trouble," he say. "We should question and question and question. Question everything."

The preacher jest look at him a long time. He done put a toothpick or something in his mouth, and he jest keep turning it and turning it. You can see he don't like that boy with that book.

"Maybe you can explain what you mean," he say.

"I said what I meant," the boy say. "Question everything. Every stripe, every star, every word spoken. Everything."

"It 'pears to me this young lady and I was talking 'bout God, young man," the preacher say.

"Question Him, too," the boy say.

"Wait," the preacher say. "Wait now."

"You heard me right," the boy say. "His existence as well as everything else. Everything."

The preacher jest look across the room at the boy. You can see he getting madder and madder. But mad or no mad, the boy ain't thinking 'bout him. He look at the preacher jest's hard's the preacher looked at him.

"Is this what they coming to?" the preacher say. "Is this what we educating them for?"

"You're not educating me," the boy say. "I wash dishes at night to go to school in the day. So even the words you spoke need questioning."

The preacher jest look at him and shake his head.

"When I come in this room and seen you there with your book, I said to myself, there's an intelligent man. How wrong a person can be."

"Show me one reason to believe in the existence of a God," the boy say.

"My heart tells me," the preacher say.

"My heart tells me," the boy say. "My heart tells me. Sure, my heart tells me. And as long as you listen to what your heart tells you, you will have only what the white man gives you and nothing more. Me, I don't listen to my heart. The purpose of the heart is to pump blood throughout the body and nothing else."

"Who's your paw, boy?" the preacher say.

"Why?"

"Who is he?"

"He's dead."

"And your mom?"

"She's in Charity Hospital with pneumonia. Half killed herself working for nothing."

"And 'cause he's dead and she sick, you mad at the world?"

"I'm not mad at the world. I'm questioning the world. I'm questioning it with cold logic, sir. What do words like Freedom, Liberty, God, White, Colored mean? I want to know. That's why you are sending us to school, to read and to ask questions. And because we ask these questions, you call us mad. No, sir, it is not us who are mad."

"You keep saying us?"

"'Us'...why not? I'm not alone."

The preacher jest shake his head. Then he look at ever'body in the room — ever'body. Some of the people look down at the floor, keep from looking at him. I kind o' look way myself, but soon's I know he done turn his head, I look that way again.

"I'm sorry for you," he say.

"Why?" the boy say. "Why not be sorry for yourself? Why are you so much better off than I am? Why aren't you sorry for these other people in here? Why not be sorry for the lady who had to drag her child into the dentist office? Why not be sorry for the lady sitting on that bench over there? Be sorry for them. Not sorry for me. Some way or other I'm going to make it."

"No, I'm sorry for you," the preacher say.

"Of course, of course," the boy say, shaking his head. "You're sorry for me because I rock that pillar you're leaning on."

"You can't ever rock the pillar I'm leaning on, young man. It's stronger than anything man can ever do."

"You believe in God because a man told you to believe in God. A white man told you to believe in God. And why? To keep you ignorant, so he can keep you under his feet."

"So now, we the ignorant?"

"Yes," the boy say. "Yes." And he open his book again.

The preacher jest look at him there. The boy done forgot all about him. Ever'body else make 'tend they done forgot 'bout the squabble, too.

Then I see the preacher getting up real slow. Preacher a great big old man, and he got to brace hisself to get up. He come 'cross the room where the boy is. He jest stand there looking at him, but the boy don't raise his head.

"Stand up, boy," the preacher say.

The boy look up at him, then he shet his book real slow and stand up. Preacher jest draw back and hit him in the face. The boy fall 'gainst the wall, but he straighten hisself up and look right back at that preacher.

"You forgot the other cheek," he say.

The preacher hit him again on the other side. But this time the boy don't fall.

"That hasn't changed a thing," he say.

The preacher jest look at the boy. The preacher breathing real hard like he jest ran up a hill. The boy sit down and open his book again.

"I feel sorry for you," the preacher say. "I never felt so sorry for a man before."

The boy make 'tend he don't even hear that preacher. He keep on reading his book. The preacher go back and get his hat off the chair.

"Excuse me," he say to us. "I'll come back some other time. Y'all please excuse me."

And he look at the boy and go out of the room. The boy hist his hand up to his mouth one time, to wipe 'way some blood. All the rest o' the time he keep on reading.

VIII

THE LADY and her little boy come out the dentist, and the nurse call somebody else in. Then little bit later they come out, and the nurse call another name. But fast's she call somebody in there, somebody else come in the place where we at, and the room stay full.

The people coming in now, all of 'em wearing big coats. One of 'em say something 'bout sleeting, and another one say he hope not. Another one say he think it ain't nothing but rain. 'Cause, he say, rain can get awful cold this time o' year.

All 'cross the room they talking. Some of 'em talking to people right by 'em, some of 'em talking to people clear 'cross the room, some of 'em talking to anybody'll listen. It's a little bitty room, no bigger 'an us kitchen, and I can see ever'body in there. The little old room's full of smoke, 'cause you got two old men smoking pipes. I think I feel my teef thumping me some, and I hold my breath and wait. I wait and wait, but it don't thump me no more. Thank God for that.

I feel like going to sleep, and I lean back 'gainst the wall. But I'm scared to go to sleep: Scared 'cause the nurse might call my name and I won't hear her. And Mama might go to sleep, too, and she be mad if neither of us heard the nurse.

I look up at Mama. I love my mama. I love my mama. And when cotton come I'm go'n get her a newer coat. And I ain't go'n get a black one neither. I think I'm go'n get her a red one.

"They got some books over there," I say. "Want read one of 'em?"

Mama look at the books, but she don't answer me.

"You got yourself a little man there," the lady say.

Mama don't say nothing to the lady, but she must 'a' grin a little bit, 'cause I seen the lady grinning back. The lady look at me a little while, like she's feeling sorry for me.

"You sure got that preacher out here in a hurry," she say to that other boy.

The boy look up at her and look in his book again. When I grow up I want to be jest like him. I want clothes like that and I want to keep a book with me, too.

"You really don't believe in God?" the lady say.

"No," he say.

"But why?" the lady say.

"Because the wind is pink," he say.

"What?" the lady say.

The boy don't answer her no more. He jest read in his book.

"Talking 'bout the wind is pink," that old lady say. She sitting on the same bench with the boy, and she trying to look in his face. The boy make 'tend the old lady ain't even there. He jest keep reading. "Wind is pink," she say again. "Eh, Lord, what children go'n be saying next?"

The lady 'cross from us bust out laughing.

"That's a good one," she say. "The wind is pink. Yes, sir, that's a good one."

"Don't you believe the wind is pink?" the boy say. He keep his head down in the book.

"'Course I believe it, honey," the lady say. "'Course I do." She look at us and wink her eye. "And what color is grass, honey?"

"Grass? Grass is black."

She bust out laughing again. The boy look at her.

"Don't you believe grass is black?" he say.

The lady quit laughing and look at him. Ever'body else look at him now, the place quiet, quiet.

"Grass is green, honey," the lady say. "It was green yesterday, it's green today, and it's go'n be green tomorrow."

"How do you know it's green?"

"I know because I know."

"You don't know it's green. You believe it's green because someone told you it was green. If someone had told you it was black you'd believe it was black."

"It's green," the lady say. "I know green when I see green."

"Prove it's green."

"Surely, now," the lady say. "Don't tell me it's coming to that?"

"It's coming to just that," the boy say. "Words mean nothing. One means no more than the other."

"That's what it all coming to?" that old lady say. That old lady got on a turban and she got on two sweaters. She got a green sweater under a black sweater. I can see the green sweater 'cause some of the buttons on the other sweater missing.

"Yes, ma'am," the boy say. "Words mean nothing. Action is the only thing. Doing. That's the only thing."

"Other words, you want the Lord to come down here and show Hisself to you?" she say.

"Exactly, ma'am."

"You don't mean that, I'm sure?"

"I do, ma'am."

"Done, Jesus," the old lady say, shaking her head.

"I didn't go 'long with that preacher at first," the other lady say, "but now — I don't know. When a person say the grass is black, he's either a lunatic or something wrong."

"Prove to me that it's green."

"It's green because people say it's green."

"Those same people say we're citizens of the United States."

"I think I'm a citizen."

"Citizens have certain rights. Name me one right that you have. One right, granted by the Constitution, that you can exercise in Bayonne."

The lady didn't answer him. She jest look at him like she don't know what he talking 'bout. I know I don't.

"Things changing," she say.

"Things are changing because some black men have begun to follow their brains instead of their hearts."

"You trying to say those people don't believe in God?"

"I'm sure some of them do. Maybe most of them do. But they don't believe that God is going to touch these white people's hearts and change them tomorrow. Things change through action. By no other way."

Ever'body sit quiet and look at the boy. Nobody say a thing. Then the lady 'cross from me and Mama jest shake her head.

"Let's hope that not all your generation feel the same way you do," she say.

"Think what you please, it doesn't matter," the boy say. "But it will be men who listen to their heads and not their hearts who see that your children have a better chance than you had."

"Let's hope they ain't all like you, though," the old lady say. "Done forgot the heart absolutely."

"Yes, ma'am, I hope they aren't all like me," the boy say. "Unfortunately, I was born too late to believe in your God. Let's hope that the ones who come after will have your faith — if not in your God, then in something else, something definitely that they can lean on. I haven't anything. For me, the wind is pink, the grass is black."

IX

THE NURSE COME in the room where us all sitting and waiting and say the doctor won't take no more patients till one o'clock this evening. My mama jump up off the bench and go up to the white lady.

"Nurse, I have to go back in the field this evening," she say.

"The doctor is treating his last patient now," the nurse say. "One o'clock this evening."

"Can I at least speak to the doctor?" my mama say.

"I'm his nurse," the lady say.

"My little boy sick," my mama say. "Right now his teef almost killing him."

The nurse look at me. She trying to make up her mind if to let me come in. I look at her real pitiful. The teef ain't hurting me a tall, but Mama says it is, so I make 'tend for her sake.

"This evening," the nurse say, and go back in the office.

"Don't feel 'jected, honey," the lady say to Mama. "I been 'round 'em a long time — they take you when they want to. If you was white, that's something else; but you the wrong shade."

Mama don't say nothing to the lady, and me and her go outside and stand 'gainst the wall. It's cold out there. I can feel that wind going through my coat. Some of the other people come out of the room and go up the street. Me and Mama stand there a little while and start to walking. I don't know where us going. When us come to the other street us jest stand there.

"You don't have to make water, do you?" Mama say.

"No, ma'am," I say.

Us go up the street. Walking real slow, I can tell Mama don't know where she going. When us come to a store us stand there and look at the dummies. I look at a little boy with a brown over-coat. He got on brown shoes, too. I look at my old shoes and look at his'n again. You wait till summer, I say.

Me and Mama walk away. Us come up to another store and us stop and look at them dummies, too. Then us go again. Us pass a cafe where the white people in there eating. Mama tell me keep my eyes in front where they blonks, but I can't help from seeing them people eat. My stomach start to growling 'cause I'm hungry. When I see people eating, I get hungry; when I see a coat, I get cold.

A man whistle at my mama when us go by a filling station. She make 'tend she don't even see him. I look back and I feel like hitting him in the mouth. If I was bigger, I say. If I was bigger, you see.

Us keep on going. I'm getting colder and colder, but I don't say nothing. I feel that stuff running down my nose and I sniff.

"That rag," she say.

I git it out and wipe my nose. I'm getting cold all over now — my face, my hands, my feet, ever'thing. Us pass another little cafe, but this'n for white people, too, and us can't go in there neither. So us jest walk. I'm so cold now, I'm 'bout ready to say it. If I knowed where us going, I wouldn't be so cold, but I don't know where us going. Us go, us go, us go. Us walk clean out o' Bayonne. Then us cross the street and us come back. Same thing I seen when I got off the bus. Same old trees, same old walk, same old weeds, same old cracked pave — same old ever'thing.

I sniff again.

"That rag," she say.

I wipe my nose real fast and jug that hankercher back in my pocket 'fore my hand get too cold. I raise my head and I can see David hardware store. When us come up to it, us go in. I don't know why, but I'm glad.

It warm in there. It so warm in there you don't want ever leave. I look for the heater, and I see it over by them ba'ls. Three white men standing 'round the heater talking in Creole. One of 'em come to see what Mama wanted.

"Got any ax handle?" she say.

Me, Mama, and the white man start to the back, but Mama stop me when us come to the heater. Her and the white man go on. I hold my hand over the heater and look at 'em. They go all the way in the back, and I see the white man point to the ax handle 'gainst the wall. Mama take one of 'em and shake it like she trying to figure how much it weigh. Then she rub her hand over it from one end to the other end. She turn it over and look at the other side, then she shake it again, and shake her head and put it back. She get another one and she do it jest like she did the first one, then she shake her head. Then she get a brown one and do it that, too. But she don't like this one neither. Then she get another one, but 'fore she shake it or anything, she look at me. Look like she trying to say something to me, but I don't know what it is. All I know is I done got warm now and I'm feeling right smart better. Mama shake this ax handle jest like she done the others, and shake her head and say something to the white man. The white man jest look at his pile of ax handle, and when Mama pass by him to come to the front, the white man jest scratch his head and follow her. She tell me come on, and us go on out and start walking again.

Us walk and walk, and no time at all I'm cold again. Look like I'm colder now 'cause I can still remember how good it was back there. My stomach growl and I suck it in to keep Mama from yering it. She walking right 'side me, and it growl so loud you can yer it a mile. But Mama don't say a word.

X

WHEN US COME UP to the courthouse, I look at the clock. It got quarter to twelve. Mean us got another hour and a quarter to be out yer in the cold. Us go and stand side a building. Something hit my cap and I look up at the sky. Sleet falling.

I look at Mama standing there. I want stand close 'side her, but she don't like that. She say that's crybaby stuff. She say you got to stand for yourself, by yourself.

"Let's go back to that office," she say.

Us cross the street. When us get to the dentist I try to open the door, but I can't. Mama push me on the side and she twist the knob. But she can't open it neither. She twist it some more, harder, but she can't open it. She turn 'way from the door. I look at her, but I don't move and I don't say nothing. I done seen her like this before and I'm scared.

"You hungry?" she say. She say it like she mad at me, like I'm the one cause of ever'thing.

"No, ma'am," I say.

"You want eat and walk back, or you rather don't eat and ride?"

"I ain't hungry," I say.

I ain't jest hungry, but I'm cold too. I'm so hungry and I'm so cold I want to cry. And look like I'm getting colder and colder. My feet done got numb. I try to work my toes, but I can't. Look like I'm go'n die. Look like I'm go'n stand right here and freeze to death. I think about Val and Auntie and Ty and Louis and Walker. It 'bout twelve o'clock and I know they eating dinner. I can hear Ty making jokes. That's Ty. Always trying to make some kind o' joke. I wish I was right there listening to him. Give anything in the world if I was home 'round the fire.

"Come on," Mama say.

Us start walking again. My feet so numb I can't hardly feel 'em. Us turn the corner and go back up the street. The clock start hitting for twelve.

The sleet's coming down plenty now. They hit the pave and bounce like rice. Oh, Lord; oh, Lord, I pray. Don't let me die. Don't let me die. Don't let me die, Lord.

XI

Now I know where us going. Us going back o' town where the colored people eat. I don't care if I don't eat. I been hungry before. I can stand it. But I can't stand the cold.

I can see us go'n have a long walk. It 'bout a mile down there. But I don't mind. I know when I get there I'm go'n warm myself. I think I can hold out. My hands numb in my pockets and my feet numb, too, but if I keep moving I can hold out. Jest don't stop no more, that's all.

The sky's gray. The sleet keep falling. Falling like rain now — plenty, plenty. You can hear it hitting the pave. You can see it bouncing. Sometime it bounce two times 'fore it settle.

Us keep going. Us don't say nothing. Us jest keep going. Keep going.

I wonder what Mama thinking. I hope she ain't mad with me. When summer come I'm go'n pick plenty cotton and get her a coat. I'm go'n get her a red one.

I hope they make it summer all the time. I be glad if it was summer all the time — but it ain't. Us got to have winter, too. Lord, I hate the winter. I guess ever'body hates the winter.

I don't sniff this time. I get out my hankercher and wipe my nose. My hand so cold I can hardly hold the hankercher.

I think us getting close, but us ain't there yet. I wonder where ever'body is. Can't see nobody but us. Look like us the only two people moving 'round today. Must be too cold for the rest of the people to move 'round.

I can hear my teefs. I hope they don't knock together too hard and make that bad one hurt. Lord, that's all I need, for that bad one to start off.

I hear a church bell somewhere. But today ain't Sunday. They must be ringing for a funeral or something.

I wonder what they doing at home. They must be eating. Monsieur Bayonne might be there with his guitar. One day Ty played with Monsieur Bayonne guitar and broke one o' the string. Monsieur Bayonne got some mad with Ty. He say Ty ain't go'n never mount to nothing. Ty can go jest like him when he ain't there. Ty can make ever'body laugh mocking Monsieur Bayonne.

I used to like to be with Mama and Daddy. Us used to be happy. But they took him in the Army. Now, nobody happy no more....I be glad when he come back.

Monsieur Bayonne say it wasn't fair for 'em to take Daddy and to give Mama nothing and give us nothing. Auntie say, Shhh, Etienne. Don't let 'em yer you talk like that. Monsieur Bayonne say, it's God truth. What they giving his children? They have to walk three and a half mile to school, hot or cold. That's anything to give for a paw? She got to work in the field, rain or shine jest to make ends meet. That's anything to give for a husband? Auntie say, Shhh, Etienne, shhh. Yes, you right, Monsieur Bayonne say. Best don't say it in front of 'em now. But one day they go'n find out. One day. Yes, s'pose so, Auntie say. Then what, Rose Mary? Monsieur Bayonne say. I don't know, Etienne, Auntie say. All us can do is us job, and leave ever'thing else in His hand....

Us getting closer now. Us getting closer. I can see the railroad tracks.

Us cross the tracks, and now I see the cafe. Jest to get in there, I say. Jest to get in there. Already I'm starting to feel little better.

XII

US GO IN. Ahh, it good. I look for the heater; there 'gainst the wall. One of them little brown ones. I jest stand there and hold my hand over it. I can't open my hands too wide 'cause they almost froze.

Mama standing right 'side me. She done unbuttoned her coat. Smoke rise out the coat, and the coat smell like a wet dog.

I move to the side so Mama can have more room. She open out her hands and rub 'em together. I rub mine together, too, 'cause this keeps 'em from hurting. If you let 'em warm too fast, they hurt you sure. But if you let 'em warm jest little bit at a time, and you keep rubbing 'em, they be all right ever' time.

They got jest two more people in the cafe. A lady back o' the counter, and a man on this side the counter. They been watching us ever since us came in.

Mama get out the hankercher and count the money. Both o' us know how much money she got there. Three dollars. No, she ain't got three dollars. 'Cause she had to pay us way up here. She ain't got but two dollars and a half left. Dollar and a half to get my teef pulled, and fifty cents for us to go back on, and fifty cents worse o' salt meat.

She stir the money 'round with her finger. Most o' the money is change 'cause I can hear it rubbing together. She stir it and stir it. Then she look at the door. It still sleeting. I can yer it hitting 'gainst the wall like rice.

"I ain't hungry, Mama," I say.

"Got to pay 'em something for they heat," she say.

She take a quarter out the hankercher and tie the hankercher up again. She look over her shoulder at the people, but she still don't move. I hope she don't spend the money. I don't want her spend it on me. I'm hungry, I'm almost starving I'm so hungry, but I don't want her spending the money on me.

She flip the quarter over like she thinking. She must be thinking 'bout us walking back home. Lord, I sure don't want walk home. If I thought it done any good to say something, I say it. But my mama make up her own mind.

She turn way from the heater right fast, like she better hurry up and do it 'fore she change her mind. I turn to look at her go to the counter. The man and the lady look at her, too. She tell the lady something and the lady walk away. The man keep on looking at her. Her back turn to the man, and Mama don't even know he standing there.

The lady put some cakes and a glass o' milk on the counter. Then she pour up a cup o' coffee and set it side the other stuff. Mama pay her for the things and come back where I'm at. She tell me sit down at that table 'gainst the wall.

The milk and the cakes for me. The coffee for my mama. I eat slow, and I look at her. She looking outside at the sleet. She looking real sad. I say to myself, I'm go'n make all this up one day. You see, one day, I'm go'n make all this up. I want to say it now. I want to tell how I feel right now. But Mama don't like for us to talk like that.

"I can't eat all this," I say.

They got jest three little cakes there. And I'm so hungry right now, the Lord know I can eat a hundred times three. But I want her to have one.

She don't even look my way. She know I'm hungry. She know I want it. I let it stay there a while, then I get it and eat it. I eat jest on my front teefs, 'cause if it tech that back teef I know what'll happen. Thank God it ain't hurt me a tall today.

After I finish eating I see the man go to the juke box. He drop a nickel in it, then he stand there looking at the record. Mama tell me keep my eyes in front where they blonks. I turn my head like she say, but then I yer the man coming towards us.

"Dance, pretty?" he say.

Mama get up to dance with him. But 'fore you know it, she done grabbed the little man and done throwed him 'side the wall. He hit the wall so hard he stop the juke box from playing.

"Some pimp," the lady back o' the counter say. "Some pimp."

The little man jump up off the floor and start towards my mama. 'Fore you know it, Mama done sprung open her knife and she waiting for him.

"Come on," she say. "Come on. I'll cut you from your neighbo to your throat. Come on."

I go up to the little man to hit him, but Mama make me come and stand 'side her. The little man look at me and Mama and go back to the counter.

"Some pimp," the lady back o' the counter say. "Some pimp," She start laughing and pointing at the little man. "Yes, sir, you a pimp, all right. Yes, sir."

XIII

"FASTEN THAT COAT. Let's go," Mama say.

"You don't have to leave," the lady say.

Mama don't answer the lady, and us right out in the cold again.

I'm warm right now — my hands, my yers, my feet — but I know this ain't go'n last too long. It done sleet so much now you got ice ever'where.

Us cross the railroad tracks, and soon's us do, I get cold. That wind go through this little old coat like it ain't nothing. I got a shirt and a sweater under it, but that wind don't pay 'em no mind. I look up and I can see us got a long way to go. I wonder if us go'n make it 'fore I get too cold.

Us cross over to walk on the sidewalk. They got jest one sidewalk back here. It's over there.

After us go jest a little piece, I smell bread cooking. I look, then I see a baker shop. When us get closer, I can smell it more better. I shet my eyes and make 'tend I'm eating. But I keep 'em shet too long and I butt up 'gainst a telephone post. Mama grab me and see if I'm hurt. I ain't bleeding or nothing and she turn me loose.

I can feel I'm getting colder and colder, and I look up to see how far us still got to go. Uptown is 'way up yonder. A half mile, I reckoned. I try to think of something. They say think and you won't get cold. I think of that poem "Annabel Lee." I ain't been to school in so long — this bad weather — I reckoned they done passed "Annabel Lee." But passed it or not, I'm sure Miss Walker go'n make me recite it when I get there. That woman don't never forget nothing. I ain't never seen nobody like that.

I'm still getting cold. Annabel Lee or no Annabel Lee, I'm still getting cold. But I can see us getting closer. Us getting there, gradually.

Soon's us turn the corner, I see a little old white lady up in front o' us. She the only lady on the street. She all in black and she got a long black rag over her head.

"Stop," she say.

Me and Mama stop and look at her. She must be crazy to be out in all this sleet. Ain't got but a few other people out there, and all of 'em men.

"Y'all done ate?" she say.

"Jest finished," Mama say.

"Y'all must be cold then?" she say.

"Us headed for the dentist," Mama say. "Us'll warm up when us get there."

"What dentist?" the old lady say. "Mr. Bassett?"

"Yes, ma'am," Mama say.

"Come on in," the old lady say. "I'll telephone him and tell him y'all coming."

Me and Mama follow the old lady in the store. It's a little bitty store, and it don't have much in there. The old lady take off her headpiece and fold it up.

"Helena?" somebody call from the back.

"Yes, Alnest?" the old lady say.

"Did you see them?"

"They're here. Standing beside me."

"Good. Now you can stay inside."

The old lady look at Mama. Mama waiting to hear what she brought us in here for. I'm waiting for that, too.

"I saw y'all each time you went by," she say. "I came out to catch you, but you were gone."

"Us went back 'o town," Mama say.

"Did you eat?"

"Yes, ma'am."

The old lady look at Mama a long time, like she thinking Mama might be jest saying that. Mama look right back at her. The old lady look at me to see what I got to say. I don't say nothing. I sure ain't going 'gainst my mama.

"There's food in the kitchen," she say to Mama. "I've been keeping it warm."

Mama turn right around and start for the door.

"Just a minute," the old lady say. Mama stop. "The boy'll have to work for it. It isn't free."

"Us don't take no handout," Mama say.

"I'm not handing out anything," the old lady say. "I need my garbage moved to the front. Ernest has a bad cold and can't go out there."

"James'll move it for you," Mama say.

"Not unless you eat," the old lady say. "I'm old, but I have pride too, you know."

Mama can see she ain't go'n beat this old lady down, so she jest shake her head.

"All right," the old lady say. "Come into the kitchen."

She lead the way with that rag in her hand. The kitchen is a little bitty little thing, too. The table and the stove jest about fill it up.

They got a little room to the side. Somebody in there laying 'cross the bed. Must be the person she was talking about: Alnest or Ernest—I forgot what she call him.

"Sit down," the old lady say to Mama. "Not you," she say to me. "You have to move the cans."

"Helena?" somebody say in the other room.

"Yes, Alnest?" the old lady say.

"Are you going out there again?"

"I must show the boy where the garbage is," the old lady say.

"Keep that shawl over your head," the old man say.

"You don't have to remind me. Come, boy," the old lady say.

Us go out in the yard. Little old back yard ain't no bigger 'an the store or the kitchen. But it can sleet here jest like it can sleet in any big back yard. And 'fore you know it I'm trembling.

"There," the old lady say, pointing to the cans. I pick up one of the cans. The can so light I put it back down to look inside o' it.

"Here," the old lady say. "Leave that cap alone."

I look at her in the door. She got that black rag wrapped 'round her shoulders, and she pointing one of her fingers at me.

"Pick it up and carry it to the front," she say. I go by her with the can. I'm sure the thing's empty. She could 'a' carried the thing by herself, I'm sure. "Set it on the sidewalk by the door and come back for the other one," she say.

I go and come back, Mama look at me when I pass her. I get the other can and take it to the front. It don't feel no heavier 'an the other one. I tell myself to look inside and see jest what I been hauling. First, I look up and down the street. Nobody coming. Then I look over my shoulder. Little old lady done slipped there jest 's quiet 's mouse, watching me. Look like she knowed I was go'n try that.

"Eh, Lord," she say. "Children, children. Come in here, boy, and go wash your hands."

I follow her into the kitchen, and she point, and I go to the bathroom. When I come out, the old lady done dished up the food. Rice, gravy, meat, and she even got some lettuce and tomato in a saucer. She even got a glass o' milk and a piece o' cake there, too. It look so good. I almost start eating 'fore I say my blessing.

"Helena?" the old man say.

"Yes, Alnest?" she say.

"Are they eating?"

"Yes," she say.

"Good," he say. "Now you'll stay inside."

The old lady go in there where he is and I can hear 'em talking. I look at Mama. She eating slow like she thinking. I wonder what's the matter now. I reckoned she think 'bout home.

The old lady come back in the kitchen.

"I talked to Dr. Bassett's nurse," she say. "Dr. Bassett take you as soon as you get there."

"Thank you, ma'am," Mama say.

"Perfectly all right," the old lady say. "Which one is it?"

Mama nods towards me. The old lady look at me real sad. I look sad, too.

"You're not afraid, are you?" she say.

"No'm," I say.

"That's a good boy," the old lady say. "Nothing to be afraid of."

When me and Mama get through eating, us thank the old lady again.

"Helena, are they leaving?" the old man say.

"Yes, Alnest."

"Tell them I say good-by."

"They can hear you, Alnest."

"Good-by both mother and son," the old man say. "And may God be with you."

Me and Mama tell the old man good-by, and us follow the old lady in the front. Mama open the door to go out, but she stop and come back in the store.

"You sell salt meat?" she say.

"Yes."

"Give me two bits worth."

"That isn't very much salt meat," the old lady say.

"That's all I have," Mama say.

The old lady go back o' the counter and cut a big piece off the chunk. Then she wrap it and put it in a paper bag.

"Two bits," she say.

"That look like awful lot of meat for a quarter," Mama say.

"Two bits," the old lady say. "I've been selling salt meat behind this counter twenty-five years. I think I know what I'm doing."

"You got a scale there," Mama say.

"What?" the old lady say.

"Weigh it," Mama say.

"What?" the old lady say. "Are you telling me how to run my business?"

"Thanks very much for the food," Mama say.

"Just a minute," the old lady say.

"James," Mama say to me. I move towards the door.

"Just one minute, I said," the old lady say.

Me and Mama stop again and look at her. The old lady take the meat out of the bag and unwrap it and cut 'bout half o' it off. Then she wrap it up again and jug it back in the bag and give it to Mama. Mama lay the quarter on the counter.

"Your kindness will never be forgotten," she say. "James," she say to me.

Us go out, and the old lady come to the door to look at us. After us go a little piece I look back, and she still there watching us.

The sleet's coming down heavy, heavy now, and I turn up my collar to keep my neck warm. My mama tell me turn it right back down.

"You not a bum," she say. "You a man."

Flannery O'Connor

EVERYTHING THAT RISES

MUST CONVERGE

Her doctor had told Julian's mother that she must lose twenty pounds on account of her blood pressure, so on Wednesday nights Julian had to take her downtown on the bus for a reducing class at the Y. The reducing class was designed for working girls over fifty, who weighed from 165 to 200 pounds. His mother was one of the slimmer ones, but she said ladies did not tell their age or weight. She would not ride the buses by herself at night since they had been integrated, and because the reducing class was one of her few pleasures, necessary for her health, and *free,* she said Julian could at least put himself out to take her, considering all she did for him. Julian did not like to consider all she did for him, but every Wednesday night he braced himself and took her.

She was almost ready to go, standing before the hall mirror, putting on her hat, while he, his hands behind him, appeared pinned to the door frame, waiting like Saint Sebastian for the arrows to begin piercing him. The hat was new and had cost her seven dollars and a half. She kept saying, "Maybe I shouldn't have paid that for it. No, I shouldn't have. I'll take it off and return it tomorrow. I shouldn't have bought it."

Julian raised his eyes to heaven. "Yes, you should have bought it," he said. "Put it on and let's go." It was a hideous hat. A purple velvet flap came down on one side of it and stood up on the other;

the rest of it was green and looked like a cushion with the stuffing out. He decided it was less comical than jaunty and pathetic. Everything that gave her pleasure was small and depressed him.

She lifted the hat one more time and set it down slowly on top of her head. Two wings of gray hair protruded on either side of her florid face, but her eyes, sky-blue, were as innocent and untouched by experience as they must have been when she was ten. Were it not that she was a widow who had struggled fiercely to feed and clothe and put him through school and who was supporting him still, "until he got on his feet," she might have been a little girl that he had to take to town.

"It's all right, it's all right," he said. "Let's go." He opened the door himself and started down the walk to get her going. The sky was a dying violet and the houses stood out darkly against it, bulbous liver-colored monstrosities of a uniform ugliness though no two were alike. Since this had been a fashionable neighborhood forty years ago, his mother persisted in thinking they did well to have an apartment in it. Each house had a narrow collar of dirt around it in which sat, usually, a grubby child. Julian walked with his hands in his pockets, his head down and thrust forward and his eyes glazed with the determination to make himself completely numb during the time he would be sacrificed to her pleasure.

The door closed and he turned to find the dumpy figure, surmounted by the atrocious hat, coming toward him. "Well," she said, "you only live once and paying a little more for it, I at least won't meet myself coming and going."

"Some day I'll start making money," Julian said gloomily — he knew he never would — "and you can have one of those jokes whenever you take the fit." But first they would move. He visualized a place where the nearest neighbors would be three miles away on either side.

"I think you're doing fine," she said, drawing on her gloves. "You've only been out of school a year. Rome wasn't built in a day."

She was one of the few members of the Y reducing class who arrived in hat and gloves and who had a son who had been to college. "It takes time," she said, "and the world is in such a mess. This hat looked better on me than any of the others, though when she brought it out I said, 'Take that thing back. I wouldn't have it on my head,' and she said, 'Now wait till you see it on,' and when she put it on me, I said, 'We-ull,' and she said, 'If you ask me, that hat does something for you and you do something for the hat, and besides,' she said, 'with that hat, you won't meet yourself coming and going.'"

Julian thought he could have stood his lot better if she had been selfish, if she had been an old hag who drank and screamed at him. He walked along, saturated in depression, as if in the midst of his martyrdom he had lost his faith. Catching sight of his long, hopeless, irritated face, she stopped suddenly with a grief-stricken look, and pulled back on his arm. "Wait on me," she said. "I'm going back to the house and take this thing off and tomorrow I'm going to return it. I was out of my head. I can pay the gas bill with the seven-fifty."

He caught her arm in a vicious grip. "You are not going to take it back," he said. "I like it."

"Well," she said, "I don't think I ought…"

"Shut up and enjoy it," he muttered, more depressed than ever.

"With the world in the mess it's in," she said, "it's a wonder we can enjoy anything. I tell you, the bottom rail is on the top."

Julian sighed.

"Of course," she said, "if you know who you are, you can go anywhere." She said this every time he took her to the reducing class. "Most of them in it are not our kind of people," she said, "but I can be gracious to anybody. I know who I am."

"They don't give a damn for your graciousness," Julian said savagely. "Knowing who you are is good for one generation only. You haven't the foggiest idea where you stand now or who you are."

She stopped and allowed her eyes to flash at him. "I most certainly do know who I am," she said, "and if you don't know who you are, I'm ashamed of you."

"Oh hell," Julian said.

"Your great-grandfather was a former governor of this state," she said. "Your grandfather was a prosperous landowner. Your grandmother was a Godhigh."

"Will you look around you," he said tensely, "and see where you are now?" and he swept his arm jerkily out to indicate the neighborhood, which the growing darkness at least made less dingy.

"You remain what you are," she said. "Your great-grandfather had a plantation and two hundred slaves."

"There are no more slaves."

"They were better off when they were," she said. He groaned to see that she was off on that topic. She rolled onto it every few days like a train on an open track. He knew every stop, every junction, every swamp along the way, and knew the exact point at which her conclusion would roll majestically into the station: "It's ridiculous. It's simply not realistic. They should rise, yes, but on their own side of the fence."

"Let's skip it," Julian said.

"The ones I feel sorry for," she said, "are the ones that are half white. They're tragic."

"Will you skip it?"

"Suppose we were half white. We would certainly have mixed feelings."

"I have mixed feelings now," he groaned.

"Well let's talk about something pleasant," she said. "I remember going to Grandpa's when I was a little girl. Then the house had double stairways that went up to what was really the second floor — all the cooking was done on the first. I used to like to stay down in the kitchen on account of the way the walls smelled. I would sit with my nose pressed against the plaster and take deep breaths. Actually the place belonged to the Godhighs but your grandfather Chestny paid the mortgage and saved it for them. They were in reduced circumstances," she said, "but reduced or not, they never forgot who they were."

"Doubtless that decayed mansion reminded them," Julian muttered. He never spoke of it without contempt or thought of it without longing. He had seen it once when he was a child before it had been sold. The double stairways had rotted and been torn down. Negroes were living in it. But it remained in his mind as his mother had known it. It appeared in his dreams regularly. He would stand on the wide porch, listening to the rustle of oak leaves, then wander through the high-ceilinged hall into the parlor that opened onto it and gaze at the worn rugs and faded draperies. It occurred to him that it was he, not she, who could have appreciated it. He preferred its threadbare elegance to anything he could name and it was because of it that all the neighborhoods they had lived in had been a torment to him — whereas she had hardly known the difference. She called her insensitivity "being adjustable."

"And I remember the old darky who was my nurse, Caroline. There was no better person in the world. I've always had a great respect for my colored friends," she said. "I'd do anything in the world for them and they'd…"

"Will you for God's sake get off that subject?" Julian said. When he got on a bus by himself, he made it a point to sit down beside a Negro, in reparation as it were for his mother's sins.

"You're mighty touchy tonight," she said. "Do you feel all right?"

"Yes I feel all right," he said. "Now lay off."

She pursed her lips. "Well, you certainly are in a vile humor," she observed. "I just won't speak to you at all."

They had reached the bus stop. There was no bus in sight and Julian, his hands still jammed in his pockets and his head thrust forward, scowled down the empty street. The frustration of having to wait on the bus as well as ride on it began to creep up his neck like a hot hand. The presence of his mother was borne in upon him as she gave a pained sigh. He looked at her bleakly. She was holding herself very erect under the preposterous hat, wearing it like a banner of her imaginary dignity. There was in him an evil urge to break her spirit. He suddenly unloosened his tie and pulled it off and put it in his pocket.

She stiffened. "Why must you look like that when you take me to town?" she said. "Why must you deliberately embarrass me?"

"If you'll never learn where you are," he said, "you can at last learn where I am."

"You look like a — thug," she said.

"Then I must be one," he murmured.

"I'll just go home," she said. "I will not bother you. If you can't do a little thing like that for me…"

Rolling his eyes upward, he put his tie back on. "Restored to my class," he muttered. He thrust his face toward her and hissed, "True culture is in the mind, the *mind*," he said, and tapped his head, "the mind."

"It's in the heart," she said, "and in how you do things and how you do things is because of who you *are*."

"Nobody in the damn bus cares who you are."

"I care who I am," she said icily.

The lighted bus appeared on top of the next hill and as it approached, they moved out into the street to meet it. He put his hand under her elbow and hoisted her up on the creaking step. She entered with a little smile, as if she were going into a drawing room where everyone had been waiting for her. While he put in the tokens, she sat down on one of the broad front seats for three which faced the aisle. A thin woman with protruding teeth and long yellow hair was sitting on the end of it. His mother moved up beside her and left room for Julian beside herself. He sat down and looked at the floor across the aisle where a pair of thin feet in red and white canvas sandals were planted.

His mother immediately began a general conversation meant to attract anyone who felt like talking. "Can it get any hotter?" she said and removed from her purse a folding fan, black with a Japanese scene on it, which she began to flutter before her.

"I reckon it might could," the woman with the protruding teeth said, "but I know for a fact my apartment couldn't get no hotter."

"It must get the afternoon sun," his mother said. She sat forward and looked up and down the bus. It was half filled. Everybody was white. "I see we have the bus to ourselves," she said. Julian cringed.

"For a change," said the woman across the aisle, the owner of the red and white canvas sandals. "I come on one the other day and they were thick as fleas — up front and all through."

"The world is in a mess everywhere," his mother said. "I don't know how we've let it get in this fix."

"What gets my goat is all those boys from good families stealing automobile tires," the woman with the protruding teeth said. "I told my boy, I said you may not be rich but you been raised right and if I ever catch you in any such mess, they can send you on to the reformatory. Be exactly where you belong."

"Training tells," his mother said. "Is your boy in high school?"

"Ninth grade," the woman said.

"My son just finished college last year. He wants to write but he's selling typewriters until he gets started," his mother said.

The woman leaned forward and peered at Julian. He threw her such a malevolent look that she subsided against the seat. On the floor across the aisle there was an abandoned newspaper. He got up and got it and opened it out in front of him. His mother discreetly continued the conversation in a lower tone but the woman across the aisle said in a loud voice, "Well that's nice. Selling typewriters is close to writing. He can go right from one to the other."

"I tell him," his mother said, "that Rome wasn't built in a day."

Behind the newspaper Julian was withdrawing into the inner compartment of his mind where he spent most of his time. This was a kind of mental bubble in which he established himself when he could not bear to be a part of what was going on around him. From it he could see out and judge but in it he was safe from any kind of penetration from without. It was the only place where he felt free of the general idiocy of his fellows. His mother had never entered it but from it he could see her with absolute clarity.

The old lady was clever enough and he thought that if she had started from any of the right premises, more might have been expected of her. She lived according to the laws of her own fantasy world, outside of which he had never seen her set foot. The law of it was to sacrifice herself for him after she had first created the necessity to do so by making a mess of things. If he had permitted her sacrifices, it was only because her lack of foresight had made them necessary. All of her life had been a struggle to act like a Chestny without the Chestny goods, and to give him everything she thought a Chestny ought to have; but since, said she, it was fun to struggle, why complain? And when you won, as she had won, what fun to look back on the hard times! He could not forgive her that she had enjoyed the struggle and that she thought *she* had won.

What she meant when she said she had won was that she had brought him up successfully and had sent him to college and that he had turned out so well — good looking (her teeth had gone unfilled so that his could be straightened), intelligent (he realized he was too intelligent to be a success), and with a future ahead of him (there was of course no future ahead of him). She excused his gloominess on the grounds that he was still growing up and his radical ideas on his lack of practical experience. She said he didn't yet know a thing about "life," that he hadn't even entered the real world — when already he was as disenchanted with it as a man of fifty.

The further irony of all this was that in spite of her, he had turned out so well. In spite of going to only a third-rate college, he had, on his own initiative, come out with a first-rate education; in spite of growing up dominated by a small mind, he had ended up with a large one; in spite of all her foolish views, he was free of prejudice and unafraid to face facts. Most miraculous of all, instead of being blinded by love for her as she was for him, he had cut himself emotionally free of her and could see her with complete objectivity. He was not dominated by his mother.

The bus stopped with a sudden jerk and shook him from his meditation. A woman from the back lurched forward with little steps and barely escaped falling in his newspaper as she righted herself. She got off and a large Negro got on. Julian kept his paper lowered to watch. It gave him a certain satisfaction to see injustice in daily operation. It confirmed his view that with few exceptions there was no one worth knowing within a radius of three hundred miles. The Negro was well dressed and carried a briefcase. He looked around and then sat down on the other end of the seat where the woman with the red and white canvas sandals was sitting. He immediately unfolded a newspaper and obscured himself behind it. Julian's mother's elbow at once prodded insistently into his ribs. "Now you see why I won't ride on these buses by myself," she whispered.

The woman with the red and white canvas sandals had risen at the same time the Negro sat down and had gone farther back in the bus and taken the seat of the woman who had got off. His mother leaned forward and cast her an approving look.

Julian rose, crossed the aisle, and sat down in the place of the woman with the canvas sandals. From this position, he looked serenely across at his mother. Her face had turned an angry red. He stared at her, making his eyes the eyes of a stranger. He felt his tension suddenly lift as if he had openly declared war on her.

He would have liked to get in conversation with the Negro and to talk with him about art or politics or any subject that would be above the comprehension of those around them, but the man remained entrenched behind his paper. He was either ignoring the change of seating or had never noticed it. There was no way for Julian to convey his sympathy.

His mother kept her eyes fixed reproachfully on his face. The woman with the protruding teeth was looking at him avidly as if he were a type of monster new to her.

"Do you have a light?" he asked the Negro.

Without looking away from his paper, the man reached in his pocket and handed him a packet of matches.

"Thanks," Julian said. For a moment he held the matches foolishly. A NO SMOKING sign looked down upon him from over the door. This alone would not have deterred him; he had no cigarettes. He had quit smoking some months before because he could not afford it. "Sorry," he muttered and handed back the matches. The Negro lowered the paper and gave him an annoyed look. He took the matches and raised the paper again.

His mother continued to gaze at him but she did not take advantage of his momentary discomfort. Her eyes retained their battered look. Her face seemed to be unnaturally red, as if her blood pressure had risen. Julian allowed no glimmer of sympathy to show on his face. Having got the advantage, he wanted desperately to keep it and carry it through. He would have liked to teach her a lesson that would last her a while, but there seemed no way to continue the point. The Negro refused to come out from behind his paper.

Julian folded his arms and looked stolidly before him, facing her but as if he did not see her, as if he had ceased to recognize her existence. He visualized a scene in which, the bus having reached their stop, he would remain in his seat and when she said, "Aren't you going to get off?" he would look at her as at a stranger who had rashly addressed him. The corner they got off on was usually deserted, but it was well lighted and it would not hurt her to walk by herself the four blocks to the Y. He decided to wait until the time came and then decide whether or not he would let her get off by herself. He would have to be at the Y by ten to bring her back, but he could leave her wondering if he was going to show up. There was no reason for her to think she could always depend on him.

He retired again into the high-ceilinged room sparsely settled with large pieces of antique furniture. His soul expanded momentarily but then he became aware of his mother across from him and the vision shriveled. He studied her coldly. Her feet in little pumps dangled like a child's and did not quite reach the floor. She was training on him an exaggerated look of reproach. He felt completely detached from her. At that moment he could with pleasure have slapped her as he would have slapped a particularly obnoxious child in his charge.

He began to imagine various unlikely ways by which he could teach her a lesson. He might make friends with some distinguished Negro professor or lawyer and bring him home to spend the evening. He would be entirely justified but her blood pressure would rise to 300. He could not push her to the extent of making her have a stroke, and moreover, he had never been successful at making any Negro friends. He had tried to strike up an acquaintance on the bus with some of the better types, with ones that looked like professors or ministers or lawyers. One morning he had sat down next to a distinguished-looking dark brown man who had answered his questions with a sonorous solemnity but who had turned out to be an undertaker. Another day he had sat down beside a cigar-smoking Negro with a diamond ring on his finger, but after a few stilted pleasantries, the Negro had rung the buzzer and risen, slipping two lottery tickets into Julian's hand as he climbed over him to leave

He imagined his mother lying desperately ill and his being able to secure only a Negro doctor for her. He toyed with that idea for a few minutes and then dropped it for a momentary vision of himself participating as a sympathizer in a sit-in demonstration. This was possible but he did not linger with it. Instead, he approached the ultimate horror. He brought home a beautiful suspiciously Negroid woman. Prepare yourself, he said. There is nothing you can do about it. This is the woman I've chosen. She's intelligent, dignified, even good, and she's suffered and she hasn't thought it *fun*. Now persecute us, go ahead and persecute us. Drive her out of here, but remember, you're driving me too. His eyes were narrowed and through the indignation he had generated, he saw his mother across the aisle, purple-faced, shrunken to the dwarf-like proportions of her moral nature, sitting like a mummy beneath the ridiculous banner of her hat.

He was tilted out of his fantasy again as the bus stopped. The door opened with a sucking hiss and out of the dark a large, gaily dressed, sullen-looking colored woman got on with a little boy. The child, who might have been four, had on a short plaid suit and a Tyrolean hat with a blue feather in it. Julian hoped that he would sit down beside him and that the woman would push in beside his mother. He could think of no better arrangement.

As she waited for her tokens, the woman was surveying the seating possibilities — he hoped with the idea of sitting where she was least wanted. There was something familiar-looking about her but Julian could not place what it was. She was a giant of a woman. Her face was set not only to meet opposition but to seek it out. The downward tilt of her large lower lip was like a warning sign: DON'T TAMPER WITH ME. Her bulging figure was encased in a green crepe dress and her feet overflowed in red shoes. She had on a hideous hat. A purple velvet flap came down on one side of it and stood up on the other; the rest of it was green and looked like a cushion with the stuffing out. She carried a mammoth red pocketbook that bulged throughout as if it were stuffed with rocks.

To Julian's disappointment, the little boy climbed up on the empty seat beside his mother. His mother lumped all children, black and white, into the common category, "cute," and she thought little Negroes were on the whole cuter than little white children. She smiled at the little boy as he climbed on the seat.

Meanwhile the woman was bearing down upon the empty seat beside Julian. To his annoyance, she squeezed herself into it. He saw his mother's face change as the woman settled herself next to him and he realized with satisfaction that this was more objectionable to her than it was to him. Her face seemed almost gray and there was a look of dull recognition in her eyes, as if suddenly she had sickened at some awful confrontation. Julian saw that it was because she and the woman had, in a sense, swapped sons. Though his mother would not realize the symbolic significance of this, she would feel it. His amusement showed plainly on his face.

The woman next to him muttered something unintelligible to herself. He was conscious of a kind of bristling next to him, muted growling like that of an angry cat. He could not see anything but the red pocketbook upright on the bulging green thighs. He visualized the woman as she had stood waiting for her tokens — the ponderous figure, rising from the red shoes upward over the solid hips, the mammoth bosom, the haughty face, to the green and purple hat.

His eyes widened.

The vision of the two hats, identical, broke upon him with the radiance of a brilliant sunrise. His face was suddenly lit with joy. He could not believe that Fate had thrust upon his mother such a lesson. He gave a loud chuckle so that she would look at him and see that he saw. She turned her eyes on him slowly. The blue in them seemed to have turned a bruised purple. For a moment he had an uncomfortable sense of her innocence, but it lasted only a second before principle rescued him. Justice entitled him to laugh. His grin hardened until it said to her as plainly as if he were saying aloud: Your punishment exactly fits your pettiness. This should teach you a permanent lesson.

Her eyes shifted to the woman. She seemed unable to bear looking at him and to find the woman preferable. He became conscious again of the bristling presence at his side. The woman was rumbling like a volcano about to become active. His mother's mouth began to twitch slightly at one corner. With a sinking heart, he saw incipient signs of recovery on her face and realized that this was going to strike her suddenly as funny and was going to be no lesson at all. She kept her eyes on the woman and an amused smile came over her face as if the woman were a monkey that had stolen her hat. The little Negro was looking up at her with large fascinated eyes. He had been trying to attract her attention for some time.

"Carver!" the woman said suddenly. "Come heah!"

When he saw that the spotlight was on him at last, Carver drew his feet up and turned himself toward Julian's mother and giggled.

"Carver!" the woman said. "You heah me? Come heah!"

Carver slid down from the seat but remained squatting with his back against the base of it, his head turned slyly around toward Julian's mother, who was smiling at him. The woman reached a hand across the aisle and snatched him to her. He righted himself and hung backwards on her knees, grinning at Julian's mother. "Isn't he cute?" Julian's mother said to the woman with the protruding teeth.

"I reckon he is," the woman said without conviction.

The Negress yanked him upright but he eased out of her grip and shot across the aisle and scrambled, giggling wildly, onto the seat beside his love.

"I think he likes me," Julian's mother said, and smiled at the woman. It was the smile she used when she was being particularly gracious to an inferior. Julian saw everything lost. The lesson had rolled off her like rain on a roof.

The woman stood up and yanked the little boy off the seat as if she were snatching him from contagion. Julian could feel the rage in her at having no weapon like his mother's smile. She gave the child a sharp slap across his leg. He howled once and then thrust his head into her stomach and kicked his feet against her shins. "Behave," she said vehemently.

The bus stopped and the Negro who had been reading the newspaper got off. The woman moved over and set the little boy down with a thump between herself and Julian. She held him firmly by the knee. In a moment he put his hands in front of his face and peeped at Julian's mother through his fingers.

"I see yooooooo!" she said and put her hand in front of her face and peeped at him.

The woman slapped his hand down. "Quit yo' foolishness," she said, "before I knock the living Jesus out of you!"

Julian was thankful that the next stop was theirs. He reached up and pulled the cord. The woman reached up and pulled it at the same time. Oh my God, he thought. He had the terrible intuition that when they got off the bus together, his mother would open her purse and give the little boy a nickel. The gesture would be as natural to her as breathing. The bus stopped and the woman got up and lunged to the front, dragging the child, who wished to stay on, after her. Julian and his mother got up and followed. As they neared the door, Julian tried to relieve her of her pocketbook.

"No," she murmured, "I want to give the little boy a nickel."

"No!" Julian hissed. "No!"

She smiled down at the child and opened her bag. The bus door opened and the woman picked him up by the arm and descended with him, hanging at her hip. Once in the street she set him down and shook him.

Julian's mother had to close her purse while she got down the bus step but as soon as her feet were on the ground, she opened it again and began to rummage inside. "I can't find but a penny," she whispered, "but it looks like a new one."

"Don't do it!" Julian said fiercely between his teeth. There was a streetlight on the corner and she hurried to get under it so that she could better see into her pocketbook. The woman was heading off rapidly down the street with the child still hanging backward on her hand.

"Oh little boy!" Julian's mother called and took a few quick steps and caught up with them just beyond the lamppost. "Here's a bright new penny for you," and she held out the coin, which shone bronze in the dim light.

The huge woman turned and for a moment stood, her shoulders lifted and her face frozen with frustrated rage, and stared at Julian's mother. Then all at once she seemed to explode like a piece of machinery that had been given one ounce of pressure too much. Julian saw the black fist swing out with the red pocketbook. He shut his eyes and cringed as he heard the woman shout, "He don't take nobody's pennies!" When he opened his eyes, the woman was disappearing down the street with the little boy staring wide-eyed over his shoulder. Julian's mother was sitting on the sidewalk.

"I told you not to do that," Julian said angrily. "I told you not to do that!"

He stood over her for a minute, gritting his teeth. Her legs were stretched out in front of her and her hat was on her lap. He squatted down and looked her in the face. It was totally expressionless. "You got exactly what you deserved," he said. "Now get up."

He picked up her pocketbook and put what had fallen out back in it. He picked the hat up off her lap. The penny caught his eye on the sidewalk and he picked that up and let it drop before her eyes into the purse. Then he stood up and leaned over and held his hands out to pull her up. She remained immobile. He sighed. Rising above them on either side were black apartment buildings, marked with irregular rectangles of light. At the end of the block a man came out of a door and walked off in the opposite direction. "All right," he said, "suppose somebody happens by and wants to know why you're sitting on the sidewalk?"

She took the hand and, breathing hard, pulled heavily up on it and then stood for a moment, swaying slightly as if the spots of light in the darkness were circling around her. Her eyes, shadowed and confused, finally settled on his face. He did not try to conceal his irritation. "I hope this teaches you a lesson," he said. She leaned forward and her eyes raked his face. She seemed trying to determine his identity. Then, as if she found nothing familiar about him, she started off with a headlong movement in the wrong direction.

"Aren't you going to the Y?" he asked.

"Home," she muttered.

"Well, are we walking?"

For answer she kept going. Julian followed along, his hands behind him. He saw no reason to let the lesson she had had go without backing it up with an explanation of its meaning. She might as well be made to understand what had happened to her. "Don't think that was just an uppity Negro woman," he said. "That was the whole colored race which will no longer take your condescending pennies. That was your black double. She can wear the same hat as you, and to be sure," he added gratuitously (because he thought it was funny), "it looked better on her than it did on you. What all this means," he said, "is that the old world is gone. The old manners are obsolete and your graciousness is not worth a damn." He thought bitterly of the house that had been lost for him. "You aren't who you think you are," he said.

She continued to plow ahead, paying no attention to him. Her hair had come undone on one side. She dropped her pocketbook and took no notice. He stooped and picked it up and handed it to her but she did not take it.

"You needn't act as if the world had come to an end," he said, "because it hasn't. From now on you've got to live in a new world and face a few realities for a change. Buck up," he said, "it won't kill you."

She was breathing fast.

"Let's wait on the bus," he said.

"Home," she said thickly.

"I hate to see you behave like this," he said. "Just like a child. I should be able to expect more of you." He decided to stop where he was and make her stop and wait for a bus. "I'm not going any farther," he said, stopping. "We're going on the bus."

She continued to go on as if she had not heard him. He took a few steps and caught her arm and stopped her. He looked into her face and caught his breath. He was looking into a face he had never seen before. "Tell Grandpa to come get me," she said.

He stared, stricken.

"Tell Caroline to come get me," she said.

Stunned, he let her go and she lurched forward again, walking as if one leg were shorter than the other. A tide of darkness seemed to be sweeping her from him. "Mother!" he cried. "Darling, sweetheart, wait!" Crumpling, she fell to the pavement. He dashed forward and fell at her side, crying, "Mamma, Mamma!" He turned her over. Her face was fiercely distorted. One eye, large and staring, moved slightly to the left as if it had become unmoored. The other remained fixed on him, raked his face again, found nothing and closed.

"Wait here, wait here!" he cried and jumped up and began to run for help toward a cluster of lights he saw in the distance ahead of him. "Help, help!" he shouted, but his voice was thin, scarcely a thread of sound. The lights drifted farther away the faster he ran and his feet moved numbly as if they carried him nowhere. The tide of darkness seemed to sweep him back to her, postponing from moment to moment his entry into the world of guilt and sorrow.

James Purdy

ENCORE

"HE'S IN THAT Greek restaurant every night. I thought you knew that," Merta told her brother.

"What does he do in it?" Spence said, wearily attentive.

"I don't go to Greek restaurants and I don't spy on him," she said.

"Then how do you know so certainly he is there every night?"

"How do you know anything? He's not popular at the college. He says he likes to talk to Spyro, the restaurant owner's son, about painting. I don't know what they do!"

"Well, don't tell me if you don't know," her brother said. He got up and took his hat to go.

"Of course," she continued, anxiously stepping in front of him to detain his going, "it isn't so much that Spyro is all at fault, you know. There are things wrong with Gibbs, too. As I said, he's not popular at the college. He wasn't asked to join a fraternity, you know. And the restaurant has made up for that, I suppose. It's always open for him day or night."

"Maybe you should make your own home more of a place he could bring his friends to," Spence said, a kind of cold expressionless tone in his voice.

"You would say that," she repeated almost without emotion. "I don't suppose you ever half considered what it is, I mean this home. It's not a home. It's a flat, and I'm a woman without a husband."

"I know, I know, Merta. You've done it all alone. Nobody's lifted a finger but you." His weariness itself seemed to collapse when he said this, and he looked at her with genuine feeling.

"I'm not trying to get your pity. I wanted to tell somebody what was going on at Spyro's is all. I needed to talk to somebody."

"I think Spyro's is the best place he could go," Spence said.

"And Spyro's awful father and grandfather!" she cried as though seeing something from far back of dread and ugliness.

"The Matsoukases?" Spence was surprised at her vehemence.

"Yes, the Matsoukases! With their immense eyes and black beards. Old Mr. Matsoukas, the grandfather, came here one evening, and tried to get fresh with me."

"I can hardly believe it," Spence said.

"You mean I am making it up," she accused him.

"No, no, I just can't visualize it."

"And now," she returned to the only subject which interested her, "Gibbs is there all the time as though it was his home."

"Do you talk to him about it, Merta?"

"I can't. I can't tell him and nag him about not going to the Greek restaurant at night. It's glamor and life to him, I suppose, and I suppose it *is* different. A different sort of place. The old man hasn't allowed them to put in juke boxes or television or anything, and you know Gibbs likes anything funny or different, and there isn't anything funny or different but maybe Spyro's. None of the college crowd goes there, and Gibbs feels he's safe there from their criticism and can drink his coffee in peace."

"Well it sounds so dull, drinking coffee in a seedy Greek restaurant, I don't see why a mother should worry about her son going there. And call me out of bed to talk about it!"

"Oh Spence," she said urgently again, "he shouldn't go there. Don't you see? He shouldn't be there."

"I don't see that at all," Spence said. "And, Merta, I wish you would quit calling me up at this hour of the night to talk about your son, who is nearly a grown man by now. After all I have my profession to worry about too...."

She stared at him.

"I had to talk with somebody about Spyro," she said.

"Oh, it's Spyro then you wanted to talk about," Spence said, the irritation growing in his manner.

"Spyro," she said vaguely, as though it were Spence who himself had mentioned him and thus brought him to mind. "I never cared much for that young man."

"Why not?" Spence was swift to hold her to anything vague and indirect because he felt that vagueness and indirectness was her method.

"Well, Spyro does all those paintings and drawings that are so bizarre."

"Bizarre," he paused on the word. "They're nearly *good*, if you ask me."

"I don't like Spyro," she said.

"Why don't you invite him here, if your son likes him?" he put the whole matter in her hands.

"When I work in a factory all day long, Spence...."

"You don't feel like doing anything but working in a factory," he said irritably.

"I thought my own brother would be a little more understanding," she said coldly angry.

"I wish you would be of Gibbs," he told her.

"Oh Spence, please, please."

"Please, nothing. You always have a problem, but the problem is you, Merta. You're old and tired and complaining, and because you can't put your finger on what's wrong you've decided that there's something wrong with your son because he goes, of all places, to a Greek restaurant and talks to Spyro who draws rather well and who is now making a portrait of your son."

"Spence! Don't tell me that!"

"You dear old fool, Merta," he said and he put on his hat now, which she looked at, he thought, rather critically and also with a certain envy.

"That's a nice hat," she forced herself to say at last.

"Well a doctor can't look like a nobody," he said, and then winced at his own words.

"What you should do, Merta," he hurried on with another speech, "is get some sort of hobby, become a lady bowler, get on the old women's curling team, or meet up with some gent your own age. And let your son go his own way."

"You are comforting," Merta said, pretending to find humor in his words.

"Was that Spence leaving just now?" Gibbs said, putting down some books.

Merta held her face up to be kissed by him, which he did in a manner resembling someone surreptitiously spitting out a seed.

"And how was Spyro tonight?" she said in a booming encouraging voice whose suddenness and loudness perhaps surprised even her.

He looked at her much as he had when as a small boy she had suddenly burst into the front room and asked him what he was being so very still for.

"Spyro is doing a portrait of me," he told her.

"A portrait," Merta said, trying hard to keep the disapproval out of her voice.

"That's what it is," Gibbs said, sitting down at the far end of the room and taking out his harmonica.

She closed her eyes in displeasure, but said nothing as he played "How High the Moon." He always played, it seemed, when she wanted to talk to him.

"Would you like Spyro to come to visit us some day?" she said.

"Visit us?"

"Pay a call," she smiled, closing her eyes.

"What would he pay us a call for?" he wondered. Seeing her pained hurt look, he expanded: "I mean what would he get to see here."

"Oh me," she replied laughing. "I'm so beautiful."

"Spyro thinks you don't like him," Gibbs said, and while she was saying *Tommyrot!* Gibbs went on: "In fact, he thinks everybody in this town dislikes him."

"They *are* the only Greeks, it's true," Merta said.

"And we're such a front family in town, of course!" he said with sudden fire.

"Well, your Uncle Spence is somebody," she began, white, and her mouth gaping a little, but Gibbs started to play on the harmonica again, cutting her off.

She tried to control her feelings tonight, partly because she had such a splitting headache.

"Would you like a dish of strawberry jello?" Merta said above the sound of the harmonica playing.

"What?" he cried.

"Some strawberry jello," she repeated, a little embarrassment now in her voice.

"What would I want that for?" he asked, putting down the harmonica with impatience.

"I suddenly got hungry for some, and went out there and made it. It's set by now and ready to eat."

There was such a look of total defeat on her old gray face that Gibbs said he would have some.

"I've some fresh coffee too," she said, a touch of sophistication in her voice, as if coffee were unusual and exotic also.

"I've had my coffee," he said. "Just the jello, thank you."

"Does Spyro always serve you coffee?" she said, her bitterness returning now against her will as they stood in the kitchen.

"I don't know," he said belligerently.

"But I thought you saw him every evening," she feigned sweet casualness.

"I never notice what he serves," Gibbs said loudly and indifferently.

"Would you like a large dish or a small dish of jello?" she said heavily.

"Small, for Christ's sake," he told her.

"Gibbs!" she cried. Then, catching herself, she said, "Small it will be, dear."

"What have you got to say that you can't bring it out!" he suddenly turned on her, and taking the dish of jello from her hand he put it down with a bang on the oilcloth covering of the tiny kitchen table.

"Gibbs, let's not have any trouble. Mother has a terrible headache tonight."

"Well, why don't you go to bed then," he said in his stentorian voice.

"Perhaps I will," she said weakly. She sat down and began eating right out of the jello bowl. She ate nearly all the rubbery stiff red imitation strawberry jello and drank in hurried gulps the coffee loaded with condensed milk.

"Spence gave me hell all evening," she said eating. "He thinks I would be happier if I found a fellow!"

She laughed but her laughter brought no response from Gibbs.

"I know I have nothing to offer anybody. Let's face it."

"Why do you have to say *let's face it!*" Gibbs snapped at her.

"Is there something wrong grammatically with it?" she wondered taking her spoon out of her mouth.

"Every dumb son of a bitch in the world is always saying *let's face it.*"

"And your own language is quite refined," she countered.

"Yes, let's face it, it is," he said, a bit weakly, and he took out the harmonica from his pocket, looked at it, and put it down noiselessly on the oilcloth.

"I've always wanted to do right by you, Gibbs. Since you were a little boy, I have tried. But no father around, and all...."

"Mom, we've been over this ten thousand times. Can't we just forget I didn't have an old man, and you worked like a team of dogs to make up for everything."

"Yes, let's do. Let's forget it all. For heaven's sake, I'm eating all this jello," she said gaily.

"Yes, I noticed," he said.

"But I want to do for you," she told him suddenly again with passion, forgetting everything but her one feeling now, and she put out her hand to him. "You're all I have, Gibbs."

He stared at her. She was weeping.

"I've never been able to do anything for you," she said. "I know I'm not someone you want to bring your friends home to see."

"Mom, for Christ's sake," he said.

"Don't swear," she said. "I may not know grammar or English, but I'm not profane and I never taught you to be. So there," she said, and she brought out her handkerchief and wiped her eyes, making them, he saw, even older and more worn with the rubbing.

"Mom," he said, picking up the harmonica again, "I don't *have* any friends."

"No?" she said laughing a little. Then understanding his remark more clearly as her weeping calmed itself, she said, commanding again, "What do you mean now by that?"

"Just what I said, Mom. I don't have any friends. Except maybe Spyro."

"Oh that Greek boy. We would come back to him."

"How could I have friends, do you think. After all...."

"Don't you go to college like everybody else," she said hurried-ly. "Aren't we making the attempt, Gibbs?"

"Don't get so excited. I don't care because I don't have any friends. I wasn't accusing you of anything."

"You go to college and you ought to have friends," she said. "Isn't that right?"

"Look, for Christ's sake, just going to college doesn't bring you friends. Especially a guy like me...."

"What's wrong with you," she said. "You're handsome. You're a beautiful boy."

"Mom, Je-sus."

"No wonder that Greek is painting you. You're a fine-looking boy."

"Oh it isn't that at all," he said, bored. "Spyro has to paint somebody."

"I don't know why you don't have friends," she said. "You have everything. Good looks, intelligence, and you can speak and act refined when you want to...."

"You have to be rich at that college. And your parents have to be...."

"Is that *all* then?" she said, suddenly very white and facing him.

"Mom, I didn't mean anything about you. I didn't say any of this to make you feel...."

"Be quiet," she said. "Don't talk."

"Maybe we *should* talk about it, Mom."

"I can't help what happened. What was *was*, the past is the past. Whatever wrong I may have done, the circumstances of your birth, Gibbs...."

"Mom, please, this isn't about you at all."

"I've stood by you, Gibbs," she hurried on as if testifying be-fore a deaf judge. "You can never deny that." She stared at him as though she had lost her reason.

"I'd like to have seen those rich women with their fat manicured husbands do what I've done," she said now as though powerless to stop, words coming out of her mouth that she usually kept and nursed for her long nights of sleeplessness and hate.

She stood up quickly as if to leave the room.

"With no husband or father to boot in this house! I'd like to see *them* do what I did. God damn them," she said.

Gibbs waited there, pale now as she was, and somehow much smaller before her wrath.

"God damn everybody!" she cried. "God damn everybody."

She sat down and began weeping furiously.

"I can't help it if you don't have friends," she told him, quieting herself with a last supreme effort. "I can't help it at all."

"Mom," he said. He wanted to weep too, but there was something too rocklike, too bitter and immovable inside him to let tears come loose. Often at night as he lay in his bed knowing that Merta was lying in the next room sleepless, he had wanted to get up and go to her and let them both weep together, but he could not.

"Is there anything I could do to change things here at home for you?" she said suddenly wiping away the tears, and tensing her breast to keep more of the torrent from gathering inside herself. "Anything at all I can do, I will," she said.

"Mom," he said, and he got up and as he did so the harmonica fell to the linoleum floor.

"You dropped your little…toy," she said tightening her mouth.

"It's not a toy," he began. "This is," he began again. "You see, this is the kind the professionals play on the stage…and everywhere."

"I see," she said, struggling to keep the storm within her quiet, the storm that now if it broke might sweep everything within her away, might rage and rage until only dying itself could stop it.

"Play something on it, Gibbs darling," she said.

He wanted to ask her if she was all right.

"Play, play," she said desperately.

"What do you want me to play, Mom?" he said, deathly pale.

"Just play any number you like," she suggested.

He began to play "How High the Moon" but his lips trembled too much.

"Keep playing," she said beating her hands with the heavy veins and the fingers without rings or embellishment.

He looked at her hands as his lips struggled to keep themselves on the tiny worn openings of the harmonica which he had described as the instrument of the professionals.

"What a funny tune," she said. "I never listened to it right before. What did you say they called it?"

"Mom," he said. "Please!"

He stretched out his hand.

"Don't now, don't," she commanded. "Just play. Keep playing."

Siblings

INTRODUCTION

COMPETITION FOR parents' affection, attention, and approval along with expressions of family loyalty characterize sibling interaction. The link between sisters and brothers is forged by sentimental memories, internecine battles, a shared heritage, and a sense of responsibility for one another's welfare. Paradoxically, while siblings feel a natural urge to staunchly defend one another against outsiders, they often exhibit hostility toward each other within the family circle.

Sibling rivalry is both natural and inevitable, whether or not parents manifest their preferences. Parental expression of favoritism toward one sibling causes resentment and hurt feelings that usually endure for years. Preferred siblings may be proud of their status but also tend to feel guilty if they suspect they have been given an unfair advantage. The reasons why parents favor one child over another are varied and complex. Parents may favor or resent a child who resembles them or feel particularly connected to a child who reminds them of someone special in their lives. Also, parents tend to identify with the child whose birth order matches their own.

Every sibling within a family occupies a particular birth-order position, which means that each sibling's perception of the family will be unique. The family an eldest sibling enters is vastly different from the family that greets the third- or fifth-born child. A first-born's primary role models and caretakers are usually the parents, while younger siblings are guided by older sisters and brothers as well as parents. Younger children typically strive to prove their power to older siblings, while the older ones learn ways to protect their senior status. Younger siblings often envy the position of older siblings, while firstborns resent having to break ground for all those privileges their younger siblings inherit with ease. Yet, there is a payoff for older siblings who gain satisfaction from mentoring younger sisters and brothers. On the receiving end, younger siblings tend to feel a mixture of appreciation and resentment, idealizing the more mature sibling while experiencing a sense of their own inferiority.

In addition to their distinct birth orders, every brother and sister has a unique role in their family's functioning. For example, one sibling may be the peacemaker, another the troublemaker or black sheep, and yet another the high achiever. Roles such as these, along with their labels, tend to adhere to individual siblings long after they leave home. As they assume their specific roles, most siblings manage to balance their individual needs with those of sisters and brothers, but this give and take is made possible only if each sibling feels sure of his or her special identity within the family unit.

The gender of siblings is also a significant variable in their interactions. Often female children in a family resent their brothers' extra freedom of movement, while male children envy their sisters' freedom to express emotions. Also, siblings close in age who are of the same gender tend to experience the most intense rivalry as they often share the same clothes, friends, and experiences.

Childhood rivalries and sibling interactions in general may change radically or may take a slightly new form when siblings become adults. Adult siblings may envy the spouses or career opportunities of one another and may argue over the treatment of aging parents. In other families, when siblings mature, they may be able to let go of past jealousy and achieve a new level of intimacy as they recall precious memories and grieve together over shared losses.

The stories included in the sibling section introduce us to brothers and sisters who are experiencing the pull between individual desires and family obligations. These stories also capture siblings in the act of clarifying their differences from one another and recognizing the common background that links them forever.

In Bambara's "Raymond's Run," a sister assumes with pride her caretaker role in relation to a retarded brother, even while recognizing how this responsibility imposes limits on her. In the three other stories, the sibling conflict and ambivalence is much more intense, and the rivalry between siblings in these stories elicits a variety of reactions. In Perlman's "Twelfth Summer," for example, a sister resents her younger brother's opportunity to earn money and her father's blatant favoritism of his son. However, the envy she experiences does not destroy her capacity to empathize with her younger sibling.

The rivalry between adult sisters in both Rich's "My Sister's Marriage" and Miriam's "Maiden Names" is richly complex. When read together, this pair of stories provides intriguing parallels and contrasts, since the narrator of the first story is the jealous sibling, while the narrator of the second is the more privileged one in her sister's eyes. In these two emotionally intense stories, the sisters experience a wide range of reactions from envy, betrayal, guilt, and rejection to affection, concern, and the underlying realization of their shared heritage.   G.C.

Toni Cade Bambara

RAYMOND'S RUN

I DON'T HAVE MUCH WORK to do around the house like some girls. My mother does that. And I don't have to earn my pocket money by hustling; George runs errands for the big boys and sells Christmas cards. And anything else that's got to get done, my father does. All I have to do in life is mind my brother Raymond, which is enough.

Sometimes I slip and say my little brother Raymond. But as any fool can see he's much bigger and he's older too. But a lot of people call him my little brother cause he needs looking after cause he's not quite right. And a lot of smart mouths got lots to say about that too, especially when George was minding him. But now, if anybody has anything to say to Raymond, anything to say about his big head, they have to come by me. And I don't play the dozens or believe in standing around with somebody in my face doing a lot of talking. I much rather just knock you down and take my chances even if I am a little girl with skinny arms and a squeaky voice, which is how I got the name Squeaky. And if things get too rough, I run. And as anybody can tell you, I'm the fastest thing on two feet.

There is no track meet that I don't win the first place medal. I use to win the twenty-yard dash when I was a little kid in kindergarten. Nowadays it's the fifty-yard dash. And tomorrow I'm subject to run the quarter-meter relay all by myself and come in first, second, and third. The big kids call me Mercury cause I'm the swiftest thing in the neighborhood. Everybody knows that — except two people who know better, my father and me.

He can beat me to Amsterdam Avenue with me having a two fire-hydrant headstart and him running with his hands in his pockets and whistling. But that's private information. Cause can you imagine some thirty-five-year-old man stuffing himself into PAL shorts to race little kids? So as far as everyone's concerned, I'm the fastest and that goes for Gretchen, too, who has put out the tale that she is going to win the first place medal this year. Ridiculous. In the second place, she's got short legs. In the third place, she's got freckles. In the first place, no one can beat me and that's all there is to it.

I'm standing on the corner admiring the weather and about to take a stroll down Broadway so I can practice my breathing exercises, and I've got Raymond walking on the inside close to the buildings cause he's subject to fits of fantasy and starts thinking he's a circus performer and that the curb is a tightrope strung high in the air. And sometimes after a rain, he likes to step down off his tightrope right into the gutter and slosh around getting his shoes and cuffs wet. Then I get hit when I get home. Or sometimes if you don't watch him, he'll dash across traffic to the island in the middle of Broadway and give the pigeons a fit. Then I have to go behind him apologizing to all the old people sitting around trying to get some sun and getting all upset with the pigeons fluttering around them, scattering their newspapers and upsetting the wax-paper lunches in their laps. So I keep Raymond on the inside of me, and he plays like he's driving a stage coach which is O.K. by me so long as he doesn't run me over or interrupt my breathing exercises, which I have to do on account of I'm serious about my running and don't care who knows it.

Now some people like to act like things come easy to them, won't let on that they practice. Not me. I'll high prance down 34th Street like a rodeo pony to keep my knees strong even if it does get my mother uptight so that she walks ahead like she's not with me, don't know me, is all by herself on a shopping trip, and I am somebody else's crazy child.

Now you take Cynthia Procter for instance. She's just the opposite. If there's a test tomorrow, she'll say something like, "Oh I guess I'll play handball this afternoon and watch television tonight," just to let you know she ain't thinking about the test. Or like last week when she won the spelling bee for the millionth time, "A good thing you got 'receive,' Squeaky, cause I would have got it wrong. I completely forgot about the spelling bee." And she'll clutch the lace on her blouse like it was a narrow escape. Oh, brother.

But of course when I pass her house on my early morning trots around the block, she is practicing the scales on the piano over and over and over and over. Then in music class, she always lets herself get bumped around so she falls accidently on purpose onto the piano stool and is so surprised to find herself sitting there, and so decides just for fun to try out the ole keys and what do you know — Chopin's waltzes just spring out of her fingertips and she's the most surprised thing in the world. A regular prodigy. I could kill people like that.

I stay up all night studying the words for the spelling bee. And you can see me anytime of day practicing running. I never walk if I can trot and shame on Raymond if he can't keep up. But of course he does, cause if he hangs back someone's liable to walk up to him and get smart, or take his allowance from him, or ask him where he got that great big pumpkin head. People are so stupid sometimes.

So I'm strolling down Broadway breathing out and breathing in on counts of seven, which is my lucky number, and here comes Gretchen and her sidekicks — Mary Louise who used to be a friend of mine when she first moved to Harlem from Baltimore and got beat up by everybody till I took up for her on account of her mother and my mother used to sing in the same choir when they were young girls, but people ain't grateful, so now she hangs out with the new girl Gretchen and talks about me like a dog; and Rosie who is fat as I am skinny and has a big mouth where Raymond is concerned and is too stupid to know that there is not a big deal of difference between herself and Raymond and that she can't afford to throw stones. So they are steady coming up Broadway and I see right away that it's going to be one of those Dodge City scenes cause the street ain't that big and they're close to the buildings just as we are. First I think I'll step into the candy store and look over the new comics and let them pass. But that's chicken and I've got a reputation to consider. So then I think I'll just walk straight on through them or over them if necessary. But as they get to me, they slow down. I'm ready to fight, cause like I said I don't feature a whole lot of chitchat, I much prefer to just knock you down right from the jump and save everybody a lotta precious time.

"You signing up for the May Day races?" smiles Mary Louise, only it's not a smile at all.

A dumb question like that doesn't deserve an answer. Besides, there's just me and Gretchen standing there really, so no use wasting my breath talking to shadows.

"I don't think you're going to win this time," says Rosie, trying to signify with her hands on her hips all salty, completely forgetting that I have whupped her behind many times for less salt than that.

"I always win cause I'm the best," I say straight at Gretchen who is, as far as I'm concerned, the only one talking in this ventriloquist-dummy routine.

Gretchen smiles but it's not a smile and I'm thinking that girls never really smile at each other because they don't know how and don't want to know how and there's probably no one to teach us how cause grown-up girls don't know either. Then they all look at Raymond who has just brought his mule team to a standstill. And they're about to see what trouble they can get into through him.

"What grade you in now, Raymond?"

"You got anything to say to my brother, you say it to me, Mary Louise Williams of Raggedy Town, Baltimore."

"What are you, his mother?" sasses Rosie.

"That's right, Fatso. And the next word out of anybody and I'll be their mother too." So they just stand there and Gretchen shifts from one leg to the other and so do they. Then Gretchen puts her hands on her hips and is about to say something with her freckle-face self but doesn't. Then she walks around me looking me up and down but keeps walking up Broadway, and her sidekicks follow her. So me and Raymond smile at each other and he says "Gidyap" to his team and I continue with my breathing exercises, strolling down Broadway toward the icey man on 145th with not a care in the world cause I am Miss Quicksilver herself.

I take my time getting to the park on May Day because the track meet is the last thing on the program. The biggest thing on the program is the May Pole dancing which I can do without, thank you, even if my mother thinks it's a shame I don't take part and act like a girl for a change. You'd think my mother'd be grateful not to have to make me a white organdy dress with a big satin sash and buy me new white baby-doll shoes that can't be taken out of the box till the big day. You'd think she'd be glad her daughter ain't out there prancing around a May Pole getting the new clothes all dirty and sweaty and trying to act like a fairy or a flower or whatever you're supposed to be when you should be trying to be yourself, whatever that is, which is, as far as I am concerned, a poor Black girl who really can't afford to buy shoes and a new dress you only wear once a lifetime cause it won't fit next year.

I was once a strawberry in a Hansel and Gretel pageant when I was in nursery school and didn't have no better sense than to dance on tiptoe with my arms in a circle over my head doing umbrella steps and being a perfect fool just so my mother and father could come dressed up and clap. You'd think they'd know better than to encourage that kind of nonsense. I am not a strawberry. I do not dance on my toes. I run. That is what I am all about. So I always come late to the May Day program, just in time to get my number pinned on and lay in the grass till they announce the fifty-yard dash.

I put Raymond in the little swings, which is a tight squeeze this year and will be impossible next year. Then I look around for Mr. Pearson who pins the numbers on. I'm really looking for Gretchen if you want to know the truth, but she's not around. The park is jam-packed. Parents in hats and corsages and breast-pocket handkerchiefs peeking up. Kids in white dresses and light blue suits. The parkees unfolding chairs and chasing the rowdy kids from Lenox as if they had no right to be there. The big guys with their caps on backwards, leaning against the fence swirling the basketballs on the tips of their fingers waiting for all these crazy people to clear out the park so they can play. Most of the kids in my class are carrying bass drums and glockenspiels and flutes. You'd think they'd put in a few bongos or something for real like that.

Then here comes Mr. Pearson with his clipboard and his cards and pencils and whistles and safety pins and fifty million other things he's always dropping all over the place with his clumsy self. He sticks out in a crowd cause he's on stilts. We used to call him Jack and the Beanstalk to get him mad. But I'm the only one that can outrun him and get away, and I'm too grown for that silliness now.

"Well, Squeaky," he says checking my name off the list and handing me number seven and two pins. And I'm thinking he's got no right to call me Squeaky, if I can't call him Beanstalk.

"Hazel Elizabeth Deborah Parker," I correct him and tell him to write it down on his board.

"Well, Hazel Elizabeth Deborah Parker, going to give someone else a break this year?" I squint at him real hard to see if he is seriously thinking I should lose the race on purpose just to give someone else a break.

"Only six girls running this time," he continues, shaking his head sadly like it's my fault all of New York didn't turn out in sneakers. "That new girl should give you a run for your money." He looks around the park for Gretchen like a periscope in a submarine movie. "Wouldn't it be a nice gesture if you were...to ahhh..."

I give him such a look he couldn't finish putting that idea into words. Grownups got a lot of nerve sometimes. I pin number seven to myself and stomp away — I'm so burnt. And I go straight for the track and stretch out on the grass while the band winds up with "Oh the Monkey Wrapped His Tail Around the Flag Pole," which my teacher calls by some other name. The man on the loudspeaker is calling everyone over to the track and I'm on my back looking at the sky trying to pretend I'm in the country, but I can't, because even grass in the city feels hard as sidewalk and there's just no pretending you are anywhere but in a "concrete jungle" as my grandfather says.

The twenty-yard dash takes all of the two minutes cause most of the little kids don't know no better than to run off the track or run the wrong way or run smack into the fence and fall down and cry. One little kid though has got the good sense to run straight for the white ribbon up ahead so he wins. Then the second graders line up for the thirty-yard dash and I don't even bother to turn my head to watch cause Raphael Perez always wins. He wins before

he even begins by psyching the runners, telling them they're going to trip on their shoelaces and fall on their faces or lose their
shorts or something, which he doesn't really have to do since he
is very fast, almost as fast as I am. After that is the forty-yard dash
which I use to run when I was in first grade. Raymond is hollering
from the swings cause he knows I'm about to do my thing cause
the man on the loudspeaker has just announced the fifty-yard dash,
although he might just as well be giving a recipe for Angel Food
cake cause you can hardly make out what he's saying for the static.
I get up and slip off my sweat pants and then I see Gretchen standing at the starting line kicking her legs out like a pro. Then as I get
into place I see that ole Raymond is in line on the other side of the
fence, bending down with his fingers on the ground just like he
knew what he was doing. I was going to yell at him but then I
didn't. It burns up your energy to holler.

Every time, just before I take off in a race, I always feel like I'm
in a dream, the kind of dream you have when you're sick with fever
and feel all hot and weightless. I dream I'm flying over a sandy
beach in the early morning sun, kissing the leaves of the trees as I
fly by. And there's always the smell of apples, just like in the
country when I was little and use to think I was a choo-choo train,
running through the fields of corn and chugging up the hill to the
orchard. And all the time I'm dreaming this, I get lighter and lighter
until I'm flying over the beach again, getting blown through the
sky like a feather that weighs nothing at all. But once I spread my
fingers in the dirt and crouch over for the Get on Your Mark, the
dream goes and I am solid again and am telling myself, Squeaky
you must win, you must win, you are the fastest thing in the world,
you can even beat your father up Amsterdam if you really try. And
then I feel my weight coming back just behind my knees then
down to my feet then into the earth and the pistol shot explodes
in my blood and I am off and weightless again, flying past the
other runners, my arms pumping up and down and the whole
world is quiet except for the crunch as I zoom over the gravel in
the track. I glance to my left and there is no one. To the right a
blurred Gretchen who's got her chin jutting out as if it would win
the race all by itself. And on the other side of the fence is Raymond
with his arms down to his side and the palms tucked up behind
him, running, in his very own style and the first time I ever saw

that and I almost stop to watch my brother Raymond on his first run. But the white ribbon is bouncing toward me and I tear past it racing into the distance till my feet with a mind of their own start digging up footfuls of dirt and brake me short. Then all the kids standing on the side pile on me, banging me on the back and slapping my head with their May Day programs, for I have won again and everybody on 151st Street can walk tall for another year.

"In first place…" the man on the loudspeaker is clear as a bell now. But then he pauses and the loudspeaker starts to whine. Then static. And I lean down to catch my breath and here comes Gretchen walking back for she's overshot the finish line too, huffing and puffing with her hands on her hips taking it slow, breathing in steady time like a real pro and I sort of like her a little for the first time. "In first place…" and then three or four voices get all mixed up on the loudspeaker and I dig my sneaker into the grass and stare at Gretchen who's staring back, we both wondering just who did win. I can hear old Beanstalk arguing with the man on the loudspeaker and then a few others running their mouths about what the stop watches say.

Then I hear Raymond yanking at the fence to call me and I wave to shush him, but he keeps rattling the fence like a gorilla in a cage like in them gorilla movies, but then like a dancer or something he starts climbing up nice and easy but very fast. And it occurs to me, watching how smoothly he climbs hand over hand and remembering how he looked running with his arms down to his side and with the wind pulling his mouth back and his teeth showing and all, it occurred to me that Raymond would make a very fine runner. Doesn't he always keep up with me on my trots? And he surely knows how to breathe in counts of seven cause he's always doing it at the dinner table, which drives my brother George up the wall. And I'm smiling to beat the band cause if I've lost this race, or if me and Gretchen tied, or even if I've won, I can always retire as a runner and begin a whole new career as a coach with Raymond as my champion. After all, with a little more study I can beat Cynthia and her phony self at the spelling bee. And if I bugged my mother, I could get piano lessons and become a star. And I have a big rep as the baddest thing around. And I've got a roomful of ribbons and medals and awards. But what has Raymond got to call his own?

So I stand there with my new plan, laughing out loud by this time as Raymond jumps down from the fence and runs over with his teeth showing and his arms down to the side which no one before him has quite mastered as a running style. And by the time he comes over I'm jumping up and down so glad to see him — my brother Raymond, a great runner in the family tradition. But of course everyone thinks I'm jumping up and down because the men on the loudspeaker have finally gotten themselves together and compared notes and are announcing "In first place — Miss Hazel Elizabeth Deborah Parker." (Dig that.) "In second place — Miss Gretchen P. Lewis." And I look over at Gretchen wondering what the P stands for. And I smile. Cause she's good, no doubt about it. Maybe she'd like to help me coach Raymond; she obviously is serious about running, as any fool can see. And she nods to congratulate me and then she smiles. And I smile. We stand there with this big smile of respect between us. It's about as real a smile as girls can do for each other, considering we don't practice real smiling every day you know, cause maybe we too busy being flowers or fairies or strawberries instead of something honest and worthy of respect...you know...like being people.

Helen Harris Perlman

TWELFTH SUMMER

T HE SUMMER my little brother went into business was a black one for me. Up until one hot evening in July, I was the self-respecting twelve-year-old sister of a nine-year-old boy, and then, suddenly, I was only a girl who was going to have to sit and wait while Sonny came and went as a person of affairs. We were all on the porch of our summer cottage at the lake that evening – my mother, my father, Sonny, and I. My mother was fanning her-herself and murmuring that if my father didn't patch some of the holes in the screens, we'd be eaten up by mosquitoes. My father said "Yes, yes" a couple of times in an absent-minded way, and kept on putting his fishhooks and flies in order. Sonny and I were playing parcheesi, and I was winning. All at once the bolt was hurled. "Son," my father said ("Son" – not "Sonny"!), "how would you like to go into business?"

"Fine," said Sonny.

"You're almost ten years old," said my father, "and I've been thinking it's time you learned something about money."

"O.K.," said Sonny, and drove me into a rage by sweeping all the men off the parcheesi board and leaning back to listen.

Sonny could have a magazine route, my father told him, and he'd make two cents on every copy he sold at five cents. My father drove back and forth to work in our town, twenty miles away, and he said Sonny could ride with him. My mother asked, For heaven's sake, what was he thinking of? What was the use of bringing children to the lake in the summer if you were going to take them right back to town again and put them to work? My father told her to hold her horses. He said Sonny would go to town only on Thursdays, his entire route would be in three big office buildings, and he'd take him to lunch every week.

"At the New Iroquois?" asked Sonny eagerly, and I knew he was already tasting the pie à la mode he always ordered at that restaurant.

"At the New Iroquois," said my father, and that cinched it. Sonny wanted to go, and none of my mother's arguments made any impression on either him or my father.

THE NEXT THURSDAY MORNING, Sonny was up early. My father thought twenty-five miles an hour was as fast as a car should be pushed, so he always gave himself plenty of time. At first, I was inclined to sulk in bed, but finally I put my bathrobe on and went and stood in the kitchen doorway. Sonny sat at the table, the shine of vaseline on his pompadour, the whiteness of his starched middy suit and his stockings, and the glory of being in business combining to make him radiant. My father sat across from him, looking pleased, and my mother buzzed about, scrambling eggs and frequently reminding Sonny that he didn't have to go if he didn't want to. Nobody even noticed me, at first. "Hello," I said eventually, and garnered some comfort from the fact that each of them said "Hello" in return.

"Looks like it's going to be a nice day," I said, and they all agreed.

"Guess I'll do some diving from the raft today," I said, pointedly, to Sonny.

"Ish ka bibble," Sonny said.

I leaned against the doorjamb disconsolately for a while, and then sat down and ate.

The fervent goodbyes my mother bestowed on Sonny, and the sight of the dust settling silently in the driveway after the car had gone, deeply saddened me, and I considered allowing myself to drown, later, when I went out to dive. The day was endless, partly because my mother kept track of the passing of each hour and wondered what Sonny was doing during it but even more because, in the course of nine years, I had grown used to having Sonny around and, reluctant though I was to admit it, I was lonesome for him. Silence lay across the lake as I swam to the raft, and though I kicked the water furiously to make some of the companionable noises of swimming, the sound died in the quiet. I dived once or twice, but the water seemed too deep and lonely, so I lay on the raft and thought, I should worry, and ish ka bibble. I kept seeing images of Sonny effulgent with success as all the men in three office buildings swarmed to buy his magazines, and I occasionally saw heady images of myself holding a silver loving cup I had been awarded for diving, or for writing a poem, or for being an actress — it was hard to decide which. I stayed there until lunchtime, and then swam back to the cottage.

After lunch, I wound up the Victrola. Alma Gluck sang "Lo, Here the Gentle Lark," Harry Lauder sang "Roamin' in the Gloamin'," Caruso's heart and voice broke in "I Pagliacci," and an infinite sadness hung over the afternoon. I asked my mother to play cassino, but she said she never could keep her mind on cards, and to wait till Sonny got home. There was nothing to do but wait.

Sonny came at last, bearing his shield. It was a large gray canvas bag with "The Saturday Evening Post" lettered on it in black. It hung from one shoulder and flapped against his white stockings. His middy suit was rumpled and so was his pompadour, but victory shone in his face. He and my father came in together, my father's arm around Sonny's shoulders. "Well," my father said to my mother proudly, "our son is a real businessman!"

I listened to every wonderful, anguishing detail. Sonny had made a big hit. All my father's acquaintances had wanted to know where he'd got such a handsome son. They'd all been glad to become regular customers, and they'd given him the names of other men. Sonny had had to go back to the magazine distributor several times to refill his bag. Then my father said that he and Sonny had better sit right down after supper and work out a system of bookkeeping. My mother said to let the child have *some* rest, and my father thought a while and then agreed, saying he'd like to get some fishing done before dark anyway.

Almost every evening, after supper, my father and brother and

I went fishing. That hour in our boat, moving toward the lowering sun and then, as the sky grew dark, coming back toward the light on our cottage porch, had always been one of the happiest of the day for me. We spoke in soft voices, so as not to frighten the fish. Sonny and I would take turns rowing, creeping by one another carefully on the boat's damp bottom as we shifted seats. After a while, my father would slip the heavy stone that was our anchor gently into the water and would stand up in the prow, silhouetted against the sky, and begin his rhythmic casting. Sonny and I would push reluctant worms or flipping silver minnows onto our hooks, lower our bamboo poles, and wait for hungry sunfish or crappies to come by. That summer, my father had decided I was getting old enough to learn to use a rod and reel, and for several weeks, whenever the lake was calm, I had been allowed to stand and cast.

On that black Thursday, it was different. We dropped anchor and my father said, "Let Sonny try casting tonight."

I was stunned. "But he's too *young!*" I cried.

"Hush," said my father. "What's the matter with you?" Then, looking over my head toward his son, he said, "If he's old enough to be in business, he's old enough to learn casting." I decided at that moment that the next day I would drown myself for sure.

FROM THEN ON, Thursday morning was a time of cheerful bustle. Sonny's hair had to be combed just right, and his breakfast had to be especially good; if it was a cool morning, there was hot cocoa for him instead of milk. Afterward, with his bag slung from his shoulder, he would be off with my father in a cloud of golden dust. Midmorning, I would walk the shady road to the post office and the grocery store. On other days, Sonny and I always went there together, and in the span of a few riddles and songs and races and arguments we were back home. Now, on Thursdays, I walked alone, and the way seemed endless. Every Thursday, the grocery-man, who was called Skipper, because he wore a yachting cap, though everyone knew he'd never been in anything bigger than a rowboat, would say "Where's that young brother of yours?" and I would answer "Sonny's gone to town today. He's in business on Thursdays."

Skipper would say, "That so? Fine boy, that boy. He'll be Some-body someday."

A glow of pleasure would rise in me then. After all, this future Somebody was my own little brother. But when the screen door had slammed behind me, the glow would drain away, and as I scuffed the dust and pebbles on the way home, I knew that some-day, dazzling in my beauty and charm, I would sweep into Skip-per's store and he would take off his yachting cap and ask "Are *you* the famous actress?" (Or "poetess," or "fancy diver.") And if he should ask "What's become of that young brother of yours?" I'd say casually "Oh, he helps me."

There was no more fishing on Thursday evenings. On the first two or three, in spite of my mother's protests, Father and Sonny went off together after supper to the library table in the living room to count Sonny's money and check his records. My father had bought him a ledger, and on its blue-and-red-lined pages Sonny wrote the names of his customers and as he made the rounds each week entered the date and the notation "Paid 5¢" or "Owed 5¢." He often couldn't collect for his magazines because the customers weren't in their offices when he made his delivery. The third week he had the ledger, he and my father got into an argument over it. Sonny said the lines were so close together they made the names squinchy; my father said he would just have to get them in some-how. Then my father said that "Paid 5¢" and "Owed 5¢" was a very poor system. He said that he had already shown Sonny how to make his entries, and that there was no point keeping books un-less you did it in a businesslike way. Sonny insisted that the system was good for *him*, and my father said all right, it was Sonny's busi-ness. After that, he just sat at the library table and read his paper on Thursday night while Sonny wrote and erased, and sometimes stopped to pour the shining money from his purse and build little towers of dimes and nickels.

Meanwhile, my mother and I did the dishes. Thursday night's dishes seemed the week's worst. The pots and pans apparently multiplied, and the kerosene stove would never heat water fast enough. By the time we had flapped our towels and hung them up, Sonny would have finished his checking and counting. He would put back in his purse the money my father had taught him to call "working capital" and drop his profits lovingly into his iron-courthouse bank. He would shake the bank and come to the kitchen rattling it and smiling proudly, and my mother would smile proudly back at him. I hated him.

ONE THURSDAY EVENING, late in August, I heard Sonny's voice rise, wailing, over the clatter of the dishes my mother and I were washing. He and my father were having another argument.

"But I have too many customers!" Sonny insisted.

"Too many customers!" said my father. "I've never heard a man in business complain of *that* before!"

My mother hastily dried her hands and went into the living room.

"This son of yours!" said my father. "The more customers he gets, the less profit he says he's made."

"Gracious!" said my mother. "How's that? Did you buy something, Sonny?"

"Buy something!" said my father. "What would he buy? *I* buy his lunch. *I* give him nickels for his afternoon root beer and cream puff!"

Sonny said, in a small voice, that he couldn't always remember who owed him from the week before, and my father replied, very quietly, that he wasn't supposed to remember — that was what the ledger was for. He added that he guessed he'd better have a good look at that ledger one of these days. He probably would have looked it over right then, but Sonny said he had a stomach-ache, and my mother said it was probably that rotten New Iroquois food and Sonny had better lie down.

Somehow, my father didn't get around to the ledger for another week. We went fishing the next evening, and visitors came for the weekend, and I suppose it just slipped his mind, then, until Thursday. I remember that evening clearly. It was the night my brother went out of business.

We had lighted a fire in the living room grate to clear out the damp chill rising from the lake. My mother and I finished the dishes, and found my father and Sonny still at the library table. Sonny was peering at the ledger, pencilling and erasing and making much ado about slapping and blowing the shreds of eraser off the paper. My father held his newspaper in front of him, but I could see he was keeping his eyes on Sonny. I had taken an extra piece of muskmelon out of the icebox, for my second dessert, and I sat on the stool in front of the fire to eat it. I was glad Thursday was almost over, and the warmth of the fire and the luscious muskmelon juice that ran down my gullet made me feel good.

Suddenly my father said "Well?" and Sonny murmured that he'd let him see it right away.

"How can you have forty-nine customers and a forty-five-cent profit?" my father asked.

"It's a profit, just the same," Sonny said. He was sitting still, staring desperately at the ledger page.

"Profit!" my father cried. "He works all day," he said, turning to my mother and me, "I transport him, I feed him, every week he says he's got more customers, and now I find he's got less than half the profit he ought to have!"

My mother set her mouth in a straight line and bent over my brother as if she were shielding him from my father. "Sonny," she said in her gentlest, most coaxing tone, "tell us what's the trouble."

"Nothing," said Sonny.

"Nothing!" roared my father. "Don't tell me 'Nothing'!"

"Sonny," said my mother, "do you want to quit this — this monkey business?"

Sonny kept looking at his ledger, and after a minute he said, in a whisper, "Yes, I guess I do."

Then it all came out. The whole trouble, Sonny said, talking fast and breathlessly, was that he had too many customers. The more he got, the messier the names in the ledger got. He sometimes had to prop it on one knee to make his entries, and his magazine bag would pull his arm down, so that often it was hard to tell whether he had written "Paid 5¢" or "Owed 5¢," and just who it was that had paid or owed. He said that he had figured most people would remember to pay him, and that sometimes some of them did, but not always.

At first, I thought my mother was going to laugh or cry — I couldn't tell which. Then she just put her arms around Sonny and didn't say or do anything. My father gave a little moan. "What grade are you in, son?" he asked.

My brother said he was going into the fifth grade.

My father shook his head as though he couldn't believe it. "In the fifth grade," he said. "Nine and a half years old. And he can't read his own handwriting!"

"The whole thing was nonsense," my mother said angrily, but my father didn't pay any attention. He stood up.

"Son," he said, "I'm sorry, but you'll have to learn to read what you write before I'll put you in business again."

My brother swept his purse, bank, and ledger from the table and bolted out of the room. No one said anything. My mother sat down in her rocking chair and looked at the cover of a magazine. I wanted to go to the kitchen to get rid of my melon rind, but I was afraid to stir the silence, so I sat there and looked into the fire until the heat made tears come to my eyes. After a few moments, my father sighed and walked out to the cold, dark porch. Out of the corner of my eye I could see him standing there, hands in his pockets, looking into the blackness.

I got up and tiptoed into the kitchen, and from there I crept into my brother's room. It was dark, but I knew that he was already under the blankets. I whispered "Sonny," and he didn't answer, so I went to his bed and felt for his face. He was crying, and he shook my hand off roughly. I stood there in the dark beside his bed, and suddenly I was crying, too. "You should worry, Sonny," I whispered. "You should ish ka bibble about that old business."

He didn't answer. I leaned against the cold brass bedpost and wept heavily and helplessly. I wept for Sonny, and for my father, and for myself, too, because I knew that I probably would never be a great actress after all.

That's about all there was to that summer. In another week, we were packing to go back into town, and Sonny and I were happy at the prospect of being in school again, although, as custom required, we rolled our eyes and groaned whenever we spoke of it.

Cynthia Rich

MY SISTER'S MARRIAGE

W HEN MY MOTHER DIED she left just Olive and me to take
care of Father. Yesterday when I burned the package of
Olive's letters that left only me. I know that you'll side with my
sister in all of this because you're only outsiders, and strangers can
afford to sympathize with young love, and with whatever sounds
daring and romantic, without thinking what it does to all the other
people involved. I don't want you to hate my sister — I don't hate
her — but I do want you to see that we're happier this way, Father
and I, and as for Olive, she made her choice.

But if you weren't strangers, all of you, I wouldn't be able to tell
you about this. "Keep yourself to yourself," my father has always
said. "If you ever have worries, Sarah Ann, you come to me and
don't go sharing your problems around town." And that's what
I've always done. So if I knew you I certainly wouldn't ever tell
you about Olive throwing the hairbrush, or about finding the letters buried in the back of the drawer.

I don't know what made Olive the way she is. We grew up together like twins — there were people who thought we were — and
every morning before we went to school she plaited my hair and
I plaited hers before the same mirror, in the same little twist of ribbons and braids behind our head. We wore the same dresses and
there was never a stain on the hem or a rip in our stockings to say

to a stranger that we had lost our mother. And although we have never been well-to-do — my father is a doctor and his patients often can't pay — I know there are people here in Conkling today who think we're rich, just because of little things like candlelight at dinner and my father's cigarette holder and the piano lessons that Olive and I had and the reproduction of *The Anatomy Lesson* that hangs above the mantelpiece instead of botanical prints. "You don't have to be rich to be a gentleman," my father says, "or to live like one."

My father is a gentleman and he raised Olive and myself as ladies. I can hear you laughing, because people like to make fun of words like "gentleman" and "lady," but they are words with ideals and standards behind them, and I hope that I will always hold to those ideals as my father taught me to. If Olive has renounced them, at least we did all we could.

Perhaps the reason that I can't understand Olive is that I have never been in love. I know that if I had ever fallen in love it would not have been, like Olive, at first sight but only after a long acquaintance. My father knew my mother for seven years before he proposed — it is much the safest way. Nowadays people make fun of that too, and the magazines are full of stories about people meeting in the moonlight and marrying the next morning, but if you read those stories you know that they are not the sort of people you would want to be like.

Even today Olive wouldn't deny that we had a happy childhood. She used to be very proud of being the lady of the house, of sitting across the candlelight from my father at dinner like a little wife. Sometimes my father would hold his carving knife poised above the roast to stand smiling at her and say: "Olive, every day you remind me more of your mother."

I think that although she liked the smile, she minded the compliment, because she didn't like to hear about Mother. Once when my father spoke of her she said: "Papa, you're missing Mother again. I can't bear it when you miss Mother. Don't I take care of you all right? Don't I make things happy for you?" It wasn't that she hadn't loved Mother but that she wanted my father to be completely happy.

To tell the truth, it was Olive Father loved best. There was a time when I couldn't have said that, it would have hurt me too much. Taking care of our father was like playing a long game of "let's pretend," and when little girls play family nobody wants to be the children. I thought it wasn't fair, just because Olive was three years older, that she should always be the mother. I wanted to sit opposite my father at dinner and have him smile at me like that.

I was glad when Olive first began walking out with young men in the summer evenings. Then I would make lemonade for my father ("Is it as good as Olive's?") and we would sit out on the screened porch together watching the fireflies. I asked him about the patients he had seen that day, trying to think of questions as intelligent as Olive's. I knew that he was missing her and frowning into the long twilight for the swing of her white skirts. When she came up the steps he said, "I missed my housewife tonight," just as though I hadn't made the lemonade right after all. She knew, too, that it wasn't the same for him in the evenings without her and for a while, instead of going out, she brought the young men to the house. But soon she stopped even that ("I never realized how silly and shallow they were until I saw them with Papa," she said. "I was ashamed to have him talk to them."). I know that he was glad, and when my turn came I didn't want to go out because I hated leaving them alone together. It all seems a very long time ago. I used to hate it when Olive "mothered" me. Now I feel a little like Olive's mother, and she is like my rebellious child.

In spite of everything, I loved Olive. When we were children we used to play together. The other children disliked us because we talked like grownups and didn't like to get dirty, but we were happy playing by ourselves on the front lawn where my father, if he were home, could watch us from his study window. So it wasn't surprising that when we grew older we were still best friends. I loved Olive and I see now how she took advantage of that love. Sometimes I think she felt that if she were to betray my father she wanted me to betray him too.

I STILL BELIEVE that it all began, not really with Mr. Dixon, but with the foreign stamps. She didn't see many of them, those years after high school when she was working in the post office, because not very many people in Conkling have friends abroad, but the ones she saw — and even the postmarks from Chicago or California — made her dream. She told her dreams to Father, and of course he understood and said that perhaps some summer we could take a trip to New England as far as Boston. My father hasn't lived in Conkling all of his life. He went to Harvard, and that is one reason he is different from the other men here. He is a scholar and not bound to provincial ideas. People here respect him and come to him for advice.

Olive wasn't satisfied and she began to rebel. Even she admitted that there wasn't anything for her to rebel against. She told me about it, sitting on the window sill in her long white nightgown, braiding and unbraiding the hair that she had never cut.

"It's not, don't you see, that I don't love Father. And it certainly isn't that I'm not happy here. But what I mean is, how can I ever know whether or not I'm really happy here unless I go somewhere else? When you graduate from school you'll feel the same way. You'll want — you'll want to know."

"I like it here," I said from the darkness of the room, but she didn't hear me.

"You know what I'm going to do, Sarah Ann? Do you know what I'm going to do? I'm going to save some money and go on a little trip — it wouldn't have to be expensive, I could go by bus — and I'll just see things, and then maybe I'll know."

"Father promised he'd take us to New England."

"No," said Olive, "you don't understand. Anyhow, I'll save the money."

And still she wasn't satisfied. She began to read. Olive and I always did well in school, and our names were called out for Special Recognition on Class Day. Miss Singleton wanted Olive to go to drama school after she played the part of Miranda in *The Tempest*, but my father talked to her, and when he told her what an actress's life is like she realized it wasn't what she wanted. Aside from books for school, though, we never read very much. We didn't need to because my father has read everything you've heard of, and people in town have said that talking to him about anything is better than reading three books.

Still, Olive decided to read. She would choose a book from my father's library and go into the kitchen, where the air was still heavy and hot from dinner, and sit on the very edge of the tall, hard three-legged stool. She had an idea that if she sat in a comfortable chair in the parlor she would not be attentive or would skip the difficult passages. So she would sit like that for hours, under the hard light of the unshaded bulb that hangs from the ceiling, until her arms ached from holding the book.

"What do you want to find out about?" my father would ask.

"Nothing," Olive said. "I'm just reading."

My father hates evasion.

"Now, Olive, nobody reads without a purpose. If you're interested in something, maybe I can help you. I might even know something about it myself."

When she came into our bedroom she threw the book on the quilt and said: "Why does he have to pry, Sarah Ann? It's so simple — just wanting to read a book. Why does he have to make a fuss about it as though I were trying to hide something from him?"

That was the first time I felt a little like Olive's mother.

"But he's only taking an interest," I said. "He just wants us to share things with him. Lots of fathers wouldn't even care. You don't know how lucky we are."

"You don't understand, Sarah Ann. You're too young to understand."

"Of course I understand," I said shortly. "Only I've outgrown feelings like that."

It was true. When I was a little girl I wrote something on a piece of paper, something that didn't matter much, but it mattered to me because it was a private thought. My father came into my room and saw me shove the paper under the blotter, and he wanted me to show it to him. So I quickly said, "No, it's private. I wrote it to myself, I didn't write it to be seen," but he said he wanted to see it. And I said, "No, no, no, it was silly anyway," and he said, "Sarah Ann, nothing you have to say would seem silly to me, you never give me credit for understanding, I can understand a great deal," but I said it wasn't just him, really it wasn't, because I hadn't written it for anyone at all to see. Then he was all sad and hurt and said this wasn't a family where we keep things hidden and there I was hiding this from him. I heard his voice, and it went on and on, and he said I had no faith in him and that I shouldn't keep things from him — and I said it wasn't anything big or special, it was just some silly nonsense, but if it was nonsense, he said, why wouldn't I let him read it, since it would make him happy? And I cried and cried, because it was only a very little piece of paper and why did he have to see it anyway, but he was very solemn and said if you held back little things soon you would be holding back bigger things and the gap would grow wider and wider. So I gave him the paper. He read it and said nothing except that I was a good girl and he couldn't see what all the fuss had been about.

Of course now I know that he was only taking an interest and I shouldn't have minded that. But I was a little girl then and minded dreadfully, and that is why I understood how Olive felt, although she was grown-up then and should have known better.

She must have understood that she was being childish, because when my father came in a few minutes later and said, "Olive, you're our little mother. We mustn't quarrel. There should be only love between us," she rose and kissed him. She told him about the book she had been reading, and he said: "Well, as it happens, I do know something about that." They sat for a long time discussing the book, and I think he loved Olive better than ever. The next evening, instead of shutting herself in the bright, hot kitchen, Olive sat with us in the cool of the parlor until bedtime, hemming a slip. And it was just as always.

BUT I SUPPOSE that these things really had made a difference in Olive. For we had always been alike, and I cannot imagine allowing a perfect stranger to ask me personal questions before we had even been introduced. She told me about it afterward, how he had bought a book of three-cent stamps and stayed to chat through the half-open grilled window. Suddenly he said, quite seriously: "Why do you wear your hair like that?"

"Pardon me?" said Olive.

"Why do you wear your hair like that? You ought to shake it loose around your shoulders. It must be yards long."

That is when I would have remembered — if I had forgotten — that I was a lady. I would have closed the grill, not rudely but just firmly enough to show my displeasure, and gone back to my desk.

Olive told me she thought of doing that but she looked at him and knew, she said, that he didn't mean to be impolite, that he really wanted to know.

And instead she said: "I only wear it down at night."

That afternoon he walked her home from the post office.

OLIVE TOLD me everything long before my father knew anything. It was the beginning of an unwholesome deceit in her. And it was nearly a week later that she told even me. By that time he was meeting her every afternoon and they took long walks together, as far as Merton's Pond, before she came home to set the dinner table.

"Only don't tell Father," she said.

"Why not?"

"I think I'm afraid of him. I don't know why. I'm afraid of what he might say."

"He won't say anything," I said. "Unless there's something wrong. And if there's something wrong, wouldn't you want to know?"

Of course, I should have told Father myself right away. But that was how she played upon my love for her.

"I'm telling you," she said, "because I want so much to share it with you. I'm so happy, Sarah Ann, and I feel so free, don't you see. We've always been so close — I've been closer to you than to Father, I think — or at least differently." She had to qualify it, you see, because it wasn't true. But it still made me happy and I promised not to tell, and I was even glad for her because, as I've told you, I've always loved Olive.

I saw them together one day when I was coming home from school. They were walking together in the rain, holding hands like school children, and when Olive saw me from a distance she dropped his hand suddenly and then just as suddenly took it again.

"Hullo!" he said when she introduced us. "She does look like you!"

I want to be fair and honest with you — it is Olive's dishonesty that still shocks me — and so I will say that I liked Mr. Dixon that day. But I thought even then how different he was from my father, and that should have warned me. He was a big man with a square face and sun-bleached hair. I could see a glimpse of his bright, speckled tie under his tan raincoat, and his laugh sounded warm and easy in the rain. I liked him, I suppose, for the very things I should have distrusted in him. I liked his ease and the way that he accepted me immediately, spontaneously and freely, without wait-ing — waiting for whatever people wait for when they hold them-selves back (as I should have done) to find out more about you. I could almost understand what had made Olive, after five minutes, tell him how she wore her hair at night.

I am glad, at least, that I begged Olive to tell my father about him. I couldn't understand why at first she refused. I think now that she was afraid of seeing them together, that she was afraid of seeing the difference. I have told you that my father is a gentleman. Even now you must be able to tell what sort of man Mr. Dixon was. My father knew at once, without even meeting him.

THE WEEKS HAD PASSED and Olive told me that Mr. Dixon's business was completed but that his vacation was coming and he planned to spend it in Conkling. She said she would tell my father.

We were sitting on the porch after dinner. The evening had just begun to thicken and some children had wandered down the road, playing a game of pirates at the very edge of our lawn. One of them had a long paper sword and the others were waving tall sticks, and they were screaming. My father had to raise his voice to be heard.

"So this man whom you have been seeing behind my back is a traveling salesman for Miracle-wear soles."

"Surrender in the name of the King."

"I am more than surprised at you, Olive. That hardly sounds like the kind of man you would want to be associated with."

"Why not?" said Olive. "Why not?"

"It's notorious, my dear. Men like that have no respect for a girl. They'll flatter her with slick words but it doesn't mean anything. Just take my word for it, dear. It may seem hard, but I know the world."

"Fight to the death! Fight to the death!"

"I can't hear you, my dear. Sarah Ann, ask those children to play their games somewhere else."

I went down the steps and across the lawn.

"Dr. Landis is trying to rest after a long day," I explained. They nodded and vanished down the dusky road, brandishing their silent swords.

"I am saying nothing of the extraordinary manner of your meeting, not even of the deceitful way in which he has carried on this — friendship."

It was dark on the porch. I switched on the yellow overhead light, and the three of us blinked for a moment, rediscovering each other as the shadows leaped back.

"The cheapness of it is so apparent it amazes me that even in your innocence of the world — "

My father was fitting a cigarette into its black holder. He turned it slowly to and fro until it was firm before he struck a match and lit it. It is beautiful to watch him do even the most trivial things. He is always in control of himself and he never makes a useless gesture or thinks a useless thought. If you met him you might believe at first that he was totally relaxed, but because I have lived with him so long I know that there is at all times a tension controling his body; you can feel it when you touch his hand. Tension, I think, is the wrong word. It is rather a self-awareness, as though not a muscle contracted without his conscious knowledge.

"You know it very well yourself, Olive. Could anything but shame have kept you from bringing this man to your home?"

His voice is like the way he moves. It is clear and considered and each word exists by itself. However common it may be, when he speaks it, it has become his, it has dignity because he has chosen it.

"Father, all I ask is that you'll have him here — that you will meet him. Surely that's not too much to ask before you — judge him."

Olive sat on the step at my father's feet. Her hands had been moving across her skirt, smoothing the folds over her knees, but when she spoke she clasped them tightly in her lap. She was trying to speak as he spoke, in that calm, certain voice, but it was a poor imitation.

"I'm afraid that it is too much to ask, Olive. I have seen too many of his kind to take any interest in seeing another."

"I think you should see him, Father." She spoke very softly. "I think I am in love with him."

"Olive!" I said. I had known it all along, of course, but when she spoke it, in that voice trying so childishly to sound sure, I knew its absurdity. How could she say it after Father had made it so clear? As soon as he had repeated after her, "A salesman for Miracle-wear soles," even the inflections of his voice showed me that it was ludicrous; I realized what I had known all along, the cheapness of it all for Olive — for Olive with her ideals.

I looked across at my father but he had not stirred. The moths brushed their wings against the light bulb. He flicked a long gray ash.

"Don't use that word lightly, Olive," he said. "That is a sacred word. Love is the word for what I felt for your mother — what I hope you feel for me and for your sister. You mustn't confuse it with innocent infatuation."

"But I do love him — how can you know? How can you know anything about it? I do love him." Her voice was shrill and not pleasant.

"Olive," said my father. "I must ask you not to use that word."

She sat looking up at his face and from his chair he looked back at her. Then she rose and went into the house. He did not follow her, even with his eyes. We sat for a long time before I went over to him and took his hand. I think he had forgotten me. He started and said nothing and his hand did not acknowledge mine. I would rather he had slapped me. I left him and went into the house.

IN OUR BEDROOM Olive was sitting before the dressing table in her nightgown, brushing her hair. You mustn't think I don't love her, that I didn't love her then. As I say, we were like twins, and when I saw her reflection in the tall, gilded mirror I might have been seeing my own eyes filled with tears. I tell you, I wanted to put my arms around her, but you must see that it was for her own sake that I didn't. She had done wrong, she had deceived my father and she had made me deceive him. It would have been wicked to give her sympathy then.

"It's hard, of course, Olive," I said gently. "But you know that Father's right."

She didn't answer. She brushed her hair in long strokes and it rose on the air. She did not turn even when the doorknob rattled and my father stood in the doorway and quietly spoke her name.

"Olive," he repeated. "Of course I must ask you not to see this — this man again."

Olive turned suddenly with her dark hair whirling about her head. She hurled the silver hairbrush at my father, and in that single moment when it leaped from her hand I felt an elation I have never known before. Then I heard it clatter to the floor a few feet from where he stood, and I knew that he was unhurt and that it was I, and not Olive, who had for that single moment meant it to strike him. I longed to throw my arms about him and beg his forgiveness.

He went over and picked up the brush and gave it to Olive. Then he left the room.

"How could you, Olive?" I whispered.

She sat with the brush in her hand. Her hair had fallen all about her face and her eyes were dark and bright. The next morning at breakfast she did not speak to my father and he did not speak to her, although he sat looking at her so intensely that if I had been Olive I would have blushed. I thought, He loves her more now, this morning, than when he used to smile and say she was like Mother. I remember thinking, Why couldn't he love me like that? I would never hurt him.

Just before she left for work he went over to her and brushed her arm lightly with his hand.

"We'll talk it all over tonight, Olive," he said. "I know you will understand that this is best."

She looked down at his hand as though it were a strange animal and shook her head and hurried down the steps.

That night she called from a little town outside Richmond to say that she was married. I stood behind my father in the shadowy little hallway as he spoke to her. I could hear her voice, higher-pitched than usual over the static of the wires, and I heard her say that they would come, that very evening, if he would see them.

I almost thought he hadn't understood her, his voice was so calm.

"I suppose you want my blessings. I cannot give them to deceit and cowardice. You will have to find them elsewhere if you can, my dear. If you can."

After he had replaced the receiver he still stood before the mouth-piece, talking into it.

"That she would give up all she has had — that she would stoop to a — for a — physical attraction — "

Then he turned to me. His eyes were dark.

"Why are you crying?" he said suddenly. "What are you crying for? She's made her choice. Am I crying? Do you think I would want to see her — now? If she — when she comes to see what she has done — but it's not a question of forgiveness. Even then it wouldn't be the same. She has made her choice."

He stood looking at me and I thought at first that what he saw was distasteful to him, but his voice was gentle when he spoke.

"Would you have done this to me, Sarah Ann? Would you have done it?"

"No," I said, and I was almost joyful, knowing it was true. "Oh, no."

THAT WAS A YEAR ago. We never speak of Olive any more. At first letters used to come from her, long letters from New York and then from Chicago. Always she asked me about Father and whether he would read a letter if she wrote one. I wrote her long letters back and said that I would talk to him. But he wasn't well — even now he has to stay in bed for days at a time — and I knew that he didn't want to hear her name.

One morning he came into my room while I was writing to her. He saw me thrust the package of letters into a cubbyhole and I knew I had betrayed him again.

"Don't ally yourself with deception, Sarah Ann," he said quietly. "You did that once and you see what came of it."

"But if she writes to me — " I said. "What do you want me to do?"

He stood in the doorway in his long bathrobe. He had been in bed and his hair was slightly awry from the pillows and his face was a little pale. I have taken good care of him and he still looks young — not more than forty — but his cheekbones worry me. They are sharp and white.

"I want you to give me her letters," he said. "To burn."

"Won't you read them, Father? I know that what she did was wrong, but she sounds happy — "

I don't know what made me say that except that, you see, I did love Olive.

He stared at me and came into the room.

"And you believe her? Do you think that happiness can come from deception?"

"But she's my sister," I said, and although I knew that he was right I began to cry. "And she's your daughter. And you love her so."

He came and stood beside my chair. This time he didn't ask me why I was crying.

"We'll keep each other company, Sarah Ann, just the two of us. We can be happy that way, can't we? We'll always have each other, don't you know?" He put his hand on my hair.

I knew then that was the way it should be. I leaned my head on his shoulder, and when I had finished crying I smiled at him and gave him Olive's letters.

"You take them," I said. "I can't — "

He nodded and took them and then took my hand.

I KNOW THAT when he took them he meant to burn them. I found them by chance yesterday in the back of his desk drawer, under a pile of old medical reports. They lay there like love letters from someone who had died or moved away. They were tied in a slim green hair ribbon — it was one of mine, but I suppose he had found it and thought it was Olive's.

I didn't wonder what to do. It wasn't fair, don't you see? He hadn't any right to keep those letters after he told me I was the only daughter he had left. He would always be secretly reading them and fingering them, and it wouldn't do him any good. I took them to the incinerator in the back yard and burned them carefully, one by one. His bed is by the window and I know that he was watching me, but of course he couldn't say anything.

Maybe you feel sorry for Father, maybe you think I was cruel. But I did it for his sake and I don't care what you think because you're all of you strangers, anyway, and you can't understand that there couldn't be two of us. As I said before, I don't hate Olive. But sometimes I think this is the way it was meant to be. First Mother died and left just the two of us to take care of Father. And yesterday when I burned Olive's letters I thought, Now there is only me.

Libbi Miriam

MAIDEN NAMES

Encased in the safety of her flesh, my sister walks down the ramp. She carefully places her new shoes with their puffy feet one in front of the other. Already I hear her voice raspy from tranquilizers, spot her forehead crouched between her finely plucked brows. Here at Gate Nine my heart heaves in cadence with my parents' voices: *Don't try to change her in a week's visit* (my mother), as if she hasn't spent years tied to Roberta's demands. *Be kind; she doesn't have everything you have* (my father), anguished by his final emptying of patience. *A parent is always a parent,* they hum in unison. *A sibling, merely a sibling.*

In a flash of memory I see Ma and Pa young and striving, Roberta once full of beauty and mischief. Where did life go wrong for her? The old Brownie snapshots with curled edges that clutter my albums, she at six skinny with dark ringlets holding me on her lap, I an infant fat and blonde. Later the four of us at Lake Michigan, the one with our matching Chinese-girl Halloween costumes that Mamma had sewn. I was only in first grade, she in seventh. And then the photos stop.

She was already difficult. Papa drove up to the lake on weekends to beat city heat; Mamma stayed at the summer resort playing canasta and cleaning the kitchenette; I was absorbed in Roberta's games of witches and princesses. She'd drag me off and then abandon me at a moment's notice. How I'd cry. How she reigned over me with terror and delight.

She's coming down the aisle now. Her huge body presses tightly against me. She was once so thin. Would anyone watching us hug know we were sisters? Yes, we certainly couldn't be friends.

"Renee, you're too skinny!" I wonder if she remembers my child's habit of stuffing food in my mouth. "And your hair. It's flat and colorless. What happened?"

"I'm not skinny; I weigh the same as I did the last time you were here. This *is* my natural color hair."

I breathe in her once dark curls, gray-rooted and red-tinted, teased into a bouffant of twenty years ago. Oh, Roberta.

The roar of the engines masks her words. I make her wait while I run to the nearest bathroom. Finally I exit more in control.

"What took so long? You didn't comb your hair. You still don't take care of yourself, do you? Why didn't you wear something a little nicer to the airport? Hurry up, I want to get to your place. I'm exhausted."

She babbles on; I eye unknown passengers wishing I were taking *them* home, people from the Philippines, South America, strangers with different values, other ways of life, anyone but my sister.

The flight was terrible; she has a chill. Will I carry her bag? She's not feeling well, her feet kill. Hurry, get the bag; it's spinning around the carousel. Him? He moved out, took everything. Not like my husband Dan, not like Joe, the sweet one who died, the one she really loved, the one whose child she lost. She's brought presents for the kids. She loves my kids. She could've had one of her own if Joe had lived. Will I take her out, will Dan?

She's all around me, arms, breasts, hair, genie out of an airplane; her arrival jets forth the forgotten years: Roberta, twelve, demanding tap lessons and a leather jacket when we couldn't afford them; Roberta, nineteen, back home after an attempt to make it in show biz; Roberta, twenty-two, after her first divorce. "Mamma loves you more because all you do is study. You never try anything else." At last I speak.

"You didn't have to bring presents. It's not necessary."

"Necessary!" she cries, "necessary! I wanted to. They're for my nieces."

I grab the luggage. The same conversation last time, but this year her eyes are more withdrawn, fearful yet unyielding. She's waving good-by to the handsome steward; he waves back as if everything's fine. He smiles at her.

On the freeway past the "little boxes on the hill," she asks, how much and can she afford one. If only she lived here, close to me, she'd feel better. More stable, secure. She'd leave that rotten job and apartment in Detroit and begin all over in California doing what she doesn't know.

Rolling through the fog across the Bay Bridge I listen to the litany of a life filled with disappointment. Yes, better to live here; she always loved San Francisco where people aren't stuffy, where they can be themselves.

We drive into the valley heat toward suburbia. She lives in a decaying part of Detroit. God, how she hates it, dull, ugly, humid. Here there're gorgeous mountains —

"They're hills, not mountains."

The most gorgeous mountains she's ever seen anywhere, but then she's not seen what I have, she's not had the chance.

I swerve into the next lane. Were we ever close? How I ran after her at five and six. "Play with me, please play with me." Was it puberty that I first closed myself off from all that I feared about her, all that I feared I might become? Was it then I turned toward school and losing myself in music to block out our parents' constant concern and deep love for their two daughters? What else could they have done to help us grow, two uncomplicated adults limited by the times, wanting to do the best for us: Ma, proud of her housekeeping; Pa, trying to be a provider.

I pull into the Safeway parking lot. Do I know how bad her neighborhood's getting? Her supermarket, old, dilapidated. Not like this gorgeous one. People ripping off food. On and on, she goes, not once asking me about myself.

My head's in a vise. I dash to the check-out stand. I'm tainted. I've become like her, whining to the clerk, I can't find anything, why's everything missing, I'm exhausted, I've got to get home. As if he cares about my self-pity, my impatience. In line my knees weaken, my vision blurs. All my effort to stay California-healthy shattered by Roberta's visit in an hour's time.

I rush back to the car where she's waiting. "What took so long?"

"God knows. That's the way they do things around here." I sound like her.

Up the driveway. Shut off the motor. Eyes close while she drones on. I know from whence I come: the family fights over Roberta's pancake make-up, her copy of *Forever Amber* hidden under our twin beds, her string of boyfriends and their disappearance, then the long black period of her staying home in bed and my attempt to pretend she doesn't exist. Now I remember, now as I think of my own daughters. Pray they don't stay locked into that kind of disturbed adolescence forever. Pray that they have the strength to make their lives as women work.

Suddenly I hear myself screaming: "Will you shut up? You've just arrived, and you haven't stopped complaining." The blood rises in my chest, my throat. "There are people who've lost everything, arms, legs, whole families in wars. Do you ever think of them? Do you see the sun shining? Look at the palms, the hills – "

She looks like a child about to cry.

"Why do you talk like that? Just because I asked you what took so long? I don't have anyone else but you. The folks are getting old. I'm the one who's there to help them out while you enjoy yourself out here."

I don't say that Ma and Pa would move out here if it weren't for their ties to her.

"You don't have to teach piano if you don't want to; I have to work. Can't you give me credit for anything, at least for helping the folks after they always favored you?"

"Roberta, you're forty-seven years old."

"Tell me, what did I say that's so bad? I told you the mountains were beautiful. What do you want? I don't have what you have. You're the one who writes me about 'identity' and 'fulfillment.' Why can't I talk about it too? You know I love you. I tell everyone in the office how you still play the piano."

Swearing in my foulest tongue, I turn the key in the lock. "You've been here an hour and you've brought death and gloom."

"Death and gloom! I brought presents. Who taught you to drive a car when you were a scared kid?"

"Listen, when we get inside I want to lie down for half an hour.

I have my own problems. I need quiet. Let's stop this stupid talk. Just don't dump on me for a little while."

"What problems? You have a good husband, great kids, a nice house. I can barely get through the day. Why should I lie about the way I feel?"

The house is strangely silent. Have the girls fled? Last time Joyce and Nina avoided her. Only Amy greeted her. She washes up in their bathroom.

Alone in my bedroom I catch my image in the mirror. Everyone in the world I try to understand; every day I search for ways to connect to others. But not her.

Not speaking, we enter the kitchen. She puts the milk in the fridge, then goes outside to the car to bring in another suitcase. With all this luggage it looks like she's come for a year.

My neighbor turns from her planting in the noon heat. A curious smile forces itself onto her lips. She wants to ask those questions I've been asked all my life: Is that your sister? How can two sisters from the same family be so opposite?

Don't be fooled. Know the similarities, our voices, our hands, our need to be recognized, our desire to escape the confines of our urban childhood.

Roberta drops her bag and helps herself to coffee. Suddenly Amy jumps out of nowhere as if she's been hiding. With her good baby instincts still alive, she runs to Aunty, kisses her, plays Welcoming Committee. Duty done, presents grabbed, paper torn off, she's gone. Aunty's eyes fill with tears for the youngest who accepts her, blessed be the child. Hers would have been like that if only it had lived. If only Joe hadn't died in that stupid auto accident, they could've tried again. She was the one who wanted children. Oh Roberta, why such godless cruelty toward your life? Why? The old traumas don't belong in my new, sunny California kitchen.

We face one another alone, like the old days when we shared a bedroom with identical twin beds and bedspreads Mamma made. She blows her nose, dabs her mascara, coughs, sips coffee, lights a cigarette, forces a wheeze. I ask her not to smoke. She's got to, she absolutely must; it's her only pleasure and don't punish her by saying no. And another thing: don't embarrass her in front of the girls like last time when she didn't know about Three-Mile Island or that someone named Virginia Woolf wrote a book about having a room when she thought that was the name of a play.

"I'm going to lay down," I say on the way to my room to dial Dan.

"She's here."

"How is it?"

"Same as last time."

"Renee, I've told you a hundred times you're not responsible for her happiness."

"She's my only sister. Be nice when you get home."

"Don't I always try?"

"She brought us presents. She doesn't have money for that. She's not selfish. She can't help herself; she's got this…"

"Don't justify her to me. You invited her."

"I couldn't say no. Maybe if she stays with us, it'll open her up, change her…"

"In a week's time? You promised a week. You sound like your parents. People have to find their way by themselves. There's only so much anyone can do."

"You never turn away from your family when someone's in need."

"With her it's endless…."

"You said you'd take her to see the city."

"I will, I will. Just don't drive me nuts with her demands."

He hangs up. I sit on the bed, get up, look out of the window. She was always the neat one, imitating Ma; I only craved inner peace and order, the kind I found through music. The importance of cleaning, the importance of external order. The window blurs pink, becomes the pink of our bedroom.

"Stop practicing. You make me sick with that King Cole record."

I get up from the piano and start to run downstairs to get Mamma who's doing the laundry in the basement of the apartment house. I trip on an old skate and tumble down half a flight. I'm screaming in agony. "My arm, there's something wrong with my arm. It's killing me! It's twisted! It's broken!"

Mamma hears me and comes up looking terrified. She starts to call Daddy.

"It's Roberta's fault!" I scream. "She wouldn't let me practice for my

recital. She always has to have her way. I never get mine! She made me do it, she made me do it. Ooo, my arm." It won't stop hurting.

Roberta hugs me. "I didn't mean to, Renee. I didn't, I love you. You can still play in the recital. I'll give you my white cashmere, the one you like. You'll be popular. Stop crying. Daddy's coming. He'll take you to the hospital.

I draw the mini-blinds across the window, go once more to look into my bathroom mirror, rinse off my face, and get ready to start dinner.

Roberta too has washed her face; it's stripped of powder. The early beauty of her mischievous hazel eyes reveals itself. She runs her hands under the water for a long time, asks me where everything is, the bowl, the lettuce, the dressing. At last she starts to make a salad.

"Amy's a doll," she says. "Smart like you when you were a kid."

"She can be a pain sometimes," I say so she doesn't dwell on the false perfection of my life.

"Don't say that, Renee; you're lucky to have her. Are you going to take me to one of your concerts this time?"

"I've told you they're not concerts. I'm only an accompanist for a local group."

"Everyone at work knows how you play concerts in California."

"Roberta, they're not concerts. And I haven't had a job accompanying for three months."

She doesn't hear me, washes her hands for the third time.

I stand there helplessly in the kitchen watching her. Our expressions, our hands, the shape of our faces, the house with the French door, the twin beds, the Halloween costumes, our initials, our maiden names: identical.

SELECTED READINGS ON FAMILY RELATIONSHIPS

Non-Fiction:

ANDERSON, CHRISTOPHER P. *Father: The Figure and the Force.* New York: Warner Books, 1983.

APPLETON, WILLIAM S. *Fathers and Daughters: A Father's Powerful Influence on a Woman's Life.* Garden City, NY: Doubleday, 1981.

ARCANA, JUDITH. *Every Mother's Son: The Role of Mothers in the Making of Men.* Seattle, WA: The Seal Press, 1986.

——. *Our Mothers' Daughters.* Berkeley: Shameless Hussy Press, 1979.

ARNSTEIN, HELENE S. *Brothers and Sisters/Sisters and Brothers.* New York: E. P. Dutton, 1979.

BANK, STEPHEN P. and MICHAEL D. KAHN. *The Sibling Bond.* New York: Basic Books, 1982.

BARNARD, JESSIE. "The Paradox of the Happy Marriage." *Woman in Sexist Society.* Eds. V. Gornick and B. Moran. New York: Signet, 1971. 145-162.

BERNIKOW, LOUISE. *Among Women.* New York: Harper & Row, 1981.

CHODOROW, NANCY. *The Reproduction of Mothering: Psychoanalysis and the Sociology of Gender.* Berkeley: University of California Press, 1978.

CROSBY, JOHN F. *Illusion and Disillusion: The Self in Love and Marriage.* Belmont, CA: Wadsworth, 1973.

DEUTSCH, HELENE. *The Psychology of Women: A Psycho-analytic Interpretation.* 2 vols. New York: Grune & Stratton, 1944-1945.

EICHENBAUM, LUISE and SUSIE ORBACH. *What Do Women Want: Exploding the Myth of Dependency.* New York: Coward-McCann, Inc., 1983.

FISCHEL, ELIZABETH. *Sisters: Love and Rivalry inside the Family and Beyond.* New York: Morrow, 1979.

HAMMER, SIGNE. *Daughters and Mothers, Mothers and Daughters.* New York: Quadrangle, 1975.

——. *Passionate Attachments: Fathers and Daughters in America Today.* New York: Rawson Associates, 1982.

KLEIN, CAROLE. *Mothers and Sons.* Boston: Houghton-Mifflin, 1984.

LEDERER, WILLIAM J. and DON D. JACKSON. *The Mirages of Marriage.* New York: W. W. Norton, 1968.

LEONARD, LINDA SCHIERSE. *The Wounded Woman: Healing the Father-Daughter Relationship.* Boulder, CO: Shambhala, 1983.

LYNN, DAVID B. *Daughters and Parents: Past, Present, and Future.* Monterey, CA: Brooks/Cole, 1979.

NEISSER, EDITH. *Mothers and Daughters: A Lifelong Relationship.* New York: Harper & Row, 1973.

OLSEN, PAUL. *Sons and Mothers: Why Men Behave as They Do*. New York: M. Evans & Co., 1981.

POGREBIN, LETTY COTTIN. *Family Politics: Love and Power on an Intimate Frontier*. New York: McGraw Hill, 1983.

RICH, ADRIENNE. *Of Woman Born: Motherhood as Institution and Experience*. New York: Norton, 1976.

RUBIN, LILLIAN B. *Intimate Strangers: Men and Women Together*. New York: Harper & Row, 1983.

SKOLNICK, ARLENE. *The Intimate Environment: Exploring Marriage and the Family*. Boston: Little, Brown & Co., 1973.

SOMERVILLE, ROSE M. *Family Insights through the Short Story*. New York: Teacher's College, Columbia University, 1964.

YABLONSKY, LEWIS. *Fathers and Sons*. New York: Simon & Schuster, 1982.

ZICK, RUBIN. "Fathers and Sons: The Search for Reunion." *Psychology Today*, June 1982. 22-33.

Short Stories

Husband-Wife

ANDERSON, ALSTON. "The Checkerboard." *The Best Short Stories by Negro Writers*. Ed. Langston Hughes. Boston: Little Brown, 1967. 207-212.

BENSON, SALLY. "Little Woman." *Images of Women in Literature*. Ed. Mary Anne Ferguson. 4th ed. Boston: Houghton, 1986. 27-32.

BONTEMPS, ARNA. "A Summer Tragedy." *American Negro Short Stories*. Ed. John Henrik Clarke. New York: Hill & Wang, 1966. 54-63.

BROOKS, GWENDOLYN "If You're Light and Have Long Hair." From *Maud Martha*. *The World of Gwendolyn Brooks*. New York: Harper, 1971. 205-214.

——. "We're the Only Colored People Here." From *Maud Martha*. *The World of Gwendolyn Brooks*. New York: Harper, 1971. 198-203.

CARROLL, JOSEPH. "At Mrs. Farrelly's." *The Best American Short Stories 1953*. Ed. Martha Foley. New York: Ballantine, 1953. 53-61.

CHEEVER, JOHN. "The Chimera." *The Stories of John Cheever*. New York: Knopf, 1979. 473-481.

——. "The Country Husband." *The Stories of John Cheever*. New York: Knopf, 1979. 325-346.

——. "The Cure." *The Stories of John Cheever*. New York: Knopf, 1979. 156-164.

——. "An Educated American Woman." *The Stories of John Cheever*. New York: Knopf, 1979. 521-535.

CHEEVER, JOHN. "Just Tell Me Who It Was." *The Stories of John Cheever.* New York: Knopf, 1979. 370-385.

———. "The Music Teacher." *The Stories of John Cheever.* New York: Knopf, 1979. 413-422.

———. "The Season of Divorce." *The Stories of John Cheever.* New York: Knopf, 1979. 137-146.

CHEKHOV, ANTON. "The Darling." *Images of Women in Literature.* Ed. Mary Anne Ferguson. Boston: Houghton, 1973. 38-47.

CHOPIN, KATE. "The Story of an Hour." *Images of Women in Literature.* Ed. Mary Anne Ferguson. 4th Ed. Boston: Houghton, 1986. 380-382.

COLETTE. "The Secret Woman." *Women and Fiction.* Ed. Susan Cahill. New York: Mentor, 1975. 38-41.

COLTER, CYRUS. "Black for Dinner." *Out of Our Lives: A Selection of Contemporary Black Fiction.* Ed. Quandra Prettyman Stadler. Washington, D.C.: Howard University Press, 1975. 238-262.

———. "The Beach Umbrella." *The Best Short Stories by Negro Writers.* Ed. Langston Hughes. Boston: Little Brown, 1967. 107-129.

DINESEN, ISAK. "The Ring." *Woman: An Affirmation.* Eds. A. Fannin, R. Lukens and C. H. Mann. Lexington, MA: Heath, 1979. 103-108.

DREISER, THEODORE. "The Lost Phoebe." *Fifty Great American Short Stories.* Ed. Milton Crane. New York: Bantam. 1965. 171-186.

EDWARDS, MARGARET. "A Wife with a Green Thumb." *Secrets and Other Stories.* Washington, D.C.: Gallimaufry Press, 1979. 69-78.

FREEMAN, MARY WILKINS. "The Revolt of 'Mother'." *Woman: An Affirmation.* Eds. A. Fannin, R. Lukens, and C. H. Mann. Lexington, MA: Heath, 1979. 322-335.

GILMAN, CARLOTTE PERKINS. "Mr. Peebles' Heart." *The Charlotte Perkins Gilman Reader.* Ed. Ann J. Lane. New York: Pantheon Books, 1980. 107-115.

———. "The Yellow Wallpaper." *The Charlotte Perkins Gilman Reader.* Ed. Ann J. Lane. New York: Pantheon Books, 1980. 3-20.

GLASPELL, SUSAN. "A Jury of Her Peers." *Woman: An Affirmation.* Eds. A. Fannin, R. Lukens, and C. H. Mann. Lexington, MA: Heath, 1979. 85-103.

GAINES, ERNEST J. "A Long Day in November." *The Best Short Stories by Negro Writers.* Ed. Langston Hughes. Boston: Little Brown, 1967. 359-402.

HARDY, THOMAS. "An Imaginative Woman. 1894." *Life's Little Ironies and A Few Crusted Characters.* London: MacMillan, 1968. 3-31.

HAWTHORNE, NATHANIEL. "The Birthmark." *Nathaniel Hawthorne Selected Tales and Sketches.* Intro. Hyatt H. Waggoner. 3rd Ed. New York: Holt. 1970. 264-281.

HAYCOX, ERNEST. "A Question of Blood." *Seventy-Five Short Master-*

pieces: Stories from the World's Literature. Ed. Roger B. Goodman. New York: Bantam, 1961. 127-130.

HEMINGWAY, ERNEST. "The Short, Happy Life of Francis Macomber." *Images of Women in Literature.* 4th ed. Boston: Houghton-Mifflin, 1986. 61-85.

HURSTON, ZORA NEALE. "The Gilded Six-Bits." *American Negro Short Stories.* Ed. John Henrik Clarke. New York: Hill & Wang, 1966.

KILLINS, JOHN O. "God Bless America." *American Negro Short Stories.* Ed. John Henrik Clarke. New York: Hill & Wang, 1966. 204-209.

LARDNER, RING. "The Golden Honeymoon." *The Ring Lardner Reader.* Ed. Maxwell Geismar. New York: Scribners, 1963. 340-355.

LAWRENCE, D. H. "The Blind Man." *The Complete Short Stories of D. H. Lawrence.* Vol. 2. New York: Viking, 1975. 347-365.

——. "The Blue Moccasins." *The Complete Short Stories of D. H. Lawrence.* Vol. 3. New York: Viking, 1975. 827-843.

——. "Her Turn." *The Complete Short Stories of D. H. Lawrence.* Vol. 1. New York: Viking, 1975. 39-44.

——. "New Eve and Old Adam." *The Complete Short Stories of D. H. Lawrence.* Vol. 1. New York: Viking, 1975. 71-94.

——. "Odour of Chrysanthemums." *The Complete Short Stories of D. H. Lawrence.* Vol. 2. New York: Viking, 1975. 283-302.

——. "Samson and Delilah." *The Complete Short Stories of D. H. Lawrence.* Vol. 2. New York: Viking, 1975. 411-426.

——. "A Sick Collier." *The Complete Short Stories of D. H. Lawrence.* Vol. 1. New York: Viking, 1975. 267-273.

——. "The White Stocking." *The Complete Short Stories of D. H. Lawrence.* Vol. 1. New York: Viking, 1975. 244-266.

——. "Wintry Peacock." *The Complete Short Stories of D. H. Lawrence.* Vol. 2. New York: Viking, 1975. 379-393.

MANSFIELD, KATHERINE. "Bliss." *The Short Stories of Katherine Mansfield.* New York: Ecco Press, 1983. 337-350.

——. "Marriage à la Mode." *The Short Stories of Katherine Mansfield.* New York: Ecco Press, 1983. 554-564.

——. "The Stranger." *The Short Stories of Katherine Mansfield.* New York: Ecco Press, 1983. 446-458.

MARCH, WILLIAM. "The Little Wife." *Fifty Best American Short Stories.* Ed. Martha Foley. Boston: Houghton, 1965. 87-97.

MAUPASSANT, GUY DE. "The Diamond Necklace." *The Best Short Stories of Guy de Maupassant.* New York: Airmont, 1968. 51-59.

——. "Useless Beauty." *The Best Short Stories of Guy de Maupassant.* New York: Airmont, 1968. 126-143.

McCULLERS, CARSON. "A Domestic Dilemma." *The Ballad of The Sad Cafe.* Boston: Houghton, 1951. 115-127.

McKay, Claude. "Truant." *American Negro Short Stories*. Ed. John Henrik Clarke. New York: Hill & Wang, 1966. 41-54.

Moravia, Alberta. "The Chase." *Images of Women in Literature*. Ed. Mary Anne Ferguson. Boston: Houghton, 1973. 300-303.

O. Henry. "The Gift of the Magi." *Perspectives on Sexuality*. Eds. J. L. Malfetti and E. M. Eidlitz. New York: Holt, 1972. 510-513.

Parker, Dorothy. "Big Blonde." *The Portable Dorothy Parker*. New York: Penguin, 1975. 187-210.

———. "Mr. Durant." *The Portable Dorothy Parker*. New York: Penguin, 1975. 35-460.

———. "The Lovely Leave." *The Portable Dorothy Parker*. New York: Penguin, 1975. 3-18.

———. "Too Bad." *The Portable Dorothy Parker*. New York: Penguin, 1975. 170-181.

Porter, Katherine Anne. "Rope." *Women and Fiction*. Ed. Susan Cahill, New York: Mentor, 1975. 78-84.

Purdy, James. "Man and Wife." *Color of Darkness*. Philadelphia: J. B. Lippincott, 1961. 67-76.

Schoonover, Shirley. "The Star Blanket." *Prize Stories 1962: The O. Henry Awards*. Greenwich, CT: Fawcett, 1962. 99-120.

Shaw, Irwin. "The Girls in Their Summer Dresses." *Images of Women In Literature*. Ed. Mary Anne Ferguson. 4th ed. Boston: Houghton, 1986. 260-264.

Steinbeck, John. "The Harness." *Fifty Great American Short Stories*. Ed. Milton Crane. New York: Bantam, 1965. 336-348.

Taylor, Peter. "Reservations: A Love Story." *Women and Men, Men and Women: An Anthology of Short Stories*. Ed. William Smart. New York: St. Martin's, 1975. 77-97.

Tolstoy, Leo. "Family Happiness." *The Death of Ivan Ilych and Other Stories*. New York: New American Library, 1960. 7-93.

Updike, John. "Eros Rampant." *Museums and Women and Other Stories*. New York: Knopf, 1968. 252-267.

Walker, Alice. "Her Sweet Jerome." *Images of Women in Literature*. Ed. Mary Anne Ferguson. Boston: Houghton, 1973. 164-169.

Welty, Eudora. "A Piece of News." *The Collected Stories of Eudora Welty*. New York: Harcourt, 1980. 12-16.

Wharton, Edith. "The Other Two." *Women and Fiction*. Ed. Susan Cahill. New York: Mentor, 1975. 7-26.

———. "The Reckoning." *The Collected Stories of Edith Wharton*. Vol. 1. Ed. R. W. B. Lewis. New York: Scribners, 1968. 420-437.

Yerby, Frank. "Health Card." *The Best Short Stories by Negro Writers*. Ed. Langston Hughes. Boston: Little Brown, 1967. 192-201.

Mother-Daughter

BALDWIN, JAMES. "Exodus." *American Negro Short Stories*. Ed. John Henrik Clarke. New York: Hill & Wang, 1966. 197-204.

BOYLE, KAY. "Winter Night." *Women and Fiction*. Ed. Susan Cahill. New York: Mentor, 1975. 86-95.

CALDWELL, ERSKINE. "Louellen." *Certain Women*. Boston: Little Brown, 1957. 111-145.

CALISHER, HORTENSE. "The Middle Drawer." *Images of Women in Literature*. Ed. Mary Anne Ferguson. 4th ed. Boston: Houghton, 1986. 214-221.

CATHER, WILLA. "Old Mrs. Harris." *Obscure Destinies*. New York: Knopf, 1932. 75-190.

COLETTE. "The Abduction." *My Mother's House and Sido*. New York: Farrar, 1953. 20-23.

——. "Maternity." *My Mother's House and Sido*. New York: Farrar, 1953. 62-64.

FERBER, EDNA. "Mother Knows Best." *Mother Knows Best*. New York: Doubleday, 1953. 1-27.

——. "The Sudden Sixties." *Gigolo*. New York: Doubleday, 1922. 222-258.

FREEMAN, MARY WILKINS. "Old Woman Magoun." *Between Mothers and Daughters: Stories across a Generation*. Ed. Susan Koppelman. New York: Feminist Press, 1985. 61-81.

FULLER, CHARLES H., JR. "Love Song for Wing." *Black Short Story Anthology*. Ed. Woodie King. New York: Columbia University Press, 1972. 141-149.

GERBER, MERRILL JOAN. "The Cost Depends on What You Reckon It In." *Stop Here, My Friend*. Boston: Houghton, 1965. 15-31.

——. "A Daughter of My Own." *Stop Here, My Friend*. Boston: Houghton, 1965. 220-234.

——. "Stop Here, My Friend." *Stop Here, My Friend*. Boston: Houghton, 1965. 45-52.

GRAU, SHIRLEY ANN. "Homecoming." *Adolescence in Literature*. Ed. Thomas W. Gregory. New York: Longman, 1978. 142-150.

HOWARD, MAUREEN. "Bridgeport Bus." *Prize Stories 1962: The O. Henry Awards*. Greenwich, CT: Fawcett, 1962. 239-250.

HOWARD, VANESSA. "Let Me Hang Loose." *Tales and Stories for Black Folks*. Ed. Toni Cade Bambara. Garden City, NY: Doubleday, 1971. 101-121.

HULL, HELEN ROSE. "The Fire." *Between Mothers and Daughters: Stories across a Generation*. Ed. Susan Koppelman. New York: Feminist Press, 1985. 114-127.

LAWRENCE, D. H. "Mother and Daughter." *The Complete Short Stories of D. H. Lawrence*. Vol. 3. New York: Viking, 1975. 805-826.

LINETTE, DEENA. "Gifts." *Ms Magazine*. March 1978. 67-71.

MARTIN, HELEN REIMENSNYDER. "Mrs. Gladfelter's Revolt." *Between Mothers and Daughters: Stories across a Generation*. Ed. Susan Koppelman. New York: Feminist Press, 1985. 131-140.

OATES, JOYCE CAROL. "Four Summers." *Wheel of Love*. New York: Vanguard, 1970. 209-231.

———. "Matter and Energy." *Wheel of Love*. New York: Vanguard, 1970. 334-361.

———. "You." *Wheel of Love*. New York: Vanguard, 1970. 362-387.

———. "Where Are You Going, Where Have You Been?" *Wheel of Love*. New York: Vanguard, 1970. 34-54.

OLSEN, TILLIE. "I Stand Here Ironing." *Between Mothers and Daughters: Stories across a Generation*. New York: Feminist Press, 1985. 179-187.

PARKER, DOROTHY. "Lolita." *The Portable Dorothy Parker*. New York: Penguin, 1976. 384-393.

PHILLIPS, JAYNE ANNE. "Home." *Black Tickets*. New York: Dell, 1979. 7-25.

———. "Souvenir." *Black Tickets*. New York: Dell, 1983. 175-196.

RUTHERFORD, DOROTHEA. "The Threshold." *A House of Good Proportion: Images of Women in Literature*. Ed. Michele Murray. New York: Simon & Schuster, 1973. 48-60.

SAROYAN, WILLIAM. "For Love of Daisy." *The Saturday Evening Post Stories 1958*. Garden City, NY: Doubleday, 1959. 48-58.

SLESINGER, TESS. "Mother to Dinner." *Between Mothers and Daughters: Stories across a Generation*. Ed. Susan Koppelman. New York: Feminist Press, 1985. 142-160.

STRAAYER, ARNY CHRISTINE. "High Heels." *Between Mothers and Daughters: Stories across a Generation*. Ed. Susan Koppelman. New York: Feminist Press, 1985. 280-284.

SUCKOW, RUTH. "The Valentine Box." *Parent and Child in Fiction*. Ed. Robert D. Strom. Monterey, CA: Brooks/Cole, 1977. 23-35.

TALL MOUNTAIN, MARY. "Naaholooyah." *That's What She Said: Contemporary Poetry and Fiction by Native American Women*. Bloomington: Indiana University Press, 1984. 251-257.

TARKINGTON, BOOTH. "One of Mrs. Cromwell's Daughters." *Women*. New York: Grosset & Dunlap, 1925. 47-62.

VALDES, GUADALUPE. "Recuerdo." *Between Mothers and Daughters: Stories across a Generation*. New York: Feminist Press, 1985. 191-196.

WALKER, ALICE. "Everyday Use." *Between Mothers and Daughters: Stories across a Generation*. New York: Feminist Press, 1985. 230-239.

WILLIAMS, SHIRLEY A. "Tell Martha Not to Moan." *Out of Our Lives:*

A Selection of Contemporary Black Fiction. Ed. Quandra Prettyman Stadler. Washington, D.C.: Howard University Press, 1975. 114-134.

Father-Daughter

ANDERSON, SHERWOOD. "Daughters." *Sherwood Anderson: Short Stories*. Ed. Maxwell Geismar. New York: Hill & Wang, 1962. 231-258.

CHEEVER, JOHN. "The Sorrows of Gin." *The Stories of John Cheever*. New York: Knopf, 1979. 198-209.

CLAUSEN, JAN. "Daddy." *Images of Women in Literature*. Ed. Mary Anne Ferguson. 4th ed. Boston: Houghton, 1986. 182-185.

DE MEYER, JOHN. "Boys Are Afraid of Girls." *Parent & Child in Fiction*. Ed. Robert Strom. Monterey, CA: Brooks/Cole, 1977. 146-158.

HAWTHORNE, NATHANIEL. "Rappacini's Daughter." *Nathaniel Hawthorne Selected Tales and Sketches*. Intro. Hyatt H. Waggoner. 3rd ed. New York: Holt, 1970. 329-360.

MANSFIELD, KATHERINE. "The Daughters of the Late Colonel." *The Short Stories of Katherine Mansfield*. New York: Ecco, 1983. 463-483.

——. "The Little Girl." *The Short Stories of Katherine Mansfield*. New York: Ecco, 1983. 138-142.

MERIWETHER, LOUISE. "Daddy Was a Number Runner." *Out of Our Lives: A Selection of Contemporary Black Fiction*. Ed. Quandra Prettyman Stadler. Washington, D.C.: Howard University Press, 1975. 32-51.

MUNRO, ALICE. "Boys & Girls." *Dance of the Happy Shades*. New York: McGraw-Hill.

PALEY, GRACE. "A Conversation with My Father." *The Short Story: 50 Masterpieces*. Ed. Ellen C. Wynn. New York: 1983. 617-622.

PETRY, ANN. "The New Mirror." *Out of Our Lives: A Selection of Contemporary Black Fiction*. Ed. Quandra Prettyman Stadler. Washington, D.C.: Howard University Press, 1975. 79-113.

SMITH, JEAN WHEELER. "Frankie Mae." *Black Short Story Anthology*. Ed. Woodie King. New York: Columbia University Press, 1972. 35-46.

WALKER, ALICE. "A Sudden Trip Home in the Spring." *Black-Eyed Susans: Classic Stories by and about Black Women*. Ed. Mary H. Washington. Garden City, NY: Doubleday, 1975. 141-154.

Father-Son

BENNETT, LERONE JR. "The Convert." *Black Short Story Anthology*. Ed. Woodie King. New York: Columbia University Press, 1972. 151-165.

CALISHER, HORTENSE. "The Sound of Waiting." *The Collected Stories of Hortense Calisher*. New York: Arbor, 1975. 246-262.

CHEEVER, JOHN. "Reunion." *The Stories of John Cheever*. New York: Knopf, 1979. 518-520.

FAULKNER, WILLIAM. "Barn Burning." *The Faulkner Reader*. New York: Modern Library, 1959. 499-516.

HEMINGWAY, ERNEST. "My Old Man." *Fifty Best American Short Stories, 1915-1963*. Ed. Martha Foley. Boston: Houghton, 1965. 49-60.

KELLY, WILLIAM M. "The Poker Party." *Black Short Story Anthology*. Ed. Woodie King. New York: Columbia University Press, 1972. 311-319.

LAGERKVIST, PAR. "Father and I." *Comparisons: A Short Story Anthology*. New York: McGraw-Hill, 1972. 10-12.

MABRY, THOMAS DABNEY. "The Vault." *Adolescence in Literature*. Ed. Thomas W. Gregory. New York: Longman, 1978. 118-128.

MALAMUD, BERNARD. "My Son, the Murderer." *Scenes from American Life: Contemporary Short Fiction*. Ed. Joyce Carol Oates. New York: Random House, 1973. 188-193.

MEADDOUGH, R. J. III. "The Death of Tommy Grimes." *The Best Short Stories by Negro Writers*. Ed. Langston Hughes. Boston: Little Brown, 1967. 408-413.

WHARTON, EDITH. "His Father's Son." *The Collected Short Stories of Edith Wharton*. Vol. 2. Ed. R. W. B. Lewis. New York: Scribners, 1968. 36-49.

Mother-Son

BERRIAULT, GINA. "The Birthday Party." *The Infinite Passion of Expectation*. San Francisco: North Point, 1982. 109-117.

CALISHER, HORTENSE. "In Greenwich There Are Many Gravelled Walks." *The Collected Stories of Hortense Calisher*. New York: Arbor House, 1975. 3-17.

FERBER, EDNA. "Old Lady Mandle." *One Basket: Thirty-One Short Stories by Edna Ferber*. New York: Simon & Schuster, 1947. 145-161.

GORDIMER, NADINE. "My First Two Women." *By Women: An Anthology of Literature*. Eds. Linda H. Kirschner and Marcia M. Folsom. Boston: Houghton, 1976. 92-103.

HARDY, THOMAS. "The Son's Veto." *Life's Little Ironies and a Few Crusted Characters*. 1894. London: MacMillan, 1968. 35-52.

LAWRENCE, D. H. "The Lovely Lady." *The Complete Short Stories of D. H. Lawrence*. Vol. 3. New York: Viking, 1975. 761-778.

——. "The Rocking Horse Winner." *The Complete Short Stories of D. H. Lawrence*. Vol. 3. New York: Viking, 1975. 790-804.

LOWRY, ROBERT. "Be Nice to Mr. Campbell." *Parent and Child in Fiction.* Ed. Robert Strom. Monterey, CA: Brooks/Cole, 1977. 99-113.

O'CONNOR, FRANK. "My Oedipus Complex." *Collected Stories.* New York: Knopf, 1981. 282-292.

PARKER, DOROTHY. "I Live on Your Visits." *The Portable Dorothy Parker.* New York: Penguin, 1976. 373-383.

WALKER, ALICE. "Strong Horse Tea." *Black Short Story Anthology.* Ed. Woodie King. New York: Columbia University Press, 1972. 133-140.

WHARTON, EDITH. "The Quicksand." *The Collected Stories of Edith Wharton.* Vol. 1. Ed. R. W. B. Lewis. New York: Scribners, 1968. 397-410.

WRIGHT, RICHARD. "Bright and Morning Star." *American Negro Short Stories.* Ed. John Henrik Clarke. New York: Hill & Wang, 1966. 75-108.

Siblings

BALDWIN, JAMES. "Sonny's Blues." *The Short Story: 50 Masterpieces.* Ed. Ellen C. Wynn. New York: St. Martin's Press, 1983. 623-654.

BENTLEY, PHYLLIS. "Kith and Kin." *Nine Tales of Family Life.* New York: MacMillan, 1960. 189-224.

BERRIAULT, GINA. "The Stone Boy." *The Infinite Passion of Expectation: Twenty-Five Stories.* San Francisco: North Point Press, 1982. 47-59.

BURNETT, WHIT. "Sherrel." *The Best Short Stories of 1932.* Ed. E. J. O'Brien. Boston: Houghton, 1932. 54-61.

CHEEVER, JOHN. "Goodbye, My Brother." *The Stories of John Cheever.* New York: Knopf, 1977. 3-21.

EDWARDS, JUNIUS. "Mother Dear and Daddy." *Out of Our Lives.* Ed. Quandra Prettyman Stadler. Washington, D.C.: Howard University Press, 1975. 223-237.

LAVIN, MARY. "The Sand Castle." *Parent and Child in Fiction.* Ed. Robert D. Strom. Monterey, CA: Brooks/Cole, 1977. 84-95.

——. "The Will." *Woman: An Affirmation.* Eds. A. Fannin, R. Lukens and C. H. Mann. Lexington, MA: Heath, 1979. 195-206.

PARKER, DOROTHY. "The Wonderful Old Gentleman." *The Portable Dorothy Parker.* New York: Penguin, 1976. 52-64.

WALKER, ALICE. "Brothers and Sisters." From *In Search of Our Mother's Gardens. Modern American Prose: Fifteen Writers.* New York: Random House, 1983. 434-438.

WELTY, EUDORA. "Why I Live at the P.O." *The Collected Stories of Eudora Welty.* New York: Harcourt, 1980. 46-56.

WEST, DOROTHY. "The Richer, The Poor." *The Best Short Stories by Negro Writers.* Ed. Langston Hughes. Boston: Little, Brown & Co., 1967. 130-133.

The book was designed by Tree Swenson

The type is Fournier

The type was set by Walker & Swenson, Book Typographers

Manufactured by Edward Brothers